D0288196

BRIDGEPORT, WV 26330

Carousel Sun

**BAEN BOOKS by
SHARON LEE and STEVE MILLER**

THE LIADEN UNIVERSE®
Fledgling
Saltation
Mouse and Dragon
Ghost Ship
Dragon Ship
Necessity's Child
Trade Secret
The Dragon Variation (omnibus)
The Agent Gambit (omnibus)
Korval's Game (omnibus)
The Crystal Variation (omnibus)
A Liaden Universe Constellation, vol. 1 (omnibus)
A Liaden Universe Constellation, vol. 2 (omnibus)

THE FEY DUOLOGY
Duainfey
Longeye

BY SHARON LEE
Carousel Tides
Carousel Sun
Carousel Seas (forthcoming)

To purchase these and all other Baen Book titles in e-book
format, please go to www.baen.com.

Carousel Sun

Sharon Lee

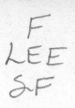

Carousel Sun

This is a work of fiction. All the characters and events portrayed in this book are fictional, and any resemblance to real people or incidents is purely coincidental.

Copyright © 2014 by Sharon Lee

All rights reserved, including the right to reproduce this book or portions thereof in any form.

A Baen Books Original

Baen Publishing Enterprises
P.O. Box 1403
Riverdale, NY 10471
www.baen.com

ISBN: 978-1-4767-3623-5

Cover art by Eric L. Williams

First printing, February 2014

Distributed by Simon & Schuster
1230 Avenue of the Americas
New York, NY 10020

10 9 8 7 6 5 4 3 2 1

Pages by Joy Freeman (www.pagesbyjoy.com)
Printed in the United States of America

Thanks are due to...

eluki bes shahar, for loaning Peggy
a Vixen the Slayer T-shirt

Jean Guerin, curator of the Harmon Museum and
Historical Society in Old Orchard Beach, Maine,
for sharing her encyclopedic knowledge of the
history of Old Orchard Beach and Ocean Park

...and Jeanne Bartolomeo, who generously hosted
the *Carousel Tides* launch party at Beggars Ride
Art Gallery in Old Orchard Beach, Maine.

Archers Beach, Maine, is a fictional town, though it owes portions of its history, coastline, and geography to the communities of Old Orchard Beach, Ocean Park, Kinney Shores, Camp Ellis, and to the Rachel Carson National Wildlife Refuge.

The Chance Menagerie Carousel at Palace Playland in Old Orchard Beach occupies roughly the spot where one would find the Fantasy Menagerie Merry-go-Round in Fun Country at Archers Beach.

CHAPTER ONE

Thursday, June 8
High Tide 9:24 A.M.
Sunrise 5:01 A.M. EDT

The sun had been up for hours, which was more than I could say for myself. I carried my first cup of coffee out onto the so-called "summer parlor," the covered porch facing the dunes, leaned my elbows on the railing, and looked out to sea.

Tide was almost in, and the sound of the waves was a constant sizzling boom. The leading edges of the breakers were brilliant with lacy white foam, while far out swells, faceted like jewels, caught the sun and gave it back in dazzling bursts of light.

Straight out, I could see the rocky islands, Blunt and Stafford, through a light haze. To my left—north, that would be—Cape Elizabeth Light was wearing a misty tutu, and Wood Island Light—south—was a silhouette inside a thicker bank of fog. What breeze there was came off the shore, bringing me a faint, sweet scent of flowers.

I sipped coffee, and sighed.

It was good to be home.

Shadow wings flashed over the sparkling water, and a gull laughed, derisive and high.

I grinned and shook my hair back from my face.

"A woman can change her mind, can't she?" I said.

❈   ❈   ❈

The laptop was chiming gently when I stepped back into the year-round parlor. I had mail, that particular chime meant. Nodding, I went past the coffee table where I'd set the machine up, temporarily, seven weeks ago, heading for the kitchen and the coffeepot.

A couple minutes later, being careful of the maps and guidebooks piled to one side, I sat down on the couch, put my refilled mug carefully to the right of the computer, and tapped a key.

I'd hit the jackpot this morning—two emails were in-queue and awaiting my attention, up from the more usual nothing, or the very occasional piece of spam that got past my filters. I build some *bad* email filters; just by way of putting my education to use.

There'd been times, during the years I'd been away from home, slinging code out in the dry lands, far removed in so very many ways from the Maine seacoast, when I'd gotten hundreds of emails over the course of a day—and answered them all, too.

Well. Now wasn't then, and two were plenty for this morning.

First up was a letter from one Peter Knorr—Painted Pony Pete, as he's known among the community of carousel-keepers. That was...mixed news. Pete wasn't exactly a rip-off artist.

But he wasn't exactly honest, either.

He was, however, a gentleman of the Old School, so he started with the courtesies.

Dear Ms. Archer:

I read with dismay that the Jewel of Northeast Wooden Carousels, Archers Beach's own Fantasy Menagerie, has met with misfortune. To have lost one of those venerable, priceless, wooden animals—my heart goes out to you, your family, and every one of the carousel's many supporters and friends.

So great was my dismay that, upon learning of this tragedy, I vowed that I would not rest until I had located a suitable replacement, and seen it installed on the Fantasy Menagerie Carousel.

You'll realize that this was no small task I undertook on your behalf, but I write to you now with news of success! I have located a replacement for the animal that was stolen: a signed and dated Looff stander. It's not perfect, of course, but it can be easily restored. And while I naturally can't reveal my sources, I will share with you, Ms. Archer, my firm belief that this horse is one of those few which were rescued from Dreamland—

"Oh, please!"

I shook my head, grabbed my mug and sat back on the sofa, trying to decide if I was offended or just blackly amused.

I mean—Dreamland? *Really*?

Dreamland at Coney Island burned down in 1911, and if anybody rescued anything from the flames beyond their lives, this was the first I'd heard of it.

Also? Looff hadn't signed or dated its horses, though the factory had branded some few inside the box with the legend, "Made by Looff."

Which any carousel-keeper over the age of eight could tell you off the top of her head, while counting people through the gate for the next ride.

"Does *Kate Archer* translate into *Born Yesterday* in some language I don't know?" I asked the empty parlor. I had another swig of coffee, and decided that I could go with being mildly amused. You couldn't, after all, blame a man for trying.

On the other hand, there was nothing in Pete's email that seemed to me to be worth the courtesy of a reply.

I leaned forward and hit the delete key.

Second email up was from Dan Muldoon, archivist for the Wooden Carousel Census. Dan wondered if I'd checked in with the Cleveland Trust for Public Land, which had the keeping of what was left of the Euclid Grand Beach Carousel. That was a Philadelphia Toboggan Company machine, Dan added, helpfully. He went on to say that there'd been talk of restoration, but it'd been thirty-seven years since Euclid Beach Amusement Park closed, and the horses and chariots were still in storage. It could be the Cleveland Trust would be willing to sell—even sell reasonably—to help keep another wooden carousel running.

As it happened, Dan wasn't the first to suggest that particular course. I'd called the Cleveland Trust for Public Land three weeks ago, on a tip from Gracie Adler, the carousel community's unofficial great-auntie. The secretary there had given me the number for the Carousel Trust.

Long story short, the carousel horses, which had been restored, were currently on display at the Western Reserve Historical Society, and Terry, the chair of the Carousel Trust, had big plans to see the machine operating again "within the next five years."

Given all the enthusiasm coming down the phone line, I

believed that, and sincerely wished them all the best of good fortune with the project.

Though it did leave my own problem in an unresolved state.

My bright idea had been to buy a new animal, and *that* led me to call an up-and-coming carver down to Binghamton, New York. We had a good, long talk, him and me—he'd been raised up in carousel-keeping, too, and knew a rounding-board from an orchestrion. Hell, he was actually excited to hear that Fantasy Menagerie's orchestrion still played its original paper rolls, and grilled me about the twenty-two animals that were left, what wood were they carved from, how many standers, how much brass did we show, did we have a working ring arm, and...

Well. Pleasant visit though it was, in the end we couldn't do business. For one thing, he needed not only the traditional arm and a leg for his work, but a couple fingers and the thumb from the remaining hand.

The second thing was he didn't have any animals under construction that weren't already spoken for, and his delivery date for a commissioned piece was well after Archers Beach Season was through.

There in the parlor, my coffee gone, I hit reply, and typed a note thanking Dan for his care, outlining the current situation of the Euclid Grand Beach Carousel, and giving him the phone number for the Trust. Good information for an archivist to have.

That taken care of, I came to my feet, stretched, and stood for a long minute, looking at nothing much, but seeing the carousel in my mind's eye.

Season Opening was just one week away, and replacement carousel animals were demonstrably *not* thick on the ground—which I'd known when I put out my call for aid. I figured my luck was about run out.

Which meant it was time to move on to Plan B.

I'd been hoping it wouldn't come to that; hoping for a miracle, really, and running the ride with one horse down. That was—not fine, exactly, but good enough for the Early Season weekend schedule, and I'd been able to string Marilyn, the park manager, on with the assurance that I was aware of the problem and was working on a solution.

Marilyn had been unusually mellow about it—which I guessed was left-over euphoria from the surprisingly successful Super Early

Season, back in April. But you betcha I'd better be showing a full complement of twenty-three animals and one chariot come Opening Day, or I'd be seeing a fine from Fun Country for every day the ride was "broken."

I sighed, ran my fingers through my hair and headed for the shower.

Some while later, showered and dressed to meet the day in sneakers, jeans, a pale green ringer tee with *Archers Beach Maine* printed on the left breast, and a long-sleeved denim shirt worn untucked over all, like a jacket, I opened the front door, and looked down.

The *Biddeford Journal-Tribune* lay facedown on the welcome mat. I picked it up, and flipped it over to glance at the headline.

AUTHORITIES BUST SIX IN COASTAL DRUG TRAFFICKING

Now, *there* was something to make the day a little brighter!

I leaned against the doorjamb and ran my eye down the front page.

Disappointingly, Joe Nemeier, Archers Beach very own drug lord, didn't figure in the thrilling story of a Coastie/MDEA collaboration, culminating in the dark moon pickup of a small barge loaded with plastic-wrapped bales of marijuana—in excess of one million dollars' worth of marijuana—at a tricksy little inlet where Elm Brook came into the ocean at Pine Point, which, as a location, was... interesting.

None of the names that did make the paper were known to me, which was a surprise. I'd've thought that the barge-runner, at least, would be local, given the piece of shore they'd been putting in to. It wasn't like Archers Beach was any stranger to the smuggler's trade. Over the centuries, anything that could be brought in illegally ran through the Beach, Surfside, or Pine Point, and there's families old in the business local to all three towns.

Well, I thought, folding up the paper and turning to toss it inside the house, it was almost certain that the bustees had been working for Joe Nemeier, and losing that cargo had to give him a pain in the pocketbook. Couple more seizures and maybe the man would catch the notion that he wasn't welcome, and leave.

Wouldn't *that* be fine?

I pulled the door shut and skipped down the stairs to the street. It wasn't all that long ago that it seemed Joe Nemeier's business was charmed—nobody could touch him or his. The Coast Guard couldn't see 'em, the Maine Drug Enforcement agents didn't know 'em, and deliveries slipped through the secret places and those who kept them like so much mist and wrack.

That situation had changed, for the better, assuming that the Coasties and the MDEA were the good guys. Joe Nemeier's concerns were no longer charmed—a condition for which I was directly responsible. I didn't imagine that Mr. Nemeier was in any way pleased with me; we hadn't met under the best of conditions and our relationship had gone downhill from a bad start. He'd twice tried to have me killed—and missed both times, which had to smart. I figured he was itching to try again, but the failure of charm and subsequent business setbacks were forcing him to keep his head down.

That was okay by me; I had plenty to keep me busy.

And right at the top of the list? Going up the hill, to see a man about a horse.

CHAPTER TWO

———— ❦ ————

Low Tide 3:10 P.M. EDT

Artie's Enterprise is 'way up the hill, across Route 5, at the very end of Adelaide Road Extended. "Enterprise" is Mainer for "junkyard," which is why Artie's sits at the end of the road, with a field behind it and plenty of room to put new pieces when they come in.

The Enterprise is old; Gran told me it'd been a trading post, back a couple hundred years ago. She didn't say whether Artie had the keeping of it then, but it was possible. After all, Gran's rising four hundred, herself. In theory, *trenvay*—that's *earth spirit*, to you—could live forever, so long as nothing poisons their rock, their patch of marsh or bit of water.

Or their tree.

However old it is, the Enterprise contains quite an astonishing collection of... *stuff*. All sorts of odd and unlikely bits and pieces of this, that, and what-the-hell's-THAT? come to rest there. Not just things you'd expect, like manual typewriters and buttonhooks, Turkish carpets, pickle barrels, ancient weathervanes, skeleton keys, glass insulators from telephone poles, and yellowed china bowls painted with pink flowers, though there are those, in good—some might say, bad—number.

7

But the Enterprise also shelters other things, and it's those that the casual shopper needs to be aware, and wary, of.

It's best to enter Artie's Enterprise with the picture of what you want to find there firmly fixed in your head. If you go in with an open mind, just thinking to see the sights, do a little window-shopping combined with a history lesson—then you're ripe for trouble. You *will* spend hours, and may spend days, inside, going from one improbable geegaw to another, beguiled and lost to time. When you do leave, you'll very likely find that you purchased something you not only don't remember buying, but that you don't actually like—and which will prove very hard to lose.

Me, now... Walking in, I *knew* what I wanted—I wanted a carousel horse carved from tupelo wood by my several times great-granduncle on the Archer side. By choice, it would be a horse, since it was a horse that had been lost. Also by choice it would have wings. It would not, however, have fangs.

"Kate." Artie came out of the back, cleaning his hands on a stained red rag. He looked faintly aggrieved, and not all that pleased to see me, which wasn't exactly a surprise. My personal popularity rating isn't high among the *trenvay* of Archers Beach; plus I'd caught the notion somewhere that Gran and Artie had old business between them.

Airing old grievances wasn't on the day's agenda, though, so I gave the man a smile and a cordial nod. "'Morning. Pretty one, too."

"It is—and I'll tell you straight out, I got nothin' like you're wishin' on here. We got our limits, y'know."

I *did* know that—we all have our limits. Still, I felt a ripple of disappointment, to have my dream summarily shot down not two steps from the front door. Dammit, I *needed* a carousel animal, and the Enterprise was my last resource.

"Nothin' wrong with dreamin'," Artie said, like I'd spoken out loud. "Only you gotta dream smaller. What's a place like this *likely* to have, in the line of what yer lookin' for—that's the question you want to ask."

It was a trick, of course—*trenvay* live to trick the unwary—and I fell for it.

No sooner were the words out of his mouth, than an image leapt into my mind—an image of a brilliantly colored Herschel-Spillman rooster, green and red tail feathers awry, and yellow legs at full stretch as he pelted toward or away from some peril, a blue saddle on his back and a wicked gleam in his eye.

Artie grinned, and I felt my stomach drop.

"Well, now, *there* yer in luck! Something a lot like that come in couple years ago..." He looked around, as if trying to remember where he'd put it, the bastard, then all of a sudden nodded and took off at an angle down an overshadowed aisle.

I followed, stretching my legs and deliberately not looking at the enticing shadowy shapes arrayed on either side of the thin way. Ahead of me, Artie pushed open a door, admitting a flash of sunlight, and went out into the side yard.

The side yard is where most of the Enterprise is stored—some stuff is under tarp, some open to the weather. There might have been a pattern and a reason to it all, but, if so, both escaped me. I kept Artie's broad flannel-covered back in view, running now, dodging a stack of hubcaps, the rusty metal frame of a slatless park bench, and a tangle of old lobster traps.

Artie stepped around the back of a wrought-iron garden pavilion. I barreled after him—and jerked up short, my sneakers skidding on the grass. I managed to keep my feet and not ram my nose into Artie's shoulder, though I didn't manage to avoid being splattered with condensation when he snapped a particularly ratty blue tarp off of—

I blinked.

It *was* a rooster.

Not, mind you, a Herschel-Spillman, sharp-painted, and clean of line.

The rooster in hand was...unfortunate. As if someone, somewhere, had tried to reproduce the original, but found their skill, or their memory, insufficient to the task...

...or both.

It was dirty, this rooster—in need of cleaning *and* a paint job—but that was just the beginning. The tail feathers weren't awry, they were downright bedraggled, the eyes were dull, both stirrups were missing, and there was a crack down the dingy yellow neck that was going to have to be—

I blinked and stepped closer, frowning at the crack and what it revealed.

"Problem?" Artie asked, obligingly pulling the tarp out of my way.

"It's fiberglass!"

Artie shrugged. "It's what I got; take 'im or leave 'im."

I threw Artie a glare, which he didn't seem to notice.

"Where'd you get it?" I asked, buying time. It didn't matter to me where he'd gotten the stupid bird. For all I knew, or cared, the Enterprise had spun it out of grass and dew.

Another shrug. "It come in, like it all does."

Which was to say: *None of your business, Kate.*

Well, okay; we all have our secrets, too.

I sighed and moved past Artie, walking around the bird in formal inspection. It was depressingly dingy, but elbow grease and paint would fix that. I knelt down and inspected the underside, which was firm and rot-free, got up, brushed off the knees of my jeans, frowned at the tangled mess of a tail, and walked on.

I came back to my starting point and stood for a long minute, considering. The only real damage was the crack on the neck— and that was why God had given us epoxy—but my inclination was to leave the damn' rooster right where he was. The thought of mixing fiberglass and wood lacerated my carousel-keeping sensibilities. But, really, prejudice aside, did I have a choice?

I thought about that hole in the menagerie, and my utter lack of success along other, preferable avenues, and the fines upcoming if I didn't do *some*thing—and reluctantly accepted that, no, I *didn't* have a choice.

"I'll buy him," I told Artie, with scant grace. "And you'll bring him."

"Be a delivery charge."

I looked him in the eye. "Really? A delivery charge, inside the Beach?"

There was a long, stretched minute while we held eye contact; the air seemed to warm appreciably, and I thought I saw a shadow move in peripheral vision. Inside my head, I heard a sound something like a warning growl. The shadow faded. I concentrated on holding Artie's eyes with mine...

...and he blinked first.

"Sorry," he said. "Delivery free inside the Beach—sure it is, Kate. When you want it where?"

I did a rapid calculation. "Today, at three, at the carousel. How much?"

"We'll have 'im down the merry-go-round at three today. Price is four bills."

Four hundred dollars was considerably less than I'd expected to pay. Unworthily, I wondered what secret flaw, hidden from inspection, the rooster would be shown to possess, and decided that it wasn't worth worrying about. I needed a fill-in animal; I had a fill-in animal. Immediate problem solved.

"I'll have cash waiting," I promised.

He nodded and tossed the tarp back over the rooster.

Archers Beach Community Federal Credit Union sits right on the corner of Route 5 and Adelaide Road. Since I was going to need four hundred dollars in a couple hours, I stopped to take care of that piece of business. When I came out again, a few minutes later, I stood on the corner and looked down Archer Avenue.

Archer Avenue is the town's main business street. It descends a long hill from Route 5 at the top, crossing the Amtrak line, and Grand Avenue, the parallel business street, before dead-ending at the dunes, the beach, and the Atlantic Ocean.

Since Archers Beach is a tourist town for part of the year, some of the businesses on Archer Avenue cater entirely to that trade. They open a week before the Season officially gets under way, and close the week after Labor Day.

When I was a kid, the Archers Beach tourist trade had a couple T-shirt and beach wear shops to choose from, an ice cream stand, couple of pizza stands, a sundry shop, Dynamite, a candy factory, a biker bar, a hobby and game store. The storefronts started out thick at the back side of Fun Country, at the bottom of the hill, but by the time you reached mid-hill, there were gaps in the line; maybe two, three empty stores sandwiched between those open for business.

Growing up, I heard a lot of grumbling among my grand-mother's friends about the Old Days, when the Beach had three Seasons full of tourists, and Archer Avenue fairly glittered with lighted shops.

Fashions change; fortunes fall. The dance bands and the off-Broadway shows stopped coming up to Archers Beach a long time ago. The Fire burned down a big swath of the posh hotels, gutted the fancy eateries. Owners chose not to rebuild—no insurance, or no heart, investors heard there was more return to be had someplace else.

The Beach had a small renaissance as a blue-collar party-place in the 1970s; rock bands instead of Big Bands came up to head-line on the World Famous Pier at Archers Beach, and things in general took an uptick.

Then, a nor'easter chewed up the World Famous Archers Beach Pier and spat it out like so many toothpicks. The town rebuilt, though slowly, with the help of a couple of angel investors with old ties to the Beach, but it was a humble thing, compared even to its immediate predecessor, and the tourist trade...fell away.

By the time I came onto the Beach, the Seasons had long been The Season, and had shrunk from twenty weeks to twelve.

A twelve-week Season might interest investors in the glamorous resorts where children of wealth go to play, but the chilly and frankly old-fashioned coast of Maine just didn't attract money from Away, anymore.

That had all been bad enough: a town gone a little to seed, but still able to show a brave front, and to keep on with its own business during the three-quarters of the year when the townies had only themselves for company.

By the time I'd returned from my self-appointed exile, though—matters had gone from bad to worse.

There was still business on the hill—a computer repair shop, a styling salon, the hobby shop and the candy store still holding firm, a tattoo parlor that was new since my time, a store sell-ing country craftworks imported from China, and St. Margaret's Catholic Church, sitting at the intersection of Route 5 and Archer like a crown atop a bald head.

The biker bar was gone, along with the antique store and the camera shop. Hell, even St. Margaret's was on reduced hours—only two Masses on Sunday, and confessions heard by appointment.

The state of Archer Avenue worried me, to tell the truth. Not that there was anything *I* could do about attracting viable busi-ness to town—that was what the Chamber of Commerce was for, and they were—reasonably enough—trying to hold their base at the bottom of the hill together. They'd managed to tempt a high-end deli into taking a chance on West Grand, along with a luxury day spa and a boutique wine store, but there they'd been helped out by the fact of some of the older motels reinventing themselves as beach condos for the pleasure of folks from Away.

It's an article of faith among most Mainers that people from Away always have money. Unfortunately, the high side of the hill was going to be a tough sell to money from Away, and if there wasn't a certain ratio of shops to empty storefronts, even the businesses that'd been hanging on would starve for lack of foot traffic.

I crossed Route 5, heading down the hill, St. Margaret's on my right. Directly ahead of me, taking up most of the sidewalk, was a pair of sawhorses, a bandsaw in close attendance, and a couple eight-foot boards propped against the window of what had four days ago been one of those empty storefronts that had recently been exercising my mind.

As I approached, I heard voices inside the place, echoing, and the sharp report of a nail gun.

I dodged the sawhorses and walked up the slight ramp, pausing with the toes of my sneakers at the line of the door, so that I was technically not trespassing, in case anybody cared.

Not one of the busy beavers inside even noticed me, so intent were they on their work.

Two young fellas in jeans and T-shirts were covering the scarred walls with honey-colored paneling. Another pair were boxing the concrete support posts with the same honey-colored wood. At the back left corner of the space, a girl on a ladder was dealing with the kraken of wires spilling out from a hole in the drop ceiling.

An empty glass showcase was set up as a barrier in front of the back wall; a thin figure bent over it, writing or sketching on a pad of paper.

I had a sense of movement behind me, unthreatening, and turned just as another young fella in jeans and a tool belt came up the ramp.

"Help you, miss?" he asked respectfully. He had a slight, not-Maine accent, a pleasant, apple-cheeked face, and serious hazel eyes. Under the Home Depot gimme hat, his hair was light brown, curling softly below his ears.

"Just wondering what you've got going in," I said, and added, by way of explaining why I cared, "I run the carousel down Fun Country."

His eyes widened as he smiled. "We're putting in an art gallery," he said.

I blinked. "Art gallery?" I repeated, and didn't add: In Archers Beach, blue-collar vacation spot as it was?

He nodded. "Would you like to meet the owner? She's right

there." He nodded toward the figure still bent, rapt, over her pad of paper.

"I'd be pleased," I said, and followed him into the store, up to the counter.

"Ms. Anderson?"

"Yes, Kyle?" She didn't look up.

"Ma'am, here's the lady who runs the carousel come to introduce herself."

She did look up then, her eyes the blue of a fog-bound ocean, set deep in the well-used face of a woman past her first youth.

"Good morning," she said, her voice smooth and calm. Her accent was New England, but not necessarily Maine. Massachusetts, maybe.

"Good morning," I answered. "I'm Kate Archer—Fantasy Menagerie Carousel." I smiled. "I saw you were fixing the place up and wondered what was going in. An art gallery, Kyle tells me. It's been a lot of years since Archers Beach had an art gallery."

"In fact," she said with a faint smile, "it's been just shy of a hundred years. You hear all about how the Great Fire took the hotels and the eating places, but you hardly ever hear that two art galleries and an art museum burned to the ground that night, too."

She held out a hand. "I'm Joan Anderson. Pleased to meet you, Ms. Archer."

"Likewise," I said, meeting her hand. We shook.

"I'm curious what made you choose Archers Beach as a location for your gallery," I said carefully.

Her smile grew more pronounced.

"I grew up here. Moved to Massachusetts when I got married. Taught school, raised kids, got a divorce. The kids are grown, the school system laid me off, and I decided it was time to come home and do what I always said I was going to do." She raised her arms, showing me the space and the busy workers.

"This gallery is going to feature Maine artists only—paintings, pottery, jewelry, furniture—I've already got fifty artists on my list, and the word's just starting to get out."

I glanced down when she said "list," but she'd been sketching on that pad, not listing. The sketch was of a horse, mane-tossed and galloping. She followed my eyes and turned the pad around so I could see it better.

"For the sign," she said.

"Nice horse," I answered. "What's the gallery's name?"

"Wishes," she said, and gave me a full-on grin when I looked up at her. "When I was younger than I was today, I used to say to my mother that I wished I could do this, or that, or that other thing. Her answer, every time, was, 'If wishes were horses, beggars would ride.'" She looked down at her horse and nodded. "Time for us beggars to mount up."

"I wish you all kinds of good luck," I said, and felt a not-exactly-welcome tingle of heat along the side of my tongue. Still, there was nothing wrong with expressing a well-wish.

Even a well-wish with a little more than simple sincerity behind it.

"Thank you, Kate. It was Kate?"

"Kate Archer—was and is."

She smiled again. "Of course. You'll come to our opening reception," she said, and it wasn't a question. "I'll send you an invitation."

"I'd be glad to," I said, nodding. "I'll leave you to it then. Think you'll be open in time for the Season?"

"In plenty of time for the Season. And the other three, too."

I stared at her. "You're gonna be year-round?"

She chuckled.

"Why not? I'm going to be living here year-round. Might as well have something to keep me busy."

"There's that," I allowed, raised my hand by way of good-bye, and turned toward the door.

Kyle turned with me.

"I'd like to take a look at your carousel sometime," he said. "I'm—I'm a big fan of the wooden ones."

"Come down when you've got a couple minutes. We're open the weekend schedule right now, but I'd be glad to give you a private tour, if you give me some warning."

"Thank you," he said, as we reached the door and I stepped over the threshold. He stopped, one step inside the shop, and inclined slightly from the waist, as if he had started to bow, and then caught himself.

"Thank you," he said again. "I'd like that a lot."

CHAPTER THREE

My grandmother lives on Heath Hill, among an old stand of mixed wood. Her nearest neighbor, as chance would have it, is that very same Joe Nemeier who stands as the CEO of the local drug trade. He'd gone and built himself a modest little Bar Harbor cottage on the high land—think Wingwood or The Willows and you won't be far afield—overlooking the Wood and, beyond it, the sea.

I came up the Hill from Heath Street, and paused outside the shadow of the trees to look up at the monstrosity sitting there—an architectural monstrosity, that was, and solely in my own opinion. A few weeks ago, the place had been truly monstrous, overlain with sticky gobs of . . . well, magic, if the word will make the concept go down easier. Those few weeks ago, Joe Nemeier had available to him, for what price I can't begin to speculate, the services and protection of an extremely powerful Ozali—magician—now deceased.

There were those of us who were glad about that deceased part, not excluding myself and my immediate family—grandmother, grandfather, and mother, too. I didn't expect Joe Nemeier entered into our feelings, but you can't please everybody.

There being nothing of interest to see up at the house, I turned my back on it and walked to the ocean edge of the Hill.

Roses softened the stony edge, tumbling over the thin grass in a froth of white and pink and dark green. Sea rose canes bear thorns, just like their hybrid sisters, so I stopped some paces back from the edge, looking down the Hill, at roses climbing rock, flowering against the sand; then raised my sights, looking out to the black, bladed surface of Googin Rock, the local hazard to navigation. Tide was going out; still, the retreating waves struck the Rock with energy, throwing thick drops of seawater up into the lagging breeze.

It was a strange and fierce place, Googin Rock, though less strange than it had been weeks ago. Magic again. And, yeah, I was in it to my elbows.

Well.

I turned toward the trees. Nine steps brought me into the shadow; nine more, and I was in the Wood itself.

Welcome, Kate...

The words formed inside my ears, shaped by the breeze. The living voice of the Wood, the unanimous greeting of the trees. Some might find it...creepy, even alarming. I found it soothing. If the trees didn't approve of me, at least they welcomed me, and they don't welcome all, or even most, visitors.

"Good morning," I said, strolling down the path that opened for me between the low growth and the mature trunks. You never take the same path through the Wood twice. Some might find that disturbing, too. For myself, I didn't question whether the Wood would lead me to the Center, or just 'round in circles until I fell, exhausted, to be strangled by vines while I slept. Yeah, I know the old stories, and I know that they're true—sometimes, and for some folk. But me, I'm not an enemy to trees; I've got close family ties.

Eventually, the press of trunk and branch thinned; the small growth fell away to grass, and the grass to moss. I was in the glade at the Center: the heart and very soul of the Wood. The place where the Lady lives.

A tupelo tree grows at the Center—what we call black gum, or pepperidge, up here in Maine. Gran took her name there—Ebony Pepperidge, which gets shortened to Bonny more often than not.

Her particular black gum tree, here at the Wood's heart, is

nine feet around, and a good hundred feet tall, with great, twisted black branches against which thin, egg-shaped leaves glow like green glass.

Sitting with his back cozily against that broad trunk was a yellow-haired man in a black muscle shirt and black leather jeans. The hair was long enough to brush his white, elegantly muscled shoulders. His face, when he looked up at me, was ageless—which isn't anything near like *young*. He had fire-red mustaches and well-opened blue eyes. If you looked close, you could see tiny blue flames dancing in their depths.

A red plastic cooler sat next to him on the moss. The leather coat and hat that completed his daily wear hung on a nearby branch. A large, soot-black bird perched on the same branch, head tucked under a wing.

"Good morning, Katie," he said with a smile. The smile was sweet, but not as innocent as it had been just a few weeks ago. Then, this man had been Mr. Ignat', my grandmother's long-time beau—a man on the far side of middle age, more than a little foolish, sweet-natured and affectionate. He'd been one of the two anchors in my life, after I'd been brought out of what was left of my home to live with my grandmother on the land my family had long ties to, and I had loved him unreservedly.

The feelings I had for the person he was now—the person he *was again*—that being specifically Fire Ozali Belignatious, formerly of the Land of the Flowers, and oh-just-by-the-way, my maternal grandfather—my feelings there were a *lot* more complicated.

Still, there wasn't any reason not to be polite to family, so I smiled and nodded.

"'Morning, Mr. Ignat'. Gran still resting?"

"She and Nessa went for a stroll under leaf. They intended to return in time for your visit." He smiled. "After all, they can't be far."

"You're a funny man," I told him, dropping to the moss and crossing my legs, Indian-style.

In the general way of things, a *trenvay*, or, hell, let's get specific—a *dryad*—is tied to her tree. An old and tree-strong dryad, such as the Lady of the Wood, might, if and when the whim took her, walk from one end of town to the other, tend a business, and live like mundane folk in a big old house overlooking the dunes. Going beyond the boundaries of the land in which her tree had roots—that couldn't happen. A dryad out of touch with her tree died. And the tree died, too.

Yet Gran, a dryad, had crossed the Wall between the Worlds, penetrating deep into the Land of the Flowers to rescue her daughter, my mother, Nessa, and lived to tell the tale—slowly, over many days, and with frequent periods of rest within her tree.

My mother, half a dryad and half something very much else, had no tree to heal her. She was, however, able to receive some benefit from all trees. So the trees of the Wood were bringing Nessa back to health, slowly, while she came to terms with the damage that had been wreaked upon her soul—and the fact that it was her own again.

I wondered, not for the first time, if there wasn't some kind of supernatural psychoanalyst we could call upon, but Gran only said that trees work slow, but certain, and Mother smiled, and told me not to worry so much.

"Will you have time for a lesson today?" I asked Mr. Ignat', by way of not being worried.

I'd lately—yes, within the last couple weeks—come into the possession of quite a lot of . . .

No, I can't call it *magic* a third time; I was raised to know better.

The formal name for the material we here in the so-called Real World prettify as "magic," is *jikinap*. It's a metaphysical substance that can be sold, stolen, earned, given away or accepted as a gift. It can also be forfeit in a variety of interesting ways, usually involving a duel between Ozali and the winner absorbing the loser's power.

The most likely outcome for a person who has accidentally contracted quite a lot of *jikinap*, and who hasn't had exhaustive training in its husbandry and use . . . is that the proto-Ozali dies, rapidly, and often enough, terribly.

Back in the day, Mr. Ignat' had been a regular on the top ten list of Ozali to Watch in the Land of the Flowers—a world rich in *jikinap*. He'd kindly—as I often reminded myself—undertaken to teach me what I needed to know in order to survive my own power. We'd been meeting two and three times a week for lessons, and while I couldn't say that I was feeling confident, at least I didn't stand on the edge of spontaneous combustion, and I could sit in peace with another Ozali without feeling compelled to absorb his *jikinap*.

Like I was sitting now, with Mr. Ignat' not two feet away, his small store of power a steady, alluring glow in the center of his chest; right where his heart would be...

"Pirate Kate? Will you dishonor your vow and your teacher?"

I blinked, feeling the taste of butterscotch along the edge of my tongue, exercised my will and sternly sent my rising power down to its proper place at the base of my spine.

"I honor my vow *and* my teacher, sir!" I assured him, playing the game we'd shared when we'd both been much simpler.

"I believe you," he said—and suddenly turned his head to the right.

I followed his gaze, saw branches shift and lift across the clearing as my mother and my grandmother stepped out of the Wood to join us.

"What's the news from town?" Gran asked, after Mr. Ignat' had dealt us each a sandwich and a bottle of water from the red cooler.

"I see in the paper that the Coasties and the MDEA nabbed some of your neighbor's hired help last night. Caught 'em at Pippin's Notch." I had a swallow of water. "You'll maybe want to keep an eye out. Joe Nemeier's a mean sonofabitch, and there's no telling what he'll do, if the law starts getting too close to home."

Gran was unwrapping her sandwich. "The Wood will protect us."

Now that the Lady was back where she belonged, even fire wasn't... much... of a threat. Joe Nemeier *had* fired the Wood when Gran was on her walkabout; happily Mr. Ignat' and his companion had been on hand to deal with it—and to guide me in crafting a shield.

I took a bite of my sandwich.

"The *big* news," I said, when I'd had another swallow of water, "is that there's an *art gallery* going in at the top of Archer Avenue, two doors down from the church. Joan Anderson—that's the owner—tells me she'll be open year-round and in plenty of time for this Season. Maine-made art only."

I raised my sandwich, then lowered it to add the rest.

"Ms. Anderson's going to be throwing an opening day reception. Says she'll send me an invitation."

"Very proper," Gran said. "I suppose she's from Away, this Anderson?"

"Not a bit of it. Grew up here, she said, got married, moved to Mass. Now the kids are on their own, and she's divorced. She says she's come back home to fulfill a dream."

"Of course," my mother said, green eyes bright in an emaciated face. "Dreams grow best at home." She turned to Gran. I noticed that, while she had dutifully unwrapped her sandwich, she hadn't made any attempt to actually eat it.

"You remember the Andersons, Mother. Julia threw pots, and John sculpted. They lived on Wintergreen Street—the house with the pottery fence."

I was reasonably certain that I'd remember a pottery fence, but that didn't ring any bells with me.

It did with Gran, though. Her face softened.

"Now, I do remember that fence! Pretty thing, set in with tiles and colored glass."

"What happened to it?" I asked, around a bite of my own sandwich.

"A car ran into it," Gran said. "Smashed it to bits. If it had been a stone wall, the driver would have been killed."

"That's recent, then?" I asked.

"Before you came on the Beach," Gran said, and looked to my mother, who moved her shoulders like she was undecided.

"Nineteen forty-six, I think it must have been," she said.

"Before my time," I agreed, and looked meaningfully at the sandwich held loosely between her hands.

She followed my glance, and lifted her head to smile at me.

"You worry too much, Katie," she said, but she did take a bite.

"Any other news, Kate?" asked my grandmother. "Have you found a replacement for the batwing horse?"

"Yes and no," I answered. "Painted Pony Pete offered me a signed Looff brought out of Dreamland."

"Kate Archer! You never—"

"No, I never. Do I look like a tourist to you?"

Mr. Ignat' chuckled at that, and Gran shook her head.

"My apologies, Kate. Of course you know better than a signed Looff."

"...though I might've fallen for it, if he hadn't mentioned Dreamland. That was a PTC machine, wasn't it?"

Gran didn't bother to dignify that.

"So you turned down Painted Pete's offer. Which any person with a grain of sense would do. *Did* you find something else?"

"I did," I said, as casually as I could. "Got a rooster at Artie's."

I'd known she wouldn't like it, but I'd miscalculated the intensity on the Richter scale.

"*You made a deal with the Enterprise?*"

It was said quiet enough, but I felt the tension in the Wood around us. Inside my head, I heard something that sounded an awful lot like a nervous whine. I sympathized. Gran in a temper is nothing to trifle with. On the other hand . . .

"I heard from you that the care and keeping of that carousel is my worry now," I said, tartly. "Did I hear wrong?"

"You did not. However, had I *ever* supposed that a granddaughter of mine would sink so low as to deal with Artie—to *willingly* take something from that damned Enterprise into our care—"

"Was there a memo?" I interrupted. "If there was, I missed it. I'm pretty sure this is the very first time I've heard that Artie isn't trustworthy."

"Oh, he's trustworthy," Gran said bitterly. "He never misses a trick."

"But, Mother," Nessa said. "Katie's the Guardian. Artie wouldn't play any tricks on her."

I felt a little wibble along my nerve endings.

Because, Artie *had* played one trick on me—and he'd gone for two. I'd called him on the delivery business, but the plain fact was that he had manipulated me into owning that rooster.

Now—of course, too late—I wondered why.

I sighed.

Gran gave me a hard stare, and shook her head, anger abruptly gone, leaving behind a strange sadness.

"Done's done," she said, sounding tired. "For future reference, Kate, Artie is—" She glanced aside. "Would you allow *mad as moonbeams* to be accurate, Bel?"

Mr. Ignat' sipped from his water bottle and carefully replaced the cap before answering.

"I allow it," he said slowly. "But I don't think there's active harm in the boy."

Boy. Artie was likely hundreds of years old.

Of course, Ozali Belignatious could easily be a thousand years old. The folk of the Land of the Flowers are long-lived, if they don't happen to die in a duel, which most do; and *jikinap*, if you manage to survive the owning of it, can extend a life-span wonderfully.

"*That* is irrelevant," Gran said.

Mr. Ignat' smiled at her, slow and sweet. She didn't smile back.

"There are things in that Enterprise that oughtn't be *any*where," she said, holding my eyes with hers. "Dangerous things. *Blasphemous* things. No one knows where most of it comes from—"

"*It come in,*" I murmured, "*like it all does.*"

Gran blinked, then nodded sharply.

"Exactly. *It come in.*" She shook her head. "It's not an easy service. Be that given, it is *Artie's* service, and he honors it as much as we honor ours. In that, yes, he's trustworthy. But in everything else—*anything* else...Be careful, Katie."

"I will," I promised, the nerve-wibble more pronounced. I might be—well, I *was*—the Guardian of Archers Beach, and that did give me a certain edge over the *trenvay* who existed in service to their small, fey places.

Being Guardian, however, didn't make me omniscient.

Or invincible.

"Have you seen Borgan, Katie?" my mother asked, by way of turning the subject.

"No," I said, more sharply than I had intended, and suddenly felt the need to move on with the rest of my day.

I rose, bringing my water bottle and the empty sandwich wrap with me.

"I've got to meet a delivery," I said, which was true, but not imminent. "Is there anything I can bring up from the house? From town?"

It was the same offer I made at the end of every visit. The answer was the same, too.

"We have everything we need here, Kate," Gran said, and Mother added, "Thank you."

I nodded, turned, and paused, as Mr. Ignat' also rose.

"I'll walk with you, if you've no objection, Pirate Kate?"

"Glad of company," I told him, which was...qualified truth.

He nodded, pulled his coat off the branch and shucked into it, settling his hat with effortless cool. His movements roused the bird, which ruffled its feathers, and gave them a quick preen.

Mr. Ignat' picked up the red cooler, stepped over to where my mother sat nibbling at her sandwich, and dropped a light kiss on her hair. He turned to Gran and took her hand to bow over.

She smiled in pleasure, meeting his eyes, and for a long moment, they were silent and motionless, existing only for each other.

I took a careful breath, my chest tight.

Gran slipped her hand away from his, her smile fading.

Mr. Ignat' straightened and turned toward me. I waited until he had gained my side before I started walking. Behind us, I heard the sound of a branch moving sharply, and looked up to see the soot-colored bird in the air.

We reached the tree line, and a path opened before us.

CHAPTER FOUR

"A ducat for your thoughts, Pirate Kate."

I shook myself, realizing that I hadn't uttered a word since we'd left Mother and Gran at the heart of the Wood.

"I was wondering why Artie wanted me to have that rooster *particularly*," I said. "I was wondering who else of the *trenvay* isn't exactly trustworthy, and I was wondering why I took this job." I shrugged, and threw him a glance, meeting the blue flames in his eyes. "Hardly worth a penny, much less a man's good gold."

"No, I think I've received value," Mr. Ignat' said slowly, as we took the short cut across Gentleman Johnnie's Mini-golf's parking lot.

We went on another half-dozen steps in silence.

"You took the job of Guardian," he said slowly, "because your grandmother rightly judged that you needed occupation, and a new direction, after Zephyr brought you away from the Land of the Flowers. You were young for it, but you had been raised as royalty; duty was no stranger to you, and you were of the blood. Archers Beach had been without a Guardian since Lydia accepted Aeronymous' bargain and crossed into the Land of the Flowers as his consort. The land had been losing its virtue . . . for some period of time."

I blinked at him, pieces snapping into place with such authority that I was sure he heard them. All the stories of the old days, when Archers Beach had been bigger, brighter, better. Then, slowly at first, then faster as entropy had its way, things began to slide downhill.

By the time Princess Kaederon came onto the Beach to take up life as Kate Archer, all that was left was the twelve-week Season, and the inevitable slide downhill...

The Old Ones—Gran and her friends—they never said right out *why* this had happened, because—well, it was implicit, right? To everyone *except* Kate Archer, who knew the Beach's history, and Lydia's story, too, and still failed to put two and two together.

If I had, I might not have...

Well, no. Knowing that the Guardian was responsible for not only the land, but the *town's* prosperity wouldn't have made any difference in my decision to leave Archers Beach when I did, given my reasons.

But before I'd gone, after the land had accepted me—those few years when I'd been...happy. During those years, there *had* been a slight uptick in the fortunes of Archers Beach. Now, I knew why. Back then—I'd just figured that these things went through cycles, if I thought about it at all.

Gran, though.

Gran had known the reason for the decline—and she had known what to do to perk things up again.

She wasn't exactly a disinterested party, either. The Pepperidges and the Archers go 'way, 'way back, to the first Archer's landing at the foot of Heath Hill, which event piqued the interest of a certain tree...

"So I was a sacrifice," I said, and felt Mr. Ignat's glance warm the side of my face.

I raised my hand before he could speak.

"No, that's all right. I *was* raised to be a princess—and Aeronymous started statecraft lessons early."

Mr. Ignat' nodded slowly. "You stood two lives from his throne," he said.

"And the politics of the Land of the Flowers being what they are, sooner or later I would have..." It hit me, then, for the very first time. Hit me, and took my breath. I slammed to a stop right there, staring very hard at absolutely nothing.

I sensed that Mr. Ignat' had stopped, too, and was waiting, patiently, for me to do, or say, something.

"I just realized," I said. "*Really* realized that—Mother and I—we're the only survivors." Of our House, that the Ozali Ramendysis had broken so he could drink our power.

Which meant that *I*, Prince Nathan's heir—I *was* Aeronymous now, Sovereign of the Sea.

"Will you return to the Land of the Flowers to take up your birthright, Pirate Kate?"

Mr. Ignat' isn't a mind reader, but he's known me a long time. Also, his rebooted self is as sharp as a drawerful of knives, like we say here in Maine.

I half-laughed.

"Y'know?" I shook my head. "This job here may be occasionally annoying, but I wouldn't survive three minutes in the Land of the Flowers."

"I think you underrate yourself," Mr. Ignat' said, "but I agree with your decision to allow someone else to aspire to Sea King."

"Well." I got my feet moving again, and Mr. Ignat' with me.

"As for which *trenvay* are treacherous," he continued, as if weighty matters of succession had never been on the table, "they all are, each according to their nature. You will have to be on your guard, and when your guard slips, you must recover."

My fencing master used to say something eerily similar to that. And then she'd add that making a recover was much more difficult than simply doing the thing right the first time.

"I'm going to have to make a recover, then."

"It may be interesting to learn why Artie wanted the rooster with you," Mr. Ignat' agreed blandly.

I laughed. "Oh, it'll be *interesting*, all right! I was just wishing for a little peace and quiet. A few mundane problems, not many, just enough to keep me on my toes. Working with the land on those spots that've gone silent. Promoting Joe Nemeier's removal from the Beach, preferably in chains, but I'll let him go under his own power, if he promises never to come back. No more... *imported* problems."

"Do you think you can expect that?" Mr. Ignat' asked seriously.

I shook my head, thinking about my life so far, not to mention my current duties and entanglements.

And nonentanglements, too.

"A girl can dream, can't she?"

"She can. She should also be well-armed and expert in the use
of her weapons." He gave me a bright smile. "Shall we repair to
the beach for our lesson?"

The sand showed scorch marks, here and there, for those
with eyes to see them, and I wasn't much more than a limp
rag. Through my exhaustion, I felt the land's worry, but it
was being good, if slightly antsy, like a dog told to "sit" and
"stay" while his master proceeds to engage in an activity that
is not...quite safe.

Spellcraft lessons aren't easy for me. I'm not one of those
crime-fighting, half-fey princesses found in urban fantasy novels,
who revel in their powers, and need no lessons in their use, or
in control.

By contrast, I'm only one-quarter fey, my power *will* turn on
and eat me if I'm not constantly vigilant, and I'm *much* better
at hacking than spellcraft.

All that said, I'm not a mundane person, either; I was born
with the ability, however small, to hold *jikinap* and bend it to
my will, and I'm not, despite what you might think by looking
at the evidence, a complete idiot.

To prove that last point, I now had firmly in my possession
three premade defensive spells and a Word to trigger each, *and*
three offensive spells, also with triggers. In theory—largely Mr.
Ignat's theory—I was now at least adequately armed and armored
against attack. The spells were, like all of Mr. Ignat's workings,
jewels of tightly woven efficiency. The six I now held in readiness
had required only a thimble's worth of *jikinap* to build—enough
to do the job, and not a dab more—and had been relatively
simple to construct.

No, the trouble hadn't been with the building, it had been
with the tuning.

See, if I was under attack, I would trigger a defense spell first.
Then, I would either run like hell, or release a counterattack. The
problem with the counterattack option is that, having triggered
my defenses, I would be enveloped by a hopefully impenetrable
shield—which I would have to breach, in order to properly answer
my enemy.

In the general way of things, it's not smart to drop your defense during battle. There are exceptions to this rule, naturally, but I'm talking about good common sense.

This general rule of thumb is even more important in a duel between Ozali, when your opponent will be most earnestly trying to wrest your power from you and make it their own. Any imperfection in your defense, any flaw in your spellcraft can and will be used against you.

That being so, the smart Ozali who wants to live to eat tomorrow's breakfast builds a replicator into his offensive spell.

It's like a computer virus, really. You trigger the offensive spell; it strikes the defense wall and forces a structural exchange. The offense is now part of the defense, and the former offense is now defense.

As the offensive spell moves toward the outside of the defense wall, the new defense spell follows it and does cleanup, stitching the wall back together almost before it's breached.

When the offense reaches the outer wall and is released to its mission, the plug is already in place—and the wall has never shown a breach.

If that explanation makes your head hurt, you'll understand why the sand was littered with the charred and pitiful remains of broken spells.

"Well done, Katie," said Mr. Ignat'. "You have reason to be proud of this day's work."

He was stretched on his back on the sand, arms crossed under his head, his hat tipped over his eyes, perfectly relaxed as he oversaw my efforts. Even the rather . . . exclamatory explosion of an unbalanced weaving had been insufficient to disturb his air of sleepy interest. I got the impression that he viewed my clumsy efforts, numerous fumbles, and frequent use of colorful language in the light of a toddler's ambitious play.

Of course, if he was old enough to consider Artie a *boy*, then I just about made rank as a toddler.

"More relieved than proud, actually," I said. "It feels better to have *some*thing in my pocket."

"It's never pleasant to be without defenses. Not only have you solved that problem, but you've learned several important principles today, which we'll be building on in later lessons."

I considered him.

"Will we?"

Eyes hidden by his hat, he smiled. "Oh, yes."

"Great," I said unenthusiastically.

Turning, I surveyed the carnage on the sand before me. An Ozali does not leave *jikinap* just lying about for another Ozali to find, absorb—and use against her.

I raised my hands, which I did purely to focus myself; put my attention on the scattered bits of my power, and breathed in.

A bright taste of butterscotch on the back of my tongue, a flash of heat along my spine. The sand before me was pure and clean, and I was again reunited with my power.

Lucky me.

To say that I was conflicted concerning my store of *jikinap* would be a masterful piece of understatement, even in Maine, where understatement is both a virtue and an art form.

On the one hand, I would sooner let it go; give it away to someone better suited to it—say, Mr. Ignat'.

But Mr. Ignat', having willingly given up, and been without the benefits of, his power for a hundred years, seemed in no hurry to increase his relatively modest magical holdings.

That he had once been a very great Ozali, I accepted as a fact—not only because I trusted and loved him still, God help me—but because the *jikinap* I now hosted had been his, before he had passed it to me, as a gift.

At his present power level, he was no match for any avenging Ozali as might suddenly happen into the Changing Land—that's what the rest of the Six Worlds call our little piece of interdimensional reality. Hell, he wasn't a match for *me*. I so outweighed him, magically speaking, that I could, even now, this minute, call up my power and allow it to absorb...

"Argh!"

I sat down, hard, on the sand, smashing the rising *jikinap* to the base of my spine so hard that I gasped. The land, apparently taking this a sign that it was released from my command for quiet, performed its version of leaping straight up into the air and licking me on the nose.

"Gently, Katie," Mr. Ignat' murmured, apparently unaware of how close he had just come to being consumed.

"Gentle?" I snapped. "Why should I be gentle with it? It's a treacherous, greedy invader, just waiting to drown me in itself and take over the world!"

For the first time, Mr. Ignat' seemed troubled. He sat up, pushed his hat back on his head and regarded me for a long moment, smooth brow wrinkled. Then, as if a breeze had wafted him upright, he rose and walked toward me.

"Stay back!" I said sharply, but apparently he'd gone deaf, too, because he kept on walking, and hunkered down on his heels not a hand's span away from me.

"Katie, Katie, what is this?" He extended a hand and casually slipped his fingers under my chin, as if I really was a toddler.

As if it wasn't really, truly dangerous for him to touch me.

I felt the *jikinap* stir, waking a sensation eerily like physical hunger. I took a deep, deliberate breath, tasting air spiced with salt and sand. The *jikinap* subsided, and Mr. Ignat' smiled.

"You are master of yourself, Pirate Kate. Never doubt it. And this notion that your power will eat you—it will not. It *can*not. Your power is you. If it eats you, it will destroy itself."

His voice was absolutely steady; truth weighted each word, and I wanted—oh, how very much I wanted—to believe him.

I swallowed.

"That's not true," I said. "Look at Ramendysis."

"Ramendysis held more power than he could absorb," Mr. Ignat' said patiently. "You are not so foolish—or so driven. In a duel between raw power and spellcraft—spellcraft will win." He tipped his head, as if considering, and added, "Unless something unfortunate happens."

"Like raw power crushing the opposition under it?"

"Rarely that," Mr. Ignat' said seriously. "Most usually, it's because a spell is flawed. Now, it is true that a certain amount of power must be maintained, as you're doing, in order to be able to mount a credible defense, if challenged. But the power you maintain, Katie, is far below a toxic dose. It does take some time to . . . integrate. But I swear to you that it will happen. The best thing you can do is learn your spellcraft, and practice it often. Your power will become accustomed to you, and you to it; it will no longer fight you, or seek to force you to its goals. Tame power is a tool. Wild power—is wild."

Most of my present power—that gift from Mr. Ignat'—was that *tame*? And what about the *jikinap* I'd stolen from Ramendysis?

I'd killed Ozali Ramendysis—*not* by the use of superior spell-craft. The plan had been to hit him with a bolt of *jikinap*—think overloading a circuit, and blowing a fuse. I had happened to hope that what would blow was Ramendysis' head, but as it happened, I missed my shot, and hit—

I caught my breath and turned my head away, squinting as I stared out over the waves. My eyes were watering, but that was because the sun was so bright on the water.

Of course.

"Katie, Borgan's well."

I looked back at him, my chest clutching.

"You've seen him?"

He shook his head.

"No, child, I haven't. But I can see the ocean."

There was, I thought, that. When I had—when I had missed Ramendysis, with all that power, I had hit Borgan, who was... call him the Guardian of the Gulf of Maine. My opposite number.

And when that bolt hit home, and Borgan collapsed onto the blades of Googin Rock...

The sea had gone dead calm. Not a wave, not a ripple disturbed its surface. It was as if the Gulf felt his absence and mourned it.

Happily, though I didn't think so at the time, I'd managed to pull my shot just enough that I didn't... entirely kill him. Thinking on it, as, believe me, I have done, hundreds of times in the weeks since it happened— Thinking back on it, it may have been that his braid had fallen into the water when he collapsed, and through that link the sea—the sea had saved him.

That was one of the things I wanted to ask, when I saw him again.

If I saw him again.

Don't be stupid, Kate, I told myself; *you know healing takes time.*

Right; I know that.

I *know* that.

"Katie?"

I took a breath and turned my head, meeting Mr. Ignat's eyes.

"I'm fine," I said, and forced a smile. "So! When's the next lesson?"

CHAPTER FIVE

We came into Fun Country from the beach side, and I left Mr.
Ignat' at Keltic Knot, stopping for a minute to admire the gleam
and glitter of the ride in the sunlight.

"It's looking good," I said, putting one foot up on the safety
rail, and propping my elbows on the top. "Better than ever."

"Elbow grease," Mr. Ignat' told me, slipping inside the fence—his
prerogative as owner-operator. "Elbow grease and virtuous living."

"Well, that sinks me," I said, smiling at the dragon-headed
lead car. The carved eyes sparkled lifelike, the scales adorning
her long, graceful neck were sharp-edged and distinct. The whole
ride looked new-made, as if it had partaken of, and prospered
from, Mr. Ignat's increased circumstances.

Which isn't really that farfetched an idea, now is it, Kate? I
asked myself.

I straightened up from my lean on the fence and raised a hand.

"I'll see you Saturday morning," I called.

"I'll be there!" He vanished behind the dragon.

I strolled off, past the Scrambler, its silver gondolas flashing
in the sun like the real thing, the plastic cushions glowing like
old crimson leather.

It being Thursday, and not yet Season, the park was pretty much deserted. Jess Robald was bucking the trend, bent over Tom Thumb's open engine with a screwdriver in one hand. I waved as I strolled past.

"Hey, Kate!" she called, straightening up and moving to the fence.

"Hey," I answered, making the slight detour. I put my hands on the rail and looked up into her face. "How's it going?"

"Going good. Well." She jerked her head at the dismantled engine behind her. "Going okay. If I can get the stack blowing smoke again, that'll notch us back up to 'good.'" She shrugged and gave me grin. "My dad always did say I was a perfectionist. Train runs fine without the smoke, and what do the kids know, anymore? But it's meant to blow smoke and I ain't happy unless it does as it's meant."

"I can understand that," I said.

"Guess you do. How's it going with finding a replacement?"

"Got one due in this afternoon."

She grinned, genuinely delighted. "That's great! Listen—why I called you over. There's a group of us getting together to talk about ways to lengthen the Season. Twelve weeks ain't enough to live on—townies *or* town! Thought you might like to be there— gonna be a breakfast meetin' up the Garden Monday 'round eight o'clock."

"The Garden?" I repeated.

"Garden Cafe; new place up the hill. The *place* is new, I'm saying. The owner—well, hell—Michelle's been on the Beach since she come up as summer help, back a time, now. Summer got over, Michelle stayed. Worked short-order for Bob that first winter, went to the Buoy next Season, then down the Brunswick—guess she's cooked in every restaurant in town, over years. Finally decided to start her own. Been open couple months now. Business was slow at first, but it's started picking up in the last five, six weeks."

"Five or six weeks," I echoed, around a funny feeling in my stomach.

Jess nodded. "Takes time for word to get out—but it's sure out now!"

"Terrific," I said, my voice sounding weak in my own ears.

"Be good if you came by, Kate," Jess said, and added, "Marilyn says the park can't get involved in town business. Says Fun Country's Season is set by the Board."

Fun Country's Board is in New Jersey, and they hadn't had one bit of trouble giving Marilyn the okay for the Super Early Season, once the sweet smell of money wafted under their pointy noses.

"Marilyn'll get on board after everybody else does the work," I said. "If we build a longer, better Season, you bet Fun Country's going to be open for it."

Jess thought about that, her head tipped to one side.

"I can see that, I guess," she said. "But you'll come by on Monday?"

One of the very few benefits of no longer being regularly employed by a dotcom is the utter lack of meetings in my life. I hated the damn' things.

On the other hand . . .

Oh, what the hell, I thought, and nodded at Jess.

"Sure, I'll come by, and have a cup of coffee."

You'd've thought I'd given her a pony.

"That's great! That's—well." She got her grin under control, and gave me an enthusiastic nod. "I won't keep you anymore, but—see you Monday, then!"

"See you Monday," I agreed, wondering what I'd just gotten myself into, and continued my interrupted trek across the park.

Fun Country's Early Season hours are Friday, Saturday, and Sunday, noon to 10 P.M. That meant things would start waking up around 11:30 tomorrow morning: the empty rides would cycle through their paces, slow and tempting; the arcade's metal doors would go up—*rattle, bang, slam!*—the avenue games would light up; the fortune-teller would hang out her shingle; the T-shirt shop owner would prop the door open with a big old piece of rose quartz, and the barkers would start humming their patter.

By noon, Fun Country would welcome maybe a dozen visitors, all adults. By five o'clock, after school let out and the kids were on the prowl, the place would be a madhouse.

Saturday, they'd be climbing the fence by ten. Ka-Pow!, the arcade, which had its own door onto Fountain Circle, might open up as early as 10:15 on an Early Season Saturday, keeping the gates between it and Fun Country shut tight until Marilyn Michaud, the park manager, hit the air horn two blasts, which was the signal to open 'er up.

Marilyn's a woman who likes her "t"s crossed, her "i"s dotted, and her clock keeping good time. The thought of all those dollar bills being spent early in the arcade was a powerful motivator, though, and more often than not Fun Country was open for Saturday business by 10:30.

Sunday was the only day of the three when the noon rule was good; an inverted day: crowds early, and the park deserted by 8:30 in the evening.

It wasn't a convenient schedule, and it didn't earn anybody what you'd call a living wage, but it did bring in coffee money. In the past, the Early Season had been the shakedown run—the dress rehearsal for the Season—when rides were fine-tuned, and patter refined; when the summer greenies who minded the hoop shoot, the duck-pick and the lobster toss perfected their skill with the game, and the guy who guessed weights and age practiced on everybody who walked by.

I passed the log flume, dry until tomorrow, and crossed the service alley to Baxter Avenue. The lights were on at Dodge City, but I didn't see Millie around. The giant samurai astride the roof of the Oriental Funhouse was silent, his swords sheathed at his back. Summer's Wheel was locked down, the gondolas swinging slightly in the breeze.

When the park's closed, the carousel's snug and safe behind padlocked gray steel storm gates. I used my key, slipped the lock through one loop and snapped it shut before I stepped inside, leaving the door standing wide behind me.

There's been a carousel in Archers Beach for coming on a hundred ten years. Not the same carousel, of course. *This* carousel—what you might call *my* carousel—has been in its current location for just under eighty-five years. Before that—from 1902 through 1923—it stood at the center of what was then called Sea Side Park.

A couple fires later, and the carousel was still standing, one of Fun Country's treasured "name" rides: the Fantasy Menagerie Carousel.

A menagerie, in carousel terms, means a ride that gives animals that aren't horses equal time—you might get a pig, a stag, or a tiger on a menagerie carousel; rarely, there'll be no horses at all.

On a *fantasy* menagerie, you'll not only see your nonequine mounts, but those out of mythology, too.

That being the case, the Fantasy Menagerie Carousel at Fun Country in Archers Beach, Maine, presents, when fully populated, twenty-three wooden animals: four traditional horses, fifteen critters of land and sea, and four fantasy figures, plus a swan chariot.

Beg pardon.

Three fantasy figures—dragon, unicorn, and hippocampus. The fourth fantasy figure—a dainty gray horse with delicate fangs and businesslike bat wings—that was the figure that had flown the coop.

Soon to be replaced by a fiberglass rooster.

That . . . It just wasn't right.

I had paused by the safety rail, my fingers curled 'round the cool metal, seeing not the carousel, a shadowy wheel encompassing forever, but the batwing horse as I had last seen her—milky eyes and lithesome form; skin so dark it had been iridescent in the sunlight; and when she smiled, she showed dainty, pearly fangs.

The Opal of Dawn, princess of Daknowyth, the Land of Midnight.

I sighed sharply, pushed a section of rail out of my way and crossed to the carousel, leaping lightly to the platform.

Before she had regained her true form—for that had been her true form, blind, farseeing eyes, fangs, and all—before she had regained her true form, the Opal of Dawn had been bound into the batwing horse, one of six beings so imprisoned within the Fantasy Menagerie Carousel.

Or so I had been told.

It seems that Gran hadn't been quite truthful with me about the whys and what-fors of the batwing horse's presence on the carousel. She'd had her reasons—good reasons—and I supposed I had no call to complain about having been left in the dark. After all, I'd been a kid, and right when I was approaching an age where a fond grandmother might expect that I might know how to value a deep and deadly secret, I left home, deliberately abandoning my duty and my family.

And yet—it had almost got me killed, not knowing. My ignorance had almost destroyed the Beach.

I sighed sharply.

Still a lot to think about *there*, obviously.

Getting back to the business at hand . . . The batwing horse hadn't been a particular favorite of mine while she was bound to the carousel—in fact, I hadn't liked her . . . at all.

She'd redeemed herself at the last, though—and stood a brave comrade when I'd needed her most.

Which was, I guess, why I missed her now, and felt a tug of real sadness as I came to stand in the spot she had occupied.

I shook my head, and pivoted slowly on a heel.

To the rear of my position were the bear and the giraffe. Ahead were the dolphin and the deer. To my immediate right, on the outside circle of standers, was the ostrich.

Well, a rooster would fit right in, I thought, but I didn't grin at my own joke.

Instead, I walked down the carousel, touching the animals as I passed, testing the poles, the bindings...

...*the bindings.*

The remaining five prisoners inhabit the hippocampus, unicorn, goat, knight's charger, and wolf. I don't know anything about them, other than they'd committed crimes so heinous that their home Lands had repudiated them and turned them over to the Wise for disposition. And the Wise, after such discoveries and deliberations as they deemed useful, if any, had bound the prisoners, all five, into the carousel.

If that sounds daft to you, well...that's the Wise.

The Wise are the final arbiters and dispensers of justice across the Six Worlds, and most sensible folk in *any* world would rather cut off their good right arm than have anything at all to do with them. Only the most desperate cases go to them for adjudication, and their judgment, no matter how seemingly crazy, is final.

That ought to give you a reading, right there, on exactly how badass the beings bound into those wooden animals are.

As to why they're bound into *this particular carousel*...

Our world—the Real World, as we call it—is the last and least of the Six in terms of the things that count—according, you understand, to the good citizens of the Upper Five. We're not only low on *jikinap*, we're *damn'* low on anybody who thinks that's a problem.

The reason there's so little magic here—*that's* what excited the interest of the Wise, and why Gran's carousel was turned into a prison.

Jikinap needs a certain stability; a lack of motion, so that it can pool, ferment, and reduce into the sticky, needy, almost-substance that's the common tool of all Ozali, across all the Worlds.

Here at home in the Changing Land, there's just too much going on, all the time; the magic doesn't have very many cozy deep places to settle into and stew.

Not only is the land in motion, but, well...

Like the name says: Things *change* here.

Which brings us to the Grand Experiment of the Wise.

If the prisoners were bound, for a period of time unknown, but assumed to be long, in the eye of a change-storm...

...would they, too, change?

Would they change *enough*—and in a...more seemly direction?

I don't precisely know how long the prisoners have been incarcerated, though I'd gotten the impression from Gran that it had been what we Mainers dignify as *a good long while*. How long it had been since anybody from the Wise's central office had stopped by to check on them was anybody's guess.

Personally, I was betting that nobody had *ever* checked on them.

I should, I thought, standing again in the place the batwing horse had occupied for all of my memory of the carousel—before she left for her own land again, I should have asked her, the Opal of Dawn, if she had Changed.

A shadow flickered across my sight; I turned, glancing up—

"Kate?" A woman's voice echoed off the steel roof and walls. "You home?"

"Nancy?" I moved across the platform until she could see me from her position just inside the open door. "C'mon in!"

She did that, moving easy and boneless, like a cat on a casual hunt. Slipping through the gap I'd left in the security fence, she hopped up onto the platform and gave me a nod, easing the gimme hat up with a nudge of her forefinger.

"Stopping by to see about Season hours, if you're gonna need me." She cast an appraising eye up and around the boards and the brass work.

"Lookin' good," she said, soft enough to have been talking to herself. She met my eye and said it again, louder, and with emphasis.

"Lookin' *damn* good."

"What can I say? You do good work."

Nancy had been my pre-Super-Early-Season prep crew, bringing the mechanicals up to spec after a winter of idleness, polishing the brass, putting in the lights, threading the paper through the orchestrion, and every other bit of fiddly, necessary work that needed to be done, with the exception of anything that touched on the carousel critters themselves.

Smart woman, Nancy Vois.

She'd stayed on as part-time carousel operator for the Super Early Season. The Early Season being what it was, I didn't have much need of her. Still, a good employee is worth holding onto, and I'd offered to split what hours there were, right down the middle, or any other way she liked it.

But, it happened that she didn't like any Early Season hours. She had work as a casual mechanic at the Little Egret Marina up on Casco Bay, working side-hours and off-shifts for cash money under the table.

"Marina doesn't need you during the Season?"

She lifted a skinny shoulder and let it fall.

"Marina needs extra hands at the start and end of *their* Season, to put the boats in the water, and take 'em out again. Reg'lar yard crew can handle it from now on t'Labor Day."

"Well, I'll be pleased to have you, like I said before. How many hours you need and what's your rate of pay?"

She shook her head and shoved her hands into the front pockets of her jeans as she took up a lean against a brass pole.

"Management's s'posed to decide that stuff."

"Let's say I'm grooming you to take my place."

She snorted delicately, then directed her gaze over my head, like she was taking counsel of the canopy lights.

"Now, see, I can always use hours. My experience is everybody can always use hours. If it was up t'me, looking at the ride open seventy-six hours across seven days, an' Management with paperwork and suchlike on top of that, I'd be thinking..."

She brought her eyes down from the heights to meet mine.

"You hiring a greenie?"

The greenies come in on a general contract with the Archers Beach Chamber of Commerce, and hail from places like Ukraine and the Czech Republic and Hungary. They work as housekeepers in the motels, as waitstaff—and as game agents and ride operators at Fun Country. The arrangement between the hiring agency and the CoC is one of long standing, and it generally, as far as I knew, worked well for all concerned.

And it wasn't like Maine college kids wanted to come down to Archers Beach to work a lousy twelve-week Season, when they could go down to Atlantic City, Rehobeth Beach, or Cape May for a longer Season, and better pay—not to mention warmer water.

I shrugged. "The park sent 'round a letter, asking us all to take on a kid or three. Frankly, I wanted to talk with you first. If you weren't interested, I was going to bring on a kid for the early afternoons, and figure on sleeping when the Season's over."

Nancy nodded judiciously. "Could be done that way. Now, what I've got in mind would get the work done, wouldn't nobody get killed, and we'd do a greenie a good turn."

"I'm all ears."

"Getcher greenie in noon to four, when it's quiet, mostly. The park feeds 'em lunch, and they get the hours on their card. The two of us'll split the night shift, when there's more likely to be trouble"—she looked owlish—"since we're able to handle trouble."

I was able to handle trouble, given one thing and another. Nancy? Well . . . yeah. I'd seen Nancy go after trouble six times her size, dig her claws in and hold on tight.

"It's a plan," I said. "The greenie's pay is set by contract, and the park matches half. What rate are you looking at for yourself?"

She pursed her lips.

"You sure I'm cut out for Management?"

"You're doing fine."

"Well." She sighed. "I'm thinking the arrangement we had during the Super Early Season was advantageous."

Nancy's Super Early Season pay had been a percentage of the net. Given that the Super Early Season had been completely new, and nobody'd known what to expect, that had sort of made sense. The regular Season, though . . .

"I've been going over the financials for the last couple years and income's been on a steady decline. I'd feel better giving you a set wage. Twenty percent—"

"Fifteen," she put in.

"—of Not Much is Pretty Near Nothing. If we settle on three hundred a week, then you know what's coming. And!" I pushed on, seeing she was about to say something else. "Wages are a business expense for Management."

"Things're looking up," Nancy said. "I think the Super Early Season was the start of luckier times comin'. Fifteen percent's fair. You can pay me extra for any repairs that need doing."

"Twenty percent," I said, giving her an ice princess stare right down my nose. "And extra for repairs."

Nancy gave as good as she got on the stare. Used to run a

Harley in a pack, did Nancy. Funny how the skills we learn young stay with us.

"You're insulting me, Kate. Fifteen percent or I walk."

Well, I knew when I was licked.

"You drive a hard bargain. Fifteen, it is. Extra for repairs."

I stuck my hand out.

"Done."

We shook on it, and Nancy looked 'round my shoulder.

"Still nothing to replace her?"

"Got something coming in this afternoon," I said, giving her a grin. "You up for earning some repair money?"

"Depends on when it's coming. I told Ma I'd be home 'bout five."

"Should be here before that," I said.

And right on cue there came a clanging noise, as if somebody was rattling the park gate, and a man's voice singing out loud and strong.

"Kate Archer? Delivery!"

CHAPTER SIX

※

High Tide 9:33 P.M.
Moonrise 5:27 P.M.
Moonset 2:40 A.M. EDT

"Seriously?"

Nancy took her cap off, rubbed her sandy going-to-gray curls, and reseated the cap, never once taking her eyes off the rooster.

I sighed. "Best I could do."

Nancy was still staring.

"Come from the Enterprise, too," she said, voice carefully neutral.

"*Now* you're starting to sound like my grandmother," I said, maybe a little too sharp, because she shifted her gaze to me and turned one hand palm up to show her lack of intentional insult.

"Sorry. Sorry. It's just...the Enterprise isn't exactly trustworthy."

"So my grandmother *also* informed me. After the deal was done."

"Right." Nancy sighed. Slid a glance at the rooster. Winced.

"My other choice was a horse of doubtful provenance from Painted Pony Pete—who is, for the record, not himself a model citizen."

"Well, but, Kate, even if the horse didn't come off the ride he said it did, or whatever, if it was a good wood horse—"

"You can stop there. If there had been any possibility of it being a *good* wooden horse, I might've gone for it. Unfortunately, the line of nonsense Pete threw down makes me suspect a knockoff—and a bad knockoff at that. Plus, he mentioned up front that it needed repairs, but not what those repairs might be." I shook my head. "I can't afford a horse that's gonna break down after two rides. And *nobody* can afford a horse that might fail and get somebody hurt."

Nancy stood a long minute, head tipped to one side, then nodded briskly. "Right you are." She raised her cap and settled it again, and looked sternly at the rooster.

"Well, let's get 'er mounted, then."

It took both of us to do the deed, after I'd done a thorough inspection, physical and magical. The body was sound, excepting that crack; neither the land nor my own awesome Ozali powers detected anything more or less than an old and ugly fiberglass rooster in need of cleaning and a paint job.

Once it was in place, I ran the carousel a couple turns to make sure everything was hooked up all tight and proper—which it was. Nancy does good work.

"Well," said the woman herself, from her lean on the safety rail beside me.

I knew what she meant. "It does change the tone, doesn't it? I'll patch him and paint him tonight; thread in the stirrups. Be as bright as a new penny for tomorrow's crowds."

Nancy laughed softly.

"Tomorrow's *epic* crowds," she murmured, and stirred slightly. "Kate?"

"Yeah?"

"If you don't mind my asking..." Her voice drifted off.

I turned my head to look at her, but all I got was the side of her face as she gazed determinedly at the carousel.

I looked in that direction myself, deliberately not sighing at the rooster.

"If I mind your asking, I'll say so. Deal?"

"More'n fair." She paused, then said, her voice too casual, "I'm wondering if you've had word of Cap'n Borgan."

It was a reasonable question, considering. I told myself that, and took a couple of deep, cleansing breaths. In spite of which, the words that came out of my mouth went off on a tangent.

"Finn's not fishing for you?"

"No, no—he is. Doing a good job. Good enough job. It's just

Ma was wondering after the Cap'n the other night. He used to drop by now and again—visit with her a bit. It's been six, seven weeks..."

Every bit of six or seven weeks, yeah. I took another nice, deep breath.

"Haven't seen him," I said, admiring how level my voice was. "If I do, I'll pass the message that your mother misses his wit and good looks."

"'Preciate it. He's a favorite, see? She doesn't get out much and—she says he reminds her of the sea."

Well, of course he reminded her of the sea. I pressed my lips tight and nodded, thoughtfully.

"Well!" Nancy pushed away from the rail. "I'd best be getting on. We'll settle on shifts solid once you got the greenie lined up."

"Yeah." I stood up, too. "I'll go down and talk to Marilyn about that now—and let her know the happy news."

"Hire a summer worker?" Marilyn looked up from behind her desk, eyebrows slightly raised, which for her was an exclamation of shock and surprise. Well, Gran didn't ever hire a greenie— not that I knew about, anyhow. It might've been a fear of what might happen, should one of the prisoners become unruly while she wasn't by. It could've been something else. Something, say, like the Ozali Ramendysis happening by one fine spring day and demanding his property back, or else he'd leave the Beach a smoking heap of slag.

Well, that particular surprise was behind us, and I was confident of the bindings on the remaining five—bindings that had been examined and approved by Gran *and* by Mr. Ignat' in his role as Ozali Belignatious.

All that being so—

"Are they all spoken for?" I asked Marilyn. "The greenies?"

She shook herself and glanced down at the top her desk, specifically at a printed list tidily lined up with the edge of the desk calendar.

"We still have several young people who need hours. Will you be needing more than one?"

"Just one should do it," I said. "Nancy Vois'll be splitting nights with me, but I can use somebody to cover noon to four."

Eyes on the list, Marilyn nodded.

"I've got one or two whose schedules might accommodate those hours. Let me find out…" She looked up at me. "Is it all right if I send somebody around to talk to you tomorrow night?"

"That's fine; you know where to find me."

"All right," she said, and frowned slightly, as if she expected me to beat a retreat now that our business was done.

Except it wasn't…exactly…done.

"Wanted to let you know, too," I said, "that I got in a replacement animal, and we'll be fully functional as of opening time tomorrow. Thanks for working with me on this, Marilyn."

It wasn't the sort of speech Marilyn was used to having from me—and I didn't blame her one bit for the blink and the moment of silence. Credit where it's due, though, she made a fast recovery and nodded, smiling as much as she ever does.

"Of course, Fun Country was pleased to work with you, Kate. The carousel has been a Name Ride, and an anchor of this park, for a lot of years, now. If there's anything else we can do to assist, you only have to let me know."

As long as it didn't cost Fun Country one thin dime, or discommode the directors any; but diplomacy counts, as my grandfather would have said, though not exactly in those words. That being so, I summoned up a stately smile, inclined my head, and eased out of the office before either one of us ran out of patience.

It was midnight by the time I'd finished patching, cleaning, painting, and communing with the newest member of the carousel.

On the communing front, all I'd gotten for my trouble and concern was the general feeling that the land didn't much care for the rooster. I couldn't get a reading on why this was so. It wasn't anything so pointed as a repugnance for something that was alien—a Black Dog, say, or a willie wisp, critters that have from time to time been known to cross the Wall between the Worlds and run along the shore. Neither one belonged, and the land was right to call foul.

The rooster, though…the rooster produced a sense of… unease; just a little niggle of something so minor I couldn't even categorize it as *worry* at the back of my mind. The proximity of the Guardian to the rooster for several hours of cleaning and painting did nothing to increase the unease.

Or decrease it, either.

I finished adjusting the stirrup leathers and sighed in irritation. I'd already inspected the thing three times with varying degrees of thoroughness.

"Which means doing it a fourth time won't kill you," I muttered. "And not doing it, might."

There was that.

I took a deep breath, deliberately setting my irritation aside, and a second, tasting tangy-cool sea air. Fortified, I stepped Sideways, and considered the rooster minutely, one more time.

Seeing Sideways is a lot like looking through infrared glasses. *Jikinap* glows thick, deep yellow; *trenvay* glamor is bright green; illusion tends toward the blue-and-silver end of things. If the object of scrutiny is a person, Sideways sight will detect, along with the aforementioned, sincerity, insincerity, pain, love. Rarely will something or someone look exactly the same in Side-Sight as it looks in real sight.

The rooster was that rare thing.

Which, yeah, made me uneasy.

I put every ounce of concentration I had on the seeing, but no matter how hard I stared, the rooster was the rooster, with no glow of *jikinap*, spell, or *trenvay* glamor about it.

Well.

I stepped fully back into the here and now—and shook my head.

The rooster would never be a thing of beauty. It was clean and sharp with new paint, but what it wasn't, was inviting. Mind you, the batwing horse hadn't been *inviting*, particularly, but she had been...*challenging*. She had appealed to the hidden Batman in some riders' psyches, and when they dismounted at the end of the ride, they felt not only merry—the usual euphoria brought on by spinning in a circle bathed in carousel music, with the sea air and the scent of Chinese cooking filling head and lungs—but accomplished. To have ridden the batwing, even in her reduced circumstances, was *something*.

To ride the rooster...I shook my head again. It was easy to see it scaring the kiddies—truth told, the really little kids hadn't cottoned to the batwing—but it was less easy to see it calling forth somebody's inner Zorro.

I frowned at it, feeling suddenly warm despite the fact that I'd pushed the storm wall back to let the breeze in. The rooster in all its motley glory filled my vision—grotesque and oh-so-slightly disturbing. If only it were...goofy, instead of grotesque; slightly welcoming instead of subtly off-putting.

The heat intensified, and I recognized the butterscotch tang of *jikinap*, rising to the will of an Ozali. That ought to have worried me, but I was more concerned with the rooster. I raised my hand, seeing the magic sparkle along my fingertips, and considered the options.

My first thought was to apply something akin to another coat of paint, this one made of inviting goofiness. My second thought was that glamor, like paint, needs to be renewed, and the better thing, by far, would be to anchor the spell inside the fiberglass body.

No sooner had I thought it than the *jikinap* dancing along my fingers grew sticky with my intent. I stepped Sideways again while I rolled a pinch of the stuff between my palms like Silly Putty. The ball warmed against my skin and I realized that I was humming the theme song from one of the cartoon shows I used to watch with Mr. Ignat' on Saturday mornings, when I was a kid.

That should do it, then, I thought, and stepped forward.

I braced one hand on the pole, and pressed the sticky ball of *jikinap* into the rooster's chest, watching it sink through the paint and the epoxy that I had used to seal the crack, to lodge, finally and firmly, deep inside the cavity.

Like a heart.

I stepped back, blinking out of Side-Sight.

Before me, the rooster was unchanged—no.

The rooster was—whimsical. Its eye was bold, its disordered feathers indicative of some late comic adventure, the details of which it just might share with someone who chose to ride it.

I let out a breath I hadn't known I'd been holding. Mission accomplished.

It was quick cleanup, then. I put the paints, brushes, and tarp away in the shed at the back wall, locked up, and made one more round of the carousel, checking the prisoners, to make sure that I hadn't inadvertently destabilized the binding spells. Everything was as it should be, and I smacked the rooster's rump before jumping down and jogging over to the storm gate.

The night was fine, and I stood for a moment on the beach, just breathing in the air, and listening to the waves. Above, the sky was clear; the stars slightly blurred in the mist off the waves. The growing moon was low on the horizon.

My house was a short walk upbeach, left, and under the Pier; I could be home in under five minutes.

I turned right, angling down toward the water and the firm wet sand that made for easier walking.

Past Fun Country, past Googin Rock and Heath Hill, the shore notches in to make a protected cove. That's Kinney Harbor, where the working boats of Archers Beach dock. On the far side of the cove is the Kinney Harbor Seafood Exchange—the 'change, according to the locals. At this time of night it was quiet, just the warn-away lamps on the corners of the deck glowing inside the rising mist.

Near to hand was a wooden pier, and it had been my intention to mount it and lean my elbows on the rail, overlooking the harbor and maybe watching Borgan's pretty little schooner dance at her mooring.

But—*Gray Lady* was at the pier.

There was a figure on deck, a shadow standing before the lantern. My heart cramped, then lifted, guilt and joy mingled painfully.

"Borgan?" I said quietly, even as I saw that the shadow was too short, and not nearly broad enough in the shoulder.

Alarm replaced both joy and guilt, and I moved forward until I was at the tie-up.

"You best of any ought to know precisely where Borgan is—*Guardian*." The voice was sibilant and low—female, I thought—and then was certain as she came into the pool of the bow lights.

Slim and blonde and perfect, she stared down at me from great black eyes, her entire body expressing distaste, and disdain.

"Actually, I don't know where he is, exactly," I said, keeping my voice level. "He was going into the sea to heal, is the last I heard."

"And there he remains," the woman on the boat told me. "Nor will he wish to see his murderess when he emerges."

That hurt, but truth is truth. "I didn't quite kill him, after all."

"Was that your intent? I had heard otherwise."

Wow, was she hard to get along with. I felt my own temper kindling and took a deep breath of sea air, touching the land for . . . equilibrium, if not comfort.

"Do I know you?" I asked.

She shook her pale hair back from her face, showing cheekbones sharp enough to cut paper.

"No, but you are correct—you *ought* to know me. My name is Daphne; I serve the Son of the Sea."

There was, I reminded my temper, serve and *serve*. And I was damned if I was going to ask Daphne which hers was. Nothing to do with me.

I nodded, easy as I could, and lifted a hand.

"Just let Borgan know that Kate was by, the next time you see him, okay?" I said, calculating the tone for insult.

At least my math skills hadn't deserted me. She straightened. She *hissed*.

"And," I continued, in that same successfully insulting tone, "please tell him that Nancy Vois' mother misses him. It's been seven or eight weeks since he's been by and she's starting to think he's avoiding her."

"These land-bound matters are meaningless to the Son of the Sea. He is of the sea. The sea gives him life, and strength, and purpose. The land gives him *nothing*." She leaned forward, long thin fingers gripping the rail so tight I'd've sworn I heard the wood crack. "Do you hear me, *Guardian*?"

I was, truth to tell, getting just a little tired of her throwing my duty around like it was a swear word.

"Nothing wrong with my hearing," I said. "You don't want to pass the message that I was by, that's fine. But he'll want to hear about Mrs. Vois—land or no land. So, don't forget that message. Please."

Daphne leaned forward over the rail.

"The land does not order the sea—*Guardian*."

With that, she turned and vanished below. The deck lights snapped out, leaving me alone in the dark.

Inside my head, the land muttered. I felt a ruffle of tenderness along my nerves; its version of *Don't worry about that harpy, Kate; the Beach loves you.*

That was nice.

I stood on the Pier for another three deep breaths, savoring the good ocean air.

Then, I turned my back on *Gray Lady*, and walked away, home.

CHAPTER SEVEN

Friday, June 9
High Tide 10:41 A.M.
Sunrise 5:01 A.M. EDT

Precisely at 11:05 A.M., I slipped into Fun Country from the beach side following the curve of the carousel's storm gate past Summer's Wheel, and toward Baxter Avenue. The shore-side breeze brought me the smell of egg rolls frying and my stomach rumbled appreciatively.

I figured it had a right. Breakfast had been some hours back, followed by a brisk walk up to the northern corner of Archers Beach, and the salt marsh where, six or seven weeks ago, I'd put a little bit of magical muscle into unfreezing a frozen sluice gate. Once the gate was up, the tide could go in and out of the marsh—Heron Marsh, by name—as it was meant to do, cleansing the waters and nourishing the small lives.

Heron Marsh, having been cut off from the beneficial influences of the tide for...a long time, had been in bad need of cleaning. I wanted to check on my handiwork, and also on the *trenvay* who belonged to the marsh, one Eltenfleur. That was something I should've done weeks ago, but I'd thought it prudent to give him a little time to mellow out after our last interaction.

That had been one of my better ideas. Eltenfleur was hardly mad at me at all anymore for having dumped a juiced-up Ozali on a mission to destroy into his marsh. In fact he'd seemed a little concerned.

"I held him as close as love, Guardian," he said, as we sat together on the edge of his marsh, "but love were not enough for him."

He was a brown-skinned and slender youth with long yellow hair, eyes the green-brown color of marsh mud, thin, sensitive lips, and a mouthful of teeth like a lamprey. His fingers were very long, and webbed, and so were his toes. As *trenvay* looks go, his trended to the middle of the bell curve. A good many *trenvay* are indistinguishable, visually, from ordinary folk. A good many more are strange-looking, and rightly absent themselves from the mundane world.

Besides the keeping of his marsh, Eltenfleur's specialty—call it his hobby—is clasping unwary trespassers in his marsh in a loving embrace and bearing them under the water. I only learned about *that* from research, after the event, but Eltenfleur had damn' near drowned *me* at our first meeting, so I'd hoped he'd be able to handle Ramendysis. I hadn't expected that a mere *trenvay* could effect the drowning of an Ozali, but I had sort of hoped that Eltenfleur would prove himself enough of a pain in the ass that Ramendysis would have gone home—and that part of the plan had worked.

Briefly.

Unfortunately for me—and ultimately for him—he'd then opted to immediately return to the Changing Land and carry on hostilities.

"I appreciate it, that you tried," I told Eltenfleur. "In the end, the land prevailed."

He nodded, politely, and changed the subject.

"The waters continue to freshen," he said, raising a languid hand to direct my attention to the marsh.

It did look considerably better; the surface moved freely, no longer bound with scum, and the water level was higher. The cattails had recovered their cheerfulness; darning needles darted through the salt hay; even the mud smelled cleaner.

"I don't take them, anymore," Eltenfleur said, almost too softly for me to hear.

I turned my head and looked at him; his face averted, as if he was studying something highly interesting among the sparse blades of grass.

"Beg pardon?" I murmured.

He looked up and met my eyes, his showing slightly red at the edges.

"I said that I don't take them anymore—the passersby. I haven't, since ... since ..." He took a breath. "For a very long time."

I carefully nodded, keeping my eyes on his.

"We get older," he said, sounding defiant. "We ... change."

"Yes," I said, feeling that resonate deep in my chest. "We change." We *change* ...

I rounded the edge of the storm gate, the aroma of egg rolls making my mouth water, and swung out into Baxter Avenue, meaning to cross over to Tony Lee's, get myself a plate of early lunch, and have a chat with Anna, Tony's wife, who knows everything going on in the park, though she hardly ever leaves the booth.

Intent as I was on this goal, I didn't see him bearing down from my right until it was almost too late—and truth to tell, I didn't *see* him so much as register something too big and too close. I'd been trained in the arts of war—House Aeronymous core princess curriculum—and training will out.

... usually at the worst possible moment.

I ducked, kicked, and connected.

"Hey!" was the first shout, quickly followed by, "Ow! Hey! Ms. Archer!"

I'd ridden the kick into a spin, now I straightened, staring up into a wholesome face that was at the moment wearing an expression more pained than pleasant.

Despite which, I recognized him.

"Kyle," I said. "Sorry about that. You startled me."

"Guess I did," he said ruefully, bending down to rub his knee. I felt a pang, remembering the solid connection I'd made.

"You okay? Let's go over to Tony Lee's and get you some ice."

"Nah, hey, it's fine," he said, sending a quick glance down, then back up to my face. He grinned, sort of.

"Good thing you weren't wearing boots, though."

That was the truth. I'd've crushed his kneecap if I'd been wearing proper footwear instead of sneakers. Still ...

"Ice'll keep it from swelling. Doesn't hurt to be proactive."

"I'll ice it and elevate it and do everything good when I get home, promise." He was looking more pleasant and less peeved now. "I've studied martial arts, off and on. You've got good technique."

I laughed. "Good technique includes being certain of your target. I didn't even get a look at you."

"I was too close, and you were spooked." A shadow passed over his face. "Sometimes, the past does our thinking for us."

I felt the truth of that echo along my link with the land. It saddened me to think that even wholesome apple-cheeked boys learned that lesson, and I gave him a small bow, in acknowledgment of a truth said well.

"I take it you're headed home, now?" I asked, deliberately breaking the seriousness of the moment.

"Roundabout," he answered. "Ms. Anderson doesn't have any work for me today, so I thought I'd come by and see the carousel, like we talked about." He held up his hands.

Which was why the lad had been lurking by the front door. True, I'd asked him to give me some notice for a private tour, but it wasn't unreasonable to think I might be at the carousel half an hour early on an open day, and be grateful for a little company.

"Be glad to give you the quick tour," I said, and firmly closed my lips before *if you think you're up to it* got loose. *A man is the best judge of his own injuries*, my grandfather's arms master used to say, and add, after a wink and a beat, *until he swoons*.

Fishing the key out of my pocket, I turned, unlocked the padlock, and opened the door.

"Go on in," I told him, putting my hands on the gate's edge. "I'll just push the walls out of the way."

It didn't really surprise me to see him set his shoulder against the opposite side, and push.

The storm walls moved, clattering and groaning as they went back on the track, meeting the stops at the sides of the maintenance shed with a clash of steel against steel.

I jumped up on the carousel, crossed the platform and dropped down into the pit, pulling open the panel, and flipping various switches. One switch snapped the lights on along the sweeps, and the outer ring. Another lit the fancy facade that hid the center of the machine from view. A third illuminated the orchestrion. I opened the door and ducked inside to kick the motor on.

By the time I was out, door latched behind me, Kyle was on the platform, both hands resting on the charger's gilded saddle, looking around, as wide-eyed as any kid. I waited at the center, loath to jump onto the platform and shatter his moment of wonder.

Slowly, as if he stood by a living animal, he raised one hand, and ran his fingertips down the proudly arched neck, armored in ebon and red. He watched his fingers move, then looked up and about again. His steps soundless on the platform, he walked down the wheel, caressing the creatures as he went.

I stepped quietly onto the platform as he vanished around the curve, walking like a man in a dream, as silent as a dream, himself.

My attention was on the ticket box when he came back into sight, walking a little brisker now, eyes still rounder than most adults allow themselves, his hands gentle on carved necks and noses.

I slapped the box back together, adjusted the stool that I hardly ever sat on, and turned to face Kyle as he slipped through the gap in the safety rail. He turned and conscientiously pushed it flush with the other sections, before facing me.

"That rooster," he said. "It doesn't belong."

"In the sense that it's where it is because I put it there, it *does* belong. On the other hand, I know exactly how you feel. Problem is that I lost a horse just at the end of April. Takes time to carve a new one—and money—and I probably don't have to tell you, they want the moon and a couple stars for one of the old animals, restored."

"Well..." He took a step forward, and put his hands on the ticket box. "I'm a finish carpenter. I can make you a horse."

I raised my eyebrows.

"Ms. Anderson doesn't keep you busy enough?"

"There's only another week until that job's done. I could go back to Amesbury and hustle work—it's summer, after all, but..." He paused, his cheeks flushing a delicate, pale pink. "See, I took the Wishes job because it was at the ocean. I thought, after it was done, I'd pick up more work here, and kind of have a...working vacation." He sighed. "I grew up on Hatteras Island—that's North Carolina. Miss it, sometimes. But, look, when I was learning—I 'prenticed with a guy up—well, down—in Glen Echo, Maryland. He made custom carousel horses, and I worked with him for almost a year. He'd gotten backed up and needed another pair of hands. I can give you his number, if you want to check."

I shook my head. "I'm guessing that I can't afford you," I said, giving it to him straight. "There's a lot of time in a horse, not to mention materials."

"Around four hundred hours," he grinned, "about a million of 'em sanding. And there's downtime, for glue to dry. But, see, I was talking to Mrs. Ellenbach the other day—you know Mrs. Ellenbach?"

I shook my head. "Townie or summer person?"

He gave the question serious consideration, brows drawn.

"Summer person," he said eventually. "She lives in the condos, marsh-side—Black Duck Manor—and she needs bookshelves built in."

The light dawned. "So you've already got some work lined up, and the more work you do, the more references you'll have in-town..."

"...and the more work I'll get, and the longer I can stay here." He finished, grinning at me like I had done something particularly clever—it reminded me, unsettlingly, of Mr. Ignat'.

"There's still the question of price," I said, getting back to brass tacks. "How much?"

He pushed the Home Depot hat back off his forehead, and frowned down at the ticket box.

"What's the wood?" he asked abruptly. "Bass?"

I shook my head. "Tupelo."

"Tupelo?"

"The original animals were carved by a great-great-etcetera-uncle, and the family woodlot had tupelo."

He nodded, but the frown was more pronounced.

"If I can get you the wood," I asked, "will that help?"

He looked doubtful. "It'll be...a hundred fifty board feet, near enough."

I nodded. "If I can get it at all, I can get all you need."

"Well, then." He tipped his head to one side. "Twenty-five hundred."

"The sea air's gone to your head, son. That hardly covers your time."

"It's my time," he said, "so I get to say what it's worth. I hardly ever get a chance to make a carousel horse, Ms. Archer. I've got the skill, and it's going to waste. Besides," he grinned, "I want to do it."

"Hard to argue with that," I said, and stepped Sideways.

It's rude to look at people in Side-Sight, like talking about someone in their presence, in a foreign language. Still, if he was an ordinary citizen of the Changing Land, he'd never know.

And if he was an avenging Ozali from another of the Worlds...
I brought one of my premade defense spells to the tips of my
metaphorical fingers, even as I looked at Kyle.

No *jikinap*, no glamor, no glow of geas or spell; nothing but
the faintest silvery shine of luck about him.

I let the defense spell go, and stepped fully back into the here
and now.

"You're provisionally hired," I said, "pending my ability to
provide the wood. Give me a cell number—yours, and that reference from down Away. I'll call you tomorrow with a yes or no."

"Great!" Forget palpable, his delight damn' near knocked me
down. "I've got a—"

But whatever it was he had was drowned out by a blare, as
rude as it was unmistakeable, followed by another just like it.

Marilyn had hit the air horn.

Fun Country was open for business.

CHAPTER EIGHT

High Tide 10:14 P.M.
Sunset 8:21 P.M. EDT

Early Season Fridays are usually slow days, and this Friday wasn't any exception. With an hour 'til closing, the ticket box wasn't quite half full. Not going to Vegas on that. Hell, not going to the *grocery store* on that.

At least I'd had time to savor the cashew chicken sent over from Tony Lee's at suppertime. The Lee Delivery Service guy on the day had been Jason, a strapping high schooler, who had given it as his opinion that tomorrow the park would be hopping.

"But there's a school rally tonight," he said, "and most of the kids are there."

"You'd think the school would check the park schedule before deciding when to hold a rally," I said, not really serious about it.

He looked doubtful. "I don't think our principal really approves of the park—at least, not the arcade. Might be just as well if we're off his radar."

"I take your meaning," I said, slipping the plastic fork out of its protective napkin. "So, why aren't you at the rally?"

"I have to work."

It was said matter-of-factly, without a trace of self-pity or irritation. The Lee ethic bred true.

"Well, if you gotta work, don't let me keep you! Tell Anna, please, that supper looks absolutely delicious. Thank you for bringing it over."

"You're welcome," he said, nice and polite, and took himself off, leaving me a little too alone with my meal.

I'd been so thin of company that I couldn't get a reading on how the rooster was doing on the popularity scales. When there's only one or two customers per ride, they've got the whole menagerie to choose from, and tend to mount the flashier critters. The unicorn got good play, and the hippocampus; the dolphin, the bronc, and the Indian pony. The poor, flea-bitten bear didn't get much love; neither did the subtly misshapen bobcat. The lion caught attention, off and on, and the giraffe was a clear favorite with certain of the very young set, as was the ostrich, but the rabbit might as well have been invisible.

Well. No accounting for taste.

So, anyway, at 9:10 on the last Friday night of the Early Season, I stepped into Baxter Avenue, and looked around me. Summer's Wheel, next door, was turning slowly, advertising its existence to any who cared to look, I guessed, since I didn't see anybody in the gondolas. Across the way at Tony Lee's, Anna was braced, palms flat on the counter, leaning out and looking down the avenue. I raised an arm and waved. She caught the motion, straightened and waved back.

I considered the aspect before me. A gaggle of middle-agers came 'round the corner from Fountain Circle, which was my cue to call out—

"Carousel's open, ladies—gents! Two tickets a ride!"

Talking among themselves, they didn't even turn their heads. I sighed, and shook mine.

People flock to carousels, even in this day and age, which is the reason I don't hire a barker. Some of the rides need them—the Terminator looks so damned scary, the barker's job is basically to *dare* the customers on to it. Carousels—even *my* carousel— look friendly; they call up memories more glad than sad; they don't demand any particular courage or bravado, just...choose a mount to your liking and relax while the music plays, and the wheel goes 'round and 'round.

Problem was, even a barker can't produce riders from an empty midway. Which was pretty much what I had. A couple was coming up the empty avenue from Dodge City: A skinny old man bent over a stick gamely followed a stout woman of about his age. She kept a uniform two steps ahead, like she was breaking trail. I sang out an invite—she didn't look, but he turned his head and smiled.

"Evenin', dear," he called, his voice high and sweet, and kept on with the task of walking.

"Evenin'," I murmured, and fell back a step, watching them round the corner into Fountain Circle. My sight flickered, and for a moment I saw a slender, bookish young man on the arm of a sturdy young woman, heads together, yellow hair and brown, matching steps, and matching smiles...

I shook my head; the image faded, and here was another potential customer, coming up from Dodge City. He was wearing a gray hoodie with the hood pulled up, head bent, hands jammed into the pockets of his jeans. His sneakers were eye-piercingly white, and his shoulders were hunched up into his ears. He might have been alone on the midway—alone on the *planet*, for all of that.

Kind of a tough sell for a ride on the merry-go-round.

Still, I stepped up to the plate, filling my lungs for a good yell. If I couldn't get him to fork over two tickets and climb on the back of a critter, at least I might be able to wake him up.

Except that, just a few feet away, he lifted his head, stared around like he'd just woke up, focused on the carousel, then on me, and walked toward us both, taking his hands out of his pockets, to reach up and yank the hood back and down.

"Your pardon," he said, in strongly accented English. "I look for Kate of the carousel."

His voice was low, but smooth; face an inverted triangle—high, broad forehead half-hidden under a fringe of reddish brown hair. Pointed chin; long, decided nose; definite cheekbones; thin lips. Brown eyes set deep under high-arching eyebrows. Pale skin. Freckles.

"I'm Kate Archer," I told him, and cocked a thumb over my shoulder. "That's the carousel. And you are?"

He looked at the carousel, then back to my face, ducking his head slightly, maybe in embarrassment.

"I am Vassily Abramovich Davydenko. Manager Marilyn sends me to you. For work."

I blinked, then nodded. He wasn't what I'd been expecting, but thinking about it, I couldn't exactly say *what* I'd been expecting.

"Have you ever operated a carousel?" I asked him.

"No," he said flatly, and, as if he realized that sounded just a thought short, added quickly, "I am very fast to learn. The hours—Manager Marilyn said every day, four hours, contract rate, and lunch."

Okay, so now I knew what was at the top of *his* mind. Fair enough. Hours and a meal every day weren't luxuries everybody had.

"I'll show you the details. Right now, if you've got time. Then you can decide if it looks like something you'd care to take on. All right?"

A faint crease showed between those high-arched brows.

"Four hours," he repeated. "Every day. And lunch. I learn, so very fast."

"You bet," I agreed, a little taken aback by quite so much desperation. "Let's go inside."

He wanted me to call him Vassily; he was from Ukraine; and he really did learn fast. By the time the five-minute warning sounded he had mastered the operator's board, the emergency stop, and could thread the Violano paper through the orchestrion faster than I could, myself, so deft that I had no fear for the fragile paper.

He helped me close the storm gates; then, at my invitation, he mounted the machine and walked among the animals, studying each one with the somber seriousness that seemed characteristic of him.

"These are good," he said. "I will like working with these."

He walked deliberately, footsteps quiet and respectful against the old wooden decking. His fingertips trailed along the sides of each critter he passed, as if he were memorizing their tactile signature.

Unlike everybody else, he neither stared, nor checked, when he came to the rooster, he merely moved gently by, fingers tracing neck, saddle, and harum-scarum tail-feathers.

When he had finished the circle, he came to the edge by the chariot, his hand resting on the curved neck of the money-side swan.

"I will like this. I will work hard. Four hours a day. Every day. All Season. Will you have me?"

I considered him. He was weird, but who wasn't? Clearly, he needed the work, and—to the point for both Nancy and me—he could *do* the work.

"Sure, I'll have you. We still need to finish up training, though. Can you work for a couple hours tomorrow? I'd like you to have some real-time operating under your belt before we turn you loose by yourself."

There was a longish pause, as if he had to work through the idiom, then he nodded. "I will come—at noon?"

"At eleven, if it fits with your other hours," I said, thinking *what the hell; might as well train him up proper.* "You can learn how to open up, too."

"Yes. I will come." He hesitated. "Thanking you."

"Nope, thanking *you*," I told him. "You're going to be a big help."

I said good-night to Vassily at Fun Country's gate, and watched him walk away, hood up, shoulders high, hands shoved down into the pockets of his jeans. He went straight down the walk, past Arcade Ka-Pow! My bet with myself was that he'd turn left on Grand, toward the motels that were the main reason for the Chamber's employment contract, where surely there was a bed for him in a dorm room . . .

As it happened, I didn't win my bet—or lose it. The gathering sea mist hid him before he hit the corner.

The mist was a little colder than was absolutely necessary for June, but that's the Maine coast for you—if you don't like the weather, wait five minutes and it'll change.

I sighed, buttoned my denim jacket and pulled the collar up. High up on Archer Avenue, the street lights were bright and clean-looking. Mid-hill, they were a little diffuse. Close in, they looked like candle flames flickering behind a spun glass curtain; even the seven-foot red letters that spelled out KA-POW! seemed a little tentative in the roiling mist.

To my right, the lights on Fountain Circle were pale, ghostly memories of lights, while the Pier showed as a multicolored smear against the thick air. I should've been able to hear the band playing at Neptune's, and the waves crashing against the beach, but it was as if the mist stifled not only light, but sound, and I shivered, though not from the cold.

"Time to get home, Kate," I said out loud, relieved to hear that my voice was crisp. I nodded, to let myself know I'd heard her. Damn' fool thing to do, just stand around in the mist and get soaked. *Past* time to get home, is what it was. I was due for a shower and a glass of wine and a chapter of the latest book before I tucked myself into bed.

My usual route home from Fun Country is up the beach, but tonight, with the mist coming on so thick, I decided to stick to the streets.

Hands in pockets, I trotted across Fountain Circle, the lights of the midway that occupied the asphalt on the other side of the Pier slipping eerily into being as I approached.

Technically, the midway is part of Fun Country, but Marilyn has nothing to do with the managing of it. In my day, the maze of carny games and concessions had been run by a woman named Phyllis Savage. She'd retired, so Nancy told me, and been replaced by the fella who had been her assistant for a good few years, name of Jens Torbin. Among his other skills, Jens apparently had a light touch with an accounts book, and at the end of last Season, Fun Country New Jersey had decided enough was enough, and fired his ass.

I had no idea who ran the place now, though my guess was nobody. It'd been locked up tight since I'd hit town in April; hadn't even opened for the Super Early Season. I wondered if Fun Country had decided that it, like Jens, was too much trouble for too little return.

Tonight, though, the lights were on.

Even more interesting, if you're interested in that kind of thing, was that the gate stood, just a little, ajar.

There wasn't much to want inside the midway—just a bunch of old games booths and concession stands tarped up for the winter. Still, it shouldn't be standing open—somebody a little tipsy with music and beer, coming down the ramp from the Pier might see a shortcut to the truck, or to the house, trip over one of the tarp-covered games and break their fool neck.

Probably, I thought, going toward the swinging gate, the chain had rusted through, and the wind had jimmied the latch. Happened all the time. I'd just pull it to, latch it up and ask the land to pile up some dirt to keep it from swinging open again.

I reached for the gate—

A hand closed over mine.

I yelled.

Somebody else yelled.

The land leapt into action, showing me a woman with bright pink hair, purple eyes, a diamond chip glittering in one nostril, dressed, like me, in jeans and a denim jacket.

"Hold it!" I snapped. "Who are you?"

"Who am *I*?" her voice was low and rough—tailor-made for singing the blues. "Who the *hell* are *you*?"

"Kate Archer. I run the carousel, over the other side."

There was a pause. The land helpfully showed me her face, which was round and slightly less pink than her hair, so I could see the moment when she decided that I could be telling the truth.

"Okay. I'm Peggy Marr, the new midway manager. I was supposed to start opening on weekends, but there was a problem at another park and Management shifted me in to sort it and fix it—" Her mouth twisted. "That's what they call me, down Jersey. *Peggy the Fixer.*"

I grinned.

"Welcome to Archers Beach. Better late than never, right?"

"I guess, except—I just got in last night and I've literally been doing nothing else but going over the old files in that...*office* back there." She shuddered. I guessed Jens hadn't been tidy.

"I'm right up against it, aren't I?" Peggy Marr said. "Season starts, what—Monday?"

"Next Friday," I said, and heard her exhale hard.

"Well, that makes all the difference. All's I have to do is come up with two dozen experienced operators and agents by Friday at...?"

"Noon."

"Noon. Great."

"I might," I said slowly, "be able to help. I can at least go over last Season's list with you and see if I know how to get in touch with any of the operators."

It would've been too much to say she got less tense, but she did look interested.

"That could be a big help, assuming they're—well, we won't know 'til we know, will we? When can you come by the office? I'll tell you the truth, I gotta get something to eat, a shower and some sleep, but I can be back down here—say, seven? Tomorrow."

The woman was driven, give her that. I nodded.

"Sure. I'll meet you right here tomorrow at seven." I stepped away from the gate, and turned left, toward Grand Avenue and home.

"See you then."

"See you then," she said behind me, and I heard a muted clang, as she latched the gate.

CHAPTER NINE

"I mean, look at these! What're they, code names?" Peggy Marr drank deep of her Starbucks Vente strong, and waved a plump, well-manicured hand at the logbook.

"And contact information! What contact information? What'd he do, whistle 'em up the wind?"

It was 'way too early in the morning, and Peggy and I were in the manager's office, a cramped little room behind The Last Mango Juice Bar.

As instructed, I looked at the logbook, seeing two names right off that I knew. I ran a slow finger down the page, concentrating my attention, and the land's attention. Yes, good. The land knew almost every name. I had, I thought, suspected as much.

Jens could very well have whistled to them on the wind. Or, more likely, they'd just shown up, when it was time, like they'd done Season after Season after...

Except, this Season, Jens hadn't called, and when they showed up, as they probably had, on the traditional Set-Up Day before the first Early Season Friday, the gate had been locked and the midway shrouded.

Was Jens *trenvay*? I let the question seep into the land, but got its equivalent of a puzzled stare for my answer. Well. Gran would know, or Mr. Ignat'. But Jens was a side issue.

I looked up into Peggy Marr's purple-that-doesn't-exist-in-nature eyes.

"I think I can help you out," I told her. "My family—well. This place is called Archers Beach, right? And I'm the Archer, great-great-great-and-etcetera-granddaughter of the guy who claimed this patch of land, and lucky he was that the local residents didn't dispute him."

"So you know everybody worth knowing?"

"Pretty much." I looked back to the list, tapping the three names that had drawn a blank from the land.

"Manny Perez, Audrey Kruger, Stilton—I don't have a clue. Could be, it'll come to me, but right now, assume you'll be short by these three."

She leaned over my shoulder; I smelled amber, orange, agar... and espresso, from the cup—and ran her black-enameled forefinger down the page, much as I had done.

"So you think you can get hold of Moss, Vornflee, Felsic..."

"And all the other weird names, but not common old Manny Perez or Audrey Kruger," I finished, taking her point. "That's right. I'm guessing that they were traveling through and took pickup work for the summer. Do you want me to pass the word to the folks I'm sure of that they're wanted?"

"Well, I'd *rather* have phone numbers, addresses, Social Security numbers and all that foolishness, but you know and I know that I'm over a barrel. I've gotta get this thing open, on time, or my ass is grass."

"After the Jersey bosses screwed with your schedule themselves?"

She straightened with a sigh, and had another chug of high-test.

"The Jersey bosses are nothing if not arbitrary. In fact, Arbitrary and Cruel is the name of the parent firm. I have an assignment. The fact that a subsequent assignment interfered with my timing on the first isn't really their problem, see?"

"At least it seems consistent," I said, bracing my hip against Jens' beat-up, Formica-topped metal desk. "I should probably say, before I put out the word—if you need Social Security numbers and home phones and all the rest of it, you might just want to make up a bunch of signs and post 'em around town. Or"—I snapped my fingers as inspiration hit—"you can ask Marilyn

Michaud—she manages the other side—if she's got any greenies who need hours."

She frowned, crossed one arm over her chest and braced the opposite elbow in her palm. Drank coffee.

Drank more coffee, staring at nothing in particular.

I let her stare, leaning across the desk to snag my travel mug from the corner where I'd put it. My perfectly good, brought-from-home brew tasted a little weak, after breathing the fumes from the Starbucks Vente. Also, quarters were a little tight, even with me hugging the desk. The main office was long and shallow and sticky-smelling. The last being a contribution from the juice bar.

Peggy shifted, decisively, and shook her head.

"If I had time to train a new crew—but I don't. I *need* experienced people, and I need 'em *stat*." Another swallow—it was starting to look like she had a bottomless Vente, there—and a firm, unflinching look into my face.

"Tell me the worst—they need to be paid in cash?"

"They do," I said, thinking that some on the list might actually possess such things as a home phone, or an address, or even a Social Security number. Some, but not all, and in order not to point up those who didn't . . .

"Well, that starts to explain Jens' *system*," she said. She lifted the cup, sighed, and leaned over to put it on the corner of the desk. "All right, I can handle cash payments."

"Getting that Social Security number might be a little tricky, too," I said, delicately.

"Also consistent with the Jens system." She looked grim. "All right. Here's how we'll handle it. We get everybody together, fill out the Social Security applications; I'll send 'em in. They can start working, pending. That's legal. Plus, Arbitrary and Cruel will have appropriate documentation. My ass will not be grass." She smiled, tightly, purple eyes glittering. "Win-win-win."

"Then I put out the word?"

"All of the words, yes. Tell them to come to work—now, today, as soon as they hear. Tell them I've got rules I have to stick by, notably from the IRS, that I'll bend them as much as I can, and that I swear to *God* I'll hamper them as little as humanly possible."

That was a lot more than I was going to pass, but I nodded and slid to my feet, bringing my traveling mug with me.

"I'll get started, then. If you need me for anything else—local guide, introductions—I'll be at the carousel, or whoever's at the carousel can find me."

She nodded and held out her hand. I took it and we shook. "Thanks, Kate. I owe you."

"Let's see if I can get your crew in first," I said.

She snorted. "If not, then I'll be asking you to hide me, so—either way, right?"

"Right," I said, and took my leave.

I figured I'd find her on the beach, working the trash cans by the dunes, but the land pushed me in the opposite direction, across the tracks, across First Street, to Lisa's Pizza, right there on the corner and already open at 8:05—and there it left me as if my next step should be obvious.

Well, no, not exactly. Here I stood at the corner of Archer and First, the red-and-white tile of the pizza stand three inches from my nose. Immediately on my right was Archer Avenue. Immediately on my left, was . . . nothing much, really—no, wait. About a dozen steps down First Street was Daddy's Dance Club. I walked thataway.

The red-and-white tiles of Lisa's facade changed to grayish barn-siding, pierced by a white utility door that was locked up nice and tight. Just beyond the utility door was a narrow space between the end of Lisa's building and the start of the dance club's building.

It wasn't nearly wide enough to qualify as an alley; it almost failed the walkway test. Breezeway, maybe. Luckily, I'm smallish and not claustrophobic. Also, I only had to walk about two dozen steps before the breezeway opened into a courtyard spacious enough to admit a trash truck, which would surely need access, given that the place was redolent with Dumpsters.

On the ground by the Dumpster nearest the dance club's back wall were several mismatched and grubby canvas bags. Protruding from the Dumpster was a bony, khaki-covered posterior; good, no-slip shoes on her feet, braced on the middle seam.

I set my shoulder against the wall, crossed my arms and waited.

Soda cans arced out of the Dumpster and clattered to the asphalt. The posterior wriggled around, one foot alarmingly rose from the seam, and I thought I heard a few pungent curse words.

Twenty-four returnables later, the scavenger turned and jumped down to the ground, landing handily amid her bounty. Immediately, she snatched up one of the bags and began to shove her take into it.

I cleared my throat.

"'Morning, Gaby."

"Eek!"

She threw the bag away from her, soda cans escaping in a wide arc, and slammed her back against the Dumpster she'd just looted, hands up at heart level, face averted, shadowed by the grubby gimme hat.

Not exactly the bravest of toasters, our Gaby.

"Oh, c'mon, Gaby, it's Kate!"

"Kate?"

She cautiously turned her head, peering at me from beneath the double protection of brim and strawlike hair.

"What're you doin' here, Kate? The returnables are mine. By arrangement."

"Sure they are," I said, soothingly. "Though it's a little rude of 'em there at the club not to set 'em out separate. You could get hurt, if you fell into a Dumpster."

Gaby snorted.

"Badder things come to me than fallin' in a trash can," she said derisively, "and I'm none the worse."

"That's fine, but there's no sense pushing your luck," I said. "I'll just talk to the manager, okay? Tell her to set the returnables out by themselves. Make it easier on you."

"That'd be a kindness," she said.

"No problem. But why I was looking for you..."

"Come *lookin'* for me!" she shrieked. "Why?"

"Well, if you'd rest a spell, I'd tell you," I said, testily.

She gulped and ducked her head. "Beg pardon, Guardian."

"I need you to pass the word, to Felsic, Moss, Vornflee and all the rest who took work at the midway. There's a new manager in and she's eager to accept their service. They'll have to fill out forms, and give a good address, but she'll pay in cash, and she needs them for setup *now*."

Gaby shifted from foot to foot, not exactly looking at me, which was Gaby's way.

"Midway's been locked up, all spring."

"Well, now it's open. Can you pass the message?"

"I can."

I considered that. Gaby was timid, and she had a certain gratifying respect for my station. But she was, blood and bone, heart and soul—*trenvay*.

"*Will* you pass the message? To the appropriate folk? Now?"

"Yes."

"Yes, which?"

"Yes, yes, and yes again!" she snapped, stamping her foot.

I'd never seen Gaby do anything as assertive as lose her temper. Truth told, it was because I knew her to be timid and accommodating that I'd chosen her as my messenger. That and the notion that Gaby was more likely to have personal knowledge of the midway *trenvay* than, say, Bob, if only because her quest for returnables would have made her a regular at the concession stands' trash cans.

Still, I hadn't meant to be rude. As a matter of fact, being rude was the one vice of all those the powerful are likely to fall heir to that Grandfather Aeronymous took the trouble to warn me about.

I inclined my head, gravely.

"Thank you, Gaby, for your service. The land and the Guardian appreciate you."

She stared at me, mouth open, then closed it with a snap, and straightened inside her patchwork jacket.

"That's no trouble at all, Guardian. Not a bit o'trouble; glad to serve. Felsic's the one who can get the others. A word to Felsic, that's all it needs."

"Thank you for taking care of it," I said. As it came about, Grandfather hadn't set a particular *value* on thanking people. He'd merely noted that a gracious sovereign tended to receive more willing service from his people, and therefore had to spend less time persuading them, *or* punishing them. Which freed up time to cruise the other Five Worlds and steal maiden lady Guardians away from their land and their duty.

But never mind that.

In the present case, I was truly grateful to Gaby for taking on the task, therefore, I shouldn't stint on my thanks.

"I'll talk to the manager here about that returnables box," I told her, moving away from the wall. "And now, if you'll excuse me..."

"No need for excuses from the likes of me! Go, go! I'll see to Felsic. Leave it to me!"

I nodded once more and left it to her.

❋   ❋   ❋

The front door of Daddy's Dance Club was ajar when I emerged from the breezeway, so I stepped in.

For something calling itself a dance club, Daddy's was tiny. The bar, such as it was, was crammed into the front corner to the left of the door; a slightly raised stage was similarly crammed into the back right corner, and the rest—was floor: black, somewhat sandy and scruffed-up floor. A white line had been painted about six paces out from the wall, all the way around the room, widening to accommodate the bar and stage areas. I guessed that was where those who were taking a breather, or who were having a drink stood.

"Club ain't open yet!" a man's voice greeted me. "Come back later, doll."

I turned to the right, where a burly, bald-headed guy with a walrus mustache, and wearing a white-and-blue-striped muscle shirt, had stepped through the door to what must be the store-room, a white carton with VODKA printed on it in red letters held on his shoulder as effortlessly as if it was a teddy bear.

"I'm here to talk to the manager."

He came across the floor and set the box on the bar, dusted his hands, and turned to look at me, hands on hips.

"You're talking to the manager. I ain't hiring, and even if I was, you're too short to see over the bar."

"I come with my own stool," I told him, crossing my arms over my chest and leaning against the wall. "But this is your lucky day; I'm not looking for work. I just want to make a friendly request."

He gave me a measuring look, up and down, sighed, and leaned an elbow on the bar.

"Look, doll, I'm restocking here, all right? Come back at closing time, and I'll maybe be open to a friendly request."

A man with priorities, by God.

"I'll bear that in mind. In the meantime, I wonder if you'd mind setting the returnables out in their own box for pickup."

He frowned, the mustache taking a threatening turn.

"Why the hell should I?"

"Because you made a deal with somebody that they could have the returnables. When you throw 'em in the Dumpster, you're making her dive for 'em; you act like you don't honor your deal; and you put your contractor in danger. Plus," I added, "Dumpster diving's illegal, and you're aiding and abetting."

His once-over this time was considerably more sour.

"You a cop?"

"Nope. You want I should call one?"

"Got 'em on speed-dial, thanks. So, who *are* you?"

"Kate Archer. I run the merry-go-round."

"She's a friend of yours? The little can freak?"

"She's somebody I know, and no more a freak than anybody else trying to get by."

He snorted, averted his gaze, looked back.

"What the hell; no skin off my nose. Sure, we'll put out a box. No sense having her break her neck." He glared at me. "I don't gotta give her nothing."

"That's right; you don't. She threaten you?"

This time, he laughed, hard and short.

"Oh, yeah, she threatened me, all right. Nah. Just ... I know some guys, all right? Went away, did a job, come back—well, maybe not all of 'em come all the way back. So, anyhow, one of them does what she does—the cans. Keeps him in smoke money. Charity. I can afford charity. I only give her the soda cans; the liquor bottles and the beer, they gotta go back to the distributor."

He looked at me hard and I nodded to show I understood.

"I'd just been throwing the soda cans into the trash, since I got three sort bins under the bar as it is. I guess I can live with four." He shrugged and repeated. "No sense having her break her neck."

"I appreciate it," I told him. "I've known Gaby a long time and I wouldn't want to see her hurt."

"Yeah ..." Another hard look. "You got everything you wanna say off your chest, now? 'Cause I still gotta restock."

I pushed away from the wall, turned—and turned back.

"What's your name?"

He was already halfway back to the stockroom door. Back to me, he raised his hands shoulder high, and shook his head.

"You just call me Daddy, doll. Now get outta here and let a guy work."

Mr. Ignat' was sitting at a picnic bench in Fountain Circle, bent over a newspaper. I sat down across from him.

"Anything interesting?"

"Good morning, Katie." He looked up with a smile, eyes shadowed by his hat. "It's all interesting, my dear. Puzzling, but interesting. There is this story, here, however ..." He looked down and tapped a column with a long, white forefinger, pushing the paper half across the table toward me.

I leaned close.

TWO MORE ARRESTED IN DRUG BUST

It was a short story, but a happy one, if you happen to be the sort of person who rejoices in the tribulations of your enemies. The two referenced were Albert Stilton and Johnny Gagnon—not Joe Nemeier. Still, it was all but certain that they worked for the man; Archers Beach wasn't big enough to support two drug lords. Nemeier had to be sweating, now. If one of those kiddies actually knew who they worked for, and mentioned it to the—

"Hold it," I said, coming out of my pleasant daydream and looking down at the paper again. "Albert Stilton?"

"So it states, Katie dear. Do you know him?"

I shook my head. "No . . . I was just this morning helping the new midway manager sort out the employee log and one of the names I couldn't help her with was Stilton. No first name."

"It's not impossible that they're the same person," Mr. Ignat' commented.

"No. And it doesn't matter, I guess. If it's the same guy, I'm guessing he's not going to be available for work for the next little while, anyhow." I looked up.

"Mr. Ignat', do you remember Jens? He was the midway manager until he got fired at the end of last Season."

He frowned slightly, and I saw him feeling back among memories that must be nothing more than mist and moonlight. After a few long minutes, he shook his head.

"I don't have much to do with the midway side, after all, Katie. What do you need to know?"

"Well, I don't exactly *need* to know; I just wondered if Jens was *trenvay*. The land doesn't seem to remember him, so I'm guessing that's my answer. Only . . ."

"Only?"

"Well, he had *trenvay* working for him—almost exclusively *trenvay* working in the midway." With the exception of three names the land didn't recognize, one of those maybe belonging to somebody who worked the dark side—who worked for *the major* dark-side provider in this section of the Maine coast.

Well, there's a Mainer for you—almost all of us hold three and four jobs, side jobs and sides of side jobs.

I'm kind of a slacker, that way.

"So!" I said brightly. "What's today's lesson?"

Mr. Ignat' folded the paper carefully and put it on the bench next to him.

"Today," he said, placing his hands, palms up, in the very center of the table. "Today, Pirate Kate, you will learn to trust your power."

Trust my . . .

I looked down at those long, white hands lying defenseless and inviting on the rough concrete, and felt my stomach clench in horror.

"No," I said, and snatched my own hands back, down to the bench, and deliberately tucked them beneath my posterior.

"Come now, Pirate Kate! Will ye be called craven?"

"Yes. *Hell*, yes! Call me every kind of coward you can think of! You want me to—what? Hold your hands? I'll *kill* you!"

"You will only do what you intend to do, Katie. If you intend to kill me, then I'll not dispute you. All I have is yours for the asking; there's no need to steal." He wriggled his fingers. "Now, come, and give me a true comrade's grip."

I shook my head, shivering with horror, feeling again the crawl of Ramendysis' power across my skin. Watching my hand rise against my specific desire and direct command that it remain at my side—

"No. I won't do this."

Mr. Ignat' sighed.

"Katie. Do you think I haven't seen that you're keeping yourself at arm's length? That you don't touch your grandmother, who would surely be glad of your comfort? Or your mother, who needs to be certain of your love? That you won't touch me—well. There are reasons a-plenty, aren't there, for you to be shy of touching me? But if you continue down that road, you'll become isolated, Katie. Just you and your power, solitary and fearful. *That* is the condition which produces the monster you so fear that you'll become. Connection and intention—those things *matter*. Your power does not shape you; you shape your power."

He lifted his arms, shot his cuffs, and put his hands once more on the table between us, palms up, fingers relaxed.

I stared at them, remembering... Remembering the two of us watching Saturday morning cartoons, laughing at the hapless coyote, falling for the millionth time into the abyss. I remembered the taste of a grilled blueberry muffin, and him smiling at me across the table at Bob's. I remembered holding his hand as we went outside so that I could explore my very first snow.

I remembered him drawing my enemy's fire, though it was certain to kill him, to give me time...

To give me time to run.

Kill Mr. Ignat'? I couldn't kill Mr. Ignat'. It wasn't in me. Hell, I'd almost gotten myself killed, because I wouldn't—couldn't—leave him to be murdered in my stead.

I slipped my hands free and brought them up to hover over the table, and then settled them, gently... affectionately... my palms against his palms.

His skin was warm, maybe a little too warm. He was a Fire Ozali, after all. I curled my fingers around his wrists and closed my eyes.

I could feel his power moving under his skin like blood. I could taste it—not butterscotch. Something... edgier. Dark chocolate and cayenne. I breathed in his power, took it deep into my lungs.

My own store of *jikinap*... stirred.

Stirred, but didn't rise. Instead, it seemed to be... interested. More, it seemed to be *learning*. Like a filtering program, I thought. And remembered that I built some damn' fine filtering programs.

I don't know how long I—we—sat there, holding hands in the morning sunshine. All I knew is that I reached a... saturation, a... certainty that I knew this man, that I treasured all that he was; that his power and mine were aligned, and I would never mistake him for an enemy.

I sighed, feeling it shudder through both of us, opened my eyes and looked into his.

He smiled, and nodded, his fingers curled around my wrists, like mine around his. True comrades.

I felt... peaceful. Calm.

I felt my *jikinap* curled at the base of my spine, comfortable as a cat.

"There, then." Mr. Ignat' said, as we slowly released each other and sat back. "Well done, Pirate Kate. Well done, indeed."

CHAPTER TEN

^〜^

High Tide 10:56 A.M. EDT

I sat at the picnic bench by myself for a few minutes after Mr. Ignat' left, just enjoying the sunshine, and the breeze. Overhead, the flags—U.S., Canadian, and Maine—snapped smartly, and eventually reminded me that I had a couple calls to make.

Gran picked up her cell almost before I hit speed-dial.

"Good morning," I said. "Expecting me?"

"Good morning," was the composed answer. "Certainly I was expecting an important call."

"I can hang up," I offered, "let you call me back after you've dealt with the big one."

"No, no. Your call came in first, after all."

"If you're sure . . ." I shifted sideways on the bench and put my right foot up on it.

"Listen, Gran, is there any cut tupelo left? I'd need about a hundred fifty board feet."

There was a moment of silence, long enough to be noticeable.

"I got somebody willing to make us a replacement horse, from scratch," I said, to save her the trouble of saying, *It depends.* "If we've got the wood, the price is reasonable. More than reasonable."

"Who?" she asked.

"Kyle Roberts, the fine carpenter who's working with Joan Anderson. That job's just about finished up and he wants to have a summer at the ocean, so he's trying to line up more work. Says he worked with a custom carousel horse-maker, and that he knows what he's doing. I still have to check that reference, but I thought first I'd see..."

"If he checks out to your satisfaction, Katie, then yes, there is sufficient wood for the project, and it can be delivered inside of Archers Beach." Another small pause. "He *will be* working in Archers Beach?"

"I'll make sure, but as far as I know, he is."

"Good," Gran said, sounding a little breathless, and again, "good."

"You okay?" I asked, concerned.

"Just tired, child. I'm a little old for adventures, you know."

Especially adventures that separated her from her tree and sent her across the World Wall, to steal her daughter back from a vindictive lord, and run home, pursued by close-enough-to-demons.

"Just...take care, okay? Oh, and Gran?"

"Yes?"

"The MDEA picked up two more of Mr. Nemeier's employees on the overnight. He's liable to be testy."

"We have nothing to do with that man," Gran said loftily. "If he comes here, the Wood will protect us."

I did not sigh.

"Okay, then," I said, briskly. "Let me check Kyle's reference, and if he's good, we'll get him the wood and let him get to work."

"Yes. Thank you, Katie. Come and see us again before the Season starts; I know you'll be too busy to come, during."

"Actually, maybe not. But, I will come up on Monday; fill you in with all the news. Give Mother my love."

Yet a third small pause, and then Gran said, "I will, of course. I love you, Katie. Good-bye now."

"Love you," I said. "Bye."

"Kyle Roberts?"

In contrast to Gran, it had taken Michael Trenton eight rings to get to the phone. I'd expected the call to go to voice mail, and jumped a little, there on my sunny seat, when a man's voice yelled into my ear, "HehLO?"

I identified myself and my mission.

"Kyle Roberts?" he repeated. "Sure, I remember Kyle. Good worker. Good eye. Not an artist. Solid, though." Pause. "You need something artistic?"

I thought about the lopsided bobcat, the scruffy bear and the out-of-proportion coon cat.

"Actually, I need solid. My machine's an original, and some of the critters are a little rugged as they stand."

"Kyle's your man, then," Michael Trenton assured me. "You tell 'im what you want, and leave 'im to it. Good worker, Kyle. Hire him back myself in a New York minute. Problem is, too much work for one, not enough work for two."

"Always the way," I agreed.

"Ain't it? Anything else I can tell you?"

"No, thanks—you've been very helpful."

"No problem at all, Ms. Archer. Glad to help out. Tell Kyle to stop on by, next time he's down in the old neighborhood. Like to see 'im. Catch up."

"I'll tell him," I promised, and we said our good-byes and hung up.

Kyle's phone *did* send me to voice mail, after three scant rings. I left a message saying that he was hired, that I needed to know where the wood should be delivered, and he should look Mike Trenton up, the next time he was in the neighborhood.

That done, I folded the phone and stood up, slipping it away into the pocket of my jacket. Between Mr. Ignat's lesson and the phone calls, it was almost time to meet Vassily at the carousel.

I stretched, took a deep breath of slightly dusty air, and strolled across Fountain Circle, heading for Fun Country.

"All right," I told Vassily a couple hours later. "I think you've learned everything I can teach you. Now, what I want to know is—how brave are you?"

He stiffened. "It is a joke?"

"Nope; completely serious." I said. "You've been doing fine while I was here watching you. I'm wondering how you'd like to run the whole thing by yourself while I take a walk."

I saw it dawn on him; that this was a test—and, more, that he was going to be running his four hours per day, every day, once the Season got under way, all by his lonesome.

"I am brave. I have learned. I will demonstrate. Please to walk and take the air. I will do everything that is necessary."

"I'm sure you will," I told him. "I've got every confidence in you. If something that we haven't covered should happen, or you need me here, for any reason at all, you just hit speed-dial on your phone and I'll come back. All right?"

One of the better ideas the Chamber had had this year was to provide each greenie with a recycled cell phone, preprogrammed with important numbers—like their contact at the Chamber, the number of the on-site boss, and the Archers Beach Fire and Police departments. Since Vassily was working for me, we'd added my cell number to the rest.

"I will not need to call you back from your walk," he told me haughtily.

"Careful." I lifted a finger. "Confidence is good. Overconfidence—not so good. I'll be back in forty-five minutes, unless you call me in earlier."

"Yes," he said.

I grabbed my jacket, though I didn't really need it, slung it over my shoulder and walked away, nodding to a young couple with a toddler, who were coming in. The toddler was riding daddy's shoulders, and yelling, "Kitty, kitty, *kitty*!"

"That's right, Sasha," the mom said, "we'll get you a ride on the kitty."

Good, I thought. *About time the coon cat got the love.* I liked it, myself, odd-looking or not.

"Welcome," I heard Vassily say behind me. "Welcome to the Carousel of Fantasy! The fare is two tickets each—but for Sasha, a free ride!"

So far, so good. I stepped out into Baxter Avenue, and looked about me.

It was a goodish crowd this afternoon, with the fine weather doing its part for fun and profit. There was a line maybe six deep to get onto Summer's Wheel, and another line at Tony Lee's. I could hear the thunder and rumble from Dodge City, 'way down to the left, and squeals and laughter from a group of preteens at the lobster toss.

"Ms. Archer?" a voice said from the vicinity of my elbow.

I turned and met the serious brown eyes of a girl about twelve years old.

"I'm Kate Archer," I admitted. "What can I do for you?"

She pulled a flat, creamy envelope about the size of her two hands together out of the canvas bag slung over her shoulder.

"I'm delivering invitations to Wishes," she said, sounding only a little bit like this part was rote. She placed the envelope into my hand. "Please come," she said, and this sounded sincere. "It'll be fun."

"I'll do my best," I promised, and slipped the envelope into the pocket of my jacket, watching absently as she made her way over to Summer's Wheel, bypassing the line to get to the operator's station.

So Joan Anderson was a woman of her word. She'd said "reception" and by gum, a reception there would be.

Determination. I like that in a woman.

Which reminded me of somebody else I ought to talk to. I turned right on Baxter Avenue, waving at Anna as I left the park, and crossed Fountain Circle.

The gate had been latched, but not locked, which I took as an invitation for those with an interest to come inside, so I slipped through, making sure the latch was secure behind me.

What a difference six hours can make.

The tarps were gone. Milk bottles were set up in a complex pattern in the center of one stand; new wire'd been strung across the main yard, and three guys on three ladders were screwing in lightbulbs fit to beat the band.

Speaking of band, somebody was dinking with the sound system—the midway had its own music piped in, not that it could usually be heard over the noise of people having fun, but it was a mood-setter for the early hours, and for other times when nothing much was doing. Over in Fun Country, each ride took care of its own ambiance, including music.

I passed two women assembling an ice cream stand. One was attaching the awnings, while the other was head and shoulders inside the giant ice cream cone, maybe working with the wiring or the lights.

Over and around the music were the sounds of hammers, bandsaws, and people calling back and forth. The place was a madhouse—no. No; it wasn't.

Madhouse implies motion without meaning; action without

purpose. There was plenty of purpose in the air, and intention so thick you could cut it with a knife.

I moved down the midway, careful to keep out from underfoot, and watchful, lest I get whacked in the head with a ladder.

At The Last Mango, I slipped behind the counter and stuck my head through the door to the manager's office.

Peggy wasn't there, which made a certain amount of sense, given all the activity going on, and really, I thought, my question was answered.

Word had gone out, and the *trenvay* had come in.

I exited the Mango, jacket held over my shoulder by a hooked finger, and looked around.

Bustle, busy bustle. At this rate, they'd have the midway good to open by noon tomorrow.

I retraced my steps, heading down the midway, and back toward Fountain Circle. At the corner, I dodged around a small mountain of ropes outside a three-sided barricade bearing the sign ROPE MONKEY.

That, unfortunately, put me into the path of an oncoming ladder. I ducked, felt my jacket slide off my shoulder, and spun—

Into something soft, that yelled in my ear.

"Kate!"

Hands grabbed my shoulders, holding me upright until I got my feet under me.

"Peggy! I was looking for you."

"Two minds with one thought," she said, letting me go, and reaching down to snatch my jacket.

"Hey, I'm sorry about—oh, damn."

She swooped down again, and came up with the jacket in one hand and the big white envelope, now slightly smeared with grit, in the other.

"Thanks." I took both and stood holding them, while she looked around, and pointed to a quiet spot in the commotion.

I nodded and followed, and we leaned our elbows against the counter of what would soon be, unless I missed my guess, a marksman's gallery.

"Thank you!" Peggy said. "I'd hoped to maybe start seeing a couple folks tomorrow—Monday. You weren't gone an hour when the first one came in, then three more, and six more after that. They all know what they're doing, and—well, hell, the best thing for me to do was just step back and let 'em do it. So! I've spread the word that, at four o'clock, we're all knocking off for pizza and introductions, followed by a form-filling session. I should have the schedules done by tomorrow, we'll do a shakedown on Tuesday and be ready for ignition Friday at noon."

She gave a deep sigh.

"Let me tell you what, this crew is *good*. No wonder Jens didn't hassle 'em and paid 'em in cash. Hell, I'd pay 'em in *gold*, if that's what it took!"

"Better not say that too loud," I said, only half-joking. "I'm glad they're working for you. I came over to ask if you'd heard, but, really—moot point."

"Yeah, but I'm glad you came by. I owe you. Big time. You need anything—a new Cadillac, a body buried—I'm your girl."

I laughed. "I'll bear it in mind. Meanwhile..."

I'd been going to take my leave, but I glanced down at the hand holding my invitation and an idea was born.

"Hey, do you know Joan Anderson?"

"Here-in-town Joan Anderson?" Peggy shook her head. "Here in town, I know you—and them." She jerked her head in the general direction of the midway.

"Then you wouldn't've gotten one of these. Hold on." I slipped my finger under the flap, broke the seal and pulled out the card.

The front was a watercolor of the horse she'd been sketching on the day I met her. The inside said:

Season Opener
Wishes Art Gallery
Thursday, June 15
8 P.M. until the food runs out
Come yourself—and bring a friend!

I turned it around so Peggy could read it.

"You'll want to know the people who are going to be at this party. The owner of Wishes Gallery is Joan Anderson. She doesn't strike me as a woman who does anything by halves, which means she'll have invited the entire town."

"Except me, who she doesn't know from—"

"You see that part, *bring a friend*? You're coming with me."

She mugged. "So we're *friends*?"

I laughed. "*You* better check up on *me*," I told her. "But I promise to be on my best behavior."

"Where's the fun in that?" She pouted, then grinned. "It's a date." She yanked her cell out of the pocket of her jeans. "Gimme your number."

We did the exchange, and I left her to the rapidly assembling midway, tucking the card back into the pocket of my jacket as I went.

Vassily worked 'til 4:00. I took several long walks during his shift, and stopped by Tony Lee's for my supper.

"Is Vassily working out?" Anna asked.

"Nothing's blown up, yet," I answered, around a forkful of steamed chicken and veggies. I looked up at her. "He'll be 'round a little later to collect his supper. If there's an extra egg roll, throw it in, hey? Put it on my tab."

Anna swung a dishcloth more or less at my head.

"Tony has already said that we should feed him up. Owner's expense."

"I know better'n to argue with Tony," I said. "Are all the greenies hungry?"

Anna frowned. "No . . . well. At first, they're shy. Then, yes—they're hungry. After that, they're family." She paused, her frown getting deeper.

"And then . . . they leave." The frown eased somewhat. "Often, though, they come back. Katrina has been back five years in a row. And this is Sergei's third summer."

"Five years? That's starting to be a career."

Anna nodded. "She says she would like to stay, and work at the Beach all year 'round."

I laughed. "So would a lot of us."

I finished up my meal and sat back with a sigh.

"That was almost too good." I sipped coffee, Katrina's wish niggling at the edge of my mind.

"There's a committee forming up, so Jess Robald tells me," I said. "Its aim is to work out a strategy to stretch the Season. First meeting's Monday morning at some ungodly hour, at the Garden Cafe, up the hill."

Anna nodded vigorously.

"Jelly will be there, for the Lees," she said. "There must be something that we can do. Other beach towns have longer Seasons. Some even have winter Seasons!"

"Unless we hire us a trail master and start cutting snowmobile trails, maybe we're not ready for a winter Season," I said.

"Well, no, Kate, but there's not one reason in the world why we couldn't be open through the end of October, even into the first week of November, for the Peepers."

Peepers is short for *Leaf Peepers*, which is to say, the folks from Away who come up to Maine in order to greet Autumn personally, and conduct her downcoast.

There's not a lot of greeting of Autumn, in terms of the Changing of the Leaves, to be done at Archers Beach, though the wood at Heath Hill puts on some fancy dress. Still, we could easily be a place to stop overnight on the way up to the mountains, or the way back down to Away.

If there were anything open to serve them breakfast and give them a place to put their heads.

Maybe play a game or two of skeeball in the arcade, or take a spin on the merry-go-round, get a beer at Neptune's...

"Kate?"

"Hmm?" I sat up, shaking my head. "Sorry. Daydreaming."

"It would be nice, wouldn't it?" Anna said wistfully. "If the town got back on its feet again?"

"Yeah. Yeah. It would." I got up and disposed of my plate, utensils and coffee cup.

"My turn to watch the painted ponies go up and down and 'round and 'round," I said. "Thank you for supper—oh! Anna?"

She turned to look at me, her head tipped to one side.

"Can I leave an extra key to the storm gate here? I'm a little nervous about just handing it over..."

Anna nodded her head. "He can pick it up from us for opening, and bring it back when he comes to get his supper."

"A plan—and a good one. Thanks, Anna."

"That's no problem at all, Kate."

"If you say so. I'm gone. Expect Vassily in moments."

"I'll get out one of the big plates," Anna said calmly. "See you later, Kate."

It was a relatively good night, by the standards of an Early Season Saturday. There hadn't been the astounding number of riders that we'd seen in the Super Early Season, but those who had come by had an...energy. A brightness of intent that was both new and fascinating. The land wriggled around on its back, metaphorically speaking, and offered its belly to be rubbed by this bright new energy. I wondered if it was just anticipation of the end of the school year—most of the evening riders had been middle and high schoolers—or something else entirely; something having to do with the *change* that was moving along the streets of Archers Beach.

Change that I'd woken, just by coming home.

I did, I thought, snapping the padlock through the loops, have a lot to atone for. If I hadn't left Archers Beach; if I'd somehow gotten past my guilt over Tarva's death and my self-loathing...

If I'd *talked* to anybody, instead of just passing judgment on myself, knowing that *I* was evil, because I was heir to every evil thing that had been visited upon me.

Well. As somebody had said, once or twice down the road of history: Life is kind of complicated.

I turned away from the storm gates, and took a deep breath, tasting salt, and sand, hot grease. The night was clear, and I could see stars in the sky beyond Fun Country's night lights.

A good night to walk home by the beach.

Light rippled and flared as I hit the sand—purple, yellow, red. I spun, seeking, feeling *heat* from the direction of Heath Hill. Heart in mouth, I flung the question into the land—

And got an answer from the Wood itself.

Calm, quiet, serene.

All right, I thought, so somebody set off some fireworks.

I scanned the sky, waiting for a second burst, but nothing came.

Heat lightning then, I thought, though it was early in the year. Maybe an aurora.

I scanned the sky again, but saw no edge of aurora. The land reported no threat or unusual circumstances.

The view from Sideways backed up the assessment of the trees—calm; quiet; serene. My power remained coiled at the base of my spine.

Heat lightning, I told myself again; that was all.

I headed down the sand, toward home.

CHAPTER ELEVEN

Sunday, June 11
High Tide 11:40 A.M.
Sunrise 5:00 A.M. EDT

The phone rang as I was pouring my first cup of coffee. Not too bad, as timing went.

"Good morning, Kyle."

"Good morning, Ms. Archer. I hope I didn't wake you."

"Just starting to get serious about my caffeine. I take it you got my message."

"I did, and—that's great, about the wood, and about Mike, too. I really owe him—a beer and a catch-up. Take care of that this winter, when I'm back downcoast. In the meanwhile, that wood. I got a workshop up Smithwheel Road; George—the guy I'm renting from—he said to tell you where Dorr's Woodworking used to be."

I sipped my coffee, thinking. In my day, Dorr's had been one of the town's bigger employers. Twenty-five carpenters turning out fine, handmade Maine furniture. It must've closed during my years away—another victim of my abandonment, or the general economy, or both.

"I know where it is," I told Kyle. "Got a bay number to deliver to?"

"George just says, 'They can drop it at the main dock,' but if whoever's bringing it gives me call and about a half-hour's warning, I can be there waiting for them. That way, no mistakes."

That way, no mistakes. I nodded at the phone.

"I'll pass that along. Just to help with planning, I'd say you're looking for delivery today—tomorrow latest."

"Sooner I can get the wood, sooner I can start work," Kyle said cheerfully.

"How's it going at Wishes?"

"Ms. Anderson's hanging art," he said. "You got your invitation?"

"I did. See you at the party?"

"I'll be there," he promised.

"Excellent. Let me get caffeinated and make a call."

"Sure thing. Thanks!"

He was gone.

I poured the second cup, walked out to the summer parlor and made my call. Kyle could, I was told, expect his wood this afternoon. Splendid.

I flipped the phone closed and tucked it in the back pocket of my jeans. Leaned both elbows on the rail and looked out over the ocean.

The water was peridot and cream this morning, the breakers starting to muscle up with the turn of the tide.

The Gulf of Maine's a pretty, mostly peaceable piece of water; the Atlantic Ocean minds its manners there. Most of that, I guessed, was due to Borgan's influence—Borgan being one of those large, peaceable, competent men who can and will knock you into next week if you aren't behaving up to his standards.

I sipped my coffee, looking out over the distant water.

I'd known him a matter of weeks; he was *trenvay*—well, no. He was the Guardian of the Gulf of Maine. And if you stipulated that *I*, the Guardian of Archers Beach, was something other than *trenvay*, then the same followed for Borgan. It was a theory, any-way. What, exactly, he—and I—were: that remained something of a puzzle, at least on my side. Granted, *I* was complicated—part of me direct from the Land of the Flowers, part of me with roots deep in the soil of Archers Beach, and another part that had given generations of human lives to the care of this land...

I was, as far as I knew, a supernatural being; mundane folk had no truck with *jikinap*, and would politely excuse themselves from any conversation predicated on a cosmology that included Six Worlds created, and linked, by the intent of a supranatural being, now possibly dead, or at least diminished past godhood.

What *else* I was, and what I was going to do with it...I could talk to Gran, and to Mr. Ignat', and, hell, to Mother. But none of them, as far as I could make out from the stories and the histories, had ever been human.

And I—despite the complications and the aftermarket bling—I felt that I was, somehow, at core, human.

Borgan...I wanted to talk to Borgan so bad it was an ache; a pain in my belly and a fever on my brow. Not guilt; just...he'd been gone long enough.

The very first thing Gran had taught me regarding the duties of the Guardian was that the Guardian of the land that was dignified on maps and such as the seaside town of Archers Beach—that Guardian owed respect to the sea. It'd been quite a while—eight weeks, in fact—since I'd *properly* paid my respects, but here I was now, having hiked across the dune, down the dry sand to the wet, until I stood with my naked toes lapped by froth-trimmed wavelets. I stood there, looking out to sea, at the humps of Blunt and Stafford Islands, straight out, Cape Elizabeth and the notch that was Portland Harbor 'way round to my left; Biddeford Pool and Wood Island to my left.

There was a sailboat hugging the rough edges of Strand Island, playing with the wind and probably aggravating the seals, and a motorboat coming out of the blur of Camp Ellis, skipping across the waves like a stone across a river.

I closed my eyes. At the edge of my attention, the land was quietly quivering with anticipation. The land *liked* Borgan. A lot. How much that influenced my own feelings, I had no idea. But...I did *have* feelings—confused feelings, granted, like most of my feelings—and I very much wanted to sit down over a cup of coffee: that same cup of coffee I'd never let him buy me...

The breeze gusted from landside, blowing my hair over my shoulders and around my face. The low-tide waves continued to plash gently against the shore.

Nothing else happened.

At all.

The midway was hopping.

I stopped outside The Last Mango and just stared. People were trying their luck at the ring toss in the center of the walk, while directly across, a lanky teenager was testing his marksmanship. Straight down the road, I could see an Italian ice concession, a duck-pick, and a ring toss, all with customers waiting. Perky popular girl hits were playing on the PA, fortunately almost completely drowned out by the yells of barkers, shots from the firing range, laughter, voices, and—

"Hey, Kate!"

Peggy the Fixer came out of the manager's cave, Vente in one hand. She was wearing black jeans and a black T-shirt showing Jack Skellington holding hands with Sally.

"It's looking good," I told her. "You're a miracle worker."

"Couldn't've done it without you," she said, shaking her pink head. "I keep pinching myself, but going by the bruises, I'm awake. So, anyhow, since you're such a big gun in the miracle business, I'm gonna ask for another one."

I eyed her.

"Shoot."

"You know anybody renting an apartment in town? I'm in a motel up on Route One, which I thought'd be close enough, y'know? Three-mile commute—people die for that where I'm from. Except I'm thinking, High Season, traffic, little country road, closing up at midnight three nights and close enough to midnight, the rest of 'em . . . the strip isn't going to be close enough." She gave me an eager, bright-purple glance. "Is it?"

"Probably not." I frowned at her. "I might know a place," I said, slowly. "Don't know what kind of shape it's in . . . Let me check and I'll give you a call, 'kay?"

"You are my go-to woman for everything in this town! I will await your call, Ms. Archer."

"Should be this afternoon. And—no promises, right? I've gotta check. If what I have in mind won't do, what do you need, baseline?"

"Baseline? A place to sleep, shower; a place to keep some food and a six-pack cold. A microwave would be swell. Washer and dryer nearby, because—schedule." She paused, added, "No wild-life," and nodded once, firmly.

Well, as baselines went, it was basic enough. I chewed my lip, debating with myself . . .

"Okay," I said, slowly. "Lemme see what I've got. Right now what I've got, though . . ."

"Is to get the merry-go-round open for business. 'Way ahead of you. I don't know why they haven't rolled back the gates over there already. The paying customers were climbing the fence when I got here, at ten."

"Marilyn has a certain fondness for order," I told her. "But, yeah, she's gonna snap soon. All that money flowing into other pockets..." I gave her a nod and started down the avenue. "I'll call you."

"I'll be waiting," she promised.

I was sipping coffee and chatting with Anna as she got the counter set up for the day when Vassily arrived, admirably punctual at eleven o'clock.

The hood was down, letting the breeze run wanton fingers through his reddish brown hair.

Boy really ought to have a hat, I thought. Skin that pale will crisp fast, even under the relatively mild Maine summer sun.

"Good morning, Kate Archer," he said, formally. "Good morning, Anna."

"Good morning, Vassily." Anna smiled at him.

Did I say that mundane folk don't wield magic? All you have to do is see Anna Lee smile and know that I'm leading you a dance.

Vassily, like hundreds before him, had obviously fallen irrevocably under her spell. Those stern, thin lips softened, just a little.

"Would you like a cup of coffee? Tea? Pepsi?"

"Thank you, I do not think any—"

"It's part of your meal program," she interrupted him, softly. "Like Kate's coffee."

Vassily took a breath, looked at me. I nodded, and raised the cup slightly.

"If that is the case, then...coffee? With...if there should be...sugar?"

"Coffee coming right up. Sugar's on your left. Show him where, Kate."

"Sure."

I used my chin to point at the condiment rack in the left corner of the counter: packs of soy and duck sauce, sugar, salt and pepper, paper napkins, and plastic utensils.

Vassily picked up four packets of sugar and came downcounter to take the Styrofoam coffee cup from Anna's hand with a tiny bow.

"Thanking you."

"You're very welcome," she told him, and vanished into the back again.

He tore open the packets, and white granules snowed into the blackness of his coffee. Enough sugar to make my teeth ache, and I'd seen this before, I realized. Gaby, who was usually on the outer edge of hungry, sugared her coffee to the saturation point, too. Kept the stomach grumbles down.

I cleared my throat, and he looked at me, face shut down again, eyes wary.

"Since you'll be opening up every day for me," I said conversationally, "I'm going to leave the key here with Anna and Tony. You come in, get your coffee, pick up the key. Bring it back to Anna when you go off-shift. That work for you?"

He sipped his coffee, and breathed in the steam.

"This works for me, yes. It works for Anna and Tony?"

"I asked them, and they're fine with it. Gives 'em a chance to see more of you."

His eyes widened slightly at that, and color kissed his sharp, pale cheeks.

"I will be...happy...to see more of Anna and Tony."

"Sounds like a win for everybody, then." I straightened up out of my lean and reached into my pocket.

The key was attached to a ring with a brass carousel horse charm.

Vassily hesitated, his eye on the charm.

"That is...?"

"Just a charm, so Anna can tell which key belongs to the carousel."

"Ah."

He slipped the ring from my fingers, careful, so it seemed, not to touch me.

"Thanking you. I will open, and work. I will work until you come at...four o'clock. If you are late, I will work until you come. If you are *very* late, I will call Manager Michaud, who is in my phone."

"I'm gonna do my level best not to be late. Otherwise, you're with the program. End of shift, you come over here, get your supper and give the key to Anna. If you need a break, or if you get in a bind, you just give me a call on the cell phone, all right?

I'll be at home, and can be here in a couple minutes. What's the first thing to do if something goes wrong with the carousel itself?"

"I say to the riders, please to dismount and exit. I will arrange a return of the fee. Then I will close the storm door, lock it, and call you on the cell phone."

"Ace." I gave him a grin. "You're gonna do fine."

His lips bent, too quick and too hard to really be a smile, but the boy was trying.

"So," I told him, "you better get opened up. If I know Marilyn, she's going to hit that horn in under five minutes."

"Yes!" He spared the key and the brass charm another hard stare, and hurried across Baxter Avenue.

I slumped back in my corner and finished up what was left in my cup, watching him open the gate, turn on the lights, and start the music playing.

Good, I thought. *Kid's doing good.*

Still, it was . . . remarkably difficult to straighten out of my lean when my coffee was gone, and turn toward home.

CHAPTER TWELVE

Sunday, June 11
Low Tide 5:18 P.M.
Moonrise 9:01 P.M. EDT, Full Moon

What with one thing and another, I got back to the carousel at the stroke of 4:00. I'd intended to arrive earlier, but, well... things had gotten complicated.

As it happened, though, my timing wasn't too bad. I walked in just as the bell sounded to end the ride. I slipped under the rail and stepped up to the operator's board.

"On your right," I murmured.

"Yes," Vassily murmured, a trifle more indistinctly than I was used to hearing from him. I waited until the riders had gotten themselves dismounted and out into Baxter Avenue before I asked.

"You okay?"

He turned, and I could see that his face was even paler than normal, and it looked—damn if it didn't look like he'd been crying.

"*Are* you all right?" I asked.

He sniffled, and nodded.

"It is to be forgiven. I was watching this, the wheel go around and the animals, and to be here...always. It...I thought of my country—my country, which is so very beautiful and yet terrible things happen. There is injustice, and of love, there is too little."

Well, I'd grown up in two countries and all I could say was

that they were both beautiful, in their particular and unique ways, and that terrible injustices occurred in each.

And that, of love, there is, according to my own observations, an ongoing general shortage.

"There's plenty of injustice here, too," I said.

He bowed his head. "Even the blessed angels in Heaven have sorrows to bear."

Well, for all I knew, that was true. I'd never had much truck with angels, myself. On the other hand, it wouldn't do to have my greenie fall any further into despondency. It was the angels that gave me my cue.

"The best we can do is try to make it better, one day, one person, one kind action at a time," I offered, broadly paraphrasing a sermon I'd heard, 'way back, about how to make Heaven on earth.

Vassily looked down at me, his face softening. He looked younger, and somehow less vulnerable.

"You love this place," he said. "This carousel; the—the creatures."

I nodded.

"I was born in another country, where there had been a war," I said, oversimplifying wildly. "When I came here, to live with my grandmother, I was . . . apprehensive at first, but then I came to love it. Even with the injustices. We make our own lives; we do what's right." This was getting a little heavier than I wanted, so I gave him a grin.

"It's your life, no matter where you are. It's up to you to make it the best life—for you and for those you love—that you can."

He gave me a long, startled stare, then he ducked his head.

"Yes," he said. And again. "*Yes.*"

"Right," I said, and jerked my head toward Baxter Avenue. "Your shift's over and Anna has your supper waiting. No work until Friday, right? And then every day until September fifth."

"I will come, on Friday," he said. "Before noon. I will get the key from Anna, and—and coffee. I will open up. At four my shift will be over. I will take the key to Anna, and have my supper."

"You got it," I told him. "On Friday, you'll meet Nancy; she'll be covering some of the night shifts. But for now—you better go get your supper."

"Yes," he said again, and added, as he always did, "Thanking you."

Then he was gone, leaping lightly over the safety rail, and jogging past the three teenage girls in pink sweatshirts emblazoned with ARCHERS BEACH MAINE, who were coming up to the ticket box.

"Afternoon, ladies," I said cheerfully. "Care to take a ride on the carousel?"

It wasn't a bad crowd, given that it was Sunday, and school was still in session. Company started to thin out around 8:30 and by 9:15 I was pretty much on my own. I wandered out into Baxter Avenue and spent fifteen minutes slaying various bovines with Brand Carver, owner-operator of Summer's Wheel.

"You comin' to the meetin' tomorrow morning?" he asked me.

"I told Jess I'd stop by for a cup of coffee," I admitted. "Sounds like she's got the whole park out."

"Lot of us, yeah." Brand pushed his cap back off his forehead. "Bunch of the folks up in town, too. Super Early Season showed we can do it. An' if we can do it once, why not every year?"

"This year might've been novelty?"

"Coulda been," Brand said, looking judicious. "But, maybe not. One of those things that we won't know 'til we try it. Thing is, nobody's been willing to try it. Super Early Season—that shook up some energy."

Well, it had done that, obviously.

"So, I'll see you tomorrow morning."

He grinned. "I'll have a big mug of coffee waiting for you."

I wandered back to the carousel, but the park was dead, now. A couple doors down, past Tony Lee's, the gypsy fortune-teller, Sylvia Laliberte, had turned off her neon tarot cards and was pulling down the door.

Across from her, the greenie minding the lobster toss started to rack up the lobsters and roll down the sides of the booth.

As I watched, the lights went out over the dart game, and the bald guy who ran the T-shirt shop came out to nudge the rose quartz doorstop inside, and pull the door to. A second later, his lights went out, too.

"I guess the weekend's over," I called across to Tony, who leaned out over the counter, to look up and down the empty avenue.

Straightening, he reached inside the booth. I heard the *snap* of a switch being thrown, and the big overhead sign that advertised LEE'S GREAT CHINESE FOOD went dark. Tony walked to the end of the counter and pulled in the condiment tray.

"See you Friday, Kate," he called.

"Take care."

He reached up, grabbed the storm shutter and pulled it down with a bang.

My cue, plain as the nose on your face.

I walked back under the carousel's roof, flicked the switch that turned off the illuminated CAROUSEL sign on the roof, ducked under the rail, and a moment later jumped up onto the decking, and down into the pit.

The orchestrion was first. I rewound the paper, and shut the machine down, then slipped through the utility door and turned off the running lights.

Back on the decking, I walked, as lately Kyle and Vassily had walked—among the animals, my hands trailing along their wooden sides.

The kid was right, I thought. I did love this place, these animals, this carousel. Loved it despite its secrets. It was home in a way that House Aeronymous in the Land of the Flowers had never been home, even though I'd had family around me. When I was a kid, it had never occurred to me to wonder why I'd had family around me. Kids don't wonder about the central facts of the universe. Since growing up, though...

Since then, I *had* wondered, and often, why Aeronymous had not only allowed Nathan to live, but named him his heir. Prince Nathan was seen as weak—half-breed that he was. Aeronymous had other children—full-blooded children, at least two of whom were pretty damn' fine Ozali. He had to have known the danger a half-bred heir posed to him, his position, and the people under his protection. And I couldn't for a moment suppose that an enduring love for Lydia Archer, the woman he had snatched at whim from her duty here in the Changing Land, was the answer to the puzzle.

I stopped and leaned my hands on the unicorn's saddle.

Half-bred Nathan would have had a soul; *voysin*. Not having souls—or at least not having souls of the same configuration, the folk of the Land of the Flowers found our *voysin*...alluring.

Seductive.

I shook my head. No, that might have been enough reason to keep Lydia around until she died, but the child?

Unless...

Unless Aeronymous had made Nathan his heir to *protect* his other children?

That was a little convoluted, even for Aeronymous. On the other hand, that was pretty much politics as played in the Land of the Flowers. The sheer number of Ozali, and the constant quest for more and more power meant that, in order to stay alive, a person had to be so insignificant they fell below the radar of the powerful...

...or so powerful that no one dared challenge them.

Most tried the powerful route. After all, most people have possessions and property, even if they don't have loved ones to protect. You might be okay with your own eventual assimilation, but watching your wife, your children, your *cat* be destroyed for the *jikinap* they held?

So, Aeronymous kept Nathan close, his heir, the wife of his heir, and their child.

Decoys, all.

Not that it mattered in the end.

Grandfather couldn't have predicted Ramendysis. Maybe. In retrospect... he must have assumed he'd be able to best any Ozali who challenged him—he *had been* old, and powerful, and accomplished. He must've felt pretty confident in his dominion.

But Ramendysis had been wily, and he had planned well, picking off lesser Ozali and banking his power until he could pick off the more powerful. Aeronymous had been near the top of the list, if not the last major Ozali Ramendysis had defeated.

Defeated. Broken like straws, and sucked dry. I remembered. I hadn't seen Aeronymous die, but I was there, standing next to Ramendysis, held there by his will, imprisoned and immobile, forced to watch my father fight for his life, while Ramendysis toyed with him, and finally, bored, made an end, snatching my father's power from him so suddenly he screamed, and fell—and misted away into nothing before he struck the floor.

Ramendysis wouldn't let me cry. Though he did allow me to survive—myself, and my mother.

Later, I came to understand what he wanted from my mother. From me—I was a toy. He wrapped me in his will, allowing me to remain just aware enough to know—and to hate—what he forced my body to do. Sometimes, he would free me to myself; at first, I would hope that he'd grown bored. But hope was what he wanted; when I had built sufficient supply, he would own me again and, slowly had my body undress itself, savoring both the death of hope, and my loathing; laughing as he walked me to his couch to perform acts no child...

I heard the land whine, felt the analog of a wet nose thrust into my hand; I smelled salt, and hot oil, and wet tarmac.

Blinking away tears, I embraced the land and moved, backing away from the memory...

...and bumped smack into the rooster.

I gasped a laugh, and shook my head to clear my eyes.

"Stupid bird," I said, and smacked its rump hard enough to sting my hand. This was reality. The other—had been a long time ago. Against all odds, I had survived.

To come home.

The air horn sounded; I jumped—and then jumped from the deck to the floor, running to close the storm gates.

"Stop here," I said, and Peggy did, pulling her Prius close in to the side of the steps, and shutting it down.

I got out and she did, and she stood looking up at Gran's house.

"I just need an apartment, Kate. I mean, the expense account is covering meals and lodging, but there's no way I can stretch to a *house*. Especially"—she pointed to her left—"a house right on the damn' beach. How does *anybody* afford that?"

"Been in the family for years and years," I said, which was true. "But I'm not renting you the house. That's where I live. What I have to offer is right over here."

I led the way around to the stairs, and the walkway hidden behind the hump of the dune, the windows sheltered by the summer parlor, directly above.

I'd left the patio light on. It shone on paving stones swept as sand-free as possible, and a couple of woven-web chairs that I'd found in the storage closet.

"You'll have to keep an eye on them," I told her. "The wind—especially storm winds—come over the dunes sometimes, and loft the furniture around. Best to keep them inside, and bring them out when you're going to use them."

"If I take the place," Peggy said.

"That's right. And don't think I'll be brokenhearted if you don't. Come on in and see what you think."

I pushed the door open and stood back to let her go in first.

As living quarters went, it was pretty basic. The front door opened into the living room, with that big window looking out over the dunes, and a concrete floor covered with indoor/outdoor carpet. At the back of the big room was a kitchenette, to the left was the bathroom, and beyond that, the bedroom.

I'd spent the early afternoon before my shift at the carousel cleaning the place and airing it out. It didn't look, or smell, too bad, and it did have, as the woman said, location.

My biggest worry had been that the appliances and heating system were as bad as I remembered them. As it turned out, I needn't have worried; Gran had updated the place sometime during the years I was away. The living room was furnished with a serviceable, middling-new sofa, a recliner, coffee table, and a television set. One corner of the bathroom housed a washer and dryer, stacked one on top the other. In the kitchen, the stove was electric; there was a microwave slotted in over it and a good range hood with lights and an exhaust fan that might've proven a danger to a cat, if Peggy had one, which I was willing to bet she didn't. No dishwasher, but the refrigerator was full-sized Frigidaire—totally up to the task of keeping the beer cold.

Peggy walked the place, opened the cupboards and the drawers, looking over the dishes and the silverware, the serviceable pots and pans.

She flicked the light on in the bedroom, tried the bed, opened the wardrobe, walked into the bathroom and turned on the shower.

Back in the living room, she flopped on the sofa and bounced—testing the springs, I guess—and looked up at me out of wide purple eyes.

"Linens come with, and all the kitchen stuff," I said, "like you see. You're responsible for doing the laundry and cleaning the place—there's no maid service here."

She shook her head.

"Kate, we're still at the same place. Arbitrary and Cruel uses the Federal per diem and lodging guidelines because that way everybody suffers equally. I got..." She closed one eye, apparently to help her calculate.

"...seventy-five hundred dollars to spend on lodging from June 'til the day after Labor Day."

Standing by the door, I shrugged.

"So? I'll charge you half that."

"No, you ignorant provincial peasant, you'll charge me *ten times* that because places like this, overlooking that"—she waved a dramatic hand toward the window—"do not grow on trees. However, if you're serious about renting to me, and because I am a big, scary fixer from the Big City, and you're not, I will trick you into taking exactly that seventy-five hundred bucks Arbitrary and Cruel is willing to pay. Done?"

It didn't actually matter to me what rent she paid, but Peggy wasn't the kind of girl who'd believe that. And she wasn't, so I strongly suspected, the kind of girl who took freebies.

"Done," I said, with another shrug.

"Thank God. Now, tell me why you don't rent this out to summer people for a thousand dollars a night."

"I don't *do* summer people," I told her, truthfully, and with maybe a little more force than necessary.

Peggy blinked.

"Beg pardon?"

"I don't do summer people—coming home drunk every night, with a new toy, and trying to go longer and louder than last night. I'm a working woman and I need my sleep. Speaking of which"—I pointed out the door and up—"that's my front porch over top, there. And over that is the window to my bedroom. Fine weather, it's usually open, so if you do bring somebody home..."

Peggy grinned. "I'll be quiet, promise."

"I'm just letting you know that privacy isn't something you necessarily get with all that." I swept my hand out toward the dunes in imitation of her gesture.

"So, you were going to let this, what—sit empty all summer?"

"No matter to me if it does," I said. "When I was a little kid, Gran used to rent it every summer to a painter. He'd come up in mid-June. If the weather was good, he'd stay through September. Never any trouble, just a slight smell of turpentine from time to time. Friday nights, he'd get in a six-pack, kick back and listen to Big Band music."

"So that's why you hate summer people!"

I ignored her.

"After he stopped coming—we got a note one May from his daughter saying he'd retired to a nursing home and wouldn't be coming up in June. Got another note in August, saying he'd gone on ahead...Anyhow, after that, Gran tried renting it by the week. It wasn't a happy experience. A couple years, she rented it out Season-long, mostly to artists, or writers, but there were years we'd air it out, then just close it up again."

"Well, I'm pleased to be able to profit from your indolence," Peggy said brightly. "When can I move in?"

I pulled the key from my pocket and held it out to her.

"Best before Friday," I said.

She took the key and stood jiggling it in her hand, looking around, as if she was thinking about what else she was going to need to make the place homey enough for the summer.

"Before Friday, absolutely."

CHAPTER THIRTEEN

Monday, June 12
Low Tide 6:04 A.M.
Sunrise 5:00 A.M. EDT

According to my phone, it had just turned eight o'clock when I pushed open the door of the Garden Cafe.

Apparently, my phone was slow.

It wasn't a big place—maybe room for fifty to sit down and eat, including the five stools at the counter. Four of the tables had been shoved together just in front of the counter, where they'd interfere least with the waitstaff's routes. All sixteen of those seats were full, and a table for two over against the wall. Five more folks holding coffee mugs stood behind the occupants of the chairs.

I recognized a good many of the faces: Jelly Lee, sitting at the head of the pushed-together long table; Joan Anderson; Brand Carver; Millie Bouchard; Henry Emerson, the Pepperidge family lawyer; Beth Abernathy, owner of Play Me; Tom Violette, owner of the Sweet Shoppe; Gregor of Gregor's Electronics; Mr. Kristanos, from Dynamite; Janice Wing, the town librarian; Johnny Gardner, the second-man at Ka-pow!; Ernie Travis, who owned the hardware store; Bob...

"Kate!"

Jess Robald got up out of a chair midway downtable, and hurried 'round to clasp my arm, like I was a returning war hero.

"Brand, get off your can and let Kate sit down. Everybody, this is Kate Archer. Kate, I think you know every—well, here's Michelle—"

A stocky woman with graying brown hair gave me a nod from behind Millie's shoulder.

"...and Ahzan Dhar..."

A slight, brown man wearing tortoiseshell glasses, nodded to me from the chair next to Bob.

"Good morning," I said, since it seemed like Jess expected me to say *something*. "Sorry I'm late."

"Not late," Brand said, leaning over my shoulder to put a nice thick white mug of coffee in front of me. "We're all just early."

"It's Michelle's fault," said Beth Abernathy. "Not only does she open at five, but she said she'd stand coffee for the lot of us."

"And then of course *some* of us," said Millie, pushing a conspicuously empty plate away from her, "wanted our breakfasts."

"So, if nobody minds," Jess said, giving Brand an especially stern stare, "let's begin this meeting of Archers Beach Twelve to Twelve."

"What's—wait." That was Gregor. "Twelve to Twelve?"

Jess looked conscious. "Well, we had to call ourselves something, and I thought, we're trying to go from a twelve-*week* Season to a twelve-*month* Season." She looked around the table, and added, somewhat subdued. "Eventually, I mean..."

"I like it," Joan Anderson said, and smiled at Jess.

"Sure, hell, yes!" Millie thumped her coffee mug on the table. "If we're in, then we're in. No sense getting half-wet."

"So we'll be all wet?" asked Tom Violette—and jerked, as if he'd been kicked. "Hey! That hurt."

"Archers Beach Twelve to Twelve," Michelle said. "That's good."

"The group has established a working name," Henry said, with an urbane inclination of the head toward Jess. "Carry on, chairwoman."

Jess gulped, then straightened her shoulders.

"So the reason we're here is that we all believe that a twelve-week Season is too short, and that for the good of the town, and the good of—well, *us*, we should work together to expand the Season. The Chamber already proved that a Super Early Season can work. We missed a trick, there, us in the park. We shoulda gone to Marilyn and fought to go right into Early Season hours, instead shutting down for two weeks after we were up and running."

"Well. Marilyn would've had to check with the Big Bosses,"

Millie said, "and by the time they'd got back, would've been Early Season, anyhow."

"Water under the bridge," Bob said. "What're you thinking, going forward?"

"The first thing I'm thinking," Jess said, looking around the table, "is there's no reason at all that Labor Day needs to be the last gasp. Sure, people go back to work, but you got your retireds, like came Early, and you got your folks who got jobs don't let 'em take time during the summer, and"—she turned her hands palms-up—"there's enough. Enough to stretch us out, what? Four weeks on either side."

"Where's President Dan by the way?" Henry asked.

"For that matter, where's the town manager?" Millie added.

"Town manager got nothing to do with how we operate our businesses," Bob said surprisingly. "So long's we don't violate an ordinance, and nobody's saying anything illegal here, right, Henry?"

"That is correct. This is a group of business owners who have formed a task force in order to facilitate efforts to increase consumer traffic and legitimately maximize profit. Nothing for the town to care about. The Chamber, however..."

"Mr. Poirier felt that this meeting was in the nature of exploration, rather than affirmation," Janice Wing said. "I wonder, Henry, if you would have time to stop by his office and share your impression of what we accomplish here today?"

"I would be delighted," Henry answered promptly. "I owe Dan a cup of coffee, come to think of it."

"Thank you," Janice said, and looked to Jess. "Excuse me, chairwoman."

"That's fine," Jess said, and added, "Thanks, Henry. Having the Chamber with us on this is going to be huge. Now, the first thing I'd like us to agree on, as a group, is that we'll commit to staying open through the end of September."

"Those of us who are in the park," Jelly murmured, "though we may agree in spirit, may not be able to honor such a pledge. Our hours of operation are set by Manager Michaud."

"Arcade's in," Johnny Gardner said. "Tell Marilyn that, an' see if she can't find the phone to call down south." He nodded to Jess. "We believe there's money to be made, and we're willing— Ms. Belleville and me—we're willing to stake a couple weeks' operating costs to see if we're right." He raised his coffee cup, his forehead wrinkling, and looked back to Jess. "And, if we're not, to see if there's a way to *make* us right. All of us."

"Problem's getting the word out." That was Bob again; downright talkative this morning, Bob. I wondered who was minding his restaurant while he came uphill to a meeting, of all things. "We can stay open all winter long, and if nobody knows it, nobody'll come."

"That's exactly right," Jess said, smiling at him. "We're gonna talk about that in a minute, okay? Just let me—" She looked downtable to Jelly. "The ride operators, we'll have a—a sub-meeting, figure out what we want to say and who'll say it, then we'll make an appointment with Marilyn. That sound good?"

"It does, thank you. The Lee family does want to be involved in this, please."

"Sure," she said.

"Send Anna to talk to Marilyn," Brand said, from behind Millie's chair. "Talking about convincing."

"That's not a bad idea, but first let's talk 'mong ourselves and see what we wanna say," Jess said. "I'll come 'round to all of you and we'll figure out a time. The park..." She frowned.

"The Fun Country subcommittee?" Henry suggested, and her face cleared.

"That's right. Thank you, Henry." She took a breath and looked around at the mob of faces. I was impressed, myself, both with Jess' command of her meeting, and with the meeting's air of serious, practical, intent.

"Okay. The next thing we have for—for Twelve to Twelve as a whole—and speaking to Bob's point—is something Ms. Wing, our town librarian, found out about. I'll just let her explain, if she would."

"Thank you." Janice leaned forward, her hands folded neatly on the table in front of her. "Some of you may know that the State of Maine government includes a tourism department. Their mission is to promote Maine to people from Away. It also offers assistance to towns wishing to...make themselves more attractive to tourists, or to, say, figure out how to expand a Season, or deepen an existing Season." She smiled a slight, librarian smile. "It may be that we are overlooking something of interest—something that we don't even think is notable, because we have it all the time."

"You mean, like the Atlantic Ocean?" asked Bob, maybe half flippant.

"The Atlantic Ocean is one thing, yes," Ms. Wing acknowledged. "Fun Country is another—it has a history, and is one of the few seaside amusement parks still operating. The carousel is another feature. Antique wooden carousels are notable, aren't they, Ms. Archer? There are, I believe, carousel tours for enthusiasts."

"That's right," I said, and, this being a brainstorming session, didn't add that we weren't really well fixed for a carousel tour, since those liked to have four or more within reasonable touring distance of each other.

"The Galaxi is also from another era; I believe that there are roller coaster enthusiasts, as well." She leaned forward, looking from face to face.

"The point is that the Office of Tourism will help us identify our strengths, so that we can promote them—as Bob said, if no one knows that we have the Atlantic Ocean; a century-old, operating wooden carousel; a classic roller coaster; the Garden Cafe—we have *many* treasures! But, if no one knows those things are here, no one will come to Archers Beach looking for them.

"I propose to make contact with the Office of Tourism and find out what sort of assistance is available, the procedure for applying, and if there are any out-of-pocket costs involved." She bit her lip and looked to Henry.

"The Chamber will, I think, need to be involved at some point, but I believe that no one can object to my mounting an exploratory expedition."

"I think it shows initiative, and an understanding that President Poirier's time is valuable," Henry said seriously. "I'll just mention to him, over that cup of coffee, that Twelve to Twelve is making sure it has all of its ducks in a row before calling on the Chamber's assistance."

Ms. Wing looked relieved.

"Thank you, Henry."

"Anybody have any objection to Ms. Wing touching base with the tourism office up in Augusta, to see what kind of help they can give us?" Jess asked.

Nobody said anything.

She nodded. "Okay, then. Ms. Wing—that's yours to do. Anybody else have something to say?"

"Just something to keep in the back of your mind," I said, and paused when all eyes turned respectfully in my direction. That wasn't how it usually went in the meetings I was used to, and it caught me off-balance for a second.

I sipped my coffee, buying balance, then addressed myself to Jess.

"The new midway manager, up from Fun Country, Jersey, is Peggy Marr. She's the woman Management sends to solve its tough problems. She has a lot of flexibility and she's not, as far as I've seen, afraid to use it. She might be a resource."

Jess nodded, and made a note on the pad.

"Thanks. Anybody else?"

"I hear a rumor," Ahzan Dhar murmured, "that the former site of the Lonely Loon is for sale."

The Lonely Loon had been a . . . seedy even for Archers Beach . . . motel directly across from Ahz's Market. It had burned down, so I'd heard, two winters ago. Suspicious circumstances, said the fire marshal, and everything froze in place until that got proved, or didn't.

Sounded now like one or the other had happened.

"Be good if somebody bought that land, and put in something useful," said Bob. "Place is an eyesore, even as a vacant lot, and it don't do you one bit of good."

"No, it does not," Ahzan agreed. "I hear another rumor."

Jess raised her head and looked at him, hard.

"What's that, Ahzie?" she asked.

"That there is a company, from Massachusetts, that has inspected this site, and considers it would be a good location for a condominium building."

The assembled Twelve-to-Twelvers blinked.

Often enough, *condominium* is fightin' words. It carries a freight of bad stuff. Condos are usually purchased as second homes—as *summer homes*—by people from Away. The places are empty for that part of the year that isn't summer; the folks who own them don't vote, or volunteer, or do much of anything at first glance, except clutter the place up during the nice weather.

Second glance, though—that reveals some details.

The summer owners use services—water, sewer, electricity, so on—for which they pay. They pay town property tax on their summer house. During the weeks they live here, they buy wine and groceries at places like Ahz's Market. They hire local folks to clean, to fix their cars and to keep an eye on their places during the months they're not around. They shop in town. They eat out. They occasionally need this or that from the hardware store.

They go to Neptune's for a beer, and to listen to the music; the kids go to the arcade, and to the amusement park.

Kind of a double-edged sword, *condominium.*

Condominium projects built by out-of-state firms, that added another level of freight, because the condo fees and the purchase price would be siphoned right out of town, to someplace Away, just like Fun Country's profits went to Jersey, and precious little trickled back up to Maine.

"I'll just do some research, if Madame Chair will approve," Henry said, "and see if I can substantiate that rumor."

"Yes," Jess said. "I approve." She looked around, making sure she made eye contact with everybody gathered in. "Anything else?"

It appeared not.

"Thank you all for coming. I thought we ought to have another meeting in about a month—I know that puts us right in the middle of July..."

"I'll stand coffee," Michelle said, "and donuts, too."

"That's great—thank you! Can everybody make it on July 17, same time?"

Nobody groaned, most replied in strong affirmative, with a couple hedging, on account of the demands of the Season.

"Sure," Jess said, nodding. "We all know how it goes. Nobody's grading you. If you can come, please come. If you know some-body who ought to be here, bring 'em! In the meanwhile, park people, I'll be stopping by and seeing when we can all sit down and talk. Might have to be after the park closes..."

"My place can be open late for a meeting," Bob said. "Coffee and muffins. Let me know ahead."

Jess beamed. "That's great!" One more long engaging look around the table, and she pushed back her chair, indicating that we were done.

I got up, caught Michelle's eye, gave her a nod, and slipped away.

"Well," Gran said, "it's quite a nice invitation, Katie. Will you be going?"

"Of course! Can't pass up the first social event of the Season. The question is, will *you* be going? Mr. Ignat' could make quite an entrance, with you on one arm and Mother on the other."

Gran smiled faintly, but shook her head. "I think I'll have to pass up the Season's first social," she said. "Nessa? Will you go?"

My mother took the invitation in long fingers and considered it—not necessarily as if she were reading it, but as if she were testing the paper and the quality of the print job.

"I think that I'll remain undertree," she said, meeting my eyes squarely. "We're going to have to come up with some . . . explanation for me, aren't we, Katie? Before I just *appear* in town."

I'd been thinking about that, off and on, though I was mildly startled to hear that she had, too.

"More than that, you're going to need—paperwork. I guess we can get Henry to work on that?" I looked to Gran.

She shook her head. "Not Henry, no. Nessa, dear, first recover your health. Once we're both . . . better able to cope, we can discuss these other matters."

I shivered, there under leaf, and looked at my grandmother hard.

"How . . . *tired* are you?" I asked.

She met my eyes, hers leaf-green and firm.

"Very. I'm glad you came by today, Katie, and not just because I'm always happy to see you, but because I'll be retiring to my tree . . . for a time. Bel thinks . . ." She took a hard breath.

"Bel thinks I may have . . . lost *voysin* in the Land of the Flowers—and that's what ails me. If that's so, then my tree is the cure."

That . . . was frightening. And certainly losing a piece of one's soul might make one tired and frail.

"I understand. Please, rest easy. Mother—" I stopped, at a loss. Because I had been about to offer to bring her down to Tupelo House, but without that *explanation*, and, worse, with the formidable Peggy Marr living in the studio . . .

Which reminded me that I hadn't imparted that piece of news. I looked back to Gran.

"I rented the studio," I told her. "To a woman named Peggy Marr. She's the new midway boss. Replaces Jens."

My grandmother only nodded.

I shivered again.

"Is there anything—"

"No, Katie, thank you." Gran smiled at me, tiredly, but with true intent. "I'll rest easier, knowing you're taking care of everything, down in the town."

"Have a good summer, Katie," Mother added. "We'll be fine here. The Wood will protect us."

Sure it would.

❈   ❈   ❈

I walked home down the beach, half-lost in thought. If Gran had lost *voysin* . . . people died from such wounds. And—Mother. It was a naked wonder that Mother had survived, given what *her* soul had been through. Most mortal people who cross over to live in Sempeki, the Land of the Flowers, succumb not to physical illness, homesickness, or even to old age.

They die because their souls wear out.

The Land of the Flowers, full to overflowing with *jikinap* as it is . . . is wicked hard on the human spirit.

I walked slowly toward Dube Street, the wind off the water braiding and rebraiding my hair as I walked. No use saying I wasn't worried; I was—and I made a note to track down Mr. Ignat' soonest, and ask him for the story on Gran and Mother's chances of full recovery. Gran had never been a stay-in-the-wood sort of dryad—or, if she had, it had been long before I knew her. And Mother was used to ordering a full and busy house, not lying around at leisure.

And I . . . I could still use somebody—some particular somebody—to talk to.

"Borgan," I said and stopped, turning to face full into the wind, and the sea. "Borgan, I miss you. Come on past and I'll—buy you a cup of coffee."

I waited; I waited for the count of one-fifty, without receiving an acknowledgment of any kind.

I took a breath. Okay, fine. Damned if I was going to *beg*.

Turning, I headed down the sand at a clip, and in a very short time was walking, sweaty and feeling grim, down the wooden walk that led over the dunes to my own front yard.

I was met, not with the usual scene of a locked studio with storm shutters across the big front window, but with bustle and confusion.

I stopped dead, trying to remember why the shutters were down and the window was open—why the *door* was open—when out of that same door came a woman with pink hair and purple eyes, wearing black jeans and a black T-shirt with a pink spider on the shoulder.

"Kate!" she called. "You're just in time for a beer!"

CHAPTER FOURTEEN

Thursday, June 15
Low Tide 8:34 P.M.
Moonrise 11:57 P.M. EDT

We arrived at the reception fashionably late, by reason of a small tussle over a Prius.

"Oh, c'mon," I'd said. "It's just right up on Archer Avenue— half a mile at most and a gorgeous night. No reason to drive."

"If you think I'm walking half a mile in *these*"—Peggy donated one of her more dramatic gestures to the cause, indicating the black lace over pink satin ankle boots with the three-inch spike heels that she wore in complement to the black lace circle dress with the plunging neckline and the short slashed sleeves—"you're not well-informed. Also? Half a mile home again, downhill—*in these*—after a glass or two of bubbly? You want me to break my neck, Archer?"

"Good God, no! I need you to live until the end of the Season."

"Or who would ride herd on the midway? You're a cold woman, but I like you. Now get in the damn' car."

I eyed the footwear.

"Can you *drive* in them?"

"I have a certificate—remind me to show it to you sometime. Now, so help me, if you're not in that car by the count of ten . . ."

It being clearly worth my life to argue with her, I slid into the passenger's seat and pulled the seat belt into place.

Privately, I thought Peggy was overdressed for an Archers Beach pre-Season reception, though I admired the foresight that had included party clothes in a road warrior's go-bag.

An analysis of my own closet, conducted prudently on Monday evening, had led to the inescapable conclusion that all I owned were work clothes—which is to say, T-shirts, sweatshirts, denim shirts, jeans—and sneakers. That being the case, I got myself down to Dynamite early Tuesday morning, to see if anything could be done.

Mrs. Kristanos listened no further than, "The reception at Wishes on Thursday—" before sweeping me into the backmost corner, into which no T-shirt, beach towel, or bathing suit was allowed to come, and shoving me into the private changing room.

Very soon thereafter, I became the proud owner of a garnet scoop-necked top that accentuated what I didn't have much of, a pair of drapey black slacks, square-toed black ankle boots with a chunky, walkable heel, and a high-necked, quasi-Oriental jacket in black-and-garnet brocade.

Mrs. Kristanos even had an answer for the accentuation, producing an item of what she called "firmware."

"Not that you need to be firmed," she told me. "You're too thin as it is. But the push-up is what that shirt needs, so you'll have this, too, Kate, *and* you'll wear it. Remember, I'll be at the reception, too."

"Yes, ma'am," I said, and bought what was good for me.

The entire effect was maybe a little somber for a kickoff party, especially since I'd done my hair in a single braid rather than let it run loose over my shoulders, as per usual—but at least it pleased me. The push-up attended to the correct portions of my anatomy, the garnet shirt felt nice, the jacket sat well on my shoulders, the slacks were silky—even the boots were comfortable.

Comfortable was good. Comfortable and neat was even better.

Peggy guided the Prius down Dube Street, turned right on Grand, drove up to Walnut, made the left, and another at Milliken, just like she'd been living in town for months, instead of three days and change. This route bypassed Fountain Circle, which was a perpetual traffic jam during the Season, and got us to Archer Avenue with no muss, and no fuss.

Two minutes later, she pulled into a parking space behind a pearly Cadillac Escalade, across the street from Wishes, which was lit up like Christmas.

"Wow."

I got out of the Prius and stared at the cars parked up and down the hill; at the people walking in from the credit union's parking lot, from around the long curve of St. Margaret's Church, and up the hill.

"This thing's gonna be epic," Peggy said, from beside me.

"Looks like she invited the whole town, and all of Saco, too," I said.

"Well, let's go in and show 'em how it's done," she said, tucking her hand in the crook of my arm and steering me across the street.

"How what's done?"

"*It*, didn't I say?"

"You did," I agreed.

We crossed the street. Peggy seemed steady enough in her unlikely footwear, but she kept a good, firm hold on my arm, anyway. Which was, I figured, only prudent. Trying to run the midway with a broken ankle would probably be *worse* than trying to run it dead.

"You know what," I said, eying a tall and very thin woman in a bright red dress walking down the hill with a man in a black turtleneck, brown cords, and a tweedy looking jacket. "I bet she invited her artists."

"Her what?"

"It's an art gallery, like I told you—Maine artists only. So, what if she invited all the Maine artists she knows, and told them to bring their friends, too?"

"Then she's a smart cookie. You will introduce me to this woman. I like cookies. The smarter the better."

"As she is our host, I will certainly do so immediately," I said, and added, as we approached the door, and stopped behind the crowd of people seeking entrance before us, "Or as close to immediately as humanly possible."

"Gotcha."

We inched our way in from the sidewalk to a space crowded with people.

As I'd expected, there were a great many faces that were unfamiliar to me, but those were balanced by the number I knew intimately: Bob was actually wearing a suit, holding a plastic wineglass and looking like he wanted a smoke. Which he probably did. I introduced him to Peggy as we inched by, and he told her to come on down for a grilled blueberry muffin some morning.

Mr. and Mrs. Kristanos came into view. I straightened, and caught her eye. She pursed her lips, looked me up and down and nodded, once.

"Pass?" Peggy yelled in my ear.

"Looks like it."

"Well, you oughta. Nice outfit; looks good on you. In case I didn't say."

"You didn't, but I figured if it was out of line you'd let me know."

"Got quite an idea of my character, don't you?" she demanded, as I waved at Henry Emerson over a sea of heads.

"Am I wrong?" I asked Peggy.

"Ah, hell, no."

We wriggled by a knot of people dressed in improbable bright colors, who were clutching plastic wineglasses and little plastic plates on which cheese and crackers and grapes balanced precariously.

Past that impediment to traffic was a wood-clad pillar that I thought I remembered, and beyond that, sure enough, was Joan Anderson, standing behind the counter, and chatting with a cadaverous woman in a black pants suit, her spiky white hair streaked with violet.

"Our hostess is in sight," I told Peggy, who was still clutching my arm.

"Thank God. Any wine?"

"Social duty first," I said, even as I wondered how we were going to negotiate the gridlock between us and the counter.

"Ms. Archer!"

That was a familiar voice, though I hadn't previously heard it at bellow. I pivoted in place and grabbed Kyle's arm.

The boy was dressed in a good sports coat over a nice blue oxford shirt, open at the neck—it's not like it was a funeral, after all.

"Kyle, this is Peggy Marr—Peggy, this is Kyle Roberts."

"Pleasure," yelled Kyle.

"Pleased to meet you," Peggy shouted back.

"Great. Kyle, we'd like to pay our respects to the host. Is there any way you can get us over there?"

He looked over his shoulder, apparently measuring the distance, and calculating his own stamina.

"Sure," he said, turning back. "Follow me."

He wasn't a tall lad, though he was taller than either of us, and wiry, rather than wide. However, he walked as if there was nothing and nobody in his way, and those people who did happen to stand in his path—

Believed him, and stepped back.

I kept as close to him as I could manage, so there was no chance of the path filing in again until we were past. Peggy clutched my arm and pressed herself against my side, which was a little disconcerting, but understandable, given the physics of the thing.

In this manner, we eventually arrived at the counter, and there was Joan Anderson, smiling with what seemed to be genuine delight.

"Kate! How wonderful that you could come! Who's your friend?"

"Joan, this is Peggy Marr, midway manager. Peggy, this is Joan Anderson, owner of Wishes Gallery, and our host for this evening."

"I'm very pleased to meet you," Peggy said, and looked around her appreciatively. "You sure know how to throw a party!"

Joan laughed. "If I'd known it was going to be this successful, I'd have gotten a permit from the town to close off Archer Avenue for a street party!"

"I thought part of the idea was to show off the gallery and the art," I said.

"It was, but who can see either in this zoo? If we'd set up outside, then people could have come inside in reasonable numbers and looked around." She laughed again. "Lessons learned for next year. But, ladies! Neither one of you has a glass! This cannot be allowed to stand. Where's—Kyle?"

He was still with us, standing off to one side, maybe a victim of gridlock, now, himself.

"These ladies need wine and something to eat. Could you possibly guide them to the buffet?"

"Sure thing," he said cheerfully, and bestowed an impartial grin on Peggy and myself. "Anytime you're ready."

"They are ready now!" Joan Anderson declared, which was a clear and present dismissal.

I nodded to Kyle.

"Lead on, Macduff."

Half an hour later, wineglass in hand, I slid through the edges of the crowd. Peggy had at long last let go of my arm and was adrift elsewhere in the sea of people. I had seen Marilyn Michaud, Jess Robald, Michelle of the Garden Cafe, Anna and Tony, Tom Violette, Ahzan Dhar, Maria Belleville, and Henry again, with Janice Wing in close attendance.

Chamber President Dan Poirier had taken over one of the rare corners and was talking to a half-circle of admirers. I even thought I caught a glimpse of the town manager, and was duly impressed.

It was, I thought, a good thing that Gran had opted out. I was beginning to feel the strain and I wasn't an elderly dryad who had stressed her system with a long absence from her tree.

In fact, I was starting to think about heading home. I'm not a big fan of large, confined crowds. First, though, I'd have to find Peggy and let her know that I was leaving, so she wouldn't spend time looking for me when she was ready to go.

Among those things I wasn't used to, was going places with a date.

I turned slightly in place, trying to remember the last place I'd seen Peggy—

"Hey there, doll. How come you ain't down at the club, dancing the night away?"

I turned back, looking up into a recently familiar face.

"Hi, Daddy. How come you're not tending bar?"

"Joanie'd kill me dead if I didn't come to her party after she sent me an invite," he said. "'Sides, what'd I be doin' for business?"

"She didn't invite *everybody* in town, did she?" I asked, only half-serious, considering the crowd.

"Sure looks like she did," Daddy answered, echoing my thought. He hefted the bottle he was holding and had a swallow of beer.

Daddy cleaned up nice, the gray silk sports jacket over black turtleneck, and black jeans looked just fine for the event.

"Known Joanie long?" he asked me.

"Just met her. I got curious about what was going in, so I came in and introduced myself."

He nodded. "Me and Joanie go all the way back to elementary school," he said, and had another swig of beer. "Glad she's back. Hell, glad *I'm* back."

"I'm glad you're both back," I said, surprising myself with the sincerity of that sentiment—and Daddy, too, if I read the look he gave me right.

"No place like home, right, doll?" Another swig of beer, which apparently emptied the bottle, because he sighed and looked over his shoulder toward the place where the bar was set up. "Good to see you again," he said. "Come by the club sometime when you're off the clock. Bring a friend."

"I'll do that."

"Sure you will," he said, and with a grin and a nod, he pushed off into the crowd.

"See you," I said to his retreating back. He didn't, I thought, think I'd show up at his club. Might be nice to surprise him. I could bring Peggy with me and surprise all of us.

Speaking of Peggy...

I straightened up as tall as I go, resumed my interrupted pivot—

And damn' near ran my nose into the golden clipper ship holding Joe Nemeier's tie in place against his bright white shirt.

"Well, Ms. Archer, isn't this a pleasant and unexpected delight!"

I went back two hasty steps—pure instinct, clearing enough room to bring my blade out, if it came to that—and looked up into his face.

Not a bad-looking man, Joe Nemeier, in an overgroomed, big-city sort of way. His nose was a little too short, and his face a little too narrow, but it was smooth and expensively tanned, like a face you might buy, mail-order, out of a models' magazine.

His hair was blond, just starting to go to silver, cut sharp as glass. His eyes were that pale blue color you find inside snow banks on really cold January mornings.

In addition to the white shirt, he was wearing a navy blue suit, and accessorized with one of the most beautiful women I have ever seen in my life—and that includes women from the Land of the Flowers, where everyone except the halflings are beautiful.

The *jikinap* at the base of my spine... stirred.

The land... quivered, ears perking.

Joe Nemeier... smiled.

The woman—girl, actually—was dressed in a simple, sleeveless mocha-colored dress. Her skin was alabaster, her hair the orange of a friendly campfire, and her eyes were amber. She was tucked between his arm and his side, one shapely hand on his breast pocket, one snaked 'round his back. Her head rested on his shoulder, orange hair spilling every which way; her belly was pressed against his side, and one long, shapely leg was wrapped 'round his knee.

She looked at me from under heavy lids, without interest, as if she were drugged.

Which, I thought with a shiver, she might well be.

"Here's someone I want you to meet," Joe Nemeier said, apparently to the girl. Her eyes opened wide; her face firmed.

"This is Kate Archer, Ulme," Joe Nemeier said.

She raised her head to stare at me, suddenly more aware, the animosity in her face heating the air between us.

"You will stop hurting Joe," she told me, her voice was quiet, but decisive, and bore a faint, seductive accent.

"I'm not doing anything to Joe," I pointed out, keeping my tone reasonable.

She shook her hair back from an oval face as lovely as the moon, and I felt the touch of *jikinap*—of someone else's *jikinap*—slide, ever-so-softly over my skin.

I shouldn't have reacted, but that touch—bad, *bad* memories woke at that touch.

"Stop that!" I said sharply. And I flicked just the tiniest warning at her, like a spark against her fine white skin.

She laughed, low and throaty.

"Joe, I *like* her."

"Well, good," he said, looking at me with a chilly smile. "I'm sure you girls will get along fine. Now, if you'll excuse us—"

"Kate!"

Peggy arrived at my side from who knew where, pink hair a little wilted, pink face flushed a darker pink, with wine, or the crowd, or both.

"Oh."

She paused, and I *felt her* looking at Ulme.

"Introduce me to your friends," she said, digging me in the side with an elbow.

Sighing, I did so.

"Peggy Marr, this is Joe Nemeier, and his . . . friend, Ulme. Mr. Nemeier, Ulme, Peggy is the manager of the midway."

"Pleased to make your acquaintance," Joe Nemeier said politely.

"Good evening, Peggy Marr," Ulme murmured, her head back on Joe Nemeier's shoulder, her eyes somnolent.

There was a pause in which Peggy simply looked at Ulme, then she turned to me.

"You ready to go? 'Cause I tell you what, I'm beat—and tomorrow's Opening Day!"

CHAPTER FIFTEEN

Friday, June 16
High Tide 2:54 A.M.
Sunrise 5:00 A.M. EDT

"So," Peggy said casually, as she slowed the Prius for the stop sign at the top of Archer Avenue, "are they *friends* of yours?"

I had been thinking—and thinking hard—about what it meant that Joe Nemeier had been among the invited guests at Joan Anderson's reception; that he arrived with a a *jikinap*-enabled houri draped around him like a fox stole; what if anything was I going—was I *obligated*—to do about either of those things . . .

"Kate."

I blinked, realized I had heard her voice, but hadn't registered the words. "Sorry; I missed what you said."

"I *asked* if they were friends of yours—Joe and Ulme."

"Friends . . ." I turned in my seat, as far as the seat belt would let me, and looked at the shadow of Peggy's face in the darkness.

"Peg, Joe Nemeier is a very dangerous man."

"Archer, I'm from Jersey; I get that."

I opened my mouth to tell her just exactly how dangerous—and closed it again.

For one thing, and Jersey or no Jersey, Peggy was a normal, everyday human person. A discussion of *jikinap*, Ozali, and interlinked worlds was therefore dead before it even got under way.

127

For another thing—despite the best efforts of the Coast Guard, the Maine Drug Enforcement Agency, and the *trenvay* of Archers Beach, Joe Nemeier remained at liberty.

And the question you had to ask yourself, if you were me, was—why exactly was that?

Possibly there wasn't enough evidence to warrant taking him up. Everybody in town knowing you're a drug lord just doesn't hold up in court like hard, indisputable *evidence* that you're a drug lord.

Or...and this was the scary one...

What if the MDEA had their evidence and were keeping an eye on their man, waiting for him to *lead them to the Big Guy*?

Peggy turned right down Walnut Street. I could feel the patience coming off of her in waves.

"Sorry..." I said again, "crowds take me that way sometimes. So—no. Joe Nemeier isn't a friend of mine, sort of the opposite, actually. And I met his lady friend for the first time about two minutes before you showed up."

She nodded.

"What's the nasty between you and Joe, if you don't mind my asking?"

At least the answer to *that* was nice and straightforward.

"Property line dispute," I said promptly.

"Well, that's something that can get ugly. Any chance of you guys kissing and making up?"

"Not too much. He not only rejected my lawyer's suggestion that he was in the wrong, he tried to make his point stick by setting my property on fire."

"On—! Kate, not your house!"

"No, no. I own another piece of land in town—a mixed wood lot. The family goes 'way back, like I told you, so there's not only Archer Park, up where the old homestead used to be, there's the parcel over on Heath Hill."

"What's old money doing operating a merry-go-round in a run-down amusement park?"

She braked for the stop sign at the end of Walnut Street, looked both ways, and took an easy right onto Grand.

"We here in Maine have a phrase for families who've held parcels of property for a long time, and still have to work for a living—*land poor*. And the carousel belongs to me, too, you know. A woman needs an occupation."

Peggy laughed.

"What do you *really* do, Archer?"

"I run the family carousel," I said. "Really. I was away for a couple years, slinging code and hacking programs, but it got old."

"So you came back home."

"So I came back home."

She made the turn into Dube Street.

"What're you gonna do when you get bored?" she asked, sliding the Prius in next to my Subaru on the gravel carport behind Tupelo House.

"I've asked myself that, but so far, I haven't been bored."

"How long you been home?"

"Eight weeks," I confessed, and she laughed.

"Jury's still out. Hell, the evidence isn't in."

"True." I hit the button, retracted the seat belt and popped my door.

"Thanks for coming with me tonight," I said, as we walked around the corner of the house.

"We should have a date night once a week," she said. "Girls need to—"

She stopped—talking and walking, her attention completely centered on the steps leading up to my front door. I'd left the porch light on, but there were still plenty of shadows...and then I saw what—*who*—she was staring at.

The land exploded into riotous, noisy hosanna, damn' near knocking me off my feet.

I kept my balance—barely—and walked forward, trying to quiet the racket at the same time.

"Hey," I said, softly.

"Hey, yourself," a deep voice answered from the shadow closest to the wall of the house, and now my stomach—or maybe my heart—joined the land in doing cartwheels.

"Everything all right, Kate?"

That was Peggy, right up beside me, glaring at the big shadow reclining on my steps. "You need me to call anybody?"

"No, it's fine," I told her. "Really. Borgan, this is Peggy Marr, replacing Jens as midway manager. She's renting the studio for the Season."

"Glad to meet you, Peggy Marr. Always glad to meet one of Kate's friends."

He didn't get up, which was probably reasonable. If it wasn't something else entirely. I felt a tiny shiver of worry, while the land continued to holler and yell its unparalleled delight.

"Likewise," Peggy said, and turned to me. "You're sure everything's okay?" she asked, by which she meant, *Is it safe for me to leave you alone with this guy?*

"I'm sure," I said, by which I meant, *Yes, I'm safe with him.*

She hesitated, then took my word for it.

"'Kay, then. G'night, both. Got to get my beauty sleep. Tomorrow's a big day!"

"See you then," I said, and Borgan added, "Sleep sound, Peggy Marr."

That...was suspicious, given the habits of *trenvay* and Guardians, but there wasn't anything overtly dangerous about laying a sound sleep on somebody coming home late from a party, with a big day directly ahead of her.

She nodded, and walked past us, giving the stairs a wide berth. I heard her heels tapping on the stone, the grate of the key entering the lock, the faint creak of hinges. The door closed with a decisive *thump,* followed by the snap of the deadbolt.

"Sounds like I might've disrupted some plans," Borgan said, as I came closer to the steps.

"Last I knew, Peggy had just recently fallen in lust with Joe Nemeier's new girlfriend, who is a *jikinap* user, by the way."

"If you say so," he shifted on the step, putting himself into what light there was, and suddenly I could see his face—broad and brown, black eyes glittering like obsidian under strong black brows. He was...thinner than I remembered, the lines at his mouth and eyes etched ever-so-slightly deeper.

He was wearing a dark—blue, maybe?—sweater. A thin braid snaked over his shoulder; here and there a bead caught what light there was.

"That's a nice outfit, Kate. Rich lookin'."

"Glad you like it; I'm afraid Peggy took the shine right out of me."

"Not hereabouts." He tipped his head slightly to look up into my face, which was as novel a viewpoint for him as it was for me. "Looking fine."

"I wish I could return the compliment." I reached out, fingers finding his braid. It was warm and heavy...seductive, and I knew better, but—

I didn't let go.

"I s'pose I'm not healed whole, yet," Borgan said, smiling up at me, and igniting a slow burn in my stomach. "Heard you call, though, and knew you wouldn't fetch me back unless it was important..."

Guilt shot through me. I dropped his braid.

"Hey, now." He extended a hand, shook himself, and let it drop before he captured my wrist. "So why *did* you call me?"

I took a breath—and another one. He wasn't well; I'd inflicted *far* more damage than I had thought—which was going a ways, since I *thought* I'd killed him—and I had been selfish enough to just *arbitrarily decide* that he'd been away long enough...

"Kate?"

"I missed you—" I blurted. "I just...wanted to...talk to you. That's all." I bit my lip and looked away, disgusted with myself.

"Well now..." he said. "That gives a man some hope, to be missed so bad after a week—"

I looked up.

"Eight weeks," I said.

Borgan's face went still, the smile fading from his eyes.

"Say again."

"You've been gone eight weeks. This is June fifteen—well, sixteen, by now. You went—you went into the sea—"

"On April twenty-seventh," he interrupted. "I remember." He looked past me, apparently at nothing, or at a memory.

"No, I won't ask if you're certain of the dates—unless sweet Peggy's fuddled, too. *Eight weeks?* It was a hard blow you dealt me, Kate, but—I missed all of May, then?" He looked back to me.

"Who's fishing Hum's boat?"

"Finn," I said, relieved to be able to set his mind to rest on this point, if on nothing else. "I—guess she didn't give you the message?"

"She?" he asked, eyebrows rising.

"Daphne," I elucidated and, when no nod of recognition was forthcoming, expanded on the theme. "I walked down to the harbor last week, just to—and *Gray Lady* was at dock. There was a woman aboard who told me her name was Daphne. She said she served the Son of the Sea. I asked her to give you a message, from Mrs. Vois—that she missed your visits and hoped to see you again, soon."

"What'd she look like, this Daphne?"

"Blonde, slender, taller than me"—that didn't really narrow the field much—"cheekbones that she probably insures. Not awfully pleasant, and wanted to make sure I caught the fact that she's not a fan. Told me that the land doesn't order the ocean, and that Mrs. Vois was nothing to concern a Son of the Sea."

"The fog's starting to burn off this," Borgan said. His mouth lifted at one side, but I couldn't tell if it was a smile or ... something else. "Daphne this time, is it? Well."

"You know her?"

"Let's say I know her kind," he answered. He stretched out a hand, this time touching me, oh-so-lightly, on the back of hand.

I shivered in delight, in ... desire.

"I thank you, for calling me back. You were right, Kate; I've been gone too long." He grinned, wide and slow. "Though I'm not sure I'm so encouraged now, that it took you *eight* weeks to miss me."

He paused. I did *not* step up to the plate to tell him that I'd missed him the instant the sea had taken him to its bosom, leaving me standing alone in the surf.

Borgan chuckled, reached up, grabbed the rail and pulled himself to his feet.

"I'll just be running along, then. Wish I could stay, but I'd better tend to this business now—tonight."

He stepped down onto the walkway beside me, and my perspective returned to the normal one, where I looked up—'way up—into his face.

"Where are you going?"

"Out to the rock, to see Nerazi. I need her to help me settle this."

"I'll come with you."

"No, you won't." He grinned.

"Now, Kate, don't look sudden death at me! I'm not trying to keep you away from seafolk secrets, and I'm not scampering off so I don't have to talk to you. I *want* to talk to you, woman, about anything—about nothing! But first I need to get the *ronstibles* off of my boat, and back to the muck that spawned them."

"That sounds like fun," I said, looking at how thin—not just his face—how thin *he* was, the sweater was hanging 'way too loose. "I could help."

"You'll ruin your nice clothes," he said to me. "Not only that—you need your beauty rest, too. Season starts in less'n twelve hours."

"Borgan—"

"Hush," he said gently, and brushed my lips with his fingertips. I shivered...and hushed.

"I'll see you tomorrow, Kate," he said, low and firm. "By which I mean Saturday morning, seven-thirty, at Bob's. We'll get breakfast and you can catch me up. All right?"

I nodded.

"That's fine, then." He stepped aside and swept his arm out and up, showing me the way to the porch.

There being nothing else for it, I climbed up the stairs, and put my key in the lock.

The door came open, and I heard his voice from the bottom of the stairs, "You sleep sound, Kate Archer."

And whether it was, in fact, a sea blessing, or only my own tiredness, I did sleep sound, and woke at eight, rested like I'd slept the clock 'round, clear-headed and full of peace.

CHAPTER SIXTEEN

Friday, June 16
Low Tide 9:16 A.M.
Moonset 10:14 A.M. EDT

I took my mug out onto the summer parlor, and stood sipping coffee while surveying the sand and the sea. It was cloudy and chilly this morning; rags of fog drifted down the beach, congregating, as they always seem to do, at the border of Archers Beach and Surfside.

There's a rock at the border of the towns—nothing as impressive or as steeped in history as Googin Rock, but a good-sized rock, rooted deep and wide. Nerazi likes to come to shore there, and shed her skin. Those who know—*trenvay*, smallkin, and plain humans, too—those who know of the place, sometimes come by in the wee hours, and if they find a naked woman sitting on a sealskin in the lee of the rock, meditatively braiding her hair, they might ask her for a hearing, or a blessing...

Or for assistance in returning the *ronstibles* to the muck that spawned them.

I drank coffee, watching the fog blow down the beach, and wondered what the hell a *ronstible* was and why the particular *ronstible* calling her- or itself Daphne had made such a point of her service to the Son of the Sea, when the man himself seemed to think the opposite.

More—and more urgently—I wondered if the man in question had found Nerazi, if she'd been of a mind to assist in ... whatever it was, and if they'd succeeded. The sea ... told me nothing. It was as lively and vital as it had been ...

... during all the eight weeks that Borgan had ...

Had been what, exactly?

Not imprisoned, obviously.

And not *in peril*—or at least not something the *sea* considered perilous.

Was a Guardian peacefully asleep upon the Gulf of Maine's tender bosom all that was required for its happiness and health?

There was an interesting question—the more so because it could be asked about a Guardian of the land, as well.

I did ... very little, beyond maintain an attachment to the land—an attachment that seemed to have an element of fortune, or ... vigor woven into it.

Gran had told me, years ago, when she had first manipulated me into taking up the duty of my ancestors, that the Guardian's purpose was to protect and husband the land.

That was all very well and good, but—

"Hey, Archer, you up there?"

Peggy's voice effectively derailed my train of thought. I leaned over the railing, but I couldn't see her, down below and behind me.

"You can see my shadow, can't you?"

"Now that you mention it, that was my hint, yeah."

"You sleep okay?" I asked. "Ready to go forth and do battle?"

"I slept great. Listen ..." There was a small pause, perhaps even a clearing of the throat. "You mind if I come up and sit on the porch with you a couple minutes? I got my own coffee."

I sighed. Quietly. And reminded myself that I was the one who'd thought renting the studio to the midway manager would be good—good for her, good for the midway and the *trenvay* who worked there. I had only myself to blame for the loss of my solitary splendor.

"Sure," I said. "Come on up."

"Nice view," Peggy said, leaning her elbows companionably on the rail beside me. She was dressed for Opening Day in black jeans, pink sneakers, and a black T-shirt featuring a scarlet rose pierced by a pink sword; below it the legend, in letters dripping scarlet blood:

Vixen the Slayer. Her pink hair positively glowed, and the diamond chip in her nose glittered aggressively in the scant sunshine.

"So, who was that guy, last night?"

"Borgan? He's a friend," I said, which was certainly true. Whether it was the complete and total truth ... well, that was one of the things I'd wanted to ... not exactly discuss with him, but to ... try to figure out.

"He a park person?"

I blinked at her, but she was staring out over the beach, sipping her coffee.

"No, he's a fisherman. Right now, he's got a contract with Mrs. Vois, to fish her husband's boat."

I saw her forehead wrinkle.

"Where's her husband?"

"He died at sea," I said. "He left his wife and daughter the boat. It's their livelihood—their business, if you want it that way. But somebody has to fish it for them. Mrs. Vois used to go out with Hum—her husband—but she's been poorly for a while. Nancy's a crack mechanic, but she's no fisherwoman. So, they hired Borgan to fish the boat, for a percentage of the take."

"Got it. So, why was he waiting on the steps at midnight like a scary guy out of a scary movie?"

"I'd asked him to come by as soon as he could. Since he knew I'd had some trouble, he took me literally."

"Had some trouble—that's the business with Joe?"

I laughed.

"You writing my biography, Jersey?"

She straightened, glared at me—then laughed, herself.

"It did kinda sound like the third degree, didn't it? Sorry. Just—if you're in trouble, I got your back, Archer, 'kay?"

"That's good to know," I said, and meant it. "So," I added, changing the subject brutally, "today's plans?"

Peggy sighed. "Get down to the midway by ten, ten-thirty, open up the office, walk the grounds, greet and make happy with the crew as they come in, and at noon!" She placed a lingering kiss on her fingertips and released it into the overcast sky. "The Grand Opening!"

She sighed again and set her elbows back on the rail. "And that's where I'm gonna be 'til midnight, one o'clock. Tomorrow, it's lather, rinse, repeat."

"You need an assistant."

"*First*, I need to make sure the midway isn't gonna self-destruct. Then, I'll think about an assistant, because you're right, if I try to fill all those hours by myself, I will shortly become a very crispy critter. You know anybody with managerial experience who needs some hours, and all the fresh-squeezed fruit juice they can drink?"

"Not off the top of my head. I'll give it some thought, though."

"'Preciate it," she said, and finished off what was left of her coffee. "'Preciate you sharing the view with me, too."

"No problem," I told her, more truthfully now than it would have been half an hour ago. "You on your way?"

"Better than late," she said.

I nodded, and went inside to show her out.

I got down to the park early, myself, and hit Marilyn's office about 10:30, just to make sure there weren't any unresolved last-minute issues between Management and the carousel. There weren't.

There *was* a manila envelope in my mailbox. It contained two sheets of murky ink-jet printout outlining procedures—such things as runner schedules, ticket counts, how a disputed count was settled, frequency of payouts. Greenies would be paid direct by the park, with our percentage deducted from receipts before payout. I was responsible for paying my non-greenie employee according to whatever arrangements we'd made between us. The park really didn't want to know what those arrangements were. That suited me fine, and I guessed it suited Nancy fine, too.

Tucking the paperwork into the back pocket of my jeans, I took a quick tour. I was pretending very hard that my hanging around the park had nothing to do with it being Opening Day and Vassily on all day, all by himself, or—the fateful refrain—*what could possibly go wrong?*

Anyhow, it was just about eleven; sunny now, though still a bit on the chilly side, and not a shred of fog to be seen. The main gate to the park was unlocked and slightly ajar, a sly invitation to those who were bold enough to come on in for some early fun. Baxter Avenue was already humming with the sound of rides running at low speed, enticing, but not necessarily working.

I walked past the log flume; the water was running in the slides, and empty sleds were circulating, all but whispering, *You could be having fun here.*

Tom Thumb was easing 'round the track, smoke coming out of the stack in convincing clouds. I heard a clatter overhead, and looked up to see one of Galaxi's two trains climbing the long hill to the apex of the route, a single passenger sitting front and center in the lead car.

I ducked around the Scrambler, which, alone in this section of the park, wasn't in motion, and came up to Keltic Knot.

There was a modest line of three of four bold gate-crashers waiting patiently for their turn, while the ride, all seats full, went through its tight, gravity-defying convolutions.

Mr. Ignat' was in the operator's tower, his back to most of the park, and his concentration obviously on his work.

I left him to it and headed back.

"Hey! Hey! Kate Archer!" came a yell as I passed the Scrambler, I turned, saw a black-haired girl waving, and made the detour.

"What's up?" I called.

"Stacey Dunlap," she said, coming to the fence. She was maybe fourteen, fifteen, her hair a riot of wind-twisted curls, a streak of grease on her chin. "My dad broke his ankle on Wednesday, and the doctor said rest, and Gwen—my dad's girlfriend—she's making sure he does. I told 'em I could run the ride—well, I can. Except something's gone bad. I need somebody to cycle it while I get under the cars and look. Can you—do you have fifteen minutes?"

I didn't really have to be any place until quarter to four, when I was meeting Nancy at the merry-go-round and introducing her to Vassily.

"Sure, I can help," I said, ducking under the rail and walking with her toward the operator's station. "What needs done?"

"If you'll just run it at quarter speed—let me get under first— and then kind of do what I yell?"

"Sure," I said again, and stepped up to the box.

Stacey ran across to the ride, ducked under and yelled, "Now!"

I moved the levers, and watched the cars start their dance, oddly compelling in slo-mo, eerie in their silence. Going at top speed, the Scrambler will describe a series of whooshes, but it's among the quietest rides in the park.

"Give 'er a notch," Stacey yelled from under the dancing cars.

I obliged her, and—

I heard something.

Something...just a very little bit...not right.

It wasn't a problem yet, but it *would be* a problem, if Stacey didn't find it and fix it, which she might do, given enough time, which was getting shorter. The Scrambler was one of Fun Country's Name Rides. If it wasn't operating at Official Opening Time on Opening Day, Stacey's dad would get hit with a hefty fine on top of the business lost on the day.

Standing in the operator's slot, I stepped Sideways.

That easy, I saw it—a little bit of heat in the shaft of the second branch of four cars. I looked closer, and saw that sand had gotten in through a crack in the metal housing. Happens, given we're at the beach.

Happens, but it's a pain to fix—a teardown, cleanout and reassemble job that would take up at least a day. A day that nobody would have for twelve weeks, starting...oh, right about now.

"Back down," Stacey yelled, and I accommodated her, my attention still mostly on the problem.

I can, I thought, *fix that.*

It would take a little bit of fine-tuning, but, I thought—no, I was *sure*—I could do something.

My *jikinap* rose easily—enough to do the job, no more—and I shaped it into the seeming of an air hose. An invisible air hose.

Using this tool as a focus for my will, I blew the sand out of the works. Then, I kneaded the *jikinap* and tugged on it until it was a sticky, thin sheet of protective material, which I caused to adhere to the outside of the breached box. It ought to last the Season; I tried to put that into the working.

That being the best I could do, I stepped fully into the Real World, and snipped the thread of magic that still held me to my work.

"Wait!" Stacey called from beneath the cars. "Stop them, please!"

I did.

A few minutes later, at her instruction, I started them again, notched them up once, and a couple more times, until they were at full speed and I could clearly hear the *whoosh* of their dancing.

"Off, please!"

I brought the dance to a slow end, so as not to tempt anything else to give, and Stacey climbed out from underneath, shaking her head.

"Find it?" I asked her.

Another head shake.

"I think it was the second arm—maybe the gearing? But I don't hear it now." She frowned slightly. "Fixed itself. For now," she added darkly, a true child of the machine age. "I'll make a note in the log and talk to my dad about it."

"Good idea," I said. "Can't be too careful."

She nodded abstractedly, then remembered her manners and gave me a sunny smile.

"Thanks for your help! I couldn't've figured it out without you."

"No problem. You're not working all day by yourself, are you?"

She shook her head. "My brother's coming down to relieve me after he gets off work."

"Really. What does your brother do for a day job?"

"He's a junior architect at Pine Point Associates, in Saco," she said, "so he can't help long-term. We're hoping Dad will be back in a week."

"Might see if Marilyn has any more greenies on the line," I said.

She blinked and perked up. "I didn't think about that! I'll talk it over with my dad."

"Good deal." I swung under the rail and resumed my interrupted tour. Behind me, I heard the Scrambler dance and whoosh.

"Hey, Kate—good you came by."

Tom Thumb was chugging 'round the track at half-speed, clouds of steam billowing satisfactorily out of its stack. Jess Robald was leaning on the safety rail.

"Was going to come by the merry-go-round soon's my greenie got here."

"Then it's really good I came by," I said. "I wouldn't've been there."

"Luck all around," Jess said. "Listen, can you be at Bob's after closing on the twenty-second? That's the meeting of all the park folks to talk about what we oughta say to Management."

"Sure, I can do that," I said. "Let me make a note, though." I pulled my phone from my pocket.

"Y'know, first time I saw a cell, I thought, Now what would I want *that* for? Turns out they're too damn' handy to do without."

"I for one welcome our electronic overlords," I said, keying up the calendar and making the note. I gave Jess a nod. "All set."

"Thanks. And thanks for coming the other morning. Really

made folks sit up and take the idea serious, knowing *you* were taking it serious."

I blinked. "Oh, c'mon. Nobody cares what I think."

"Yeah, they do," Jess said, and suddenly turned her head, as two of the small set accompanied by two grown-ups approached Tom Thumb's boarding platform.

"Gotta go," she said. "See you Thursday!"

"Nancy," I said, "this is Vassily Abramovich Davydenko. Vassily, this is Nancy Vois; she'll be relieving you every other day, more or less. Starting with today."

Vassily gave his grave sort-of bow.

"Nancy Vois, I am pleased to meet you. I work from noon to four, every day."

"That's good," Nancy said, easily. "Real pleased to have you helping Kate and me out. They feeding you good over at Anna and Tony's place?"

"They are everything that is kind. The feeding is . . . excellent, and there is coffee early, when I come to get the key, to open."

"That's right. They're good people over there, and they'll take good care of you."

"Nancy, you got a cell number we can add into Vassily's phone?" I asked. "Chamber gave all the contract workers hot-number cells."

"Sure, I got one. Vassily, let's you and me swap contact numbers, right?"

That done, and the boy gone across to collect his dinner from Anna, I said to Nancy, "I saw Borgan last night and gave him your message."

She nodded, grinning. "I know you did, 'cause he was coming up the walk just as I was leaving. Said he knew he'd been a time away, but there'd been a situation he'd had to take care of. Left him sitting in the rocker with a beer in one hand, talking to Ma and Aunt about fishing up Nova Scotia."

It was a little startling, the crimp I felt in my chest, that he'd gone to visit Nancy's mother—and that, I told myself firmly, was idiotic. I'd seen the man in the wee hours of the morning. I had a breakfast date for tomorrow morning. I'd passed the message myself about Nancy's mom, and I would not—*would not*, I told myself sternly—tolerate petty jealousy.

"He's a man of his word," I said to Nancy, as she ducked under the rail and got herself set up at the operator's station. "You good to go? Need me to stick around?"

"I'm good," she said. "And you'd *best* go—get yourself a nice supper, glass of wine, have a relaxing evening. Because tomorrow, you got the long shift."

"You make a persuasive argument," I said. "I'm outta here. If you run into any trouble, you know who to call."

Despite it being the first day of the Season, the beach was uncrowded, in deference to the chill riding the breeze. There were a few hardy souls out with umbrellas, and one semienthusiastic game of bocce being played on a field marked out on the wet sand, but on the whole there were more seagulls than tourists on the beach.

Being the sturdy Maine girl that I am, the feel of the sun on my skin outweighed any minor discomfort brought by the chilly breeze. In most respects, it was a fine day for a walk.

I walked up the beach from the park, but when Dube Street and my own boardwalk over the dunes came into sight, I didn't turn away from the ocean and angle across the dry sand to home.

Instead, I kept walking.

Like I said, it was a fine day for a walk. That, and the fact that I was just the least little bit restless must have been the reasons I continued on down the beach toward Surfside. After all, I *knew* it was 'way too early to look for Nerazi at the Boundary Stone, though I suppose I could've been looking for something else.

The bodies of dead *ronstibles*, maybe.

Whatever a *ronstible* was.

I supposed it made a certain amount of sense, given the number and kinds of seafolk of which I was aware, that there would be some ... philosophical problems among them. Didn't I have my share, with the *trenvay*?

Each *trenvay* is guardian of a particular piece of land, marsh, water, tree, or whatnot. Each *trenvay's* life is inextricably bound with the life of that which she guards, so it makes perfect sense that each *trenvay* is stubborn, opinionated, proud, and very, very protective of what Gran calls *their service*. Being *trenvay*, they had a little tiny bit of trouble, now and then, with the idea of a Guardian of the land entire. And especially with *me* as the Guardian of the land entire. I don't blame them; they've got cause. Two good causes, in fact.

Cause Number One: Despite being an Archer of the Archers,
I'm not from around here, having been born in the Land of
the Flowers, and there's no Mainer breathing who believes that
somebody from Away has their best interests at heart.

Cause Number Two: I walked out on *my* service.

Hell, half the time, *I* didn't trust me.

So far, though, and with the possible exception of Artie, I'd
managed to get work done without getting badly burned.

But, what if a particular *trenvay* or group of *trenvay* decided
to take me down and replace me with themselves?

I shook my head as I walked, shivering a little, hardy Maine
girl or not, as I passed from the sunshine into the shadow cast
by the Tides In Condominiums.

Wouldn't work. If they were determined, they could get rid of
me, sure. But they couldn't set up as Guardian. The land chose
the Guardian, and for hundreds of years, it had chosen Archers.

Or nothing.

That sort of begged the question of what would happen
when there were no more Archers, but for today I was more
interested in the notion that there were a group of seafolk—let's
call them *ronstibles*—who thought that they could take over the
Guardianship of the Gulf of Maine just by...suppressing the
seated Guardian.

That—

"Good-day to yer, missus," a high voice said from the vicinity
of my ankle.

I blinked out of my web of conjectures and looked down.

"Good-day to you, Heeterskyte," I said politely. "Is there a
service I may perform for you?"

Heeterskyte are smallkin; virtually indistinguishable from your
ordinary Maine sandpiper. If anything, they're rather more reserved
than your ordinary Maine sandpiper by which, I saw now that I
was less abstracted, I was presently surrounded.

"I beg your pardon, Heeterskyte," I said, with real regret. "I
allowed my thoughts to swallow my sense. I had no intention of
disturbing the flock."

"That's well said," my particular heeterskyte said approvingly.
"But we know you, missus, and we know you're no threat to
us or our feeding. I was wishful of telling you a thing, which
might've escaped notice."

Heeterskyte are also fond of gossip—and they're *accurate*. I don't know how they do it.

"I'd be very interested," I said, truthfully.

"Something's here that don't belong," the heeterskyte said sternly. "Knows it don't belong, is what I think, missus, though there's those who think that might change."

Well, as gossip and rumor went, I'd had vaguer. But not by much.

"Do you have a range?" I asked it. "Are we talking Black Dogs? Snallygasters? Willie wisps?"

"No, none of that," the heeterskyte said, slowly. "I don't say it's much, but it's something. Trouble is, it happened up near the Old Woman's landhold. Thought at first it was something of hers. Talked to a nighthawk who'd seen it, though. Said the flames came from the house, and that he heard somebody just after, cryin'."

CHAPTER SEVENTEEN

Saturday, June 17
High Tide 3:50 A.M.
Sunrise 5:00 A.M. EDT

I hit Bob's at 7:15—early for my date, and a good thing, too.

I'd forgotten how it was during the Season—when places that had been comfortably half- or uncomfortably quarter-full were suddenly standing-room-only. It probably wouldn't have hit the restaurants downtown yet—the places that catered exclusively to the tourists—not on the second morning of the Season. Bob's, though—Bob's was year-round: a townie place, first and always. Back in the day, it'd been quaint and "Maine" enough to attract headliners from the Pier, many of whom had signed the photographs that still lined the walls.

Being a townie place, on the morning of the second full day of the Season, when mundane folk and *trenvay*, too, needed a good breakfast to see them through the long working hours ahead, Bob's was packed. The dividers had been pushed back, opening up the summer dining room, and as far as I could tell, every booth, every table, and every place at the counter was taken.

I hesitated, looking around, saw a hand go up from the booth in the back, by the kitchen door, and started in that direction.

"Guardian."

It was a low voice, not immediately recognizable as to gender. I turned and found myself surprisingly eye-to-eye with a person wearing a long-sleeved brown-and-black-striped sweater and well-worn jeans. His or her eyes were either brown or black—the shadow of the gimme hat made it hard to be sure. The face was broad, nearly chinless; the mouth wide and thin-lipped.

"Yes?" I said politely.

"Just wanted you t'know—Gaby said you wasn't clear how t'get hold—I'm Felsic. You got need, I'm down t'marsh, right close in town. Step behind the Sand Dollar and you'll find me."

"Thank you," I said. "I'm happy to meet you, and glad you could work for the new manager."

Felsic lifted round shoulders; let them fall.

"Been doin' it years. Ain't hard, 'n' spills honey on the land t'sweeten the sour times."

"Still, it's good of you," I insisted. Then, because it *had* been worrying at me: "Do you know what happened to Jens? Is he..." I let it trail off in deference to the three definite non-*trenvay* eating their breakfasts approximately two inches from where we stood, taking up precious floor space.

The broad head tipped, evoking a feeling of owlishness. "Phyllis, she was one of us. Jens...belonged to Phyllis. Y'could say it that way. Stayed on, after she'd faded. We knew 'is service, an' he never shorted it. Did like he was taught to do, and no blame on 'im. Was folk from Away pushed 'im out, not us."

I nodded. "Do you know where he went? Jens."

Another shrug.

"Off outta Archers Beach s'all we know, Guardian."

"Kate," I said gently. "It's my name."

"Kate, then." Felsic put up a stubby hand and tugged on the rim of the gimme hat. "Pleasure. Won't keep you no longer from your meal. 'Morning."

"Good morning," I said, and watched Felsic pivot in place and move back to a table where two companions waited, coffee mugs at half-mast, eyes round. I wondered if they might be Moss and Vornflee, but it didn't seem polite to go over and ask.

And, besides, there was that hand still up in the back, steady as she went, but probably getting a little tired of it by now.

Borgan was wearing a denim shirt with the sleeves rolled, and the top two buttons undone. The nacre stud was in his ear, which it wasn't always, so he must consider that this was a special occasion.

My stomach certainly agreed, and while the land was being circumspect, I could feel it quivering with pleasure.

To be perfectly honest, I was quivering myself, under a strong desire to fling myself against his chest. Fortunately for *that*, the table was between us. I took a breath, grinned at Borgan, and slid into the booth across from him.

"Sorry 'bout the delay; Guardian politics."

"No problem," he said, pushing a heavy white mug toward me. "Little worried your coffee'd get cold, though."

"Which would make it worse, how?"

I pulled three creamers from the saucer in the center of the table, and emptied them into my mug before tasting.

Every bit as awful as always. And hot, to boot.

"Wouldn't want it any warmer," I told Borgan. "Nancy told me you dropped by to see her mother last night."

"That I did. Me an' the ladies had a free-rangin' chat about the fishin' here as opposed to other pieces o'water. Turns out Hum'd been part of a commercial fleet for a while, as a young man, sailing out of Nova Scotia. Come home to tend matters when his father fell sick. Met the missus, and it turned out that she'd have him, so they bought the boat with his portion of his father's death, and he never went back up north." He picked up his mug and gave me a grin. "Beer was good, too."

"Very important to have good beer for a free-ranging conversation," I said, and drew in a breath—

"What can I get you two?" came a familiar voice from just in back of my shoulder. I turned my head to look at Bob, who hefted the coffeepot in his right hand and warmed our cups for us.

"I'd like a ham and cheese omelet with a toasted blueberry muffin on the side, please," I said.

Bob nodded. "You got it. Cap'n Borgan?"

"Two eggs over easy, home fries, sausage, wheat toast—that'll do me."

"Beans or doughnut?" Bob asked. "Looks like you could use a little weight put on."

"It'll come," Borgan said. "If I'm still peckish after, Kate here'll gimme an ice cream."

Bob snorted. "Breakfasts comin' right up. Good you're back, Cap'n."

"Good to be back," Borgan returned.

Bob left us, vanishing through the swinging door into the kitchen. I added more cream to my mug, and looked up at Borgan.

Yes, he was too thin, and yes, he looked worn. But beyond all of that, he looked like Borgan, and the simple fact of him being himself contented me in ways that I suspected were deeply dangerous to my future peace of mind.

"So," I said, keeping my voice as casual as I could, with the land wanting Borgan to rub its ears in the worst possible way... "what's a *ronstible*? And did you...retire it or them in good order?"

Borgan laughed out loud, and picked up his mug.

"That's our Kate—a point like a needle."

I glared at him.

He grinned, drank coffee, put his mug down and leaned his elbows on the table.

"Seeing me here and awake might give you an answer, eh?"

"I saw you and you were awake Thursday night. Friday morning. And the sea..."

"Right," he interrupted. "Well, then. *Ronstibles* are..."

"Here y'are," Bob said, dealing plates like a poker hand.

He was gone, wading out into the main room with tray at shoulder level. A round-faced woman with gin-blonde hair came out of the summer parlor, coffeepot in one hand and a pad in the other. She dodged Bob neatly, stepped over a boot in the aisle, glanced at our full cups on the way past, and pushed through the swinging door into the kitchen.

"Who's that?" I asked.

"JoAnn. Bob's daughter."

I blinked. I hadn't known Bob had a daughter, though I'd certainly known he'd been married. Lillian had died back when I was still a kid, killed by the toxins that had leached into and poisoned her pond. Now, was Bob's daughter *trenvay*, or—

I forcibly yanked my thoughts back from that fascinating line of speculation and looked at Borgan, who was grinning, damn him, as he addressed his breakfast.

I picked up my fork. *Let the man eat*, I scolded myself, and sampled a forkful of omelet. Perfect, as always. If Bob ever learned how to brew coffee, world domination was his.

When the omelet was gone, and half the blueberry muffin, I looked up to see Borgan regarding me seriously over the rim of his coffee cup. His plate was shoved to the outside edge of the table, silverware neatly stacked, all ready for pickup.

"So," I said, trying to sound cool and calm, "you were telling me about *ronstibles*."

"Wouldn't you rather know about JoAnn?"

"No."

"You're a hard woman, but have it your way. To tell it short, *ronstibles* are . . . sea witches. They're the ones who guarded the waters . . . a long time ago."

"So they're the original guardians, that you displaced."

Borgan gave me another glance over the rim of his cup. "That's right."

"And they hold a grudge."

"In a manner of speaking. Most times, they're not a bit o'trouble. But—" He stopped abruptly, looked down and reached for a piece of toast.

"But I'd almost killed you," I finished, and the edge on my voice made *me* wince. "They took their chance to, what? Keep you drugged and asleep?"

He looked up. "Something close. Good thing you eventually missed me."

"*I missed you*," I said, perhaps unwisely, "the minute you went into the sea, after the Opal opened a door in the air and went home."

He smiled.

"Now that," he said, "does give me some hope."

I shook my head, drank coffee; feeling the laughter rise—and rise, until I couldn't keep it bottled up anymore, and threw back my head to laugh.

"I hope that's not a commentary on my chances," Borgan said.

"No, it's—one of the things . . . I wanted to talk to you about . . . being human."

"Well, I can talk about that, if you want to. As human as you are, if older. Which reminds me to say that you could show more respect for your elders."

"I could, but I probably won't. It just doesn't," I said apologetically, "seem in character."

"Well, you're right about that." He glanced over my head.

"Looks like there's a line of hungry folks out front," he commented. "Want to come for a walk on the beach? I still need to get caught up on the news."

Archers Beach's claim to fame is seven miles of sand beach—a true rarity, given Maine's rocky, not to say perpendicular, seacoast—and of course the folks that advertise such things mean from one end of town to the other. It's just coincidence that it looks seven miles from dune to breakers, when the tide was 'way out, which it was now.

From Bob's, Borgan and I walked up to the top of Dube Street. Peggy's Prius was in the carport, which didn't tell me anything regarding her whereabouts, seeing as my car was right beside it.

"How's your roomie workin' out?" Borgan asked, picking up my thought.

I snorted and shook my head. "Fine, for somebody who moved in less than a week ago. She's a hard worker, and *not* my roomie. I don't think I'd do well with a roomie."

"Now, see, that's an important piece of information right there," Borgan said earnestly. "How d'you feel about visitors?"

He dropped back to let me mount the boardwalk over the dunes first. I glanced at him over my shoulder.

"You proposing yourself?"

He looked innocent—an expression that, for some reason, he seemed to have pat.

"Just tryin' to get a range, is all."

"Because, see," he continued from behind me, "there's plenty room on *Gray Lady* for you to leave some things; drop by whenever you like to."

What with one thing and another, and some personal trauma, my experience with boyfriends is...*almost* nonexistent. I'd dated a little when I'd been out west, but, frankly, it had been a lot easier to throw myself into my work. Let's just say that I'm bad at relationships.

And yet, I felt...an attraction to the idea of leaving a fresh change of clothes aboard Borgan's boat, and having the option to drop by whenever I'd like to.

I jumped from the end of the boardwalk to the sand, and turned in time to see him do the same.

"Borgan."

He smiled at me, and I felt the air go out of my lungs. I took a deep breath to replace it.

"What you said to me"—almost the very last thing he had said to me, before he'd gone into the healing of the sea—"that there was no keeping the land and the sea apart. Was that—" My breath was short again. I inhaled, deliberately.

"Was that—" Worse than my breath, words failed me.

He smiled, a little wistfully, I thought.

"A threat?" he said, and shook his head. "Truth is, I was thinking in terms of a promise, Kate."

Oh, well. A promise. That was fine, then.

Wasn't it?

I sighed sharply, turned and stalked—sloshed—through the dry sand, and stopped when I gained the firmer stuff to let him catch up.

He did, and stood quiet at my side, hands in the pockets of his jeans, looking chilly, despite the sweater.

"Where's your jacket?" I asked, not meaning to sound like his mother and probably failing miserably.

He half-laughed.

"Well, y'know? I had that jacket for a long time and liked it real well. But, here's the thing, Kate. Even though I know it wasn't responsible for Mr. Wonderful's using it to pull me in to 'im like a hooked sculpin—that it would've kicked 'im in the balls, if it coulda done—I just don't seem able to favor it anymore. Funny, eh?"

I felt my eyes sting. Happens sometimes on the beach, when there's a lot of salt in the air.

"No," I said. "Not funny."

Slowly, I reached out and tucked my arm through his.

I felt a jolt of connection—I'd expected that. What I hadn't expected was for the jolt to fade to a simple, warm pleasure. I sighed, and felt Borgan sigh, too.

"I'll buy you a jacket," I told him, and turned downbeach, toward town, tugging lightly on his arm. "Let's go."

He didn't move. I felt his arm...twitch. When I looked up into his face, he was half-smiling and shaking his head.

"Summer's here—or will be, next week. I'm fine for now, Kate—thanks for the thought."

It hit me then, what I'd almost done. Giving a *trenvay* a gift was a tried-and-true way of binding him to you. He'd owe you a favor, according to the rules he himself played by—

"Do Guardians and *trenvay* play by the same rules?" I asked, trying to sound matter-of-fact and just curious.

The half-smile twisted.

"I'd say it depends on who they're playing with."

Well, that put me in *my* place.

I nodded and slipped my hand out of the crook of his arm. The breeze being a little chilly, I tucked both hands into the pockets of my jacket, and started to walk, toward the Pier and downtown, since I was going that way, anyhow. Borgan walked with me.

Well, at least he wasn't so insulted that he was washing his hands of me. That was, I thought, something. Even though I was an idiot.

The breeze was coming from landside; the low-tide surf more on the order of a whisper than a roar. There were people on the beach—a good couple dozen, walking mostly, like we were; it was probably too early for bocce.

Eventually, Borgan cleared his throat.

"So," he said. "What've I missed, bein' away all that time?"

Right, the news.

"Well, let's see...the Coasties and the MDEA made two busts over the last couple days, and cleaned up a bunch of what has to be Joe Nemeier's property, and a good number of his kiddies, too. Unfortunately, they don't seem to be able to lay hands on the man himself. Or," I added, recalling my previous speculations on the topic, "they hope he'll lead them to somebody bigger, up the chain."

"Shame what happens to a man's investments when he don't have an Ozali on retainer."

"About that," I said. "I told you the other night that he was at the reception at Wishes with a new lady friend, who—"

"Got ahead of the story," he interrupted. "Wishes?"

"A year-round art gallery, believe it or don't. Owner's Joan Anderson, a returning daughter. She threw a Season Opener reception Thursday night—that's where Peggy and I were coming home from. For some reason, Joe Nemeier was there..."

"Easy reason. Man's got money. Makes good sense for the gallery owner to sweeten up the folks who have pockets deep enough to buy her artists' stuff."

He was right, of course. I sighed.

"Didn't think of that. Anyhow, the man was there, and he'd brought his lady friend. Ulme, her name is."

"The Ozali you told me about."

"No," I said slowly. "Not Ozali. I don't think. She has *jikinap*, but I think she...just does. Like almost anybody from any of the other Worlds, well, except Sempeki."

"So Ozali is different from just having magic?"

"An Ozali has studied spellcraft—which is the loophole that lets me into the club. This girl—Ulme. I don't think she has any training. I think *jikinap* is just...a sense to her. Like touch, or hearing."

"So, not a replacement for Mr. Wonderful?"

I chewed my lip.

"Beats me. I guess if Joe Nemeier's shipments go invisible again, we'll have the answer. Otherwise, the good guys'll eventually pick him up and put him away. Couldn't happen soon enough, as far as I'm concerned."

"Any other news?" Borgan asked, after we'd gone half a dozen steps in silence.

I shook myself out of my Nemeier-tainted funk.

"Sorry. Lots more. There's a citizen committee got up by Jess Robald—Archers Beach Twelve to Twelve, they're calling it. They want to lengthen the Season; eventually get to being year-round. You met Peggy. I pissed off my grandmother by dealing with the Enterprise for a replacement animal—"

"How's Bonnie doin'?" Borgan interrupted.

That was an on-point question. Borgan was one of Gran's allies—he'd not only been in on the secret of the Ozali who wasn't in Googin Rock, he'd been an important part of making the con work. That meant he ought to have—no. He *deserved* the truth, so he'd know how much he could depend on her right at the moment.

So—"She says she's fine, just a little worn out, but...she's under Wood, and spends a lot of time in her tree. Mother... the trees are tending to her, too, but she's frail, and not getting less frail as fast as I'd like."

"This is when I say that it's *only* been eight weeks," Borgan murmured. "And when you've got a soul to regrow, and a body to heal, that's no time at all."

"I guess." I stared down at the sand. "I just...I *hate* it, that they're up there, vulnerable, no matter what Gran says about how the Wood will protect them, with the local drug lord right next door. The local drug lord *who we know* holds a grudge."

"Ozali Belignatious went back to Flowerland, did he?"

I jerked my head up to stare at him.

"Mr. Ignat'? Of course not! He'd never leave Gran—" I stopped, feeling like an idiot, again.

"Okay," I acknowledged. "Not *completely* vulnerable."

"Not to say that I heard there was a granddaughter who was a dab hand at magic, too," Borgan said ruminatively.

"A *dab hand*! I'll have you know I've been taking spellcraft lessons from the best!"

"Well, there y'are. An' I'm betting, tired or not, Bonnie's nothing like a pushover, either."

"No," I agreed. I took a breath. "Anyhow, the upshot is that the carousel's mine to run, and the house, to keep."

"So you was saying you got that replacement animal?"

"I did, right. Pissing Gran off in the process. After the process," I added, in the interest of being totally honest.

"Bonnie didn't want you dealin' with Artie?"

"Well... not Artie so much as the Enterprise, is what I gathered. Not that I had a choice. Long story short, Artie tricked me into taking a fiberglass rooster; either a bad copy of a Herschel-Spillman or... just an ugly rooster. But relief is in sight. The rooster *also* offended a fine carpenter named Kyle, who'd done some 'prentice time with a carousel animal carver. He offered to build another horse. So... *next* Season, we'll be back up to speed. *This* Season... we have a rooster."

"What'll you do with it, after the new horse arrives?"

I shrugged. "Hadn't thought out that far. Might just store it, as a spare. Maybe auction it off on eBay."

We passed under the Pier; footsteps sounded on the wooden planks over our heads, drowning out the murmur of the waves. On the far side, Borgan waved his hand toward the carousel.

"Gettin' off here?"

I shook my head.

"I've got some business down Goosefare Brook at dead low. I'll walk you to the *Lady*, if you don't mind my company."

"Always pleased with your company," Borgan assured me, with a look that made my chest go tight again.

I took a breath, and said, not *quite* at random. "My shift doesn't start 'til four."

"That a fact?" He snapped his fingers. "Nancy did say she was working the merry-go-round this Season."

"She is, and so is Vassily Abramovich Davydenko, Greenie Extraordinaire. He's from Ukraine; he's morose; *and* he's hungry! Anna's taken it on as a personal mission, to feed him up."

"No hope for the boy then," Borgan said with a heavy sigh.

"Yeah, he's pretty much doomed."

"Which puts me in mind of your not-roomie. Her being from Away, how's she handling the *trenvay*?"

"All good so far. She's a fixer, so she tells me, and her job first and foremost is to get the midway operating and making lots of money for Management in New Jersey. To this point, she's pulled at least one stunt, and agreed to pay in cash. My personal belief is that she'll get through the Season before one of the big bosses realizes what's she done and reels her in."

"Likely to lose her job?"

"Depends on how good she is, generally," I said, slowly. "Free-wheels have their place in corporate culture, so long as they don't wheel too far or too free."

"Well, I wish 'er well. The midway needs a firm hand."

"Don't we all?"

He gave me a sideways glance.

"That a call on my good nature?"

"What do you think?"

"I think it's what *you* think," he said, somewhat heatedly. "An' I can see that I didn't do myself any good, trying to work it around so you wouldn't think one thing in particular; then damn me if you didn't go and think something *else* that wasn't even on my radar." He sighed deeply. "Never knew such a woman for thinkin'."

I blinked. That had sounded genuinely aggrieved.

"Runs in the family," I admitted, only half-flippant.

"Bonnie does have a long head on 'er."

"You never met Aeronymous," I said, "speaking of long heads. Ozali Belignatious isn't a slouch, either."

"Sliest man in Six Worlds, when he has his whole wits about 'im."

"There you have it."

"I'll just have to learn to be quicker on my feet. Gotten lazy all these years without anybody to gimme an edge."

We'd passed Fun Country's far boundary. Ahead of us was Googin Rock, almost entirely exposed at low tide.

Borgan stopped on the apron and stood regarding the rocky length of it.

"Does look different," he said after several long minutes of study. "Always was a nasty bit of navigation hazard, but I'd gotten so used to seein' the balefire over it and the glamor we'd woven that I'd all but forgot that all it is—is a rock."

"I never knew it any other way," I said, standing next to him, my hands in my pockets. "Every time I look at it now, I get a little catch around my heart, like—*oh, no, what's it planning*?"

He laughed, deep in his chest.

"I expect we'll get used to it in another hundred years, and not be able to remember there was balefire at all."

"I'm not likely to be here in a hundred years," I said, as we moved on down the beach.

"No? Now I'd've said so when you first come back. Didn't look likely you were gonna last a hundred hours, what with phasin' in and out. But once you got connected up with the land again, that little problem fell away."

I frowned at him. "You think being Guardian makes me . . . immortal?"

"Not immortal, no. Everything ends, eventually. But a hundred years? No reason not."

"From what I've been told, most of the Archer Guardians went before their time, rather than wear out their welcome."

"Well, there is a family tendency to put yourselves in harm's way," he allowed, as one being fair.

I took a breath, realized I didn't have anything in particular to say, and shook my head.

Borgan grinned.

"Best you ask your gran," he said kindly. "She'll know how long-lived the family is, in general."

"I'll do that," I said.

We followed the hard curve of the beach 'round the foot of Heath Hill, and there was Kinney Harbor. *Gray Lady* was out at her mooring, looking sprightly and spirited.

"So," I said. "What did you *do* with the ronstible—ronstibles? I only saw Daphne, myself. Was there more than one?"

"There was the one you're calling Daphne, on the *Lady*—"

"Hey, I'm only calling her Daphne because that's what she said her name was!"

"It's not," Borgan said grimly. "But like I was saying—there was the one aboard the *Lady*, and her sister, at one with the waters. It was her was keeping me slow, but their problem, see, is that they have to *keep* me."

"I see," I said, and breathed a wish that they wouldn't soon figure out a way around that little inconvenience. "How's *Gray Lady*?"

"Had some cleaning to do," he said, leaning his arms on the dock's rail. "Nerazi come by last night and made sure of what I'd done, but we're still not fit for company." He turned his head to look at me, lazy, if you didn't mind the tension in his shoulders.

"You'll come aboard for coffee, once she's shipshape again?"

It's dangerous to go—especially to go invited—into a *trenvay's* private space. On the other hand...

"Well, I'll have to inspect, won't I? To see if there's a reasonable place for me to keep those clean clothes?"

His face lit with laughter.

"Hadn't thought o'that, but you're right." He straightened and looked down at me.

"I'm going to have to leave you here," he said. "The news wasn't the only thing slipped by while I was dozing, so I got some few things to tend to. Tomorrow, I'm fishing."

I nodded. "Hum's boat?"

"Oh, aye; that's the contract. Finn's a happy man, going back to pickup crew."

"Who wouldn't be happy to be left off the hook?" I said, pushing away from the rail. "I'll leave you to it, then. See you around."

I thought I'd hit just the right note of casual, there, as I turned.

"Kate."

I turned back.

He took my face between both of his warm, broad hands, callused fingers sliding into my hair.

"I'll see you Midsummer Eve," he murmured, while I stood still and tried to pretend that I wasn't shivering in my shoes from his touch.

He snorted lightly, mouth twisting toward a smile. Then he bent, and kissed me on top my head.

"You be careful, Kate," he said, and let me go.

CHAPTER EIGHTEEN

Low Tide 10:09 A.M. EDT

Goosefare Brook enters the Gulf of Maine past Kinney Harbor. The pool it forms just short of the narrow mouth is a favorite hangout for egret, heron, and the occasional very bewildered swan. In addition to being narrow, the mouth sports a mess of broken pilings, like rotten teeth, visible at low tide, invisible at high, and at all times a threat to the navigation of any vessel but those with the shallowest draft: kayak, canoe, barge. Captains of such craft can easily come ashore at a pleasant little apron beach on the marsh side, perfect for a picnic and a spot of bird watching.

There's another hazard to navigation in the area, too: a wrecked ship sitting well out on the shelf. I've seen it exactly once, myself, at dead low water during the lowest low tide in thirty years, according to Nerazi, who'd shown it to me. Mostly, its black and broken hull is covered by the kindly waters, but it remains a risk, not for that barge or kayak so much as any ocean-going rig whose skipper hasn't done his homework.

To the best of my knowledge; despite—or maybe *because of*—the navigational challenges, the little beach has been used off and on for smuggling operations. Not lately, if what I read in the paper was so. Or maybe whoever was using the beach just hadn't been caught.

Yet.

My interest today, however, wasn't smuggling, past or present. It was the little beach itself, which showed up—or, say, *didn't* show up—in my Guardian-gestalt of the land as . . . call it a dead zone. No—call it a *still zone*.

When I'd first come back home to Archers Beach, my two pressing problems had been:

One, make sure that the prisoners on the merry-go-round were secured beyond any possibility of breaking away—a significant challenge, given the state of my health (dying) and mage-craft (rudimentary).

Two, find Gran, who had gone missing at just about the worst time possible, though, to be perfectly fair, no time that springs to mind would have been good.

In the process of my search, my subsequent reconnection with both the land and my duties to it, I had become aware of certain . . . specific areas that seemed to need . . . help. Maybe even the help of the Guardian of the land.

The first of those had been Heron Marsh—Eltenfleur's territory. I'd tended to him first because, well . . . because Eltenfleur hadn't been remotely still or quiet or quite yet dead. He'd been *dying*. He'd been *in pain*, and he wanted everyone within the sound of his voice to know it.

Since the end of the Super Early Season, in my spare time, which had amounted to a fair number of hours, I'd been trying to map out exactly where those others—the quiet spots—were.

This wasn't as easy you might think, for the simple reason that the land doesn't do maps, or driving directions. Of course, the land could just *walk me* to anyplace I expressed an interest in, but I liked to think that I'd learned better than that.

After my experience with Eltenfleur—especially the almost-getting-killed part—I wanted to have some idea of where I was going, and what I was likely to find there.

Before I arrived.

The rewards of practice were that I could, with concentration, sense the direction of a particular location, and . . . sometimes . . . bring the land's perception into some kind of relationship with how I saw the world.

What that meant in practical terms is that I'd been spending a lot of time flat on my back on the living room floor, feeling out the size and shape of one quiet zone at a time, the flavor of the land to all sides of it, then rolling over to stare at the map until, suddenly, something just...clicked, and I *knew*.

Or, as was more often the case, I *didn't* know and all I had for my trouble was a headache. At that point, I'd take a couple aspirin before hitting the guidebooks, and the local histories, again.

Goosefare Brook had come through pretty clear: the first certain location, after Heron Marsh. Maybe I should have visited immediately, but early on I'd had the idea that I'd do better by pinpointing all the quiet zones first, nice and neat on the map, and see if there was—oh, a pattern, or a proximity, or a theme. But the truth was that my other fixes were still kind of...fuzzy.

And it had finally come to me that I was shirking my duty, by withholding the Guardian's aid, such as it might be.

Since it was low tide, the marshside beach was at its widest, which suited my purpose perfectly. Assuming that the quiet tentativeness was a sign that there *was* something wrong or in need of repair, I'd have most of the problem area above water and open to observation.

Which was why I was skinning down the side of an embankment, using various exposed roots for handholds, and startling a blue heron taller than I am, which was standing out near the center of the pool.

The land was right with me, curious as a puppy dog, which is its usual mode of operation. In the land's view, I was endlessly fascinating, and thought up so very many *interesting* things to do.

I did feel a tingle of puzzlement regarding today's adventure, and a certain wistfulness, which I took to mean that it was sorry Borgan hadn't come along, too.

The roots under my hand, and the embankment itself, hummed as I worked my way down, as things do. Generally, I wouldn't experience them this clearly, as individual melodies; but as two strands of the ongoing symphony of the land that infused me, constantly. I'd gotten to the point where I didn't consciously hear the racket, anymore.

But I sure did miss it when it stopped.

I dropped the last few inches to the little beach—landing inside a silence both absolute and terrifying. My knees buckled and I hit the sand hard, and there was nothing—so much nothing that for a wild second I thought I'd gone deaf.

But no.

Out beyond the broken pilings, I could hear the whisper of waves against sand, under the growing roar of a speedboat's engine.

But the land, the ongoing symphony of *all's well...*

Was gone, as if I'd never heard it.

I took a hard breath, stilling a surge of panic. After all, I'd lived like this; lived like this *for years*, by my own choice. I could certainly bear a few minutes' separation from the voice of the land while I looked around and tried to figure out just what the hell was going on here.

Slowly, I got my feet under me and rose. I brushed the sand off my jeans, and walked forward until I was at the water's edge. Out in the heart of the pool, the blue heron observed me with a critical golden eye.

The sand on the little beach was orange in color and gritty in texture, same as the sand on the ocean side. Used to be the sand at Archers Beach was white, and fine as powder. That was before the Army Corps of Engineers built the jetty at Camp Ellis, in a effort to save the town. My friend Tarva, the selkie, had strongly disapproved of the Camp Ellis jetty—or as strongly as a selkie can disapprove of anything. They're a fairly easygoing lot, and committed to their own comfort.

In fact, Tarva's disapproval had its roots in his comfort. Before the jetty, according to him, the Saco River and the sea had been free to comingle at Camp Ellis. This action of the waters coming together had produced that exceptionally fine sand—sand eminently suitable for a seal to cuddle into for a well-deserved nap.

The Corps' meddling had not only removed the refining process, so that the sand that now came onto the beach was two steps up from orange gravel, but too much of it passed up the coast, adding to the shelf, and producing dunes, destroying what had once been a wide, firm, glistening beach of white sand.

The same high-handed meddling might also have produced a silted-up, choked, marsh pool, but that wasn't what I was seeing. Even at low tide, the pool was wide and deep, almost up to the blue heron's knobby knees.

So, no Eltenfleur problem here, where the marsh had been cut off from the ocean's healing touch.

I walked from the front of the tiny apron of sand, around to the left, until I came to the bank I'd climbed down. Just for kicks, I put my hand on an exposed root.

The song of the land soared into being, strongly laced with worry. I tried to be reassuring, but probably wasn't all that successful, given that I let go of the root, instead of climbing back up to unity. Alone once again in silence, I moved along the bank to the right edge of the beach, and down to my forward starting point.

The silence was absolute. The land was not present, and my land-attached powers were not available to me.

Jikinap, however, *was* available to me. More, it was aware and, slowly, with what felt like a good deal of caution, it was uncoiling from its nestling place at the base of my spine.

Two things interest *jikinap*—more of itself, and a vacuum that can be filled with itself. Either is dangerous.

I exerted my will, firmly but gently, and stopped the rise of my power. Then, I stepped Sideways.

Bars of light snapped into being around me—following the contour of the tiny sand beach. In Side-Sight, they coruscated slightly, as if the light were contained in tubes. I extended my will to embrace the one nearest to me, intending to give it a closer inspection...

Except that my will slid off of it like the tubelike construct was greased. It stayed where it was, and my will rebounded to me—hard.

It stung, but I'm nothing if not stubborn—get that from all sides of the family, as far as I can tell. I extended my will again, this time making sure that it was sticky with a light coating of *jikinap*.

I got a firm, metaphysical grip on the tube this time, but it didn't budge. It felt as if the thing was rooted in the land—hell, as if it was rooted in the *rock*. I tightened my grip, raised a little more juice—

I heard a crack, saw a flash, then stars.

When the stars had faded, I sat up, crossed my legs tailor-fashion, and considered the situation.

"Ouch."

The blast that had blown me off my feet had also blown my sight back to the everyday world. From my cross-legged seat in the sand, I blinked Sideways again.

There they were—bars of light, glittering at me coyly. This time, I managed to resist the temptation to get hold of one, and studied the big picture.

In total, there were twelve bars, six on the left side of the beach, starting at the bank, and six on the right side. The colors were in prismatic order: red, orange, yellow, green, blue, purple, with the purple bars at the front of the beach, but twice as far apart as any of the others.

A faint bell rang in the back of my abused head.

Slowly, I stood up, staring around me at the bars of light, and at the space, ready to receive the thirteenth—white—bar, which would gather and focus the energy of all the bars, in order to open...

A wild gate.

...which is to say, a Gate between one and another of the Six Worlds that has not been put into place, and registered, by the Wise.

Mind, it's not necessary to have *any* kind of Gate—sanctioned or not—in order to cross from one world to another. The old stories are full of Ozali and mages and just plain desperate persons of more power than sense singing themselves across the World Walls.

The problem with that is that the environments and the societies of the Six Worlds tend to rub along about as equitably as you might imagine. You've only got to look at Joe Nemeier's success here in the Changing Land—a success dependent upon a hefty magical assist from an Ozali of Sempeki, the Land of the Flowers—to see why free and easy commerce between the Worlds might not be...an unmixed blessing.

The most puissant Ozali in all the Six Worlds hail from the Land of the Flowers; and the lives of the people of Sempeki are one long struggle not to be absorbed by someone stronger. The Ozali of Sempeki—call them the mid-list Ozali of Sempeki—had in fact begun to shop elsewhere for sources of *jikinap* to help even out the survival game...

And it was then that the Wise acted to close most of the existing Gates, and to make it much harder—though obviously not impossible—to cross, except at the authorized Gates, with their authorized Gatekeepers and the ear of the Wise at least cocked in their direction.

Gran, now...

I froze in place, looking at the bars of light rooted down through the sand and, for all it had felt like when I'd tried to heft one, through the earth's own heart.

Gran.

Among its other virtues, the Fantasy Menagerie Carousel is an Authorized-by-the-Wise Gate. The carousel-keeper, which for a long, long time had meant Ebony Pepperidge, Dryad and Ozali, was the designated Gatekeeper. Right now, being able and qualified, I was the Gatekeeper. Not that anybody had informed the Wise of the change in personnel. Most reasonable people tend to avoid the Wise. For good cause.

Be that as was, and no matter the manner of her going, I didn't for one minute believe that Gran had opened the Authorized Gate and strolled into the Land of the Flowers. The Gates are noisy—anybody who possessed *jikinap* or land-magic would hear it open—and Gran's mission had been one of stealth.

I'd never asked her how she'd crossed. If I'd thought about it at all, I'd just assumed she'd sung herself across, since that was how the business was handled when she'd been young and learning her spellcraft from the Abenaki wise women and medicine men who had once lived on this land.

But I *hadn't* asked. Gran did change with the times, after all. Hadn't she gotten herself a cell phone?

If this Gate was Gran's...

I rolled to my feet, blinking Sideways one more time, as I approached the leftmost red tube. My power stirred, and I gently pushed it back where it belonged. This wasn't a frontal assault; it was a taste test. I wanted to know if this construct had been made by Gran.

Every Ozali has a signature, a...magical scent that lingers in her workings. I knew Gran's signature—green growing things, damp soil, and leaf mold. If she had...called this thing into being, then I would know.

My nose damn' near on the red bar, I breathed in.

And smelled nothing.

Not even salt.

CHAPTER NINETEEN

High Tide 4:36 P.M.
Sunset 8:25 P.M. EDT

Gray clouds were starting to gather as I climbed Heath Hill, and the Wood itself looked darker than was strictly necessary.

Up on the height, Joe Nemeier's house sat in its own pool of sunlight; the abode of a righteous man, picked out by God's spotlight.

Or not.

I stepped into the Wood, took a deep breath, tasting pine, and announced myself: "It's Kate."

Welcome, Kate, came the reply. A path opened at my feet.

My mother was standing in the center of the clearing when I emerged, a thin woman in a short green shift, brown hair curling loose to her bare shoulders. Her long naked feet were half-hidden in the soft grass.

"Katie," she said, and walked forward, hands outstretched. "What's wrong?"

I slipped my hands into hers, and felt my power stir. My mother was of interest—I focused on her, and drew in my breath.

My mother was of interest because she was an empty vessel.

"Katie?"

Nessa Pepperidge was a child of the Changing Land. That

169

meant she had *voysin* and a soul as part of the standard package. *Jikinap* ... she had been a member of Aeronymous' household; patriarch that he was, he insisted that all of his people were capable of defending themselves. That meant, if she hadn't possessed sufficient resources for self-defense when she arrived in the Land of the Flowers as Prince Nathan's wife, she would have been given the means.

"Katie?" my mother said again. Her fingers pressed mine and I felt my power stir more strongly.

"I was looking for Gran," I said, slipping my hands free with a smile. "I've got a question about Goosefare Brook."

My mother shook her head.

"She's in-tree," she said, moving her head a little to indicate which tree, as if I wouldn't know. "She's—I'm afraid she took more harm than she'd admit, crossing over to rescue me." She smiled slightly. "It was very brave, but not at all necessary."

"Not necessary?" I repeated, looking at her, wraith-thin and powerless. "You were—she must have thought that you were dying."

"She did—she told me that much. Ramendysis ... Well. We all know what Ramendysis was."

Some of us—like the woman whose soul he had taken for his own—more than others.

"But the fact of the matter is that, by the time he came to Mother with his bargain, I was ... on the mend. The plants in our formal gardens remembered me kindly, and they each gave a little of themselves so that I would grow and ... prosper. Yes, Ramendysis knew where I was, and he could have uprooted me. But time—the disparity of time between the Worlds was working against him. That, and his own power. He might *easily* have given some of it away ... but he was so terribly afraid."

I stared at her, remembering Ramendysis the last time I'd seen him—triumphant, certain of victory, disdainful of those weaker than he.

And, yet ... the man had held her soul. She would know him ... as well as she knew herself.

"It might have been better for everybody," I managed, "if he'd found other ways to handle his fear."

Mother laughed.

"There's no arguing with that. But, Katie, lacking Mother, is there anything I can do for you?"

"A couple things, actually. I have it from a heeterskyte who has it from a nighthawk that there's something on the Beach that doesn't belong. Apparently a door opened up here, on the hill, a few nights back. The heeterskyte thought it might be something of Gran's working, but his friend the nighthawk said he was up this way when the deal came down. *He* said he heard someone crying, after."

"It was nothing of ours, obviously," Mother said. "I'm scraped dry and Mother's hardly any better. Father..." She shrugged. "I don't think Father would bring something across the Walls." The look she gave me was 'way too earnest.

"Unless it was of the utmost importance," I agreed, dryly.

"Well, of course; you couldn't expect him to leave a princess in peril. But, no; if there was a disturbance here on the hill, it can probably be laid at the feet of our good neighbor."

"That," I confessed, sending a glance toward the house I couldn't see for the trees, "is what worries me. If he's got another Ozali on the hook..."

It was then that the penny dropped, and I swung my eyes back to her.

Mother raised her eyebrows. "Yes?"

"Gran says the trees will protect you, and they will, I know. But with Gran in-tree and you... not yet up to speed, I'd feel better if you had a little something in the arsenal. I've got plenty of *jikinap*, and I will very happily make you a gift."

My mother shook her head.

"I appreciate your concern, Katie, but I don't dare."

"You handled *jikinap* at—in Grandfather's house," I pointed out. She'd had a mean way with a spell, too.

"Yes, but then I had a robust soul, and a strong body. Right now, I have neither. You know as well as I do, that the power will fill any void, and seal any fracture."

She was right. I bowed my head.

"I wish there was something," I said. "I hate the two of you being..."

"I know," she said.

I looked up. "At least I can reinforce the fireproofing." Mr. Ignat' had guided me through that spell, and it still hung over the Wood. It could probably use a little more juice—but Mother was shaking her head again.

"If what you suspect is true—that our neighbor has another Ozali in his employ—then we're better not to tempt them with more power. Your net is so subtle, and uses so little power, that it's barely noticeable."

It was also twisty and inwoven with traps. An Ozali might dismantle it, with care, but he wasn't just going to snack it down in one bite—not without getting a really nasty case of indigestion.

"We'll be fine, Katie," my mother said, and smiled at me. "Really."

I didn't like it, but her objections were reasonable, and I couldn't think of anything else to...

"Father sleeps here every night," Mother continued, her smile deepening. "Not that the night is all that long during the Season. His winged friend graciously gives us his company during the times he's away, so you see we're not entirely without security."

"Right," I said. "If you can think of anything I can do—"

"I'll call," she promised. "Did you want me to ask Mother your question?"

I considered that, then shook my head. "There's somebody else I can ask. If I draw a blank there, I'll be back."

"All right," she said, and opened her arms. "Give me a hug."

It started to drizzle just as I hit the corner of Dube Street. I ran to the top of the street, clattered up the stairs, and let myself into the house.

By the time I'd had a quick shower and washed down a Swiss cheese sandwich on rye with a big glass of orange juice, the drizzle had turned into a downpour. Not the sort of weather to entice epic crowds to the amusement park, though the arcade ought to make out fine. And you never knew. People did occasionally pull on their slickers and brave the damp.

After all, rain did, eventually, stop.

It was a little early when I donned my own slicker and headed back downtown, but there was somebody I wanted to see before I relieved Vassily at the carousel.

The midway was effectively deserted, though there were two hardy pleasure-seekers at the baseball toss. As I watched, the little kid in his miniature Red Sox jacket and matching cap reached up over his head to put a quarter on the counter.

The operator whisked the coin away and replaced it with three regulation hardballs.

"Want a boost?" The man who asked was either a much older brother or a very young dad, wearing an identical, if larger, jacket-and-hat ensemble.

The boy nodded. "Yes. Please."

"Okay, then, champ, here we go."

The bigger guy—I was going for dad, myself—hoisted him up and held him tight around his hips.

"Okay?"

"Yes!"

"Then show me what you can do!"

The kid picked up his first ball, weighed it in his hands, snapped forward and threw.

It bounced off the backboard and disappeared noisily into the depths of the booth. The game agent, wisely, did not immediately pursue, but stayed tucked into the far corner.

The second ball hit the rim of the center basket, and fell away.

"One more, champ," the kid's dad said. "Make it count."

The boy drew a deep breath. He brought the ball up in both hands. He squinted at the basket—and threw!

The ball hit the rim, teetered...

In the dim back corner, the agent shifted, very slightly.

The ball fell into the basket.

"The young man is a winner!" The agent announced loudly enough to be heard across the almost-empty midway.

"I won!" the kid yelled.

"I knew you could do it!" his dad didn't quite yell. "Good job!"

"For the winner!" The agent reached under the counter and came up with a stuffed baseball bat approximately as tall as the boy, who took it with a grin, and hugged it close.

"Thank you!" he said.

The agent's smile was broad, to go with the Maine accent.

"Your skill did it, deah. Got the ahm of a pro!"

The kid grinned and hugged his bat.

"Thanks," the dad said to the operator. "Okay, champ, hang onto the prize. And down we go!"

He set the kid on his feet and offered a hand.

"Now what would you like to do?"

"Ice cream!" the kid said, and his dad laughed.

"Coulda guessed." He gave me and the game agent an all-inclusive grin as the kid dragged him down the midway to the sign of the lighted ice cream cone.

When they were out of earshot, the agent came forward to lean elbows on the counter.

"Guardian."

"Kate," I corrected.

Felsic nodded slightly. "Kate."

"I've got a quick question, if now's a good time."

"Best time all day, so far," Felsic said.

"Good. I just wondered if you know anybody living hard by the Dummy Railroad bridge."

Felsic frowned, and nudged the gimme hat up a centimeter.

"Let me think."

"Dummy railroad?" demanded a familiar voice from behind me. "What the hell's a dummy railroad?"

I turned around to grin at Peggy, who was wearing a safety green slicker that must've belonged to Jens—the hem hit her slightly below the knee and the sleeves completely engulfed her hands.

"Have a little respect," I told her. "It's history."

"So tell me," she said, pushing the hood away from her face. It immediately fell forward again. "If you don't, you don't know what I'm likely to imagine."

"Actually, I have a pretty good idea. But, see, back in the Eighties—that's the *Eighteen*-Eighties, when Archers Beach was *the* place to come on your summer vacation, there was a branch line of the Boston and Maine put in directly to serve Archers Beach, Ocean Park, and Camp Ellis—that's way down Saco, on the point. Some smart fella dubbed it the Dummy Railroad 'cause it made the return trip from Camp Ellis with the engine pushing the train, it allegedly not being smart enough to turn around."

Peggy had another go at pushing her hood back. This time it perched uneasily on her pink hair for a second before falling over her face.

"So why *didn't* it turn around?" she asked, slightly muffled.

"You ever been to Camp Ellis? Then as now there's no room to build a turntable, or to lay a turnaround track. The train *had* to go backward, or not go at all."

"Only, it doesn't still run?"

"Nope, closed down in the Twenties, I think—the *Nineteen*-Twenties, just to be clear. The track's long gone, but you can still see the trestle, where it went over Goosefare Brook. It's a local landmark."

"Oh." Peggy pushed the hood back again, and held it in place with one hand. She looked at Felsic, who looked back at her from the shadow of the gimme hat.

"I was going to ask if you thought we should close," she said, when Felsic continued to say a lot of nothing. "Call it an impromptu poll."

Felsic shrugged. "Rain'll clear out soon. I don't mind waitin'."

"So noted," Peggy said, and gave me a nod. "See you later, Kate."

"Have a good evening." I stepped aside to let her go by, then looked to Felsic. A head shake was my answer.

"I'm not bringing anybody to mind. I'll ask around. Somethin' we need to know about?"

"I'm not sure," I said, slowly. "There seems to be something... peculiar going on with the marsh beach, and I wanted to talk to somebody familiar with the area, compare notes."

A slow nod. "I'll ask around," Felsic said again.

"Thanks," I said, pulling the hood of my slicker up nearer my face. "'Preciate it."

"Pleased to help, Guar—Kate. Stay dry, now."

"You do the same."

Ka-Pow! was doing a healthy business, to judge by the sounds of gunfire, revving motors, and screams that echoed over Fountain Circle as I left the midway.

Fun Country, on the other hand, was deserted. Baxter Avenue looked downright unwelcoming. The gray air leached the bright colors from Summer's Wheel, reworking it in monochrome. Brand was nowhere to be seen; probably taking shelter in the utility shed.

Down the avenue, the greenie tending the lobster toss had let three of the canvas sides down, and was leaning against one of the corner posts, staring out at the rain and smoking. Directly across from him, the Tarot cards glowed bravely against the gloom, but the gloom was winning.

Anna was behind the counter at Tony Lee's, her arms crossed over her breast, leaning back into Tony, who had one hand on her shoulder. I waved, and got under the carousel's roof, pulling the slicker's hood back as I did.

There wasn't anybody waiting in line; I hadn't expected it. The carousel wasn't running; I hadn't expected that, either, though sometimes people will come in under the roof to ride the merry-go-round when it's raining.

I *had* expected to see Vassily at the operator's station, and in that expectation I was disappointed.

Well, he liked to commune with the animals; doubtless he was around the other side of the wheel.

I ducked under the safety rail, unzipped my slicker—and paused.

I heard a sound...a tiny sound, as if someone had gasped.

Around on the far side of the merry-go-round.

Letting the slicker hang loose, I slipped under the inner rail and moved toward the dim back corner where I'd heard the sound.

My sneakers were wet, but I managed to move without any telltale squeaks, 'round the wheel, to the corner opposite the supply shed...

Where Vassily was in a clench with a girl as tall and as slender as he was, her hair bright enough to illuminate the gloom.

"Am I interrupting something?" I asked, loudly.

They leapt apart, the girl tugging her violet hoodie back up onto her shoulder. She looked at me, amber eyes wide in an oval, alabaster face, and I sighed.

"Ulme," I said, nodding politely before I turned to deal with my employee.

"Your pardon," he said quickly. "I am at fault. There was no one, and I thought we would not be so long. We only needed to—to speak, since we are both strange here."

"So you thought it was okay to leave your post and make out with your girlfriend on my time?" I asked interestedly.

He flushed, his pale skin taking on a rather alarming shade of red. I would have thought he'd go dark pink, with his coloring. The red really was too much.

"Please to forgive me," he said. "I know it was...not done. It will not be done again. Please."

"I'll let it go this time," I said, including Ulme in my very best serious, no-nonsense stare. "But if it happens again, Vassily, you're fired. Understand me?"

I didn't even bother to try to get into what would likely happen to him if Joe Nemeier found out Vassily'd been canoodling with his decorative wrap. For all I knew, they were all three very good friends.

"I understand. Never again. I swear. Here." He snatched Ulme's arm and hustled her past me. "I see you out," he said to her. "You will remember."

"I will remember," she said, sounding cowed. She went with him until they reached the edge of the roof, then she suddenly balked, yanking her arm free, and staring out into Baxter Avenue.

"It is only rain," Vassily told her roughly, and pushed her shoulder, which was kind of harsh treatment, given what they'd just been doing in the back corner, there.

"Go," he said, giving her another push, this one a little less bracing than the first. "There is no harm."

Ulme swallowed, her eyes on the soggy outside, then pulled up her hood and darted out into the weather, her sneakers splashing loudly as she ran for the gate, and Fountain Circle, beyond.

Vassily stood until I couldn't hear her anymore, then sighed. He pivoted and gave me his almost-bow.

"Good-night. I will be back tomorrow, to open, and to work until four o'clock."

"With no girlfriend to keep you company," I added. "That stuff's for your own time."

"Yes," he said. "My own time. Thanking you."

And he turned and stalked out into the rain, head down, headed for Tony Lee's.

CHAPTER TWENTY

High Tide 10:31 P.M.
Moonrise 12:22 A.M. EDT

The rain continued.

I amused myself by running the carousel as slow as it would go, and cranking the volume on the orchestrion. "The Battle Hymn of the Republic" made for nice uplifting background music as I walked counter to the wheel's turn, spotting the rib lights. When I was satisfied that each bulb was bright and flicker-free, I hopped onto the decking and, again walking against the wheel's turn, made a close study of the illumination around the central column.

That vital inspection complete, I walked between the rows of animals until I was standing beside the wolf. I put one hand on the saddle and one on the fierce head, and stepped Sideways.

It was busy work, that was all, like making sure none of the lights had burned out; I didn't expect to find anything wrong with the ties that bound the prisoner.

...and I wasn't disappointed.

The being at the wolf's core slumbered in enchanted sleep; the ties binding it to its wooden prison were as smooth as glass, and as tough as titanium, showing neither crack nor mar.

All righty, then.

I blinked into the Real World, and walked back to the goat, where I repeated the exercise, with the same results.

The knight's charger and the hippocampus were likewise bound and unaware.

The unicorn...

A blare of light hit me the moment I stepped Sideways, igniting an instant flare of headache. Involuntarily, I closed my eyes and threw myself back into plain sight.

For the space of a couple of deep breaths, I stood there with both my hands on the unicorn's ornate saddle, listening to my head ring. When the pain had eased off some, I allowed my power to rise and, eyes still closed, waited for it to...become interested.

It didn't take long. *Jikinap* was very close by. It had the feel of something that had once been shaped, but because of poor spellcraft, neglect, or over-powering, it had oozed out of its intended shape into a sticky puddle of purposeless goo, burning 'way too bright.

I swallowed, hard, and, eyes still closed, moved in the direction my power urged me.

It wasn't far. Not far at all. And when I opened my eyes, I saw, not one of the prisoners, standing free amid their shattered chains, and fully awake to their own power. No...

It was the damn' rooster.

Something...

I went Sideways and brought all my attention to bear; not easy with the bright, unformed power pounding at my senses. Another case of stubbornness proving more of a virtue than a vice.

Indeed, the little working I'd placed within the rooster's fiberglass breast had...melted. That was odd in itself. I hadn't infused it with any heat beyond a hint of eccentric charm; as such things go, it was cool-running, and about as complex as a ball of Silly Putty. I forced my attention closer, and saw what looked like... secretions inside the cavity. If the rooster had been a living thing, its autoimmune system might have produced such secretions, as an allergic reaction.

I blinked, inadvertently snapping myself back into the everyday world.

An allergic reaction? Inanimate objects didn't have allergic reactions.

I frowned at the rooster.

"How about," I said to it, "an inanimate object that came from the Enterprise?" An object that Artie had been awfully eager for me to have, for reasons as yet murky, and all the more unsettling because of that.

The carousel's stately progress was taking me past the intake gate. I looked 'round, but there was no one in line. Good.

I put my attention back on the rooster.

"Look, you," I said. "I'm not hard to get along with; I don't want to make you sick, or break you. But you're going to have to work with me, here. You've got to be welcoming to the paying customers, okay?" I paused, listening with the land's ears, and with the ears of my power, just in case...

But I heard nothing.

I sighed. "Right. Let's see if we can come up with a compromise."

Carefully, I called my power out of the rooster and into my palm. I inspected the spellwork... the smallest bit of glamor, of charm. Well, and maybe I *had* misjudged the amount of power necessary to carry so light a burden. It seems to be a universal constant, no matter what the craft, that the little, fiddly stuff is the hardest to get right.

I halved the little blob of *jikinap*, reabsorbed one half and rolled what remained into a ball, making sure the suggestion of zany charm was evenly distributed, and unlikely to cause the magical equivalent of a hot spot.

When I was satisfied with my work, and that the spell was as balanced and as inoffensive as I could make it, I returned it to the rooster's chest cavity, and blinked back into the real world.

There was no denying that the rooster was a little odd. But odd in an endearing sort of way, like an ugly puppy.

It would, I decided, have to do.

I turned and jumped off the merry-go-round, making a note to pay close attention to the rooster, while he continued as part of the carousel's company.

The rain was still coming down, and Fun Country was still deserted. I retired to the stool at the operator's station, snapped my phone open and punched up my most recent book.

I'd only read a couple paragraphs when the sound of a fire engine's siren roused me. I lifted my head, listening, hearing the truck come down Archer Avenue... and turn right maybe a block short of Fun Country. Frowning, I stood and walked to the edge of the carousel's roof, hearing more sirens now, as the cops came in down East Grand and West.

It was, as I'd suspected, still raining, but if Lisa's french fry oil had caught fire, say . . .

Anna stepped up to the counter at Tony Lee's and waved to me with one hand, the other holding a cell to her ear.

"Tony went to see," she called. "He says it's a Dumpster fire behind Daddy's Dance Club. The fire department has it under control."

"Great!" I called back. "Thanks!"

She nodded and stepped back into the depths of the kitchen.

I returned to the operator's station, and my book.

I was well into it when I heard a sound, like a wet sole gritting on dry cement, and looked up to see a man in the omnipresent hoodie approaching the carousel, the hood casting his face in shadow.

I snapped the phone shut and slid it into my pocket, simultaneously coming off the stool and onto my feet.

"Good evening!" I said brightly, mentally snapping my fingers for the land's attention. "Like a ride on the carousel?"

The guy hesitated, then laughed, and reached up to pull the hood back, rumpling his pretty brown curls in the process.

"Actually," Kyle said, "I wouldn't mind a ride, but I came to talk to you about a horse."

I considered him, and gave the land leave to sit. "Decided the project's too much for you?"

"Oh, no! I want this! I got started—and that's when I realized . . ." He paused, a delicate rosy blush more suited to Vassily's coloring tinting his round cheeks.

"I was getting ready to cut the pattern, and I realized that I never asked you what kind of horse you might want—or if you wanted a horse at all."

I blinked at him, and then laughed.

"We're both idiots," I said. "I just assumed—well, that's the problem, right? Come on in and let's survey the situation."

He ducked under the gate, unzipped his hoodie and hung it neatly over the rail before following me to the carousel.

I led him around to where the rooster stood in all his zany glory, and nodded at it.

"Not a rooster," I said.

"Got that," he said, pulling a pad out of his back pocket and a pencil from somewhere else. "What was here before? It was stolen, I think you said?"

"Right. It was a unique piece—a fantasy horse. I told you the animals were carved by family, so there's not going to be a pattern..."

"I can make the pattern," Kyle told me, flipping the pad open. "Do you want a—well, it won't be *exact* replacement, but as close to the animal that was stolen as I can get?"

I thought about that. Thought about the image I'd had in my head when I walked into the Enterprise a week ago.

"I'd like it," I said slowly, "if we could get something close to what was here. I was...kind of used to it, tell the truth." I looked around at the animals in sight. "You work with something most of your life, you get attached."

"*Yes,*" Kyle said, with more emphasis than I would have expected, given such a saccharine offering. He brought his pencil to the ready. "So, what did he look like, the horse that got stolen?"

"She," I said, giving him a half-grin. "Just a little gray, dainty as you like her, head up and neck proud. Black mane and white socks."

Kyle was making notes on his pad, nodding. "Lot of that will be with the painter," he said, "but I'll just note it down..."

"Sure," I said, and waited until his pencil stilled before adding, "she had batwings, black to match the mane, kind of half-furled along her sides. Also, fangs."

He looked up.

"The fangs aren't important," I told him. "In fact, it'd probably be a good idea to lose the fangs. She was a hard sell sometimes, that horse, even to the kids who loved the idea that she could fly."

He nodded and went back to his pad.

"Stander, prancer or jumper?"

"Prancer."

Another nod, then a quick look up.

"If you don't mind...I can sketch you out something in a couple minutes, make any adjustments right here."

"Sure; take your time. It's not like we're real busy at the moment."

Another nod, this one considerably more abstracted as he stared at the rooster—or maybe at the space the rooster occupied.

I left him to it, and returned to the operator's station and my book.

I hadn't read more than a chapter when I became aware of a certain lack in the background. I raised my head and looked outside.

The rain had stopped.

I checked the phone's face: eight o'clock. Early enough that we might get some action out of the night, yet. I slipped the phone into my pocket and went outside to survey the situation.

It was coolish, with the breeze off the ocean, and things were pretty drippy, but I could see streaks of pink and orange through a wide break in the cloud cover—sunset, coming right up.

"Think anybody'll come out, after all that?" Brand called over from Summer's Wheel.

"Not impossible," I called back. "It's been raining a good while. Adults locked in motel rooms with antsy kids have been known to do strange things."

"True," he said, and reached over to his operator's station, flipping the running lights on to their brightest setting, and nudging the Wheel into a stately spin.

"Let's see what happens," he said.

Beyond him, the Samurai warrior drew his swords and invited those who were honorable and worthy to accept the challenge of the Oriental Funhouse. As counterpoint, I heard the cars at Dodge City start to rumble and snap. The kid at the lobster toss stubbed out his latest cigarette, straightened, and began rolling the sides of the booth back up.

"I guess it's unanimous." I gave Brand a wave, and went back underroof.

Kyle was waiting at the operator's station, pad in hand.

"Right with you," I said, reaching over to start the carousel spinning again, before jogging over to crank the orchestrion up as far as it would go.

"Okay," I said, coming back to the station and putting my hands on the safety rail. "What've you got?"

He had several sketches. I flipped pages, looking at them.

"Her head was a little longer," I said slowly. "Think delicate, but strong. And the wings were broader—you looked at her and you really did think she could fly."

Kyle nodded, took the book back, and made some adjustments on the sketch I had settled on as the best. "Like this, here? And then the wings..."

"Yes. Yes, that's right."

"Great!" He looked up with a grin. "I'm glad I came down here. You're right—that's a unique design. Do you have any idea who stole the original?"

"No," I said untruthfully.

"You filed a report with the local police?"

I hadn't, since I knew full well what had happened to that "horse." For half a second I thought about lying, but the question had been, to my ear, just a little too casual, so I told him a version of the truth.

"No, I never did file a police report. Carousel's not insured, and the cops don't tend to take the problems of 'carny folk' too serious. Whoever took that horse wanted her, I'm sure. I have to believe they'll take good care of her."

He gave me a long, expressionless look. I stared right back, eyes wide. He blinked first, glanced down, and flipped the pad shut with a snap.

"All right, then. I'll get on back to the shop, and start work." He turned—turned back.

"Another question, if I might."

I raised my eyebrows and waited.

"Joe Nemeier wants some cabinets built. I saw you talking with him at the reception. Give me a reference?"

I shook my head.

"I'm not friends with the man—we've got a property line dispute going, which never makes friends. I never heard that he didn't pay his debts." I hesitated, then added, carefully, "Rumor is he's a dangerous man to cross."

Kyle gave me a grin.

"Then I won't cross him," he said, and turned to go just as the first group of five—four kids and one harassed-looking woman with several ticket books in her hand—walked under the carousel's cheery roof.

CHAPTER TWENTY-ONE

Tuesday, June 20
High Tide 6:57 A.M.
Sunrise 5:00 A.M. EDT

It was 7:30-ish on my day off, but I was already in the kitchen, priming the coffeepot and singing along with Marc Cohn, really putting my all into... *the middle of a pouring rain*...

The doors to the summer parlor were wide open, the front door was on the latch, and, unlike the Memphis of my duet, the sun was out, up, and very much on the job. A warm breeze explored the living room, rustling the map spread on the floor, and riffling the pages of the guidebook I'd left open on the coffee table. Outside, I heard seagulls screaming insults at each other, and the occasional crash of a wave, as the ocean danced away from the land.

To my observation, it was a perfect early summer day—which the weather guy on WBLM confirmed as I opened the refrigerator: Sunny, bright, breezy, zero chance of precip, highs in the mid-seventies. The theme continued tonight: clear and temps in the mid-fifties; with more of the same on tap for tomorrow.

I pulled out eggs, milk, cheese, closed the refrigerator door with my hip and headed over to the stove, asserting my love of rock 'n' roll in sync with Joan Jett.

"Somebody's in a good mood," Peggy said, closing the front door behind her. It had gotten to be a habit, already, that we had a cup of coffee together on the summer parlor in the morning. Mostly, we talked about nothing much—her parents in Hoboken; the kid sister taking Library Science at Rutgers...

"My God, Archer, are you making *breakfast*?"

Peggy, I knew by now, didn't indulge in breakfast. She apparently ran on caffeine, and the occasional hot dog or slice of pizza.

"Scrambled eggs," I said, looking over my shoulder at her. "Just as easy to make two helpings as one. Want some?"

"You a good cook?"

"No, I'm a lousy cook. But even I can make scrambled eggs. Which I'll just be doing, whether you want any or not."

"Sure, what the hell," she said. "You want I should make toast?"

"Think you can handle it?"

"You're lookin' at a pro, Archer. Where's the bread?"

"Fridge."

I started the frying pan warming, cracked eggs into a bowl, added milk, shredded cheese, pepper, whipped it all up with a fork and got down to business.

We carried our plates and mugs out to the summer parlor, sitting cross-legged on the deck rather than bothering to unfold the chairs, and had breakfast, bathed in sunshine.

Peggy sighed, put her plate aside, picked up her mug and leaned against the railing.

"So, what's the occasion?"

"For making breakfast? I was hungry."

She shook her head. "I don't think I've heard you sing before. Pretty good voice, but you could use better music."

I eyed her. Today's T-shirt was black, with a bat picked out in black sequins on the chest.

"What do you suggest, musically?"

"Rasputina. The Creatures. Abney Park. Vernal Equity. Poe... You never heard of any of these bands, have you, Archer?"

"I'm a classic rock kinda girl," I confessed.

"Sometime when I'm not working my butt off, I'll get you down to my place and play you some real music. With beer. And a pizza. I know what's due a guest." She sipped her coffee, staring at me over the rim.

I picked up my own mug, and glanced out over the beach. A perfect day.

"I hear there's a big party tonight," Peggy said. "The crew were talking about it. You going?"

Still looking out over the beach, I blinked, feeling like an idiot.

So, about that good mood, Kate, I said to myself, kindly. *That wouldn't happen to have anything to do with the fact that today is the day before the summer solstice, would it?*

Midsummer Eve. The day that Borgan'd said he'd see me again.

The day that all of the *trenvay* and those townies who did gather on the beach at the base of Heath Hill at full dark, and threw themselves a helluva party.

I hadn't been to a Midsummer Eve in years, naturally, but I had vivid memories of it. Tarva had been my escort, under strict orders from Nerazi and Gran, I now suspected, to be on his very best behavior.

"Did I spoil a surprise?" Peggy asked.

I shook myself and looked back to her.

"Sorry; got caught up in a memory," I said, trying to sound matter-of-fact. "It's the Midsummer Eve party—kind of a townie tradition. Sure, I'll be there. You?"

"I don't wanna crash a private gig," Peggy said, sounding careful, "being as I'm from *Away...*"

Oh. So she'd found out what Away meant, in the context of a Mainer's conversation; and it sounded like she'd found out from one of the folks who used it as a pejorative, instead of a geographical distinction.

"Well, you're in an interesting position," I said, employing what I liked to think of as tact. "You're from Away, sure. But you're working with Jens' crew. If they didn't want you to know about the party, they wouldn't've let you overhear them talking about it. So, I'm guessing you've got a sideways invitation."

"Sideways invitation?"

"Nobody's *invited* to Midsummer Eve. People just show up. If somebody *invited* you, then they'd be treating you like a stranger."

"But they made sure I heard them, so now I can show up, too? Just like a regular?"

"If you *want to,*" I said, because this was important, too. "No pressure. If you think it's going to be outside your comfort zone, you're not required to come."

Peggy chewed her lip, eyes half-squinted.

"So, I can compromise? Come by, show the flag, and duck out, if it's too wild for a Jersey girl?"

"That, too," I agreed. "It's up to you."

I finished off the last of my coffee, and nodded at Peggy's mug. "Refill?"

She shook her head. "Nah. I better get down to The Mango."

"Awful early."

"Got paperwork."

"Keep this up, you're going to be a crispy critter a lot sooner than later."

"I'm tough," she said and rolled to her feet.

I did the same; we gathered up the plates and silverware and carried them back to the kitchen.

"Thanks for breakfast; it was great," Peggy said. She opened the front door.

"See you tonight."

"Good deal," I said, but she'd already closed the door behind her.

If you turn your back on the ocean and walk up Walnut Street, over the train tracks, past the old condos, and on up the hill past the new condos, too; about three-quarters of the way to Portland Avenue you'll come to a place where a blacktop driveway intersects the sidewalk between two pretty white houses.

Nothing unusual there. But, if you follow this particular driveway back between the houses, and keep on walking straight into the trees at the place where the drive elbows to the right, you'll strike the remains of an old road.

Follow that to the edge of the marsh, and you'll come to the place where the Kite Track used to be.

Back in 1892 or so, the Kite Track had been a big deal—a mile-long trotting track made out of hard clay, said to be the fastest track in the world. When light harness went out of style as a sport, in the mid-1920s, the track closed. It reopened in 1936 as a pari-mutuel track, a stop on the Grand Circuit; closed again in the 1950s, and opened for one last, halcyon fling as a motorcycle track in the late 60s.

After that final closing, the marsh took back its own. Nobody remembers the old track anymore, or would much care, if you told them.

I knew about it because when I was a kid I'd *listened* to the stories my gran told me. And, as Guardian, it was my business to know.

The reason I was walking out to the remains of the Kite Track on this particular and perfect Midsummer Eve morning was because I'd caught my second positive ID on a quiet zone last night, and I'd come to see what there was to see.

The sense I got from the land was one of informed curiosity, something like having a seasoned young hound at my heels; alert, but relaxed. The marsh was pleasantly bustling as birds, insects, mice, and other small creatures got on with their lives, and the growing things drank down the sunshine in quiet satisfaction. Underfoot, the ground was slightly spongy.

Behind me, I heard the full-throttle roar of a speeding motorcycle. I spun, *jikinap* tingling at my fingertips, ready to blast the fool coming down here on a cycle, along the broken road, *at that speed* . . .

But there was no motorcycle racing toward me over the marshland. At my heel, the land stood calm. According to my eyes, I stood among the brush and bramble of the marsh. My hair was warm under the sun's persistent caress, and I smelled salt and mud and grass on the moving breeze. I heard the sweet, piercing song of a hermit thrush, stitching through the cycle's roar like gold thread.

I closed my eyes. Carefully, trusting the land to keep me from a misstep, I walked forward, the sounds of the marsh enclosing me, including the constant noise of a racing motorcycle.

The land barked a warning.

I stopped and opened my eyes. Just three steps ahead was a pool of black water.

Mindful of the ground, which had gone from spongy to soggy, I approached the pool, squatted down on my heels, and sent out a small feeler.

I received various impressions: cold, brackish mud, an insistent tug that must, I thought, be the tide going out. Nothing else. Marsh water, that was all. No sign of *trenvay* care or consciousness.

I retracted the feeler and straightened slowly. I could still hear the cycle, roaring along a track years ago returned to marsh.

Now, I've never met a ghost. I won't say that there aren't any—a woman in my position has to keep an open mind—but, as far as I understood the literature, if the cycle was a ghost, it ought to keep running the track that wasn't here, 'round and 'round, 'round and 'round. The noise I heard was constant; unmoving; one sound among all the myriad sounds of the marsh. Almost as if the marsh had gotten the sound of a racing motorcycle engine stuck in its collective consciousness, like I'd had "Walking in Memphis" stuck in my head since breakfast.

I frowned, turning that last thought around so I could get a good, hard look at it.

Well, why not? The Kite Track had been on the land here for almost eighty years—not a long time, as the land measures time, but certainly long enough to be noticed. There was also a certain intensity of emotion attached to racing—from the spectators and the participants, human and equine.

What if the marsh *remembered* the track? If that was the case, and its memory was motorcycles—a sound already starting to fade—then it might be that when it faded completely, the marsh would grow less...contemplative, and return its voice more fully to the united song of the land.

It was a theory, anyway.

And, if true, it meant that there had to be, somewhere within the confines of the old track, a *trenvay*—the spirit and the heart of this place.

Eyes open, I walked the outline of the old track, the land coursing ahead of me now, questing. The motorcycle stuck with me, snarling against the everyday sounds of the marsh.

I saw two white-tailed deer, startled a fox, and got cussed out by a blue jay, but otherwise managed to return to my starting point without encountering a *trenvay* of any description.

Well, then.

I turned and strode off, striking for the track's center, the land running ahead—

The land barked; the impression I had was one of tentative welcome. In the next instant, I saw her...and teetered on the edge of revising my opinion about ghosts.

She was tall and naked, and she was so very thin that it seemed the strong sunlight shone through her. She glowed like an emaciated moon, twiglike fingers twisted together before her.

Then she spoke, and laid the notion of ghost to rest.

"Guardian?" Her voice was sweet, weirdly evoking the song of the hermit thrush. "Do I hear *Guardian?*"

"You do," I said, coming close, until I heard the land whine softly. "I'm Kate Archer."

"Why are you here? Nobody comes here. Not anymore. I'm all alone."

"Not alone," I said, taking one step closer, ignoring the land's worry. "In fact, I was coming to see why it was so quiet hereabouts, and to remind you..." I let that trail off...temptingly, I hoped.

She shook long, verdant hair back from her face. Her eyes were as black as marsh water.

"Remind me? All I have are memories."

"You have more—or less, according to your own choice. As Guardian, I've missed your voice in the land-song, without ever having heard it. You sequester yourself with your memories and impoverish us all." I bowed my head. "Which is, as I said, your choice. I only came to remind you that—today is Midsummer Eve."

The black eyes widened in the narrow face.

"It means nothing to me."

"As you say," I answered, and turned toward the entrance road.

I hadn't gone a dozen paces, when I heard her say, sharp and sweet: "Wait."

I stopped.

"Do you know my name?"

I felt the question vibrate through me and connect with the land; felt the answer weigh on my tongue.

"Cathahouris," I said.

I heard her whisper the syllables; then came a rustle, like a deer moving through high grass. Carefully, I queried the land; received the impression of absence.

Well.

I closed my eyes where I stood, and detached the tiniest possible grain of *jikinap* from the store coiled at the root of my spine. Gently—gingerly—I extended the very thinnest of feelers to the crumb of magic, and let the symphony of the land flow across it.

The process was roughly—*very* roughly—like copying music from a laptop to a cell except there weren't any devices and the whole transfer was taking place on a metaphysical level not normally accessible to mp3 players.

Still, when I felt I had my recording firm, I hunkered down and planted the tiny seed of *jikinap* in the spongy marshland. It wouldn't last long. I hoped it would last long enough.

A reminder, that was all. In case she needed one.

Spell set, I came to my feet, snapped my fingers for the land and asked it to come to heel.

It did that, willingly enough, with a flutter that may have been a happily wagging tail.

I took a couple of nice, deep breaths, then walked away, back out the way I'd come in.

CHAPTER TWENTY-TWO

High Tide 7:28 P.M.
Sunset 8:26 P.M. EDT

The bonfire was going a treat by the time I arrived at the party beach, a minute or two after nautical twilight. I'd figured that nothing would really get started until Fun Country and the midway had closed for the night, but it seemed I'd figured wrong.

I walked into the fire's shadow and added my offerings to the pile of driftwood and other fuel. I'd brought two good, dry tupelo branches, so Peggy was covered, in case nobody'd told her about the tradition that everyone brought something for the fire.

"Kate." Bob came out of the duneside shadows, and gave me a nod. "Glad you're here."

Bob had mellowed somewhat toward me since my return, but this was almost effusive.

"Glad to be here," I said truthfully. "They didn't do Midsummer Eve, out where I was, Away."

He shook his head, apparently over the strange ways of folks from Away, pulled a hardpack out of his shirt pocket and extracted a cigarette.

"Heard you took a walk out the Kite Track this mornin'," he said, looking down while he fished a lighter out of the pocket of his jeans.

Well, *this* was interesting. I tried not to look too interested, though. No sense spooking the man.

"I had some concerns about the state of the land thereabouts." Bob lit his coffin nail, took a long drag, and sighed out smoke. "How'd you find things?"

"Puzzling," I admitted. "I did what I thought right—what I thought I *could* do. But I'm not sure I did any good."

He nodded again, and slipped the lighter back into his pocket.

"Lillian and Catha were—I guess you'd call 'em best friends. Both liked the dances, the races, all the excitement, back when. Party girls." He snorted; maybe it was a laugh.

"Lillian was the level-headed one—hey, she married me, right? Catha was wild. You'd've thought that track was her own personal party; that the owners and the bettors—hell, the horses and the dogs! That it was all hers. Her service. While Lillian was alive, Catha kept ties with us. But...after...the track was long gone, the people—well, I don't have to tell it to *you*—and now Lillian was gone, too. Catha...she didn't so much break with us, as she just drifted away."

"I did what I thought best," I repeated.

"I believe it," Bob said, and gave me a grin. "In the job description."

Startled, I laughed.

"More or less it *is* the job description," I agreed and hefted the increasingly heavy grocery bag dangling at the end of my right hand.

"Where do I take the goodies?"

"JoAnn'll take those off your hand," he said, and pointed over my shoulder. I turned to look.

Strings of fairy lights straight out of somebody's stored Christmas decorations glittered among the sea roses at the rocky foot of Heath Hill; tables had been set up in front of that natural boundary, and people were moving around them.

"Good deal," I said, and headed that way.

Bob's daughter was setting up the sweets table, carefully placing plates of brownies, cookies, whoopie pies, cupcakes and other temptations to their best advantage. She looked up as I approached, then straightened, a firm smile on her lips. The land fed me a sense of a deep reserve.

"Good evening, Guardian," she said primly. "It's good of you to come."

"Good evening," I answered. "My name is Kate. This," I hefted the bag, so she could see it, "is homemade potato salad and a block of cheddar, for the feast."

"You didn't..." she began.

I hefted the bag higher. "Freely given, freely shared, between true companions and friends."

That was an old phrase, but Gran had made sure I knew *all* the old phrases. JoAnn looked—and according to the land, felt—startled. For a long moment, she didn't move, then she smiled again—a little less firmly—and took the bag from me.

"The feast increases, with the goodwill of all."

And that, by God, was the authentic, complete response. Bob had seen his kid educated, so he had.

"Is there anything I can do to help out?" I asked.

She glanced up the row of laden tables, and the folks still fitting in plates and bowls and tubs...

"It looks like we're set here. Thank you for asking, Kate."

"No problem. Thank you for organizing all of this; must be the last thing you want to do, after working in the restaurant all day."

She shook her head, and this time the smile was almost warm.

"This is nothing like waiting tables. All we have to do is put the food out ahead, so everybody can help themselves. *I'll* be dancing while they do."

"Put that way, it does seem a lot less work. Maybe Bob can reorganize as a smorgasbord."

"Not a chance," she said.

I felt someone moving behind my right shoulder, and stepped left to make room for Henry Emerson, who was carrying an enormous cake pan in his two arms.

"How'd you get that down here without getting mugged?" I asked, while JoAnn darted two tables down to pass my donation off to the guy working there.

"I drove to the bottom of Heath Street, and walked across the dunes," Henry said.

"Pretty clever."

"Native slyness and a strong will to survive," Henry agreed, and gently placed his burden in JoAnn's outstretched arms.

"There won't be a crumb left," she said. "Henry's cakes are wonderful!"

"Flatterer," he said. "Has Andy arrived yet, Jo? He has my fiddle."

"They're setting up in the usual place."

"Excellent!" He smiled, gave me a nod. "If you'll excuse me, Kate?"

"I know better than to get between a man and his fiddle."

He hurried off. JoAnn had already taken the cake away.

I turned back toward the bonfire, walking softly, watching the crowd.

"Evenin', Guardian," Gaby said breathlessly as she hurried toward the tables, a bag in each hand.

"Good evening, Kate," said a woman I didn't immediately recognize, walking briskly toward the fire, with a nice thick stick in her hand.

By the time I did, and answered, "Michelle," she was gone.

Shaking my head, I barely missed stepping on a short fella with pointed ears—and pointed teeth, too, as I saw when he grinned at me. He dodged under my arm, and ran toward the ocean, kicking up great gobs of sand as he went.

I queried the land as I angled toward the dunes, where the beach was less congested, and received an impression of sea roses growing in tangled profusion over a tumble of rock. Someplace up toward the Enterprise, I thought; it had that kind of feel—

"There she is! Hey, Kate!"

I turned as Peggy rushed up, flanked by the two *trenvay* I had figured for Moss and Vornflee. She was wearing the same T-shirt and jeans I'd seen her in this morning.

"You're gonna freeze!" I told her, seriously alarmed.

"That's what these guys said, but, hey, there's a bonfire, right? How cold can it get?"

Her escorts exchanged a look over her head.

"It can get plenty cold. It's only June. Here, I'll give you my shirt." I was wearing long-sleeved denim over a T-shirt.

"So then *you* freeze?"

"I'll be fine," I told her, which was true; the land would keep me toasty, if I asked.

"Not necessary, Guardian," the *trenvay* I had figured for Moss said. "Felsic went to fetch down a sweater."

"Is that where she went?" Peggy glared at them over her shoulders. "What'm I, three?"

"Six?" the one who must therefore be Vornflee suggested.

Peggy didn't quite not laugh, though she made a noble effort. "The pair of you are insubordinate."

"We're on our own time," Moss said, placidly.

"Wise guys, too."

The land twitched an alert ear, and in the same instant Vornflee said, "Here's Felsic."

I glanced to the left, and nodded at the stocky *trenvay* sloshing through the dry sand toward our position.

She, huh? I thought, as Felsic joined the group. I was still undecided, myself. The land, queried, returned its equivalent of a baffled stare, and a repeat of the assurance that Felsic was trustworthy.

"Kate," Felsic said, returning my nod. "Peggy, you'll catch your death."

"So I'm being told. I was *also* told that you went to get me a sweater." She actually sounded stern.

"A lend only, now," Felsic said, managing to sound both soothing and amused. "Try this."

This was a purple sweatshirt with a bright yellow fish of indeterminate species embroidered on the chest. At a guess, it was in size giant. Peggy eyed it without favor.

"It'll spoil my look."

Felsic continued to hold the shirt out to her by the shoulders.

"C'mon, Jersey," I said. "Pretend it's a Halloween costume."

"Oh, cute. *Cute*, Archer."

At that moment, a breeze obligingly ran among us, straight off the ocean, damp and, yeah—definitely chilly.

Peggy took the sweatshirt from Felsic and pulled it over her head. For a moment, she stood there, the headless purple Fixer, then the shirt rippled, as if the fish was trying to swim off of it, and Peggy's head appeared. Her hands, not so much, and the hem of the shirt hit her slightly below the knees.

"You look adorable," I told her.

"I'll get you for that. Later." She looked around at us—the Guardian and the three *trenvay*. "So, what's to do?"

"Beer," said Moss.

"Cupcakes," said Vornflee.

"Music," said Felsic.

"Music?" Peggy asked, looking at me.

"Sure thing. Fiddle, guitar, harmonica, spoons—like that. Soon's they get tuned up, there'll be dancing." I *did* remember the dancing. I must've danced a marathon at my first Midsummer's Eve, carried on the double wave of hormones and the land's exuberance. The second year, I had better control, but the music had still beguiled my feet until dawn.

"Beer," Peggy said decisively. "And a cupcake."

"First," Felsic added. The four of them started to move as a unit toward the mobbed goodies tables.

"You comin', Archer?"

Well, why not? I thought.

I fell in beside Felsic, at the rear of the group; Peggy was walking ahead, still bracketed by her loyal insubordinates.

"She's not likely to find trouble here, is she?" I asked.

"No worry, G—Kate, she's safe with us."

Which, come to think about it, was just a teensy bit disturbing.

"And *without* you?"

An oblique look from under the rim of the gimme hat.

"Safe enough."

Yes, *definitely* a little frisson there.

"Don't break her, unless you want the owners from Away up here, asking questions and upsetting things."

Felsic snorted. "We know a gift when we see 'er, Kate. Don't fatch."

"Now," Felsic continued; "it's good we come up on you. Wanted to let you know I'd done some asking about on that question you set me t'other day. I'm hearing there'd been somebody—I'm tellin' Seasons here, a lot of 'em—somebody whose service was bringing ships in 'til they was torn open by the rocks or run t'ground at the narrow. The black wreck, that's one of hers."

I shivered, and Felsic threw me a look, unreadable in the fire-laced dark.

"Long story short, she had 'er service took from 'er—all proper done, with the *trenvay* in support of the then-Guardian—and there ain't been nobody else since come into service near the mouth. That was a risk, which the then-Guardian knew it to be, but the other—that was worst."

"I agree," I said. There'd been a *whole lot* of information in that squib. If I was lucky, it'd only give me things to think about for the next decade or so. "Thank you for checking it out for me."

"Happy to be of service to the Guardian. Well," as we came to the tables, "don't that look *fine*."

I checked, but Felsic kept going. Peggy and Moss were three

tables up, apparently having decided that beer came before any other pleasure. I didn't see Vornflee. Felsic was already working the sweets, filling a plate with the clear intention of eating desserts first.

I wasn't hungry, necessarily, so I stepped to one side, watching the crowds around the smaller fires, and the drift of bodies from group to group. The majority seemed to be *trenvay*, with a leavening of not-exactly-mundane humans.

Henry was human, of course—and as if the thought had called it, I heard a fiddle start up, playing something bright and bluegrassy.

I saw Joan Anderson go by on the arm of a tall, cadaverous woman with white-and-violet hair, and Mrs. Kristanos, wandering slowly by herself, drinking beer from the bottle. Nancy Vois passed within an arm's reach, pacing a ginger-haired guy in a leather motorcycle jacket, who could've been her brother.

The fiddle had been joined by guitar and pipe, and my feet were getting itchy. Inside my head, the land jumped and swung. I exerted my will—to not very much good effect, and realized that I'd started to move, lightly dancing toward the music across the joyous land.

I forced myself to stop, and took a couple of deep breaths.

A hand fell on my shoulder, and the land gave full tongue.

"Dance with me, pretty lady?"

CHAPTER TWENTY-THREE

Tide was going out, expanding the dance floor with each short-ened wave. I didn't want to think about what would happen when the tide turned.

Actually, I didn't want to think—at all.

I wanted to dance.

I was holding Borgan's hand, and he was breaking trail, dodg-ing and weaving in time to the music's beat, dancers dancing with the dance.

There was a sharp tug on my hand; we dodged to the right, and Borgan spun, claiming three square feet of sand. At the end of his arm, I spun, too, and let myself be drawn close, the music informing us, moving feet, and blood—

My connection with the land, which had gotten loose and warm under the suasion of the music, suddenly snapped tight. The weight of its attention crushed the music beneath it. I stopped dead, turning my head. Borgan, caught on the edge of a swing, staggered, recovered, and stood, holding my hand and watching the side of my face.

Guided by the land, I . . . was staring into the duneside shad-ows cast by the bonfire, my eyesight sharpened well beyond the ordinary, so that I clearly saw the tall, thin figure standing there, wearing a red circle skirt and a white twinset, a pair of strappy shoes hanging from the fingers of one hand. Her eyes were wide, her lips half-parted, and I felt her trepidation as if it were my own. In another minute, unless something happened, her courage would fail her and she'd bolt.

I took one step...

The firelight flickered as Bob moved between it and us. He threw his cigarette into the fire, and half-danced toward the thin, hesitating figure, his arms opened wide.

"Hey, sweetie; lookin' good! C'mon, gimme smooch!"

She dropped the shoes and ran to him, throwing her arms around his neck. I blinked away tears of relief, my heart slamming against my ribs as he hugged her tight, lifting her a little off the sand, and spinning her around.

I backed away from the land's perception, turned and looked up into Borgan's face. He had been watching the pair at the bonfire; now he looked down to meet my eyes.

"Who's that?" he asked.

"Cathahouris," I said, "from the Kite Track. I went out and talked to her this morning. Reminded her it was Midsummer Eve. She said she didn't care."

"Looks like she changed her mind," Borgan said. "You still feel like dancin'?"

I grinned at him, the music filling me again, heating my blood, brain and heart; and the land already dancing.

"I don't think you can stop me."

Midsummer is one of the most-celebrated days in the world; a festival of light that outshines even Christmas. Longest day, shortest night, the sun at the height of his powers, recharging the whole world, and everyone on and in it.

Is that a great excuse for a party, or what?

Some traditions have an element of spirituality—of ritual. Some are not much more than a bonfire, and a dance.

Those two things right there—the fire and the dance—those are the two constants, across the world.

In Archers Beach, dancing is the reason for the season. Oh, sure, we have a feast, but that's because dancing's hungry work.

It's a free-form affair; nobody'll stop you ribbon-dancing 'round a pole, stipulating you could find room on the beach to pitch one, and space enough to swing out. Mostly, though, folk dance with a friend, friends or by themselves—uplifted and informed by the music.

It's the music that ties us all into a whole; that lifts us out of ourselves and connects us; the music that makes us one will and whole desire; that washes our souls and pours the combined golden energy of us over our land, and everyone on and in it.

I don't know how long Borgan and I were part of the dance. The music flowed around, through, and between us. We kept hold of each other's hand, and it seemed that the music became the tide, flowing from me to Borgan; returning from him changed in some infinitely precious way.

It was, if you'll excuse the expression, magical, and utterly different from dancing down Midsummer Eve with Tarva.

Borgan and I slowed, in obedience to the music's tempo. We drew nearer, my hand found his shoulder, his palm molded my waist, and we moved, effortless as water, perfectly matched in the music. I looked up, met his eyes, black and brilliant in the fire light. He bent his head, and I raised my face . . .

The music shattered.

We stumbled, snatched at each other, and managed to stay upright, which wasn't the case for everyone who had been motivated by the music. Nearby, I saw Gaby sprawled in the sand, shaking her head. Further on, there was Moss down on one knee, and Felsic with an arm around Peggy's waist, and a shoulder against Vornflee's chest.

The fiddle carried on alone for another bar, two, three . . . and drifted into silence. Land-sharpened sight showed me Henry turning questioningly toward his mates, bow at his side. One of them stepped forward, coming from the dark into the light, and slinging his guitar around to hang down his back by its strap. He was staring to the left, a frown on his not-quite-ordinary human face.

The land murmured then, pleased, but muted. I turned to follow the guitarist's gaze, saw dazed dancers move aside, opening the way for . . .

Mr. Ignat' . . .

. . . with my mother on his arm.

She looked like a child, her light curls tousled and tumbled by the breeze, dressed in jeans and a bulky sweater that might've been handed down from an older, bigger cousin.

"*Nessa?*" The guitarist sounded disbelieving.

"Andy." She slipped away from Mr. Ignat' and walked forward until she was standing in the light cast by the stage lanterns. "Good to see you. It's been a long time."

"A long time," he repeated, and shook his head, his gaze never leaving her face.

"I haven't danced at a Midsummer Eve since I went Away, all that time ago," she said softly. "May I dance at this one?"

"Anybody who can hear the music can dance Midsummer in. That's the way it is. Always been so."

"Yes," my mother said, quietly. She paused before adding, "It was wonderful, the music. I'd like to hear more."

Andy's mouth twisted. "You home, now?" he asked, like the question had been knocked out of him by a sharp slap on the back.

"Yes," Mother said. "I'm home now."

Andy sighed, and didn't say anything for what felt like a long time. Everyone—dancers and musicians waiting, breath caught—sighed as one being when Andy gave a sharp nod, pulled his guitar 'round and ran out a lick so bright and brittle it might've drawn blood.

The bass took up the line, dulling the edge with drive; and the fiddle came in again, singing joy and welcome home. Hearing it come together, instrument by instrument, it struck me that Henry *was* only human; perhaps the only human among the players. He must, I thought, be the safety valve; the guarantee that the music stayed within bounds; that it delighted, healed, and informed without jumping the line to possession, doom, and damage.

"And me without a pair of red shoes," I muttered, watching my mother sway into a dance all of her own, her eyes still locked with Andy's. Mr. Ignat' had stepped back into the crowd; after a search, I spied him, dancing as one of a circle of six.

The music picked at my feet, tempting me, but my stomach had other ideas. Dancing with the fairies is hungry work.

"Something to eat?" I asked Borgan.

"Sounds good."

We carried our beers and our plates out of the crowd, down to Googin Rock, and made a picnic on the dry apron, the timid plashing of the waves restful and blessedly ordinary, after our immersion in the dance.

"Folk still give it a wide berth," Borgan commented, after our plates were empty, and our beers nearly so.

"It's not exactly the most inviting seat in the house," I answered, downing what beer was left, and setting it and the plate carefully on the stony surface.

It wasn't, I realized as the silence stretched, the best answer I might have made. A better one might have offered some opportunity for continued conversation.

"How's *Gray Lady*?" I asked, introducing a topic with more scope. I hoped.

"She's all cleaned up and shipshape. I built some wards so they won't be able to do *that* again, at least."

"And Daph—the *ronstibles*, themselves?"

He snorted, drank off the last of his beer and set his bottle and plate with mine.

"Let's just say that good fences make good neighbors."

That was Maine wisdom, right there. Still...

"Are they *really* good fences?"

"Think I don't know how to build a ward?"

"I know you can build a ward. Saw what you did with this very rock, didn't I?"

"Fairly speaking, I had help."

"Borgan, seriously—what happens if they get loose again? The *ronstibles*?"

"Well, this is the first time in a lotta years they had a chance to set up an ambush. Generally, I'm careful, Kate—don't you worry." He paused, and then said, just a little too casually, "So I was thinking, if you don't mind walking down to the harbor, I'd introduce you to the *Lady*, an' you could see if that shelf I left for you's gonna be enough."

I stared at him. "You left me a shelf?"

"For your things, like we talked about. You thought maybe you'd only want that change of clothes, but if you need room for more or other, I don't grudge the space."

I stared at him. He stared back.

"You're serious," I managed.

"Weren't you?"

I closed my eyes. I had been—serious. Sort of. And now, tonight, having danced, I was even more serious. Borgan was...safe?

No, I told myself; he *wasn't* safe. In fact, I had the fixed notion that Borgan could be extremely dangerous.

But I trusted him.

"Borgan," I said.

"Kate?"

I took a deep breath, opened my eyes and said steadily, "Kiss me."

He glanced aside, and my chest cramped so hard I felt tears come to my eyes.

"Well, now," he said softly. "I wouldn't object to a kiss. Not at all."

"You—" I began, and stopped. Because he was right, damn him. It was my move. *I* was the one bringing the baggage into our relationship, if any. *I* was the one who'd kept pushing him away. *Dis*trusting him. That had changed, for me. As he told it, Borgan had been constant as the tides.

"You sure know how to take the spontaneity out of a moment," I said, and stood up.

He looked up at me, black eyes wistful. I put my hands on his shoulders, bent down and kissed him as best I knew how.

It was clumsy—even I knew that, and my experience could be counted on the fingers of one hand. His lips were warm, and firm, and exciting in a way reminiscent of the rising of power. I felt a pressure on the back of my head and realized he was holding me, pressing me into the kiss.

The added pressure overbalanced me; my feet slipped, and slid in the sand; and I broke the kiss, grabbing Borgan's shoulders for support. He gave before me, going flat on his back, his arm around my waist as I fell—

Onto his chest.

He was laughing. I was laughing. I got my hands flat on the rock on either side of his head and levered myself up, looking down into his face.

"Now you're sorry, aren't you?" I asked him, meaning it for a joke.

"No," he said, and pulled my face down to his.

It was sweet. As sweet as anything I can remember in my life. I learned that kissing his ear made him shiver and laugh, and that having my throat nuzzled made *me* shiver and laugh.

I learned that it was . . . immensely satisfying to sit on Borgan's lap, his braid lying heavy between my breasts; my head against his chest, listening to his heartbeat.

We had been arranged like this for some amount of time—I don't know how long—when the music began again. Whether the band had taken a well-deserved break, or whether Borgan and I had been too involved in each other to pay attention to the music—I didn't know that, either.

What I did know was, my toes were twitching and my body was responding to the energy of the music.

"Is it too late to inspect that shelf?" I murmured.

"Not late at all," Borgan answered, which was only true in the context of Midsummer Eve. "Now?"

"I think I'd better not start dancing again."

"In that case, now it is.

"No navigatin' through that," he said, after we'd both gained our feet and stood for several long seconds staring at the dancer-clogged sands.

"And if we tried, we'd be dancing again, no matter what our intent," I agreed. "Just have to go around, then."

I grabbed his hand and started walking at an angle, toward Heath Hill, keeping the dancers on my left. Borgan followed without comment—like a cruise ship being pulled along by a tug—his fingers warm 'round mine.

We were halfway up the hill when the land *screamed.*

I threw myself up the remaining vertical feet. Before me was the Wood, slumbering and black . . .

An orange flicker caught the side of my eye and I spun, running toward the fire burning within the shadow of the Wood itself.

The land was barking furiously. Panting, I summoned my power, and threw it like a blanket over the flickering flames.

They went out at once, almost apologetically.

I dropped to my knees and stared at the place the fire had been, butterscotch and adrenaline mixing badly on the back of my tongue, shivering with remembered horror—

And, throughout the whole, there had been not one ripple in the serenity of the trees.

I swallowed, and took my *jikinap* back to myself as Borgan knelt beside me.

"Fire?"

"Fire," I confirmed.

Truth told, and in the calm of hindsight, it hadn't been much of a fire. It left behind an extremely modest patch of scorched grass, and two singed leaves on a nearby sapling.

Still, there came no word of complaint or alarm from the Wood.

I stepped Sideways; looking first to the wards.

They were intact, which raised the musical question: How the *hell* had someone managed to build a fire here, *right here* on the very edge of the Wood, under the nose of the trees and the wards?

That was an interesting question, I thought. I'd have to ask the perpetrator, when I caught up with him.

I turned my attention to the surrounding area, looking for clues to the identity and means of my arsonist.

I found nothing, save that lingering, vague impression of embarrassment.

Blinking back into the Real World, I stared down at the scorched grass.

"This," I said to Borgan, who was still kneeling patiently at my side, "should not have happened. The wards didn't even notice it."

"Natural fire, then," he said. "Little one, too."

Borgan had been present when Mr. Ignat' had guided me in the construction of the wards; he knew as well as I did that they . . .

. . . had been built to respond to intended threats against the Wood.

I rubbed my forehead.

"So you're thinking because it was *natural*, it didn't trigger the threat key?" I asked.

"That, and it being so small—might've blown out all on its own, if we hadn't happened by. If it'd been a bigger, bolder fire, the wards would've seen it, I'm betting."

Thinking about it, I was willing to bet the same way. The fire had been so small, it hadn't even gotten the attention of the Wood.

"The land is traumatized," I commented. Inside my head, I heard a long, doggy sigh of contrition and smiled. "That's okay, so am I. Well."

I came to my feet, and Borgan did, too.

"Doesn't look like there's anything more for us to do here," I said, and offered him my hand.

He took it and together we approached the trees.

Welcome, Kate. The voice of the Wood was as always, but no path opened before me. That might have to do with the fact that I wasn't alone; which meant that it was time to bring out another of the old forms.

"I ask safe passage, for myself and my true companion," I said. "We wish to pass through, and arrive safe above Kinney Harbor."

There was a pause, as if the Wood were giving due consideration to the matter. Borgan gave my hand a reassuring squeeze—and a path opened before us.

We entered... but we did not enter the Wood I knew.

The path shone, dimly, before us; the trees were fearsome, hulking shadows, and no breath of air or breeze disturbed their black leaves. For the first time in my life, I was aware of the Wood's power and presence—not as old tales, but right in the pit of my stomach.

I gripped Borgan's hand so tight my fingers ached, and asked the land for night-sight.

After a moment, it seemed as if the pathway glowed a little brighter; the trees became more distinct, as if they were merely shrouded in fog; and a very small breeze kissed my damp brow.

I took a breath, tasting salt, kept my eyes on the path, and my fingers around Borgan's.

The path curved sharply to the left; the trees thinned...

Between one step and another, we were out, looking down the Hill to the sea, and the boats that lay asleep in Kinney Harbor.

CHAPTER TWENTY-FOUR

Wednesday, June 21
Low Tide 1:45 A.M.
Sunrise 5:00 A.M. EDT

Gray Lady was as gracious and winsome belowdeck as she was above. Her paneling was cedar; her saloon neat; and her tiny galley thoughtfully laid out.

I followed Borgan into said galley, and leaned against the wall, watching his back as he opened an overhead cabinet and took out a can of coffee.

"That shelf we're talking about's forward," he said, without turning his head. "If you wanna take a look. Coffee'll be a minute or two."

"Okay. Coming through behind you."

I'm neither tall nor broad; thin as the passage was, it was plenty wide enough for me to pass behind Borgan without touching him. So, it was purely to please myself that I put my hands on his waist as I skooched by—and gasped as I received the certain knowledge that the contact didn't *just* please me.

Shaking, I made it to the far side of the galley and stepped into a stateroom.

Like the rest of the *Lady*, it was shipshape and sharp. There were books in the shelves at the head and foot of the bed, and storage lockers over the length. More storage was built into the bulkhead opposite, with a metal mirror over. I glanced into it, seeing nothing markedly different in my face. My hair was snarled beyond belief—not surprising, considering what I'd put it through tonight. What did surprise was how much it irritated me. Maybe it was the spray of pine needles tangled in above my left ear.

There was a comb on the shelf to the right of the mirror. I picked it up and waged a brief, vicious war with my hair. When the knots were vanquished, I braided it, which, since I didn't see any elastics to pilfer, would keep me neat for exactly as long as it took the braid to unravel.

Feeling somewhat less harum-scarum, I called to mind the reason why I'd come into Borgan's bedroom, and turned to survey the shelves built into the short wall at right angles to the mirror.

Borgan had been generous—there were *two* empty shelves, low, where they'd be the most use to a height-challenged woman. They weren't wide, but they were deep, each shelf fronted with a rail, to keep things from flying all over the room, in rough weather.

I smiled, and felt the land's pleasure, fainter than I was used to, echoing my own.

"Coffee's done," Borgan said from the galley. It came to me that he sounded *careful*. "That's three creams, right?"

"Only if your coffee's as bad as Bob's. Two usually does me fine," I said, reaching in my pockets, searching for something—it suddenly seemed important, absent those "things" we'd euphemistically talked about, to leave *some*thing. To let him know that I was pleased.

I didn't have much beyond the necessary in my pockets—ID, a couple of dollars, my house key. What else do you need at Midsummer Eve?

Biting my lip, I dug deeper, knowing that there was nothing more.

"Kate?"

"Just a sec."

My fingers touched something hard and smooth at the bottom my pocket, hiding under the house key.

I coaxed it out—a plain white beach stone, cool against my palm.

Perfect.

I put it on the topmost of the two empty shelves and went out into the galley.

"I like the braid," Borgan said. "Oughta do it more often."

"I ought to," I said cordially, taking the mug out of his hand. "I got used to having my hair all around my face—protective coloration, I'd guess you'd say."

He nodded, frowning slightly.

"One thing, though. It's gonna come undone. Hang on."

He put his mug on the counter and slipped past me, with no extracurricular touching, into the stateroom.

I felt— through the land? the sea? *Gray Lady* herself?—a jolt of surprised joy, and then Borgan was back, looking utterly matter-of-fact, a leather string in his hand.

"Here we go," he said. "Turn around."

Meekly, I put my mug down, and did as I was told. I felt him fiddle with my braid, and tie off the string. His hands settled, big and warm, around my shoulders.

I felt his lips against the nape of my neck.

Molten power shot up my spine; I moaned, knees suddenly soft, gasped—and gasped!

"Wait!"

He let go of me immediately, even as I extended my will to banish the rush of *jikinap* back where it belonged, only to be met by—nothing. I did the metaphysical equivalent of the stagger-and-snatch you do when a surface you expect to be firm gives—

And began to laugh.

"Kate?" Borgan *definitely* sounded careful. Well, who could blame the man?

"Wait," I said again, gasping, one hand raised. "I don't—" I lifted my face to his. "I—I thought it was my power, rising..." I said, unsteadily. "I—that felt really good, by the way."

I love Borgan's laugh; it's deep and rich and generous.

"Don't remember a time I had a better recommendation," he said at last, raising a hand to wipe his eyes. He shook his head. "You want to go topside? Nice night to drink coffee and look at the stars."

"Sounds great," I said, truthfully.

The waning moon had risen; the tide had hit dead low and turned.

What I'm saying is, it was late. Or really, *really* early, depending on your referents.

We leaned against the rail. I was tucked under Borgan's arm, snug in the curve of his chest. The coffee was long gone, and we'd done some more kissing, though it must be noted that Borgan stayed strictly away from the back of my neck.

Have to do something about that, I thought drowsily, looking down at the dark water.

Something moved in the depths, and I half-stirred—but it was only a harbor seal, breaking the surface in a lazy roll and vanishing again, below. I resettled with a sigh. Sadly, though, I couldn't *quite* settle back into mindless contentment.

"Borgan?"

"Hmm?"

"Tell me about the *ronstibles*."

"Thought I did that a couple days ago."

"Well, bare bones, sure. But if they were the old Guardians, and you displaced them—how did that happen, exactly? And why are they around to hold a grudge? And—"

"Mercy, woman." I heard his laughter rumble in his chest. "All that, right now?"

"Right now, I've got the upper hand," I pointed out.

"You do at that," he agreed, deadpan. "No sense to wastin' an advantage." He took a deep breath, and sighed it out.

"So . . . *ronstibles*."

He was quiet for a minute or two—organizing his thoughts, maybe. I snuggled closer, content—and content to wait.

"Some claim Lorelei for a *ronstible*, and the Siren sisters, too," Borgan said conversationally. "So far's I know, though, those ladies took shape from the terror of mariners and the cunning of rocks. The *ronstibles*—the ones Nerazi and I know—they might be as old as the sea itself.

"Sea witches, *ronstibles*—whatever you might call them, they're of the sea and for the sea. If a man should sin against the sea, then they made his life payment for the sin.

"Not all the sea's waters hold a witch; not every witch born of the sea's genius thrived. The *ronstibles* of the Gulf of Maine, they weren't the worst; they didn't tempt men to drowning, though they had no pity for those who died on their waters."

Borgan paused, took another breath, and pulled me closer to him. He rested his cheek on my hair and sighed softly. When he spoke again, his voice was low and slow, like he was talking in his sleep.

"The sea is older than any man, and the sea has her own ways and meanings. It's in her nature to be bountiful, and it's in her nature to be deadly. The people of the land, they fear what might kill them. The people of the land feared the sea, though she fed them, but they feared the *ronstibles* more.

"The sea, she might kill them, but the *ronstibles* were cruel.

"That's how it was, and that's how it stayed, until, like everything, it changed.

"Change was a man. Warrior, Hunter, Fisherman. The man, this man, he loved the sea, and all the creatures within her bounty. The sea noticed. The sea became interested in the man.

"The man, this lover of the waters, he took from the sea's bounty, but only enough, and never more. He took a loon chick from Old Man Turtle's mouth, and gave Turtle fish from his own net. That loon, he raised him like a brother.

"The sea fell in love; she granted favors to the man. The *ronstibles* did not love the man.

"And, then... it changed a second time. The man went away.

"The sea mourned her loss, and the *ronstibles* had their way."

He paused then, and I kept very still in the shelter of his arm, not wanting to disturb him until the story was done.

"For a third time... it changed.

"The man returned to the sea. He was a chief now, with people to protect from the sharp knives of a rival.

"He wanted to take his people to the islands. It was an easy trip by canoe, on a fair day.

"The day the man came back, it was not fair. He and his people, they were closely pursued.

"As dirty as it was, they could not wait for the weather to turn. If his people fell into the hands of their enemies, they would all die. If his people put themselves onto the sea, they might, most of them, survive.

"The canoes took the women, and the children, each with a warrior to paddle. The chief and three of his best warriors stood on the land to guard their retreat.

"Their enemy arrived, and the battle was terrible. The chief, once beloved of the sea, prevailed. At the end, he alone remained standing among all who had fought there. Bleeding from many wounds, he turned to see what progress his people had made across the water.

"It was then that he saw the *ronstibles*, attacking the canoes, flinging his people into the cold, stormy waters—his people who could not swim.

"The man cried out to the sea, begging that his people be spared, and offering himself in their stead.

"The sea heard him. The sea . . . *remembered* him.

"The sea extended her power.

"A great wave gathered in the gray waters, and sped toward the shore. The chief saw it, and straightened, even as a loon—his very own loon, that he had rescued so many moons past—settled between his feet. The wave sped toward him; beyond it, he could see his people—his people . . .

"His people, swimming gracefully toward the islands, changed by the sea's mercy—into seals.

"The last thing he saw, before the wave took him to the sea, were the *ronstibles* being drawn beneath the waters, wailing."

I took a very, very careful breath.

"Borgan?"

There was no answer.

"Borgan," I said again, slightly louder.

"Kate," he answered, and raised his head.

"Was that you?" I asked. "The warrior on the shore?"

But I knew the answer to that—I had seen him, in his leathers, with his loon nestled by his foot . . .

I heard a sharp intake of breath.

"I told you *that* story?"

"If *that story* is how the *ronstibles* fell into disfavor with the sea, and Strand and Blunt Islands came to have seals—yes."

He closed his eyes.

"Why didn't the sea unmake them?" I asked, eventually, and hoping I wasn't venturing onto unwelcoming waters.

"Well." He opened his eyes. "The sea can't unmake a part of herself, and the *ronstibles* are just that: a part of her nature."

The piece clicked into place.

"And that's the reason there wasn't anything to clue me—or anybody—into the fact that everything wasn't perfectly fine. The *ronstibles* are part of her nature, and you were with her." I drew a breath. "How long could they have kept you . . . subdued?"

He sighed.

"I'm thinking the longer they have me, the easier it is *to* have me, if you take my meaning."

I shivered.

"Kate, they're weak and—"

"I know," I interrupted. "You built wards, and that ought to hold them. Unless something weakens *you* again, and they slip the leash."

"This is getting 'way too serious," Borgan said, and turned, bringing me with him, so he could kiss me, an exercise I entered into with enthusiasm.

"It's late," he murmured some little while later, nuzzling my throat, and I had just enough wit online to realize that was a question.

Well, Kate, I asked myself kindly, *staying what's left of the night, or not?*

"I think," I said slowly, holding onto his braid. "I think I'd better go home."

He raised his head. "If that's what you think, I'll walk with you."

We walked empty streets, under a sky already beginning to lighten. Hand in hand by mutual choice, not talking; there wasn't really any need to talk. Just holding hands, and walking...that was good enough. No. It was as near to perfect as made no difference.

We turned the corner from Grand and I could see the porch light glowing like a moon at the top of Dube Street. Home again, not quite the same day.

The steps being narrow, I went up first, Borgan coming after. The key was in the lock before I realized that I had another decision to make. After all, Borgan had made me free with his space. It was only, and at the very least, polite, to reciprocate.

I turned toward him.

"Do you—" I began and got no further, because he'd pressed his fingers gently against my lips.

"No need to do anything rash," he murmured. "You hardly know me, after all."

I laughed against his fingers. He smiled, and moved his hands to cup my face. Holding me still, he bent down and kissed me.

Thoroughly.

"Hey!" a familiar voice hollered. "Get a room!"

Borgan broke the kiss, and I turned my head.

Peggy the Fixer stood at the bottom of the flight, Felsic's arm around her waist.

"You drunk, Jersey?"

"She's not," Felsic said quickly. "Only danced-up a little, G-Kate. I'll see to her."

The land swore Felsic was as steady as they went, as trustworthy as the tides. I took that as absolutely true, with one caveat.

Felsic was *trenvay*.

And Peggy...wasn't.

I went down the steps, nodded to Felsic, put my hands on Peggy's shoulders, and looked into her face. Her eyes were wide, her color high; she was animated and burning so bright I could feel her on the land, almost as if she was *trenvay*.

I looked back at Felsic.

"I think I'd better take it from here," I said, courteously. "Thank you for your care, and your service, Felsic."

There was a small pause as Felsic looked over my shoulder, and nodded politely. "Cap'n Borgan."

"Felsic. Good to see you. 'Morning, Peggy Marr. You'd best let Kate get you in to bed."

"Kate's busy," Peggy announced, purple eyes very bright, "in case you hadn't noticed. Besides, I can get myself to bed."

"Sure you can," I said, taking her arm and guiding her to the studio's door. "Where's your key?"

"Right here." She fumbled it from her pocket, and held it out. I used it and let us in, shoving the door closed behind. Peggy was showing a tendency to break into dance, which was probably why Felsic had taken firm hold. I got my arm around her shoulders, left the key on the kitchen counter, and steered her into the bedroom.

"You bi?" she asked, doing a little heel-and-toe in place.

"Straight as a pine tree," I told her.

"*Damn*, my luck's lousy," she said, feet stilling for a moment, and shoulders drooping, just a little.

I took a chance and let her go while I yanked the blankets down on the bed.

"Take your shoes off, Jersey, and get under the covers."

She obediently toed out of her sneakers and slid, fully dressed, even unto the purple sweatshirt, into bed.

I pulled the covers over her, and she crossed her hands on top.

"I won't sleep a wink. I'm too full. So *much* energy. I could dance to the moon..."

Under the covers, her feet were shifting in what looked like the heel-and-toe. This would *not* do. It was possible to draw too much from the music; a mundane human might even—according to the old stories—dance themselves to death.

I sat down on the edge of the bed and put my hand over Peggy's, folded on her breast.

She smiled at me. "You're cute when you're worried, Archer."

"Who says I'm worried?"

"If I wasn't so, so—*I'd* be worried. Gotta work tomorrow. Today. Whatever."

"You do, and you will," I said, and made the request of the land, feeling its willingness come back to me.

"Go to sleep, Peggy," I murmured, the land's gift flowing through me, to her. "Wake up well rested, full of joy and energy." But not, I added, just between me and the land, *too much* energy.

Peggy's errant feet stilled beneath the covers, her eyelids drooped, and her breathing smoothed out. I kept my hand on hers for a long count of ten, then rose, checked to make sure the alarm was on, and tiptoed out.

Borgan was sitting on the steps when I came out, locking the door behind me.

"Where's Felsic?"

"He thought he'd better go 'long home, too. Said to tell you, you was right—he didn't mean her no mischief, but he's a little danced-up himself."

"Him, is it? Peggy says her."

Borgan looked unsurprised. "What's Kate say?"

"Kate's not sure," I confessed, and he nodded.

"I'm thinking that's the right of it." He tilted his head toward Peggy's door. "She'll be all right?"

"The land put her to sleep. She ought to wake up rarin' to go, in about"—I winced, remembering the tale told by Peggy's alarm clock—"four hours."

"And you'll do the same for yourself," he said, rising easily.

"I'll be fine," I said. "One way or another. You, though—"

He put his hands on my shoulders and smiled down at me, softly. My heart flipped over in my chest. I swallowed, hard, and Borgan's smile widened.

"I'll just go back the sea route," he said. "That'll set me up for the day. You—you'd best go in, now." He bent and kissed my forehead. "I'll see you tomorrow, Kate," he said, and stepped back, clearing my path to the stairs.

He was leaving. Suddenly and very badly, I wanted him to stay. I wanted to throw myself on his chest and kiss his chin, his ear, the corner of his mouth...

"Kate?"

"Right. Bedtime." I nodded, sharply, and forced myself to go up the stairs, slide the key into the lock, and push the door open.

I paused then, and looked down. Borgan was standing at the foot of the stairs, his hands in the pockets of his jeans, his face tipped up and bathed in light.

My heart flipped again. I wondered if that was going to become a habit, and whether I'd eventually get used to it.

"See you tomorrow, Borgan," I said, feeling the promise resonate in the land.

Then I stepped inside and shut the door.

CHAPTER TWENTY-FIVE

Wednesday, June 21
Midsummer Day
High Tide 8:02 A.M.
Sunrise 5 A.M. EDT

I woke refreshed, with no assist from the alarm, from a sleep so sound it seemed as if a cat had guarded my dreams.

That was an odd fancy, I thought, lying there and not exactly in a hurry to rise. It'd been years since I'd lived with a cat—Gran's big old Maine coon, that would have been—Bowditch, by name.

I'd been wounded when I arrived, suddenly and without warning, long years ago, on Gran's doorstep. Not just your garden variety gunshot wound, either; I'd been elfshot, and I should've died, because that's what people who've been elfshot do.

Gran said that *I* hadn't died because Zephyr had gotten me across the World Wall almost immediately after I'd been hit. The poison had changed, said Gran, before it had a chance to kill me.

As guesses went, it was as good as any.

Though it hadn't killed me, being elfshot didn't made me any stronger, either. I was sick for months, needed a lot of feeding up, and sun, and sleep. Bowditch, being a past master in the art of napping, had guarded my sleep by day. At night, I'd had Snow, the wolf dog, beside me. Bad dreams got past Snow—she wasn't anything like as resty as Bowie—but I never feared that anything *but* a dream would get past her.

That'd been important, in those days.

Well, I thought idly, *maybe I should get a cat.*

I stretched, and threw the covers back, glancing at the clock as I did.

Seven forty-five. Perfect.

I went downstairs to take a shower.

The day's agenda took shape while I showered. I had to relieve Vassily at four, naturally, but before that, there would be low tide. After sleeping on it, my back brain had decided that the better part of valor was the immediate closing of the wild gate at Goosefare Brook.

I considered that idea narrowly as I shampooed my hair, but—aside from the fact that I had no idea how I'd go about closing a working that had literally knocked me on my ass—the concept seemed sound. Sort of implicit in *protect the land* was the notion that there shouldn't be random mystery Gates spotting the landscape.

They say that water's therapeutic, that there's something about taking a bath or a shower that stimulates the creative process. That was certainly true for me, today at least. By the time I'd turned the water off and was toweling off, I had figured out one possible approach to my problem.

If that didn't work, I promised myself, I'd apply to Mr. Ignat' for high-level assistance.

In the meantime, and before either low tide or Gate-crashing, came breakfast, which was fortunate, because I was *starving*.

I heard Peggy's door close as I was pouring my first cup of coffee.

What I *didn't* hear, a minute or so after, was her step on the outside stairs.

Frowning, I walked over to the door, which was on the latch, per recent habit, and pulled it open. Peggy was most of the way to the corner, walking fast, a short, pleasantly rounded figure all in black, with a purple sweatshirt thrown over one shoulder.

I watched her swing left onto Grand, then closed the door, feeling...sad, I guess it was. Upset, even. If Peggy was mad at me—but I hadn't done anything to make her mad! I thought.

Had I?

I am so very bad at people.

Mug in hand, I stalked to the summer parlor. Midsummer Day had dawned in glory: brilliant, bright, and already starting to warm up nicely.

I stared out over the sparkling waves and sipped coffee, gloomily.

It occurred to me that Peggy might be less angry than embarrassed about our last meeting. That got me off the hook, socially, but it didn't make me feel any better. I'd gotten used to Peggy; I *liked* her, and I didn't want anything unpleasant—anger or embarrassment—sitting between us like a toad on a birthday cake.

Which meant, I thought, finishing my coffee, that I'd better get my ass down to the midway right now, before the place was a screaming madhouse, and try to smooth it over.

Before I left, though...

I ran upstairs to my bedroom, and pulled open the bottom bureau drawer. It's a drawer that doesn't get much use; I don't have a lot of stuff, and four drawers is about two more than I need. In fact, there were only three things in the drawer.

A pair of venerable canvas work gauntlets, scored and stained, the wide cuffs a badly faded blue, the palms and fingers grubby pink—and a slim knife in a slim sheathe, the hilt wrapped in leather. The knife's name was Mam'selle. If the gloves bore names, nobody'd bothered to tell me.

I hung the gauntlets on my belt, and slid the sheathed knife away safe along my spine, where she could keep my magic company.

Then I closed the drawer, straightened, and left the room at a brisk walk.

The little office behind The Last Mango was empty, though the purple sweatshirt was lying, rumpled and forlorn, in the middle of the desk.

I nodded and went back outside.

Despite it wasn't even ten o'clock, the midway was moderately busy. About half the games were open, and there were a good couple dozen early birds wandering leisurely about, surveying the offerings and weighing their chances, coffee and soda cups in hand.

Peggy wasn't immediately in sight.

I queried the land, got a fix and directed my own wandering feet toward the climbing wall at the dune's edge, about as far from The Mango as you could get and still be in the midway.

I reached the place, and spotted my quarry inside the safety rail, looking up the wall while a scrawny white-haired guy, shorter than she was, pointed and talked. Squinting, I looked, too, and could just make out what seemed to be a tear around the "rock" at the tippy-toppest right-hand corner.

I made a request of the land, and looked again with sharpened sight. It wasn't a tear, but more like a chip in the wall, as if somebody had climbed up and taken a rock hammer to the plaster surface. A thrill-seeker, I thought, had come in from the ocean-side after the midway was closed, climbed up the wall and thought they'd get themselves a souvenir.

So, they'd managed to chip the plaster, and expose the wood beneath, but they hadn't managed to get the prize, which was firmly attached with big, businesslike bolts.

Some people really aren't very bright.

Peggy and the guy spent a few more minutes waving their hands at each other; then the guy nodded energetically and bustled off toward the operator's shed, while Peggy headed out of the enclosure.

I straightened up from my lean on the rail, and moved over to the gate.

Peggy was looking good, I thought; her step was springy; her face was smooth, and her eyes were sparkling, like she'd had twelve hours of sleep...

...or danced Midsummer in with the fey.

"Hey, Kate," she said, giving me a nod as she came through the gate. "What's up?"

"I missed you this morning for coffee," I said, falling in beside her, "and wanted to be sure everything was all right between us."

She stopped and turned to look into my face.

"You put me to bed last night when I was drunk and disorderly," she said. "I was rude to you..."

"Not a bit of it. At least, Felsic said you weren't drunk, and I trust Felsic's judgment. At no time were you disorderly."

Her pink cheeks flushed even pinker.

"Made a pass at you, didn't I?"

"You asked an honest question, and I gave an honest answer, which you took with good grace." I gave her a grin. "Truth told, I'd've been miffed if you *hadn't* been disappointed."

She laughed.

"All right, Archer. We're good. I missed you this morning, too, but I figured the boyfriend might think three was a crowd."

Kate, I told myself, *you're an idiot.*

I'd forgotten Borgan—or, not *forgotten* him, but forgotten that Peggy had good reason to suppose I had other company for breakfast.

"He went back to his place. But you couldn't have known that."

She nodded, and started moving again; I kept pace.

"Go away from me!" an angry voice cut across the midway's muted roar.

Peggy and I turned as one woman, both of us running toward the man and woman, who were glaring at each other. The man had the woman by the wrist. The woman, clearly angry and frightened, was trying to break his grip.

"Go away from me!" she shouted again. "I don't go with you!"

I grabbed the guy's free arm and twisted it behind his back hard enough to get his attention.

"Let her go," I snapped.

At least he didn't have to be told twice.

Peggy snatched Ulme—for it was Ulme—and walked her rapidly away, leaving me holding the guy. I dropped his arm, and spun to face him.

"Kyle, what the hell's wrong with you?"

He was mad—*really* mad, judging by the glitter in his eyes and the color in his cheeks—but not mad enough to be stupid. I knew that because he didn't take a swing at me, or try to push by to run after Peggy and Ulme.

"Well?"

He took a hard breath.

"She was leading me on," he said, sullenly.

"Leading you on? Are you stupid?"

He blinked, the color fading slightly, and shook his head.

"I hope not," he said. "I really hope not."

I stared at him, trying to square this episode with what I thought I knew about him. But that was the problem, wasn't it? I *didn't* know him; I'd only seen a little of him, and liked what I saw—a fresh-faced, hard-working, even-tempered guy, with just that little bit of lucky shine to him.

He didn't seem like the kind of guy who would provoke a scene in public and grab a woman against her will...

I shook my head, more distressed than mad, and more puzzled than both.

"You're doing work for Joe Nemeier?" I asked.

"Yeah," he admitted.

"So, *leading you on or not*, I don't have to tell you what a bad idea it is to get involved with his girlfriend?"

"No, you don't."

"And I don't have to tell you it's wrong to assault people?"

"No," he said, and sighed. "I'm sorry."

"I'll pass it on to Ulme. In the meantime, if I was you, I'd be thinking about getting a nice big cup of coffee and proceeding with my day."

"That sounds like a good idea. Good morning, Kate."

He gave me a sharp nod, and walked away, heading into the midway; maybe making for the gate on Fountain Circle.

I watched him until he rounded the corner, then asked the land to do the honors, while I headed for The Mango.

Ulme was sitting cross-legged in the center of the desk, the purple sweatshirt draped over her shoulders. Her sleek orange hair was tangled, and she was shaking. Peggy was holding her hand.

"It's going to be fine, sweetie," I heard her say as I entered. "Kate won't let that guy get past her."

"He's gone," I said, the land having reported that Kyle had passed out of the midway and was walking up Archer Avenue toward Jay's Eatery.

I stopped a couple steps out from the desk, tucked my hands in the back pockets of my jeans and stared at Ulme.

"You want to tell me what that was about?"

"He wants me to hurt Joe," Ulme said, and her voice was shaking, too. "I tell him it is impossible for me to hurt Joe. Impossible! But he will not understand!"

I considered her. "Is it? Impossible to hurt Joe, I mean."

Her chin came up. "For myself, yes," she said, daring me to make something of it.

"Easy," Peggy said, and threw me a look that I interpreted as *cut the kid some slack, Archer.*

I sighed, and blinked Sideways, just for a couple seconds; long enough to see the flames dancing in Ulme's aura, and to catch the scent of her signature. Her power smelled like daisies, fresh and innocent.

Back in the Real World, I frowned, trying my best to look stern.

"Look, Ulme, this is twice now I've seen you with guys who aren't Joe: Vassily, and now Kyle. Kyle in particular says to me that you were leading him on. Obviously, that's no excuse for him grabbing you, or for not taking *no* for an answer, but, at base, Kyle's a decent guy. After he blows off this head of steam, he won't give you any more trouble.

"But *you*—I'm not sure you understand where this could go. Because Joe Nemeier is *not* a decent guy. He's a bad man, with a *seriously* bad temper. I'm telling you this from personal experience—I crossed him once, and he sent one of his kiddies down here to cut my face. Do you believe me?"

Chin still elevated, Ulme swallowed, and gave a hard nod.

"Right. Now, what do you think Joe might do if he figures either Vassily or Kyle—or, hell, Vassily *and* Kyle—were bothering you? Do you think he might send another kiddie with a knife—or a gun—to teach them a lesson?"

I leaned forward, a little, and stared hard into her eyes.

"Do you think," I asked, very gently, "that Joe might do that to *you*, if he got mad?"

"It is," Ulme said, her voice just above a whisper, but firm, for all its faintness. "It is . . . possible."

She had an idea of what she was dealing with, then, I thought, and couldn't decide if that was a good thing or a bad thing. Either way, I pressed on with the lecture.

"You say it's impossible for you to hurt Joe—great. Along with that, I'd recommend making sure you don't hurt anybody else. Got it?"

The chin quivered. She got it under control and replied firmly, "I will not be foolish again."

It was on the tip of my tongue to tell her not to overreach herself, but one look at Peggy's face convinced me to keep the snark to myself, so I just nodded.

"Good. None of us wants any trouble."

"That is correct."

Ulme uncrossed her legs, slid off the desk, pulled the sweatshirt from her shoulders, rolled it sloppily, and held it out to Peggy.

"Thank you, Peggy. Thank you for helping me."

"Women don't get beat up by creeps on my watch," Peggy said, taking the roll and hugging it against her chest. "But look, sweetie, if what Kate says is true, you need to stay away from

Joe. Guys like that, it's not a question of *if* he'll hurt you—it's when. You don't want to be there."

"I must be there," Ulme said, with dignity. "I will be careful."

She turned to face me.

"Thank you, Kate Archer, for coming to my aid, and for sending—for sending Kyle away from me."

"You're welcome," I said neutrally, and stepped aside so she could get past without touching me.

She nodded and was gone, disappearing into the midway.

"So," Peggy said, still hugging the sweatshirt. She put a hip against the edge of the desk and looked closely into my face. I raised my eyebrows and waited.

"So," she said again. "No scar. Plastic surgery?"

I stared at her, completely at sea.

"One of Joe's kiddies cut your face?" she prompted. "Or was that just to scare the poultry?"

Oh, right.

I shrugged, trying for casual.

"It happened a while back," I said.

"Couldn't've happened too far back," Peggy pointed out. "You've only been home eight weeks."

Woman had a memory like a steel trap.

"I heal quick," I said, and when she frowned, added, "Really."

Peggy sighed.

"Sure you do."

'Way too close, a buzzer voiced a staticky Bronx cheer. Peggy frowned, dumping the poor abused sweatshirt back onto the desk.

"My master's voice," she said. "I've gotta go whirl up some smoothies. See you later?"

"You know where I live."

I followed her out, and made good my escape.

CHAPTER TWENTY-SIX

Low Tide 1:58 P.M. EDT

According to Mr. Ignat', there are three basic levels of spellcraft: intuitive, which is to say, no crafting involved. Black Dogs, willie wisps, and other vermin fall into this category, as does Side-Sight, the ability to speak Words of Power, and people who just happen to be born with *jikinap* as part of their biological makeup—Ulme being a case in point.

The second level is your basic magecraft: an individual who may willfully and mindfully manipulate *jikinap*, weaving spells to answer a specific purpose, which may last for some time, absent operator oversight.

The third level is group-work, which is just what it sounds like: several Ozali get together, pool their power, submit their will to the group vision and create something that any single one of them could never build, no matter how powerful or well-versed in spellcraft they are. And that working, once built, takes on a solidity, a purpose, and a *reality* of its own. Once created, it needs nothing more from its creators; it is—complete.

The Wise's authorized World Gates are just such workings, *real* across the strange and not necessarily compatible interfaces of six separate worlds. Mr. Ignat' says—and I have no reason to doubt him—that the World Gates exist not in any one world, but in all six simultaneously. Being a toddler in the realm of spellcraft, I can't even begin to figure out how the makers did that.

However it was done, though, I was willing to believe it had required a hell of a lot of very sharp coding.

Happily, I wasn't here to take down a World Gate. A straight world-to-world Gate was a far simpler thing. Or so I theorized. All I had to do, in theory, was dismantle the Gate on my side and the rest of the working should simply unravel.

I knelt on the lip of land over the apron beach, and laid my tools on the grass before me.

Gauntlets, shabby, faded, and stained.

Knife, slim and deadly.

A fist-sized chunk of stone from the base of Heath Hill, sharp-edged and gritty.

I also had, on call, the three defensive and three offensive spells that I'd built with such effort two weeks ago. Frankly, I didn't think today's work would end in a duel, but it was best to be prepared.

So, then. The tide was as out as it was going to go, and I was due at the carousel in a little less than two hours.

Time to get busy.

I slipped off my sneakers, tucked my socks inside them; rolled my jeans to the knee; slipped the sheathed knife away; pulled the work gauntlets on; and picked up the rock.

The land whined anxiously, and I paused a moment to rub its ears, and assure it that I would be perfectly fine. Which, in theory, I should be. The land whined again, sounding resigned.

"Back before you miss me," I told it.

Then I got to my feet, rock in hand, swung over the edge, and dropped to the beach below.

I landed flat-footed, knees flexed, the rock held before me like a candle. Straight ahead, knee-deep in the pool, was a blue heron—possibly the same blue heron from my previous visit. It spared me a single weary and incurious glance before bending its attention once more to the water. Lunch must go on, I guess.

I put the rock carefully on the sand by my feet, straightened and stepped Sideways.

The twelve rainbow pillars snapped into being along the edge of the sandy apron. I glanced at my own hands, and the gauntlets I wore. Neither shabby nor stained, in Side-Sight I wore the battle gauntlets of an Ozali warrior, palms and fingers sheathed in supple crimson leather, wide night-blue cuffs richly embroidered with flames; gemstones winking cunningly among the threads—citrine, or yellow diamond, or some other precious stone that exists only in the Land of the Flowers.

Carefully, I approached the red bar that had kicked my ass on my last visit; I extended one gauntleted hand, and wrapped my fingers around it.

The bar felt gratifyingly solid; the gauntlet gave me the kind of purchase I needed without bringing a stranger's *jikinap* into the equation. I grabbed on with my other hand, braced myself... and tried to pull the bar up and out of the land.

I had a sense of shifting...a very *slight* shifting, but noticeable. Possibly, I thought, loosing the bar and stepping back to consider the matter...possibly the Gate was Changing. That, in fact, the bars might eventually just...fall over, breaking the pattern and the spell, without any encouragement from me.

I considered that idea; that I just let nature take its course...

...and reluctantly decided against, *eventually* being as fluid as it was.

So far as I knew, there wasn't anything like an established decay rate for change, and even if there had been, I had no idea how long the wild gate had been in position.

I wondered if there was a way to learn at least that much. I wrapped my fingers around the red bar one more time, and opened myself, like I did when searching for dead zones, only not so far.

It seemed as if I stood there a long time, listening with all of me. I heard the breakers, soft and distant; I heard gulls, swearing overhead, and a prop plane, which may have been the cause.

I heard someone crying—the wrenching sobs of heartbreaking loss—I saw a flicker, as if of wings, and a glissade of color, like a rainbow...

Nothing else.

I took a breath, opened my eyes, and nodded.

Best get this over with.

From time to time Mr. Ignat' has had reason to remonstrate with me for a certain lack of...elegance and subtlety in my spellcraft. In my defense, I also tend to program in a straightforward

and frank manner. I'm good, and I'm original, but elegant...
not so much.

Physically dismantling the wild gate had been my first prefer-
ence, but even the work gloves weren't going to give me the edge
I needed for that.

Which left me with my Plan B—blow the thing up.

I released the red bar, and crossed the beach, pausing to pick
up the rock I'd left in the sand. This, I carried to the front of
the apron, to the spot where, if I had been intending to complete
the magical circuit that would open the gate and send me to
wherever the other side was, I would place the white rod.

The white rod would have contained a locator spell, which would
focus the energy gathered from the other twelve rods, and open
the gate onto the correct world. The energy would then dissipate,
flowing through the gate at the opposite end.

With the stone—the very essence of Archers Beach—closing
the circuit, the energy would try to open the side of the gate
it was already on, which would create a feedback loop, which
would melt the circuits.

I was pretty certain of my theory, but, still, I was glad that
my unknown Ozali had chosen such an out-of-the-way place to
build his or her gate. I wouldn't have wanted to try this up in
the populated areas of town. In fact, I did pause, and rerun the
scenario, just by way of settling my stomach, before I stepped
through the gap in the circle, which put me off the beach and
in water almost up to my knees.

Safely outside the overload zone, I bent and placed the rock.

Then I stood back and held my breath.

The air began to buzz, ratcheting up from contented honey bee
to angry hive in less than thirty seconds. The bars of light began
to flash, deliberately, in order: red, orange, yellow, green, blue,
purple, synchronized down both sides of the beach. The flashes
grew quicker as the buzzing became angrier, until all I could see,
mundane sight, or Side-Sight, were two blurred rainbows, locked
on either side of the beach.

That was when the rock screamed.

My throat caught. I hadn't planned on the rock cracking under
the strain.

And what will happen, Kate, I asked myself kindly, *if the rock
does break?*

It was a good question, and one for the research files, because even as I raised my power to do...*something*...

The rainbows expanded, until the whole area of the beach marked out by the light bars was full of racing, buzzing light, and there was no room for any of it to go—

Except up.

Which is where it went—up into the blue daylight sky, blossoming like flowers, each petal limned with power, before melting into glowing droplets, and raining down upon the sea and the land.

The apron beach was empty. Quiet. Directly before me, half-buried in feather-soft white sand, was a sundered rock, the broken faces fused like glass.

Carefully, I stepped out of the water, onto the soft white sand.

The land barked, loud with joy, and leapt up, knocking me to my knees.

It was a good night at the carousel; busy enough that all of the animals got the love—even the stupid rooster. The crowd started to thin around quarter to ten, and by the time the closing whistle sounded, with the exception of a few stragglers, the park was empty.

I waved good-night to Anna when she came to the window to bring in the condiments and napkins. She waved back and yanked down the metal shutter, the sign proclaiming LEE'S GREAT CHINESE FOOD snapping off in the same instant.

A couple seconds later, Summer's Wheel went dark, and I took that as definitive.

I'd turned off the big sign on the carousel's roof, and was heading for the storm gates, when the land muttered irritably.

Pulling a defense spell into ready position, I turned.

The guy who had stepped under the carousel's roof, raised his hands and shook his head.

"Just me, Kate. Artie. Got something for you."

Really? Now that was a surprise. I put the defense spell away.

"Help me close the storm walls," I said, and saw by his posture that I'd surprised him.

"Sure," he said, and walked toward the back, angling right.

I continued on to the left, grabbed the loop and hauled. For a minute, the rumble of moving metal filled my head, then Artie and I met in the middle with a crash and a clash.

"'Preciate it," I told him, giving him a civil nod. "What can I do for you?"

"Couple things, as it happens," he said, sounding... unsure in a way he hadn't sounded, up at the Enterprise.

From the back pocket of his jeans, he produced a flat booklet about five-by-three, with longer, folded, papers tucked between the covers, and held it out to me.

I raised my eyebrows.

Artie had the grace to blush.

"Naw, now; it ain't what you're thinkin'. It's just—it come in like it does, and I thought I'd better bring it direct." He paused, lips pursed, then shook his head. "Might should've taken it up the Wood, but it's around that your gran's not feelin' herself and shouldn't get stressed. I go up there, you bet she'll get stressed. So, anyway..."

He shook the folder and papers a little. I tucked my hands into my back pockets.

"What is it?" I asked.

Artie pushed his cap back with the hand not holding the papers, maybe so I could see his frown better.

"Papers, for Nessa."

"Really?" I said, letting my voice echo disbelief, even though the land assured me Artie was telling the truth. "Where'd you get papers for Nessa, if you don't mind my asking."

"They come in," he repeated, and sighed sharp and hard. "On the land itself, Kate, I don't know where they come from. Wha'dya think, I order 'em outta some catalog?"

"Well, but I don't know the system, and after the rooster, you'll see where I want to be a little careful, especially where it concerns my family."

"Oh, *hell* yes, who wouldn't wanna be careful, with the Enterprise in it? But—hey, the rooster. I heard at Midsummer Eve you was worried, an' your gran, too. Shouldn'a done it, prolly, not with what's between Bonnie an' me, but I couldn't seem to help myself. Just some mischief, that's all; fool the Guardian, that's good for some free beers, yanno? Truth of it, you near weren't tricked, and then you 'bout skinned me when I pushed it."

He took a breath, and gave me a nod.

"It wasn't right. I might've been a little set up by what you come lookin' for, but I coulda handled it better. That rooster— ain't no harm in it that I could see."

"And you weren't after anything more than earning points?" I asked. The land was letting me know that Artie was telling the truth. He'd tried to trick me because he was *trenvay*, and *trenvay* trick people. Tricking the Guardian? Definitely bragging rights, there.

"Just stretching my muscles, in a manner of speaking," Artie agreed, and shook the papers again. "This here, now . . . birth certificate, driver's license, Social Security card, United States passport . . ." He rolled his eyes and I could read the thought, *like she's gonna need* that.

"That's all. That's *everything*. Nothin' to upset your gran, once she gets over it comin' in. Just *did* come in, not twenty minutes ago. Found it sitting on my desk chair when I come back from getting a cup o'Jack."

I slipped a hand out of a back pocket, but I didn't take the papers yet. Not quite yet.

"What's between you and Gran?" I asked.

Artie blew air noisily, like a horse kept waiting too long.

"Somethin' come in—a long time ago, okay, Kate?—and I'm sayin' *it come in*, just . . . it wasn't what your gran wanted it to be." He waggled the papers he still held, and shook his head.

"Packet a lot like this. No passport, not them days, nor Social Security, neither. Birth record, that was there. And so was the death certificate. Your gran, she was mad, and considering how it happened, I couldn't blame her. She blamed me, though. Said I'd done it a'purpose, when it wasn't, and it never is—which she knew, but she chose to forget."

That rang true—rang like a bell, from the land and up all the bones in my body.

I extended my hand and took the little packet of papers.

"I'll take them up to Mother," I said, gently. "Thanks for bringing them right away, Artie."

He swallowed, and nodded.

"No problem. And, listen, you wanna lose that rooster . . ."

"I'm having a horse carved," I told him, still keeping my voice soft. "Why don't I give you a call when that's delivered and you can come down and collect the rooster?"

"Sure. Sure, I can do that." He grinned. "Give you a refund, too. Half."

"Half?"

"Well, you had use."

"I made improvements."

"Well . . . I'll tell you what. You get that new horse all delivered and set up, and we'll dicker serious when I come down to get the rooster. Deal?"

"Deal," I acknowledged, feeling the rough vinyl of the passport's cover against my fingertips. Artie stood there like he didn't know quite what to do, so I gave him a hint.

"I gotta finish closing up, here," I said. "Then I'll walk this up to my mother."

"Right," he said, and pulled the brim of his hat down a bit. "Right. See you 'round, Kate."

"See you around, Artie," I answered, and watched as he crossed to the door, paused, then stepped through muttering, "Thanks."

Half a second later, Borgan stepped through the door, using his chin to point at what I guessed was Artie's retreating back.

"Everything okay?"

"Everything's fine," I said, slipping my mother's paperwork into the back pocket of my jeans. "He came down to deliver something for Mother. Thought he'd upset Gran, if he went to the Wood, himself."

"Good thinking," Borgan said.

"In fact, it was. But it did set me back a little on shutting down. You mind waiting—and then walking up Heath Hill with me?"

"Pretty night for a walk," he said. "Lots of stars. Anything I can do?"

"Wait right there," I said. "Won't be a sec."

"Wouldn't know anything about a big magical light show earlier in the day, would you?" Borgan asked, as we strolled, hand-in-hand, down West Grand toward Heath Hill.

"Now that you mention it, I was the cause of a fairly impressive explosion this afternoon, down Goosefare Brook," I admitted, and looked up at the side of his face, glowing in the starlight. "I didn't break anything, did I?"

"Nothing I know about. Was bright, though. And noisy. Mind telling me about it?"

I obliged him as we walked, and by the time we were going up the side of the hill, he was in possession of all the pertinent facts.

"It more or less worked like I thought it would," I said, as we gained the top of the hill. "But I underestimated the amount of energy that would be released."

Borgan cleared his throat.

"You could've asked me for help, if Ozali Belignatious was busy," he said mildly.

"I would've asked Mr. Ignat', if it turned out I couldn't handle it," I assured him. "But I thought I should try it myself, first, since protecting the land is pretty much my job."

I heard a small intake of breath, as if Borgan was about to say something—and then nothing, as if he'd thought better of it.

We were under the edge of the Wood now. I stopped, Borgan right beside me. Uphill, Joe Nemeier's overgrown "cottage" had every window aglow. The man must be throwing a party.

I turned my face to the Wood, Borgan's hand warm in mine, and spoke, quietly. "Mother?"

A small breeze disturbed the branches directly overhead, and I thought I heard my voice, repeating against the leaves.

"Just bear in mind," Borgan said softly, "there's those you can ask for help. Sometimes, it's . . . prudent to call in help *before* you try it yourself."

I thought about that; remembered the broken and glassed-over rock.

"How much of a disaster did I make today?"

"Today," Borgan said seriously, "you were lucky."

I was still digesting that when the shadows between the tree trunks parted, and Mother was with us. She was wearing the sleeveless green shift, her legs and feet bare; light brown curls were tangled on her shoulders and her eyes seemed heavy.

"Katie—Borgan! How nice of you to visit." She sounded genuinely pleased, if slightly sleepy.

"I hope I didn't wake you," I said, reaching around to my back pocket. "Artie said this had just come in. He was eager for you to have it quick."

She took the folder and attendant papers from me, and stood holding them in her hand.

"I'm told there's a Social Security card, driver's license, birth certificate and passport in there," I said. "Nothing else. Artie was extremely clear on the point."

I saw her shoulders lose some tension and she breathed a laugh.

"Poor Artie. As if it was his fault."

"Told me he'd delivered a death certificate with the packet once," I said. "What happened?"

"Mostly that," Mother said. "The certificate had a date on it and a cause—*Act of God*. We all—Mother, Aunt Alba, and I— we thought it was a joke. She was young, and healthy, after all. There was no reason she and her tree couldn't stand for another hundred—two hundred—years."

"What happened?" I asked again, when she didn't go on.

"What happened?" Mother shook her head. "There was a storm. Her tree was hit by lightning."

CHAPTER TWENTY-SEVEN

Thursday, June 22
High Tide 9:21 P.M.
Sunset 8:26 P.M. EDT

Five tables had been pushed together in the middle of Bob's main room. Two coffeepots, cream, sugar, and two plates of muffins were set out. Each attendee was nursing a mug; a couple had heard the siren song of the blueberry muffins and were happily indulging.

The Archers Beach Twelve to Twelve Fun Country subcommittee meeting had ten members in attendance: Henry and Bob, and eight Fun Country folk. The rest, Jess said, had other commitments.

"Except Doris Vannerhoff, who says that we're all cracked in the head if we expect Management to go against its own interest, and if any of us had an ounce of gumption, we'd go down Florida in the winter, like she does, and do some work for a change."

Jess frowned down at the paper lying on the table in front of her, possibly reading over a note, nodded, and looked 'round at us.

"That's it. I made her say it out slow for me, so I could take it down and be sure to get it right."

Millie laughed.

Brand shook his head dolefully. "One thing about Doris," he said, "she's got such a retirin' nature, you can never be sure where she stands."

That made the whole table laugh.

"Scrambler's Dunlap says he's in," Jess continued, after the general merriment had died down. "Says keep 'im posted and tell 'im what to do when. Broken ankle's slowing 'im down, 'swhy he's not here tonight."

She looked around the table again.

"Why we're here, is to figure out how to get Management on board with a longer Season. One thing I thought we should point out right up front is Ka-Pow!'s serious about staying open through the end of October. If Fun Country closes Labor Day night, any money that comes rolling down Archer Avenue after that will go right into the arcade."

"Management'll just say that a hundred percent of nothin's still nothin'," Millie said.

"The Super Early Season gives us leverage," said Sylvia Laliberte, the fortune-teller.

"Well, *we* think that," Brand said. "No telling what Management will think. Or say."

"Knowing Marilyn," said Donnie Atkins, owner-operator of the Galaxi, "what she's most likely to say is that the Chamber arranged for the Super Early Season, and that it was a one-off, because they won that contest." He took half a muffin in a bite, raised his coffee mug and looked around at us.

Apparently he was not reassured by what he saw, because he had a swallow of coffee and expanded.

"Chamber's official, see? We're just . . . carnies. Got no standing."

"Speaking to that point," Henry said, "I have, as instructed by our chairwoman during Archers Beach Twelve to Twelve's first meeting, spoken with Mr. Poirier of the Chamber concerning the committee's existence and what it hopes to accomplish. Mr. Poirier believes that the Super Early Season has given us evidence that the Season can begin weeks earlier, with profit to all concerned. He's very interested in gathering similar evidence for the end of the Season. While he stopped short of promising our committee Chamber resources, I think that he could very easily be persuaded to lend his support"—a nod to Donnie—"and standing to the committee in talks with Fun Country management."

"So," Jess said, "we start talking with Marilyn, and if she stalls, like Millie thinks she will—well, like we all think she will—then we'll ask Mr. Poirier to step 'round and have a word?"

"Depending on *how* Marilyn stalls," I said, "Dan Poirier's in a much stronger place to pick up the phone and put a call through to the New Jersey office."

"Oh!" Jess blinked, then smiled. "All right. Thank you, Henry. Good work."

"My pleasure," Henry said gallantly.

"So, number one talking point is the Super Early Season," Jess said, and made a tick mark on her pad.

She looked up. "How many weeks longer should we go this year?"

"Six," Brand said decisively.

"Six full weeks?" Donnie shook his head. "They won't go there."

"One full week and five Late Season weeks," said Anna, who was sitting next to Tony at the far end of the tables. "To match the five weeks of Early Season plus the Super Early Season."

"That seems fair," Millie said.

"Symmetrical," I said, because Jess looked at me like she expected pearls to fall from my lips.

Jess smiled. "That's good. And it plays into Mr. Poirier's evidence gathering. The only way it's a fair test is if we try it for the same amount of time."

She made a note on her pad, nodding slightly.

"Last question. I think." She smiled around the table. "How do we approach Marilyn? If we all go into her office together, that's gonna look threatening. And if we just pick somebody to be spokesperson, then how does Marilyn know it's not just one of us gone off our head and sayin' stuff?"

"We take a letter around to everybody, and ask them to sign it," Sylvia Laliberte said. She glanced up and down the table. "*If* there's more than eight of us who agree that extending the Season has to be tried."

"I talked to everybody," Jess said, turning toward her. "Why we're so thin here tonight is because it's full Season and folks don't have time or patience to come to a meeting after working all day. Everybody I talked to was interested in trying for a longer Season. Well. Except Doris."

"There's something," Brand said. "Doris goes south the second the park closes for the Season. She's not going to want to stay up here six weeks longer for weekend pay."

"Flume's not a Name Ride," Donnie pointed out.

"I don't like that," Millie objected. "If the park's open, then it ought to be with everybody up and running. Doris is the only one of the operators goes away; the rest of us are local. Might be able to get somebody else to keep the flume open."

"*You* try to get Doris to agree to that, and let me know how it works out," Donnie said sourly.

"Now, you can never tell about September," Brand commented. "Sometimes, it's chilly. The flume don't draw much, cold days."

"There's that," Millie said thoughtfully, and shrugged, looking over to Jess. "Just let Doris shut it down, then, I guess. But most of us ought to be open."

"That's where the letter does double duty," said Sylvia. "We take turns hand-carrying it to folks, and explaining what the committee is and what we're trying to accomplish, and reminding them of the Super Early Season." She looked around the table, a little militantly, I thought.

"If we can't sell *ourselves* on this idea," she said, "how are we going to sell it to Marilyn?"

I was starting to be pretty impressed with Sylvia Laliberte. I'd known who she was, in the general way that people who work in the same place, but whose paths rarely cross, know each other. It was good to find out that she had a hard edge of practicality to her.

Jess, however, was looking troubled. "That leads to another question," she said, apologetically. "Who's gonna write this letter?"

There was an uncomfortable silence around the table. I saw Henry's eyebrow twitch, but he didn't say anything. He was probably waiting for Jess to think of him herself, which she wouldn't, not being much used to the ways of lawyers.

I cleared my throat.

"As the group's attorney," I said, "Henry could draft a letter and run it past you." I paused, then thought, *what the hell.* "I'd be glad to look a letter over, too, if you think that would be useful."

Jess' face cleared. "That would be great."

"Then it will be done," Henry said. "I'll bring a draft around on Monday, if that will do?"

"Fast," Jess said, giving him another smile.

"We have to act fast," said Sylvia Laliberte, "if we want to get *this* Season extended."

"That's right," Donnie said, wolfing down another muffin. "Gotta move while Marilyn still remembers how much money the park made during the Super Early Season."

Jess sat up straight, and looked around the table, meeting everybody's eyes.

"Thank you all for coming, so late an' after a full day. Bob— thank you for giving us a place to meet—and snacks, too! I'll be back in touch, once Henry and Kate have the letter ironed out. For tonight, though . . ." She grinned, wryly.

"For tonight, I think we oughta call this meetin' over, and go home to get some rest."

"Second!" Brand called, getting to his feet with a clatter of the chair.

Henry and I stayed to put the tables back where they belonged, while Bob washed up, then let ourselves out onto Grand Avenue after calling our good-nights.

"Don't know how we became coauthors on the letter," I said, looking up at Henry, as I settled the handles of the canvas bag over my shoulder. "You know where to find me, if you need me."

"I do, and I will welcome your input first, if you'll indulge me, Kate. You've been around the world a little more than Jess has."

"And seen lots of business letters, too," I acknowledged with a grin. "Sure I'll look at it first."

"Excellent." He smiled. "Good-night, Kate."

"'Night, Henry," I answered, and watched him cross Grand before I turned and walked up Dube Street, across the dunes, to the beach.

Last night, after the visit to Heath Hill, I'd taken Borgan to Daddy's Dance Club.

"Hi, Daddy!" I said, as we slithered up to the bar. Tiny as it was, the place was packed with more gyrating bodies than I would've thought possible. The band was playing classic rock, because that's what bands play in Archers Beach.

Daddy finished with the rum and coke he was putting together, skated it downbar to the man wearing a white silk shirt unbuttoned almost to his navel, and caught the bill the guy tossed to him.

"Keep the change," the guy said, and melted away into the crowd standing against the wall.

Daddy snorted, and finally looked my way.

"Hey, doll," he said, with a half-smile to maybe show that he remembered me. His gaze moved past me, then, and up.

"Brought a friend, I see."

"Told you I would," I said. "Borgan this is Daddy; Daddy—Borgan."

"Pleased to meetcha," Daddy said. "Something to drink?"

"Got Sea Dog?" asked Borgan.

"Why wouldn't I?" Daddy asked.

So we got our ales, and drank them, tucked close together in the marked area, while we watched the dancing. When the ales were gone, we indulged in some dancing ourselves, until we slipped out into the cool night, and walked, hand-in-hand, down to the beach, to watch the stars.

When the breeze made star-watching too chilly, we walked up the beach to Dube Street, content with each other, and thoroughly in tune.

Or so I thought.

"G'night, Kate," he said, when we got to my front door. He bent and kissed my forehead. "Sleep deep."

That quick, he was gone, down the steps and over the dunes, bound, as I supposed, for *Gray Lady*.

So, maybe we hadn't been as much in tune as I'd...

"Good evenin', missus," a high voice spoke at my knee, rousing me from my memory.

The Pier was now far behind me, and Googin Rock, too. I was approaching the notch at the base of Heath Hill.

It was...somewhat unusual to find heeterskyte here, though in theory you could find them anywhere at water's edge. In reality, they tended to prefer the beach up toward Nerazi's rock, which was less crowded with humans. I hoped nothing had gone wrong with the nests.

"Good evening to you, Heeterskyte," I said, politely. "Please forgive my inattention. I have much to think on."

"That's all right," said the heeterskyte. "Just a friendly word, deah: There's some business goin' on up north tonight, and us who've come down thisaway for a spell, so's to give it a miss."

I stared down into the bright beady eyes.

"What kind of business?"

"Man Business," the heeterskyte returned, unconcerned. "Nothin' to do with us or ours, 'ceptin' to crowd the beach. Best you stay clear of it, too."

"I thank you, Heeterskyte, for your care," I said, keeping my voice low.

"That's all right," the heeterskyte said again, and darted away toward the notch.

I stood where I was and posed a question to the land.

At once there came before my mind's eye Nerazi's rock, the boundary marker between Archers Beach and Surfside. I saw three men at the stone, all wearing dark clothing. One had a gun in his hand, muzzle pointing at the sand; another was fiddling with his ear, fingertips following what must've been a wire down into his collar.

All three had the unmistakeable bearing of policemen—efficient and apparently happy in their work. My assumption was that they were observers, and backup, and that the real action was further upcoast, beyond the boundary, where I had no eyes or ears.

Thoughtfully, I moved on, 'round the base of Heath Hill, to the harbor.

The dock was empty. I could see *Gray Lady* at her mooring, deck light on, and felt a flash of disappointment—which immediately turned to self-mockery.

I'd said I'd stop by tonight after my meeting, but I hadn't set a time, having no clue how long that meeting would run. And had I had the wit to call the man when the meeting was done and I was on my way? Not Kate Archer.

Honestly, Kate; he's not a mind-reader.

I dug my phone out of my pocket, flipped it open and hit speed-dial.

"'Evenin'." Borgan's voice was warm in my ear.

I smiled. "Good evening," I answered.

Across the water, I saw a dark shadow come out onto the *Lady*'s deck. I raised an arm and waved vigorously. "Visiting hours over?"

"Not a bit of it. You stand right where you are for a tick."

The phone went dead. Borgan vanished toward the stern. The next moment I heard a quiet splash, and saw a dinghy advancing across the dark water, propelled by a lone oarsman.

My stomach fluttered; but it was, I decided firmly, a good flutter.

Smiling, I settled the bag over my shoulder and walked down to the ladder to wait.

❈　　❈　　❈

"You go ahead and claim a chair. I'll just nip down and pour you a glass of wine," Borgan said a few minutes later.

"If you don't mind," I said, feeling shyer than I hoped I sounded. "I brought a few things." I settled the straps of the canvas bag on my shoulder again.

He blinked, and for a heartbeat I thought he was going to cry. Then he wrapped his arms around me and drew me close. I put my arms around his waist, and leaned my head against his chest.

"Sure you did," he said, his voice rumbling against my ear. I felt him kiss the top of my head. Then he let me go, and led the way below.

T-shirt, jeans, socks, underwear, toothbrush, and comb all fit comfortably into the lower shelf. I folded the canvas bag and put it on the top shelf, next to the beach stone, and went out to the galley.

Borgan had two wineglasses out on the counter, and was addressing the bottle with the corkscrew in a manner than suggested very little familiarity with the process. I propped myself against the bulkhead at the end of the counter and crossed my arms over my chest, wondering if I should offer to help.

"Any news?" Borgan asked, his attention on the corkscrew. It was a ferocious-looking contraption all of silver-colored metal, with a cork-hat, and wings, and a screw that looked like it'd been a drill to China in its previous life. It seemed obvious from his question that I shouldn't offer to help, so I obediently delivered up news.

"Heeterskyte says there's Man Business going on up north. I saw three at Nerazi's rock, but nothing else, which I guess means the action's at Surfside. Or even Pine Point."

Borgan nodded, having finally gotten the corkscrew's hat positioned properly over the cork.

"Coasties been out in numbers, with their stealthy hats on. I'm figurin' your neighbor's got another load of never-you-mind comin' in tonight."

"So we'll find out if Ulme's an Ozali, real soon now."

"That'll be interestin'."

"It will," I agreed, and paused, considering if I had any other news.

"I took a walk around town today, just to see how things were looking, with the Season started, and I—I don't want to jinx anything, but we have crowds; we have people walking all the way up to almost the top of the hill to check out the art gallery.

Joan Anderson says business is rocking. She's been talking to the other shop owners up at the top, and they're going to the town for a permit to block off Archer Avenue from Route Five down to Seavey Street some Wednesday night real soon now, and throw a multiple open house street party."

"Ambitious," Borgan said. He put the corkscrew down with a sigh.

"That's quite an instrument," I said, picking it up; it weighed at least half a ton. "Where'd you get it?"

"Ahzie sold it to me, with the wine."

I turned the bottle so I could see the label: Snow Pond Chardonnay. There were worse bottles of wine in the world. And, to Ahz's credit, there were more expensive bottles of wine in the world, too.

"Sold me the glasses, too," said Borgan. "Told me it was bad form to give a lady her wine in a coffee mug."

I grinned. "That Ahz is a classy one."

"I was grateful for his advice. Just shoulda had 'im give me a tutorial with that thing, is all."

"I can do that," I said. "If you still want one."

His lips bent into a slight smile and he nodded.

"Sure could use some help," he said.

We carried our glasses topside.

I was wearing one of Borgan's sweaters, with the sleeves rolled, so I could use my hands, because the breeze had acquired some teeth.

At the rail, I stopped, and raised my glass.

"A toast!" I said, feeling equal parts giddy and shy.

Borgan raised his glass and waited.

"To the land and the sea," I offered.

"Stronger together than apart," Borgan added, and we drank.

"That's good," he said, sounding surprised.

"You thought Ahz would sell you bad wine?"

"No, Ahzie's solid. It's just that I don't know wine; didn't know what to expect, exactly."

"Well, now you know. You may," I said magnanimously, "invite me over whenever you care to have wine."

"I'll remember that."

We pulled our chairs close and leaned against each other, watching the stars, and the dark waters, sipping our wine.

The wine wasn't calming me down; it was bringing me an edge, not unpleasant, but not familiar, either. The breeze whispered starry promises in my ear, and I leaned closer to Borgan...

"Coasties're closing up," he said quietly. "Guess they got their lads against the shore."

I queried the land, receiving, as I had expected, a tight view of the Boundary Stone. The three men had gone; I saw no sign of Nerazi.

"Can you tune in to the whole Gulf of Maine?" I asked with some interest.

"Can, but there's no sense to be got out of it, if I do. Best just to let things float to the top."

I nodded.

"I hear music," I confided. "Like an orchestra playing in my head, all the time." I grinned in the dark. "Unless there's an emergency. Then, it gets noisy."

"Goes without sayin'. But an orchestra, that makes sense, the land havin' so many different parts."

There was a loud splash, just beyond the deck, as if somebody had thrown a rock into the water.

"Now, what...?"

Borgan got up, and looked over the rail. There came another splash, slightly louder than the first.

"Damn it."

"Problem?" I asked, rising and moving to the rail. I looked over, but all I saw were waves, running a bit rougher than they had been—no.

Running a bit rougher, yes.

But *only* under *Gray Lady*.

"Let me guess—you're needed elsewhere."

Borgan turned to face me, mouth wry.

"Timing," he said. "I'm wanted upcoast where the action is. The seafolk are mustering an assist on the side of the law."

I laughed, and after a moment, he grinned.

"You're right; it is comical. 'Specially the part where I'm to keep matters from crossin' a line. Still, though—I'm wanted, and I need to go."

"Go on, then," I said. "Duty is duty." I hesitated. "Can I ask you to row me over to the dock, or will that slow you down too much?"

"Won't slow me down at all."

He slipped the glass out of my hand, and vanished belowdecks, reappearing almost immediately to lead the way to the dinghy.

"Here we go." He swung me onto the dock, and came up to stand beside me, looking down with that rueful look.

"You'll be all right, walkin' home?"

I laughed up at him.

"Exactly as all right as you're going to be keeping the seafolk out of the Coast Guard's way."

He snorted.

"I'm guessing that's fair," he said. "Be careful, Kate."

He bent and kissed me, quick, but sweet, and stepped back.

"You be careful, too," I told him.

"Carefullest thing in all the Gulf o'Maine," he promised.

And without further ado, he dove off the dock, into the black water.

I stepped up to the rail and looked with land-sharpened sight, but I didn't see him surface. After a while, I turned and walked up the beach, toward home.

CHAPTER TWENTY-EIGHT

Friday, June 23
High Tide 10:04 A.M.
Sunrise 5:01 A.M. EDT

The coffee was brewing, the bagel was toasting, the french windows onto the summer parlor were open, curtains dancing in a stiffish breeze off the ocean. It was a good morning, all things taken into account, and I sang along with the Black Crowes, as I poured cream into my mug.

There was a step on the outside stairs. I reached into the cabinet for another mug, and had it down by the time Peggy pushed open the door, newspaper in hand and asked, "Breakfast club still open?"

"Sure," I said. "We can split the first bagel while the second one's toasting. There's cream cheese and peanut butter in the fridge."

She came in, put the paper on the kitchen table, and opened the fridge while I poured coffee, got a second plate out of the cabinet, and scooped a couple of butter knives from the silverware drawer.

"How's it going?" I asked, carrying the plates to the table. The breeze was 'way too stiff for alfresco on the porch.

"Going good. *Really* good."

I glanced down at the *Journal-Trib*'s front page.

PUC Considers Rate Increase Request

...and sighed.

"Not what you were hoping to see?" Peggy asked, bringing peanut butter, strawberry jam, and cream cheese to the table.

I shook my head, half in self-mockery. Whatever Man Business had gone down last night had certainly been concluded long after the *Journal-Trib* had gone to bed.

"Just looking for word of a friend," I said, and tossed the paper at the couch. It fell short, pages fluttering; spreading full color advertising inserts over the floor.

"So," Peggy continued, "what d'you want on your bagel?"

"Cream cheese."

"I will deal," she said. "You go hack another one in half and get it toasting."

"Sure thing, boss." I turned to the counter.

By the time the second bagel was toasting, both first courses had been spread handsomely with peanut butter—her—and cream cheese—me.

I sat down, took a sip of coffee, and grinned at her.

"So, it's going *really* well?"

"I shouldn't say more." Her eyes were wide. "Don't want to jinx a good thing." She took a bite of bagel; I did the same, and for a little while the only thing that was going on was concentrated chewing.

"I still need to get somebody to help out at The Mango," Peggy said eventually, "so I don't have to be Wonder Woman and do it all. I got a greenie in, like you suggested, but the intricacies of the juicers were beyond him. Also, I think he didn't like getting all sticky and berry-spattered."

"Seriously?" I asked, sipping coffee.

"There's no accounting for some people's foibles," she told me earnestly. "Anyhow, I'm keeping up so far, mostly motivated by fear, because it's *fatal* to fall behind on Arbitrary and Cruel's reports. Unfortunately, I see a day when I'm going to fall behind, because I'm tellin' you, Archer, there are people in this town who are *serious* about their smoothies."

"Well, I'm an idiot, which we know because I used to sling code for a living, but I could probably learn to make smoothies, and I don't mind getting splattered—" *which I wouldn't be*, I added silently. "I'm available 'til three-fifty, most days."

Peggy snorted. "After which you go to do your thing with the merry-go-round until ten or midnight."

"Every other day," I pointed out.

She shook her head.

"I think the goal here has to be that *neither* of us gets toasted. Speaking of which..." She got up, plate in hand.

I chewed the last bite of bagel, nodding my thanks when a second toasted half hit my plate.

This time I went with strawberry jam.

"That looks good," Peggy said.

"Is good," I told her, pushing the jar toward her. "Homemade."

"Seriously? You know somebody who makes jam?"

I laughed. "Mrs. Kristanos makes her own jam, and, before you ask, she told me that she finds time by putting her kids to work her shifts at Dynamite."

"For which small sacrifice, they get homemade jam," Peggy said, applying jam with a will. "There's no place else on *earth* where you can get a deal like that."

"Point."

I got up to fetch the coffeepot and the creamer, and freshened both of our mugs.

"So, everything's going good for you?" Peggy asked eventually, over the dregs of her bagel. "The boyfriend's not being an ass?"

"Not an ass," I said. "He does have some attitude, though."

"Well, you want that; otherwise you'd walk all over him, and then you'd get bored."

"True. I'm a terrible person."

"You are, but I like you." She cocked a sapient eye. "Something bothering you?"

"Well..." I sipped coffee while I weighed whether or not I wanted to bring this up. On the one hand, Peggy was almost certain to have more practical experience in the area than I did. On the other hand, I wasn't used to discussing private matters with, well...anyone.

I set my mug on the table, picked up the bagel, and met her eye.

"It's going a little slow, I think."

"Yeah? He didn't strike me as the shy type."

"Not shy." I felt compelled to defend Borgan's honor. "Just..." I took a bite of bagel and chewed, considering.

"Careful," I said eventually. "I've got some...bad history."

Peggy nodded. "He know that?"

"Yeah..."

"Well then, it's your move, Archer! If he's worth having around, he won't want to hurt you *or* rush you, right?"

I sighed. "Right."

"So if you want to go faster, woman—go faster!" She eyed me over the rim of her mug. "You didn't want to do *any* of the work?"

"I'm lousy at relationships."

"Only way to get better is practice," she told me. "Just like everything else."

"And if I make a mistake and screw everything up?"

"That sucks," Peggy said. "It really does." She gave me a lopsided grin. "See, I know that because I'm lousy at relationships, too."

"What a team."

She laughed and chugged what was left in her mug.

"We should do this at my place sometimes, so you don't have to do all the work."

"My God, but the labor of making a pot of coffee I was going to make anyway, and toasting a bagel I was going to toast anyhow will wear me to the bone! Besides, you don't make breakfast."

"A little respect, please. I have two *different* kinds of Pop-Tarts in inventory!"

"I had no idea."

"Yeah, well now you do." She gave me a grin. "I better go. I'm glad the breakfast club hadn't shut down."

"Me, too," I said truthfully. "If you can hold up a sec, I'll walk down with you."

"Sure thing," she said. "Pretty morning for a walk."

I left Peggy at the midway gate, and crossed to Fountain Circle.

Even so early on a Friday, the place was crammed. The cement tables were full of people and their breakfast picnics of dough-nuts, coffee, french fries, pizza, soda. The air was redolent with hot grease, and the sound of voices wove into the background of gull calls, surf, and simulated mayhem from the arcade, to make a kind of music almost as seductive as Henry's fiddle.

I found a place to sit on the edge of the fountain, and turned my face up to the sun, letting the murmur and shout of voices wash over me. So far the Season was a success. The hope now being that it would continue as it had begun, that the weather would hold, with every weekend sunny, and rain falling tidily, and only after midnight.

Not anything I had control over; I wasn't a weather-worker. In fact, I wasn't sure that weather-working was really viable, given the various balances and checks imposed by the environment. Be an interesting thing to ask Mr. Ignat'.

I sighed and opened my eyes.

To my left on the fountain lip was a middle-aged woman in a pretty print dress and sensible flat sandals; her eyes hidden by sunglasses, her fingers wrapped in the leash of the tiny, fluffy black dog asleep on her ankle.

To my right, a boy in what looked to be his late teens had a baby in a chest sling. The baby was zoned out. The boy had his eyes closed and his face tipped up toward the sun, as if taking the benediction of the light.

Honey on the land—who had said that? I wondered, and then had it: Felsic. Something about the work in the midway pouring honey on the land to sweeten the sour times.

Odd sort of person, Felsic.

A shadow passed before me; the little dog jumped up from his nap with an excited yap, and his mistress said, "You're late."

"I couldn't find a place to park," a potbellied man in a Hawaiian shirt, blue shorts and flip-flops told her. "This place is *packed*."

"It's summer," the woman said, standing, and slipped her hand into his. "Let's go down to the water."

Hand-in-hand, they crossed the circle, the little dog gamboling at the end of his string.

I sighed, relaxed under the sun's grace...and felt a tiny tickle along my spine, as if someone had touched my *jikinap*.

Relaxation fled; I closed my eyes again, listening with every sense available to me. The tickle came again—and I had it.

Something was going wrong again with the rooster.

"Damn the bird," I muttered, and opened my eyes.

A little girl with flyaway yellow curls, her outfit a cacophony of pinks to match her round cheeks, was staring at me—or maybe she was staring at the place to sit, next to me, where the woman and the dog had been.

"Sally, don't bother that lady," said a plump woman with the same flyaway curls, who was pushing a stroller with one hand and trying to balance two coffees and a bag of doughnuts with the other.

Senses tingling, I got up and gave the woman a smile.

"In fact, I've got to be getting to work," I told her. "Have a seat."

She returned the smile, and steered the stroller in. "Thank you!"

"No problem," I assured her.

I angled across the circle and up, toward the beach, jogging by the time I hit the tarmac.

Not too many minutes later, not jogging so much as bouncing, I came 'round the curve of the carousel's storm wall, key in hand—

And braked hard, staring at the door.

Which was *already* unlocked.

I queried the land, which assured me that Nancy was *not* inside the storm gates; nor, when that question was put, was Vassily.

I pulled out my cell, and hit speed-dial.

Nancy's cell rang in my ear—once, twice, three times, four...

And went to voice mail.

"It's Kate, Nancy. Give me a call when you get a chance."

I flipped the phone closed and slipped it away, staring at the door with a decided feeling of ill-use.

Only one way to find out what's going on, Kate, I told myself.

I pushed the door open, quietly, and stepped inside.

Hot air rushed at me, my senses near overpowered with the scent of ripe peaches. *Jikinap* shot up my spine, questing, even as I turned and saw that the carousel was turning slowly inside a curtain of living green flame, like the Northern Lights made small and contained... and shimmering with power.

Somebody—some unknown Ozali doubtless shielded by the coruscating flames—was trying to open the Gate!

I brought my power to hand, hefted it like a broadsword and brought it slashing downward.

Mr. Ignat' would have chided me; there was neither finesse nor elegance in the action.

It did, however, *work*.

The curtain shredded, blowing in the hot air before dissipating, leaving a fading trail of golden sparks. Beyond, I could see the carousel slowing, the animals—*all* of the animals, including the rooster—glowing as if they possessed *voysin* of such purity that it shone through the wood that encased them...

Except *voysin* was a substance irretrievably attached to the soul... which carousel animals, saving five very special carousel animals, do *not* possess.

I ducked under the safety rail and moved toward the carousel, *jikinap* and the land questing. According to those various sets of senses, I was alone inside the enclosure. Whoever had set up the Gate-crash had fled—possibly camouflaged by the twin bursts of heat and stink...

It occurred to me, as a peripheral thing, that it was still too hot inside the storm walls. I waved a hand, and a breeze sprang up, cool and damp and tasting of salt. Nodding approval, I jumped onto the carousel.

The first thing I did upon stepping Sideways was to check the master spell and the wards on the Gate. Which were intact, of course. I couldn't have avoided hearing the noise, if the Gate had actually been opened.

Next, I brought my attention to the animal nearest me, which happened to be the moose. In Side-Sight, it contained a bonfire; blue-hot at the center and burning with a clear actinic light—*jikinap*, certain enough, with a little extra juice that might have been a pinch of *voysin*. I didn't quite see what the use of it all was—then hunger roared through me, leaving me weak-kneed, and I had the answer.

My arm around the moose's neck, I breathed in, tasting ripe peaches, and accepted that each and every animal on the carousel had been filled with *jikinap*.

Never mind *open*; I'd interrupted an attempt to *blow* the Gate wide.

And, I thought, looking around me, feeling my power yammer to consume more of itself—and, if they had just left the rooster alone, rather than trying to displace the working I'd left in it...

They might have succeeded.

That would have been bad. Even magical explosions can destroy real things.

Kill real people.

My stomach clenched and I swallowed bile. I closed my eyes and concentrated on taking deep breaths.

When I was feeling steadier, I opened my eyes, and straightened from my lean against the moose. The glow of *voysin* was bright enough to make me squint.

Well, I couldn't just *leave* it here, potential threat to life as we know it.

And there was only one way that I knew of to render loose power harmless.

Accordingly, I centered myself... and breathed in.

CHAPTER TWENTY-NINE

Low Tide 1:58 P.M. EDT

I was sitting in the chariot, hot, bloated, and shivering, when I heard a step in the door, and a voice call out.

"Who is here?"

"Kate," I managed, making some shift to sit up straight and get my eyes decently open. Wouldn't do for the help to find the boss falling down drunk.

Not that I could think of a way to avoid it.

I heard footsteps crossing the floor, and then a light thump, which must have been Vassily jumping to the platform.

More footsteps, and here the child was, his *voysin* burning in his breast like a votive table in a church.

He stopped a prudent distance from me, his hand on the lion's rump.

"Are you ..." he paused, perhaps hesitating over the proper word. He licked his lips and tried again. "Are you an angel from heaven?"

I blinked at him, having expected that "well?" would be following "are you." It was on the tip of my *jikinap*-loosened tongue to tell him to stop talking nonsense, and I looked down to gain some measure of control.

Whereupon, I saw my own hand, resting on my knee. The glow of my newly increased power made a fairly pedestrian brown and work-roughened member into a thing of strength and beauty. Tears rose to my eyes, just looking at it—absolute perfection, the ideal to which all hands must strive...

I yanked my thoughts back from *that* edge, before I took a nasty tumble, and looked back up to Vassily.

"No," I said, wisely not shaking my head. "Not an angel."

He nodded. "Are you in pain?"

That was better, I thought, peach and butterscotch at war on the back of my tongue.

"I'm a little under the weather, nothing to worry about," I told him, hoping that wasn't mere optimism.

It had by now occurred to me that I might have done something that wasn't particularly smart. Though I'd imbibed *jikinap* previously, I'd apparently not noticed an important fact.

Mr. Ignat' had *given* me his magic, and, beyond finding myself the unwilling vessel, I'd borne no ill effects.

I'd also stolen *jikinap*—a boatload of the stuff. And that had gotten me power-drunk, out of control, and slightly mad. That time, the survival of the land had been on the table, and I wasn't tracking very well, anyway—see drunk, crazy, and beside myself, above.

This time, there wasn't any deadly enemy into whom I could more or less immediately release the power I had ingested. The only thing I could do was digest what I had eaten, and endure until the new power settled in.

"The door was open," Vassily said, carefully, "and you are here. Am I...dismissed?"

The kid's worried about his job—and his dinner. Focus, Kate.

"No," I assured him, taking care with my diction. "I just... stopped by. The door was open when I got here."

His eyes widened. "The animals—the wheel—there is no damage?"

"Everything looks good. Guess Nancy just forgot to put the lock through the loop on her way out last night."

"This does not seem like her."

"No," I agreed, "it doesn't." I leaned forward, testing my balance. I'd been unsteadier.

The worst problem was my head, which was pounding like a

Ginger Baker drum solo. I really didn't relish the prospect of taking it outside to meet Midsummer's brilliant sky. Lesser problems were my stomach—definitely queasy—and my balance—not great.

"Why don't you open up," I suggested to Vassily, "while I finish getting myself sorted out here? I'll be out of your way in a couple minutes."

"Yes," he said, and crossed the platform, jumping lightly to the floor.

I heard his steps, and then the clatter of the storm gates being opened.

Tentatively, I slid carefully across the bench, got to my feet, and exited the chariot from the money side, holding tightly onto the edge so that I didn't overbalance on the climb to the floor.

By the time I'd gotten myself onto solid land, Vassily had the walls locked back. I straightened, forcing my spine straight by millimeters. My mouth tasted too much of magic, and my nasal passages seemed to have captured the odor of ripe peaches, so that every breath brought me the scent.

I've never really liked peaches.

"Am I to bring Anna?" Vassily asked from beside me. "You do not look well."

"Just a little bug; gone in no time," I assured him. "I'm going to go home and lie down. Be back at four."

"If you are ill later," Vassily said, sounding stern, "you will not come. I will work longer, or Nancy will come."

"You got it, boss man."

"This is a joke?"

"Joke," I affirmed, swallowing hard, and tasting only peaches. I reached out and patted him on the arm. "I'll be fine."

I could walk a reasonably straight line, if I concentrated and took it slow, which I did, leaving the carousel by the exit gate, rather than risk ducking under the safety rail.

Outside, the sunlight was a hammer, striking my head. And with each blow, I tasted more peaches and less butterscotch.

Kate, you idiot, what did you do?

I could barely see in the blare of sunlight; it felt like the next hammer blow would knock my head clean off. Eyes watering, I let the land guide me, staggering like your drunken sailor, to the fountain.

I collapsed to the lip, closed my eyes against the punishment of the sun, and concentrated on not throwing up. The land whimpered, and pawed my hand, but I didn't dare...didn't dare open myself to its healing until I knew what I had taken on. Poisoning the land—not in the job description.

Phone, I thought laboriously, and, eyes screwed shut, fished it out of my pocket, flipped it open and hit speed-dial, wondering who I'd just called.

"Kate?" Peggy's voice was brisk. "Listen, can I call you back?"

"I need help," I said, my voice slurring.

"Where are you?" she asked, sharp now.

"Fountain."

"I'm sending somebody. Stay on the line."

"Thank you."

"Stay on the line! Kate?"

"Here."

"What happened?"

What happened, the woman asked.

"Kate. *Tell me what happened.*"

"Ate something...that didn't want to be, to be..."

"Have I *told* you never to eat the blue cotton candy?"

I half-laughed, which was almost disastrous, and swallowed hard.

"Here you are, now, Guardian," a low familiar voice was cool in my ear; a hand comfortable on my shoulder.

"Felsic," I said.

"That's right." I felt something settle on my head. "This'll help, maybe. Wicked bright today. Now, you just lean on me; we'll get you up an' out o'the sun in a shake."

"Felsic, am I glowing?"

"A mite; nothin' to notice—not in this light. Come on now, I'm putting my arm 'round you."

True enough, a strong arm came around my waist and the next moment, with no real sense of how I'd gotten there, I was on my feet. I felt a touch of vertigo; opened my eyes to slits. The brim of Felsic's gimme hat threw an improbably deep shadow; I felt like I was standing in a cave.

"Nice cap."

"Does what it's s'posed to. Had it donkey's years. Peggy?"

"Here," she said. Hell; I'd forgotten about the phone.

"We'll be at The Mango in a few—Kate needs to take it slow. Best if she puts the phone away."

"Got it. Should I call an ambulance?"

"No!" I said sharply. "I just...need a place to sleep it off."

There was a slight, charged pause, before Peggy spoke again.

"If, in my sole judgment, based on what sort of hell you look like when you get here, you don't need an ambulance, you can sleep in the office."

"You're a champ, Jersey," I said, and signed off, sliding the phone into the pocket of my jeans.

We'd gone two slow, easy steps, when I noticed a cool, salty energy seeping into my veins. It cooled the fever and for a moment only, I was profoundly grateful. Then, I remembered.

"Don't!" I snapped, stumbling in my distress. "I *don't know* what I got into. You don't want to—don't want to share this."

"That's all right," Felsic crooned, adjusting for my stumble with no noticeable strain. "Don't fatch, Kate. Just a little home brew; nothin' taken; only givin'."

"I can't wait to see the bill for that," I muttered.

Felsic laughed.

"You look like hell," Peggy said, staring hard into my face. "Falling-down-drunk hell. Or maybe epic-migraine hell. Not ambulance hell." She pointed at the desk. "You may use the emergency couch."

"Thank you. 'Preciate." I sat on the edge, and took a deep breath. Felsic's little draught of home brew had settled my stomach, and cooled the fever; but my tongue was still saturated with peach; my nose clogged with it.

"Just by the way," Peggy said. She pulled Felsic's hat off my head, and held it out to its owner. "You *are* glowing. I *knew* the blue stuff is radioactive."

"Cracks in the head?" I asked.

"None visible. You want some Advil?"

"Won't help, thanks."

She looked like she was going to argue that, but the buzzer rasped, cutting her off.

"When do I wake you?" she asked, moving toward the door.

"In time to relieve Vassily at four."

"Got it." She passed through the door into The Mango. I heard her voice, brightly suggesting today's special smoothie, banana-raspberry.

Felsic had replaced the gimme hat, and gave me a hard look from under that deep brim.

"What happened?"

I sighed. "Somebody was trying to take out the Gate."

Felsic's eyes widened.

"Anything we ought do?"

I sighed. "If you see an unfamiliar glowing Ozali come into the midway, run."

Felsic nodded, looking serious, patted my shoulder, and went away.

I got myself into the middle of the desk, rolled up the purple sweatshirt for a pillow, closed my eyes and willed myself to sleep.

I dreamed.

I dreamed that I stood in a world strange to me, dazzled by a landscape so saturated with light that the very air burned. There was music—singing, so I thought, and then thought that what I heard must be the voice of the wind in this place.

The light was thick and heavy, like honey, or molten gold. It coated me where I stood, binding me to the brilliant land.

Before me, I descried bell-shaped flowers on bending stalks lining a winding path, and in the distance, trees with branches limned in silver, leaves dripping with the heavy light.

The golden air rippled above the path, and a shape appeared— manlike, tall and lissome. Rainbow wings arced from his shoulder blades, each feather as sharp as a shard of glass. He was quite naked, and, to my dream-eyes, sexless.

"Release me!" The voice that disturbed the wind's whisperings was raw, dark with anger and pain. "Release mine!"

"I'm not holding you," I objected, my voice a meager thing against the majesty of this place.

"Who are you?" the angry voice demanded.

"I'm the Gatekeeper," I said.

"Gatekeeper! Say, more truly, jailer!"

"That, too," I agreed. "We're all of us many things."

"Then, hear me, Jailer. I give you the opportunity to avoid mayhem. Release what is mine!"

"To the best of my knowledge, I don't have anything of yours," I said.

"You hold Jaron, Varoth's fairest son, my second self. Release him to me." Slowly, he sank to one knee. "I abase myself. I beg you."

"I am powerless," I told him, spreading my hands against the heavy air. "It's not given me, to know who the prisoners are. Petition the Wise—"

"The Wise!" He came to his feet with a great clashing of wings. "It was the Wise who tore him from my arms!"

"I am powerless," I repeated—

The rainbow wings clashed. The light tore, the landscape shredded, and a maelstrom shrieked from the black air; I took flight on wings of my own, battling the winds, until I rose, panting, into my own body...

...and woke to the scent of pineapples and strawberries, on the desk in the office behind The Last Mango.

I sat up, shaking my head to clear the vision of the angry Varothi.

"I definitely need a cat."

The door opened, and Peggy put her head into the room.

"It's three-forty. You good to go, or you want to call in relief?"

I took stock. The inside of my head felt tender with the aftermath of the headache, but it wasn't actively throbbing. The queasiness had passed off, leaving me hungry, and I felt like my skin was a good fit for me, neither too loose nor too tight.

"I'm good to go," I told Peggy, rolling off the desk. "Thirsty."

"I'll make you a smoothie," she said. "Dinner *and* a thirst quencher, all in one handy cup. In the meantime, the bathroom's back there." She pointed. "You need to wash up and rebraid."

I nodded, and turned in the direction of the point.

"Oh, and—" Peggy said. I looked at her over my shoulder.

"You're not glowing anymore," she said, opening her eyes wide before she ducked back through the door.

CHAPTER THIRTY

———— ᖫᖰ ————

High Tide 8:25 P.M.
Sunset 8:26 P.M. EDT

I reached the carousel, smoothie in hand, on the stroke of four, to find a line snaking from the operator's station all the way back to Fun Country's front gate. Vassily reported that he had been exactly this busy all day. Apparently, overwork agreed with him. He seemed almost happy, his face animated, and his eyes sparkling.

"It is beautiful."

He actually smiled, waving at the carousel, a rider on every animal; random rays of sunshine caressing the brass and teasing glints from the mirrors.

"It is," I agreed. "Very beautiful."

His hands resting lightly on the controls, he turned his head to look at me.

"You are well?"

"I'm well," I told him—not a complete fib. "It's after four. How 'bout you go get your dinner and let me have some fun?"

He started and blinked, as if I'd derailed a serious train of thought.

"Yes," he said after he'd caught up with himself again. "My shift is over and I will eat my dinner. Good-night, Kate Archer. Thanking you."

"You're welcome—now, git!"

He got.

I stepped up to the control board after putting the smoothie out of harm's way on the floor, rang the bell twice to signal the end of the ride, and slid various levers gently downward.

The carousel spun slowly to a stop. Riders disembarked, and headed for the exit gate.

I turned to the first person in line, and gave her a smile. "Good afternoon. Two tickets, please."

...and that was pretty much my next eight hours. The crowd started to thin around 11:30. At 11:50, the lights began to go out on Baxter Avenue. I took that as a sign, turned off the roof light, and shut the storm walls, locking myself inside the carousel's enclosure.

Privacy thus assured, I did a complete inspection—physical and magical—of the carousel, its critters and keepings.

Everything was as it should be; I detected no secret stashes of *jikinap,* nor any rogue wards. The animals were as they should be; the prisoners were as *they* should be; the wards and spells associated with the Gate were intact. Even the damn' rooster was looking good.

Mindful of my bad reaction earlier in the day, I stepped back and considered the state of myself. The headache had completely vanished, my stomach was steady, and my mind was clear. When I breathed in, all I tasted was salt, sand, hot grease, and sea rose.

It would appear that my unwilling prize had been assimilated.

A trill sounded from the depths of my pocket. I fished my cell out and flipped it open.

"Sorry I'm so long calling back, Kate," Nancy Vois' low, raspy voice told me.

"Not a problem. I just wanted to let you know that I came down to the carousel early this morning—and the door was open."

There was a longish pause.

"I locked 'er up good 'n' tight last night before I left," Nancy said. After a much briefer pause, she added, cautiously, "Is everything...good?"

"A little mischief made; no lasting harm done."

"That's all right, then," she said with a sigh. "You change the lock?"

"Haven't yet. Will by tomorrow. I'll leave the new key with Anna."

"Right."

"Thanks for calling back," I said.

"No problem. You take care now."

She hung up.

I looked up at the carousel as I slipped the phone back into my pocket.

Eight hours of honest labor had given my brain time to sort out what it was willing to believe and what it wasn't willing to believe, leaving me with a list of what I was willing to call facts.

One, the dream I'd had in The Mango's backroom? Wasn't a dream; it had been an actual conversation with an Ozali of Varoth, the Land of Air and Sunshine. Considering that I'd consumed a good amount of his *jikinap*, such a conversation was completely in the realm of the possible.

Two, the Varothi threatened mayhem, unless I freed his lover.

Which—point three—I couldn't do. I didn't know who the prisoners were. *Gran* didn't know who the prisoners were. The *prisoners* didn't know who they were, because the Wise had taken their memories.

Four, the Varothi felt that a petition to the Wise would be useless. Happens I agreed with him there.

Five, his plea to myself having gained a negative result, he was going to try to free Jaron again.

I sighed, and wondered if *I* should call the Wise. I was loath to do it, for all the usual reasons. And, even if calling the Wise *was* the best course, a call tonight was unlikely to garner an instant response. I'm not precisely sure on what plane or land beyond time the Wise dwelt in—if they even lived together—but the mail delivery to wherever they were was wicked slow.

All of which meant that the Gate had to be warded like hell, right now, tonight.

I frowned at the unicorn, thinking.

The Gate was heavily warded and opening it in a nonexplosive sort of way required a very tricksy bit of magecraft. Screw up, and all that would be left of the carousel would be a smoking crater. Given what I'd found cooking here this morning, it seemed safe to assume that the possibility of an explosive outcome didn't bother the Varothi.

Which meant that I was, right now, going to build the biggest, baddest, toughest ward possible, and then I was going to take advice on how to proceed on the larger questions of the Varothi, his lover, and the Wise.

Wards are easy, relatively speaking. Righteous wards that won't buckle under a bulldozer just wanted a lot of power to fuel them. I thought about that, given the amount of power I'd seen burning here this morning, and flexed my fingers.

A medium heavy-duty ward with a reflector woven into it, I thought, so that anything tossed at it would bounce.

I could do that.

Tomorrow, early, I'd get with Mr. Ignat' about building something more flexible. I also wanted to talk with Borgan, Nerazi, and Gran about the situation and the pros and cons of calling in the Wise.

Hell, it was late enough, I'd probably find Nerazi at her rock, if I cared to walk that way after I got done here.

First, though, I needed to get done here.

I straightened, centered myself, and called upon my power.

It flashed up my spine, burning, searing every cell, filling me with light so heavy I crashed to my knees. I gasped, gagging on peach-tainted air as thick as cream. Heart pounding, half-strangled, I thrust the power back to the base of my spine with the strength of pure panic, filled my lungs with salt-soaked air—

And the burning flare of *jikinap* came roaring back, knocking me flat to the floor, my mouth clogged with too-thick air.

Instinctively, I snatched for the land, but the land couldn't help me, not with this.

Or—

I brought the land . . . close, and I whispered into its distressed, doggy ear: *I need help.*

Every *trenvay* in Archers Beach would hear that message. Which begged the question of what they might *do*, that the Guardian herself could not.

In the meantime, the situation had gone from bad to worse. My lungs were burning; it felt like my *blood* was burning, while the weight of the light ground me into the floor.

If I didn't do *some*thing, I was going to die. Right here.

Right now.

I gathered my fragmented will, dark spots swirling before my eyes, and *pushed*.

The punishing power retreated, just a little.

Just enough.

I could breathe.

One breath. Two.

Again, I gathered my will.

...and the door in the storm gate, that I had so carefully locked from the inside, blew open.

"Kate!"

A wave of blessedly cool water lifted me above the agony, my skin tingled with salt, and the air was fresh, bracing, and plentiful.

I slammed my will against the burning power. It gave, but not much. I hit it again, but it was like punching a rhinoceros; my puny efforts were only making it mad. A little tongue of flame tickled the center of my chest; my heart cramped; I lost my concentration, and the rogue power flared.

I think I screamed.

"Kate!"

I was...somewhere else. If I had a body, I couldn't feel it. The only thing I could feel was Borgan, holding me—holding me in his strength, inside his power—and if I exploded, or ignited, would I poison the sea?

"No..." Somehow I struggled; felt Borgan's grip tighten.

"Kate. Listen to me, now. Let it go."

Well, there was a simple solution. Why hadn't I thought of that? Oh.

"Don't know how."

"Relax," Borgan told me. "Open your will and just—don't fight. *Do it now.*"

And he thrust me back into my body.

I couldn't have screamed if I'd tried, though I surely wanted to. As for relaxing my will...

The best I could manage was to curl into a ball, there inside my burning body, and hide.

It seemed that the attack abated; that the enemy within me withdrew somewhat to survey this new situation. In that moment of withdrawal, I heard the land whimper, and I reached out to comfort—

A blast of heat blew up my spine, exiting through the top of my head, like a lightning strike in reverse. The shock wave knocked me out of my protective curl, and I felt a tug, as though my soul, loosened by torment, sought to follow the lightning.

I embraced the land, and breathed in. My soul hesitated... and settled back into place.

At which point, I do believe that I blacked out.

I opened my eyes and looked up into Borgan's face, no more surprised to see him than to be lying against his chest, his arms supporting me.

"Timing," I said, my voice hoarse, "is everything."

"Lucky I came by," he agreed with a lightness that was belied by his eyes. "What happened?"

"You saved my life."

"Before that."

"I was trying to seal the carousel so the Ozali who tried to blow the Gate open earlier today doesn't get a second chance."

It was ridiculously hard to lift my hand and curl my fingers 'round his braid. I managed it, though. Cool comfort spread through me, and I pressed my forehead against his chest, so he wouldn't see the tears.

"Before *that*," I said hoarsely, "I ate something I shouldn't've and it was causing all kinds of hell."

"It was that." His arms tightened. "You're good, now."

"If only. Peggy saw me glowing, and I just used the land to broadcast the fact that, as a Guardian, I'm kind of a fuck-up."

"What I heard you say," Borgan said, "was, *I need help*. I might've decided not to come in past the lock if you hadn't, and gone on home with my feelin's hurt."

I laughed, which made my chest hurt—and turned my head toward the shredded metal wall. Nobody could accuse Borgan of not being thorough.

A shadow hovered at the edge of the wreckage. I couldn't quite see—but the land knew who it was.

"Gaby?" I said, knowing that she'd hear, despite my voice being so weak.

The shadow shifted, and she stepped through the hole in the wall, stopping just inside the enclosure.

"Heard a whisper, that the Guardian needed help," she said, with dignity. "Others're comin', but I was closest." She looked at Borgan, long and hard. "*He* ain't the problem."

"No, he's not the problem."

"What sort o'help, then, Guardian?"

I looked up into Borgan's face.

"Got to seal the carousel."

"I'll take care of that," Borgan said.

I shifted, meaning to stand up and let the man work—and realizing at that exact moment that there was no way my legs were going to hold me.

His arms tightened, not so much to keep me in place, I thought, but to prevent my falling.

"No need to go anywhere," he murmured. "Won't take a minute."

I smelled salt, and a rich, effervescent tang—Borgan's magical signature. His power rose around us, silky and cool; as unpretentious as the tide. Mist formed, alive with color, like sunlight seen through sea spray.

The mist expanded, rippling like spun-glass curtains, and draped itself 'round the carousel, peak to floor. I could see it still, but as if from a distance, filmy and not quite real behind the spray.

"That'll hold 'er," Borgan murmured, his power spiraling away, leaving us sitting dry and content on the gritty cement floor.

I looked over to Gaby, who'd been waiting, if not with patience, then at least without fuss. I thought I saw other shadows behind her, and outside the wall.

"If there's those among you who can repair the door, and lock up for the night, that would be a welcome service," I said.

Gaby tipped her head as if listening, then nodded.

"We can do that, Guardian. No cares."

"Good," I said, truly grateful. "I'll leave you to it, then."

Whereupon Borgan stood up, holding me in his arms as if I weighed exactly nothing, and was too fragile to go on my own two feet down the land of which I was Guardian...

...and I let him.

CHAPTER THIRTY-ONE

Saturday, June 24
Low Tide 4:39 A.M.
Sunrise 5:01 A.M. EDT

Fun Country's gate being locked, Borgan carried me out the back way, over the dunes to the beach.

He kept on carrying me, too, all the way to the surf line, and I kept on letting him.

The waning moon hadn't risen yet, and the tide was going out. The night was clear; the stars so bright even the lights from the Pier couldn't take their shine. Neptune's was open, naturally, with live music, too—one guy accompanying himself loudly on electric guitar. The song was either "Crimson and Clover" or "The Star-Spangled Banner"; I couldn't really be sure.

I'd almost died, I thought, and I shivered in Borgan's arms. If I'd had the energy, I might've laughed, too.

Ten weeks ago, I'd been well on my way to dying, and had made my peace with both the reality and the process. Or so I'd thought. Now, I wanted to hold on to life with both hands.

That's called irony.

"I'm taking you home," Borgan said, his voice a growl deep in his chest. And he waded into the sea.

"Deep breath," he commanded, and I managed it, holding the air in my lungs as a wave broke over our heads.

There was a moment, not unpleasant, and not long, where I was just floating, cool, fluid, and bodiless, surrounded by Borgan's power even though I was not aware of his arms.

Then my body returned, cradled in strong arms. I heard the crash of a wave, looked down to see foam curling 'round booted feet as Borgan strode up the beach.

We were both perfectly dry, and I was still hanging on to his braid like it was a lifeline.

He carried me over the boardwalk, and up the steps to my front door.

"Key," I muttered.

I raised my free hand, trying for the pocket, and the key in it, but it was too much effort, the pocket light-years away.

"May I enter?" Borgan asked, and his voice had changed again; it almost had a physical weight, and a resonance that brought tears to my eyes.

"Yes," I whispered. "Please enter and be welcome in my house, Borgan."

There came a click, distinct and sharp. Then the door—the same door that tended to swell and stick against the frame, and then required a firm kick to open—the door swung open and Borgan carried me into Gran's—into *my*—house.

The door closed behind him and I heard the snap of the lock engaging.

"Bedroom?" he murmured.

"Porch," I cleared my throat. "I don't want—to be locked in."

He paused, then turned to the right. The french doors swung open before him, and he carried me onto the summer parlor, and there he paused, where we could both overlook the sea.

"How d'you feel, Kate?"

"Like I've been poisoned, and had half the life choked out of me," I said, too exhausted to be anything but completely truthful. "Like I'd fall down if I tried to stand up."

"Do you need to go uptown?"

To the old Archer homestead, he meant: a place of power and renewal for those of the blood.

"This'll do fine," I assured him. "I'll—I just wish I had a cat."

"Cat?"

He sounded bemused, and who could blame him?

I made an effort to explain. "To keep the dreams away."

"Right."

He dropped smoothly to one knee; then, without jarring me in the least, arranged himself cross-legged on the deck. Carefully, he settled me on his lap. I lay against his chest, fingers twisted in his braid, a boneless thing, almost without will.

"Call the land," he murmured, his voice a comforting rumble in the ear I had pressed against his chest. "Heal yourself. There's no dream that'll get by me."

"You don't need to stay here."

"It's too late to get you a cat tonight. *Go to sleep*, woman."

Plainly, there was no arguing with him. I settled my cheek against his sweater, eyelids drooping, opened myself fully to the land...

...and went to sleep.

I stirred, and half-opened my eyes, seeing Borgan's face above me in the gray predawn.

His arms withdrew and I realized he had carried me inside to the couch and thrown the old afghan over me.

"Hush," he said, though I hadn't said anything. "I'm gonna go fish. You go back to sleep, Kate. And you call me when you wake up, all right?"

"All right," I said, still two-thirds asleep.

I felt his lips against my forehead, and closed my eyes, the land cuddled close, like a teddy bear.

The last thing I remember hearing was the lock snapping shut.

At 7:30, I woke again, fully this time, and fully healed, to a room overflowing with sunlight from the wide-open French doors, the curtains fluttering in the breeze. I took a deep breath, and for long moment could do nothing but marvel at how *well* I felt, and consider what a precious gift life was.

Then I remembered that I was supposed to call when I woke, and I pitched back the afghan and came to my feet, digging in my pocket for my cell phone...

...which, despite its dunking in the Atlantic Ocean early this morning, functioned just fine.

"Kate?" His voice was sharper than I was used to; I could feel the tension coming through the airwaves.

"Good morning," I said. "I'm awake, I'm rested, and I'm starving."

The sense of tension eased considerably.

"That sounds encouraging. How else do you feel?"

"Perfect," I told him honestly.

Relief positively flowed through my phone.

"I'm sorry I worried you," I said truthfully.

Borgan laughed. "I'm thinking that's going to be the state of things," he said ruefully. "From how you tell it, I'm not exactly a worry-free proposition. What're doin' today?"

"First thing after a shower and breakfast? Buying a lock."

"Good plan. This is your night off, right? Want to have dinner?"

I smiled. "Sounds great."

"Good, then. I'll be by your place around five-thirty."

"See you then. Be careful."

"Always."

The call ended.

I stood there, just holding the phone for a couple of heartbeats before I put it, with the rest of my pocket things, onto the coffee table, and skipped down the hall to take a shower.

Peggy hadn't come to breakfast. As near as I could tell, she hadn't come home last night.

While I walked up the hill, I tried to figure out if worrying about that was a sign of a control freak, or just normal concern for a friend who might be getting into something trickier than she knew.

Not to say that Peggy wasn't competent; she was damn' competent, and she'd obviously been taking good care of herself for a number of years. Except not in Archers Beach, which had peculiar dangers—not so much for plain vanilla folk, as for those who could hear the music on Midsummer Eve.

So, then: she was a competent woman who could take of herself . . . until she couldn't. Which pretty much put her on even footing with everybody I'd known, at home and Away, even as far as the Land of the Flowers.

That knotty problem settled, I swung into the hardware store. Ernie Travis was pulling the shades up on the big front window; I gave him a nod and a brisk "Good morning!" and headed for the back of the store.

A couple minutes later, I met him at the counter, carrying a Mul-T-Lock C padlock.

"Good lock," Ernie said, aiming the scan gun at the bar code.

"Hope so," I answered. "Somebody got around the one on the carousel yesterday."

He frowned, and shot a quick look into my face. "Everything okay?"

"Nothing broken or defaced. Still, it seems like a message from the universe about changing the lock."

He nodded. "It's a wonder how communicative the universe can be, sometimes. You're gonna be wanting extra keys for that?"

"Three, if you could."

"No trouble, just take a few." He punched keys on the register. "With the keys, that's one-thirty-two."

I offered my credit card, he swiped it and gave it back, then broke open the blister pack, extricated the key and moved to the other end of the counter, where the key machine crouched like a rust-colored tarantula. I broke the lock the rest of the way out of the packaging while Ernie fitted a blank onto the cutting surface, lined up the live key on the tracer, and hit the button.

There came a brief scream of metal; a spark flashed from the edge of the blank, and another. Then Ernie liberated the new key, gave it a quick grind on both sides, and tossed it onto the counter in front of me.

"Give that a minute, then see if it does what it oughta," he directed, and got busy fitting another blank onto the board.

I tried the new key in the padlock; it turned smoothly, tumblers clicking, and the shackle snapped open.

Excellent.

Keys number two and three speedily appeared; they also performed as they ought.

"Thank you!" I said, tucking them into the pockets of my jeans.

"Say, Kate?" Ernie said, his voice pitched a little lower than it had been.

I looked at him over my shoulder. "Yeah?"

Ernie frowned slightly, glanced down at the counter, then met my eyes.

"I'm wonderin' if you noticed anything...*funny* 'round town."

Let it be said that Ernie Travis is *not trenvay*; furthermore, he has my vote for the man least likely to hear the music at Midsummer Eve. So it was with considerable care that I repeated, "Funny?"

"Yeah..." He looked aside, like he was embarrassed, which he probably was, poor normal. *Funny* didn't have any place in Ernie's life. Nerazi in all her opulent nakedness might walk past him of a moonlit night, and the only thing Ernie'd see would be the moon.

"You're gonna think I'm nuts, maybe, but it's just—some of these guys—?" He waved a hand toward the front windows, by which I understood him to mean the summer people and tourists.

I nodded.

"Some of these guys ain't—they ain't *havin' fun*. It's like they're lookin' real hard at everything an' everybody, like—well, hell, like we're all under suspicion."

Well, here was something. And I was willing to bet that Ernie was as little inclined to see undercover cops as he was to see selkies. I thought about the heeterskyte's Man Business, and the three undoubted cops at the Boundary Stone; and I shook my head.

"I didn't notice anything this morning," I told Ernie, with perfect truth, "but they might not like merry-go-rounds. I'll keep an eye peeled. Anybody else notice?"

Ernie nodded.

"Beth up at Play Me. She's the one brought it to me. I hadn't noticed, but once you start lookin', it sorta stands out." A faint smile. "Like when you get a new car, suddenly the only thing you see on the road is your model."

So far as I knew, Beth Abernathy was an observant, no-nonsense, down-to-earth woman. Not the kind of person to start seeing boogeymen among the nice tourists.

"I'll keep an eye out," I said again.

"Thanks," he said, and produced another faint smile. "Like to get a reading on if I'm losing my mind."

"Sounds reasonable to me." I hefted the padlock. "I better get down to the carousel."

"Oh, hell, yeah! Good choice, by the way—nobody's gonna break that lock."

If I hadn't seen what Borgan had done to it last night, I wouldn't have thought the storm gate had ever been dented, much less sustained an explosive blow that shredded metal, and produced a hole big enough for a big man to leap through.

I wasn't seeing illusion, either, but a true and lasting repair.

I touched the healed steel and received a jumble of signatures: Gaby, Feesila, Carn, and Artie.

Artie? I thought, and then realized that of course Artie would have to be involved—he was, after all, a backyard mechanic of no small skill, and he'd probably done the giant's share of the repair work.

So, then, I thought: Good work, team!

The old lock was in place, its shackle seemingly through the loops. That, however, was seeming, only. Borgan's burst of power must have been the magical equivalent of a solar flare. When I looked at the lock with the land's eyes, I saw that it was friable, its shattered form stitched together with strands of sea grass and homey land magic; the shackle was gone completely, and the only thing holding the lock near the loops was a dollop of some unmundane substance that reminded me of pine sap, and that bore Gaby's signature.

I put my hand on the lock. The land magic unraveled with a vibration that I felt at the center of my chest. In my hands was ... nothing; my fingertips showed dusty red, as if I had touched something rusty. I dusted them off on my jeans.

Then, still entwined in the land's regard, I pushed the door open.

Nothing happened.

Well, *of course* nothing happened, I scolded myself.

But I stood on the threshold, anyway, and allowed a tendril of *jikinap* to quest before me, while I queried the land regarding any possible presence within the storm gates.

My magical feeler reported Borgan's curtain—and nothing else. The land discovered no one within the gates, save myself.

I stepped through the door, walked over to the utility pole and threw the switch for the lights.

Even in the flood of artificial light, the curtain 'round the carousel glowed and shimmered, a thing of grace and ...

From the depths of my pocket, my cell phone sounded. I dug it out and flipped it open.

"Kate," Peggy said grimly. "Where are you?"

I blinked.

"At the carousel."

"Thank God. You'd better get over here. We've got a problem."

CHAPTER THIRTY-TWO

High Tide 10:59 A.M. EDT

Ulme was crouched in the center of the desk in the office behind The Mango, feet flat, like she would take off running at the first hint of threat. Her glorious hair was a knotted mess, and her face...

...her face was swollen, the pale skin mottled with interesting colors; her mouth was crusted with blood. I could see bruises in a black bracelet around her wrist, where the sleeve of her sweater had ridden up.

"Okay," Peggy was saying. "I get that you're not going to call the cops. Joe's a bad dude, bad dudes work for him. I get that. But, sweetie, we've at least got to take you to the ER!"

"ER?" Ulme's voice was strained and high—a peculiar combination of stress and exhaustion. "What is that?"

"Emergency room," I said, stepping nearer, and keeping my hands in plain sight. Her eyes turned to me, brilliant in the mask of bruises. "Hospital."

"Hosp—" She shook her head. "No hospital."

Peggy looked at me. "She's got to get checked over."

"No," Ulme repeated. "Joe must send me home."

"Joe's done enough!" Peggy snapped. "You wanna go home? Fine. Where do you live? *I'll* take you home!"

Give it to Jersey, her heart was in the right place, but that was a dangerous thing to say, right here and now, to this particular person, occupying what was probably an extremely volatile emotional space.

Ulme smiled; she seemed to glow a little, along her edges, as if a candle had been lit inside her.

"Will you?" She leaned towards Peggy, her lips slightly parted, and her eyes glowing warmly amber. "Promise?"

"No," I said firmly—okay, maybe a little *too* firmly. "She can't take you home. *That's* a promise."

Ulme wilted; Peggy swung 'round to stare at me, anger in her purple eyes.

"What the hell's wrong with you, Archer?"

"So it is true, what Joe says," Ulme whispered. "Only he can send me home."

"Well, no," I said, considering her. "That might not be *exactly* true. Am I right in thinking you're from Kashnerot?"

Ulme nodded, watching me with hot amber eyes.

"Do you know it, my land?"

"Never been there, but I've heard stories." I bit my lip, thinking. This business about only Joe being able to send her back...

"Does Joe have something of yours?" I asked.

"Yes, he has my...my *vishtayre*. The amulet of, of my clan." She took a breath, and winced. Might be some bruised ribs there, too. "Joe said that you are a malicious enemy, without glory or honor."

And I'd thought the man didn't care. I shook my head.

"Takes one to know another," I said. "How did Joe bring you here?"

"By the virtue of the Great Star; for bait, his *voysin*. He had learned this, he said, from a Great Flame. Are you a Great Flame?" Plainly, she doubted it.

"No, I'm a Small Flame. But I *am* a Flame. I'm also Guardian of this land—it's small, too, but not without virtue. I might be able to send you back home, given luck and a tailwind, but before I can even try, you're going to have to get that amulet back."

"Yes," Ulme said, her mouth tightening. "I cannot go home without my amulet."

"Do you know where it is?"

"My *vishtayre* is part of me. Always, I feel it."

"I don't suppose you can call it to you?" The question had to be asked, but I wasn't really surprised when Ulme shook her head.

"Here, it is not possible; I have tried." She sighed. "So many things here are not possible."

"We've got a whole 'nother set of values," I told her.

"Yes?" she said vaguely.

I sighed and got back on topic. "Joe's using the amulet to hold you here."

"*Yes*," she said. Firmly.

"And you can feel it." I chewed my lip. "Do you know *where* it is?"

Ulme drew a sharp breath, and her eyes flickered, bright and hard, as if she'd reached her limit on stupid questions—and then suddenly she must've understood what I meant, because she sighed and lowered her gaze.

"No. I do not know where it is being kept."

"Okay, let me think about that. I might have to bring in a consultant."

I took a breath.

"The cops confiscated Joe's shipment the other night, didn't they? That's what this"—I moved a hand up and down, showing her battered self to her—"is all about, isn't it? You were supposed to protect the runners and the cargo. What happened?"

Ulme sat up a little straighter.

"I tell him—I am not a Great Flame—no! Not even a small one. I am only myself, Ulme, and I have in my care the children of the clan, to teach them their lessons, and their manners. Joe does not believe this; he believes that I prevaricate; that I am lazy, and do not wish to help him. Which I do not, now. Then... I was dazzled; his *voysin* enwrapped me; I forgot myself; and I wanted only what Joe wanted. But even then—" She stared at me. "*Even* then, I said to him that I was no one—a...a governess. He asked could I shift from sight, and of course I could do that! I showed him, and he said that, for him, I should shift many persons from sight—which, I have not the heat, nor the way of it. Joe did not believe me. He hurt me, and sent me to punish his enemies with fire..."

I looked at her, dawn breaking.

"You set the fires at the Wood, and at Daddy's?"

"Yes, although I did not wish to do so. Joe's *voysin* had begun to thin, and I knew myself again, a little. I was also to fire the carousel, but the Flame at duty there did not allow."

"Vassily's not a Flame," I objected, but I felt something funny going on in my stomach.

"Vassily is a willing vessel," Ulme said, with conviction.

Possibly, I blinked. *A willing vessel?* I repeated to myself. *For what, exactly?*

"Kyle—" Ulme said, disturbing what passed for my thought processes.

Peggy shifted, but didn't say anything, smart girl.

"What about Kyle?" I asked.

"He is hunting Joe," Ulme said simply. "Maybe he will kill him. I did not want that, but now, I think it would be a good thing." Her shoulders drooped. "I should have helped him, when he asked, but I was afraid."

There wasn't much to say to that, and the silence grew a little unwieldy, until Peggy broke it.

"So, if we're not going to the ER, you can stay here, sweetie, okay?"

Ulme nodded. "Thank you. It is a kindness."

"You could put her to work making smoothies," I suggested, only half serious.

Peggy took it as offered, though, looked momentarily thoughtful—then shook her head.

"I would, but I can't put those bruises behind the counter; they'd freak out the paying customers."

I sighed, and eyed Ulme.

"I can do something about your hurts, if you're agreeable. Get you some ease, and give you a chance to pay Peggy back for sticking her neck out for you. If Joe figures out where you are..."

"I will help Peggy," Ulme interrupted. "Joe will not hurt her."

"That's fine, sweetie, but I can take care of myself. Kate—"

"I am agreeable," Ulme overrode her. "Please. I submit myself to your fires."

"All right, then."

I stepped up to the desk, and held my hands out, palms up.

"I've got to touch you," I told Ulme. "Avert your eyes, Jersey."

"Up yours, Archer."

"Have it your way."

I took Ulme's outstretched hand between both of mine. Her pale skin was hot; hotter even than Mr. Ignat's skin.

I closed my eyes and breathed in, allowing the healing virtue of the land to rise and pass through me, to Ulme.

There was a sharp intake of breath. I opened my eyes, saw Ulme's face, smooth and white; her perfect lips moist and full. A downward glance showed that the black ring of bruises 'round her wrist was gone as if it had never been.

I nodded and dropped back, releasing her.

She bowed her head, a formal gesture.

"I thank you, Kate Archer. May your fires burn hot and ever bright."

"You're welcome," I said, and looked to Peggy, who was standing a bit stiffly, I thought, her face bland and somewhat less pink than usual.

"Good?" I asked her.

She swallowed; gave a brisk nod.

"Perfect!" she said brightly. "I knew you'd know what to do. C'mon, Ulme, let me show you how the juicers work."

It was a little after 10:30 when I arrived at the carousel for the second time that morning. I used one of the new keys on the new lock, shot the hasp through one loop and let the door fall closed behind me.

I'd left the lights on, and even if I hadn't, Borgan's spell was plenty bright enough to see by.

The curtain 'round the carousel not only glowed, it was a thing of rare and supple beauty.

. . . and not a little power, I realized as I extended a tentacle of my own power toward it.

There was frisson at contact; the curtain flared bright; and Borgan's signature was suddenly strong.

I paused, my hands tucked into my back pockets, and considered the artifact before me, remembering how easily—how effortlessly—he had produced this subtle and complex working. The power that I wasn't using for the tentacle stirred, and rose, the sense of it more akin to curiosity than avarice. I allowed it to regard the working, even as I tried to memorize its subtleties.

I could have looked at it all day; it was that beautiful. But the land interrupted my reverie with a tiny, undignified jolt accompanying the realization that time marched, and Vassily would soon be reporting in for work.

I sighed, and bowed slightly, acknowledging the work of a master. All that remained to me was to release it.

Which was when I realized that I should've asked Borgan how, exactly, his beautiful spell was to be released. In theory, I could just absorb the *jikinap* that had been used, thereby collapsing the spell, but, truth told, I was off absorbing *jikinap* for the foreseeable future.

In which case, all I had to do was dismiss the working, and allow the power to return to its rightful master...

...and that brought me right back around to *how?*

I glanced down at my fingers, still reddish with rust, and looked again at the shimmering curtain.

Borgan knew my skill in spellcraft was fairly basic. He would, I thought, have built in a simple and easy trigger for me, which would, at the same time, be completely impervious to the meddling of others.

Which meant—first—that the spell needed to know that I was me.

I stepped up to the curtain.

"Thank you," I said quietly, and put my hand into the coruscating colors, feeling them flow over my skin, each one distinct.

A small breeze sprang up, as if I'd called it; I tasted salt. Before me, the curtains blew—and disappeared, taking the sense of Borgan's presence with them.

I sighed, mounted the carousel, and once more toured the animals, inspecting them with every sense available to me. In addition to wanting to be sure that the various wards still held, I was looking for clues, *any*thing that would help me to find the Varothi before he tried again.

While I was there, I turned on the running lights, and the orchestrion, and went into the center to start the motor.

I'd just stepped back onto the deck when the door opened.

Vassily stepped through, and stopped, the door held open on the tips of his fingers.

"Opening time?" I asked, dropping to the floor.

"It is, yes," he answered gravely. "Are you well?"

"I'm well," I assured him. "Just came down to replace the lock, and to—spend some time in meditation."

"It is good, to meditate upon beauty," Vassily agreed.

I beckoned him nearer.

"I've got a new key to open the new lock," I said, showing him one. "Give me the key ring and I'll make the exchange now."

He dropped the key and ring onto my palm, then turned his attention to rolling the storm gates back.

"Here you are," I said to him when he returned to the operator's station.

"Thanking you." He put the key carefully into his pocket, and turned to the ticket box, opening it up and making sure the bag was present and empty.

"Vassily," I said.

He turned his head to look at me, thin reddish brows drawn. "Yes?"

"I hear from a source that you're a *willing vessel*. You wanna tell me about that?"

"Do you not know, of yourself?" He looked faintly surprised when I shook my head, then moved his shoulders in a tiny shrug.

"It is simple." He glanced at me. "Understand, I did not think that; I did not believe my uncle, the priest, when he said to me that it is simple. Worse than this, I did not care. I was...very bad. I did bad things. I hurt people.

"Then, on a day, I met my Alisa. And I stop being bad. I am... transformed, you see? It is her. She makes me good." He paused.

"I was new, but the past...it follows. Bad deeds want blood for balance."

Another pause; and a tiny sigh.

"My Alisa, she says, there is a program. We will get jobs in America. We will lose the past, she says. I say, yes, we will do this. And so we sign the papers and are told that Samuil will come for us on a day, to bring us here, to America, with all the rest.

"Two days before Samuil is to come, the past...finds me. I had, before my Alisa transformed me, I had hurt, you will say, a wrong person. I did it for money. That person had...a protector, a lover. He found me. He found Alisa..."

He bowed his head abruptly, shoulders stiff. I wanted to tell him to stop, to not go there, that I hadn't meant...

He raised his head.

"So, this terrible thing. My Alisa is dead. I am...It is..." He catches his breath in what sounds like a sob.

"I have the gun in my mouth when Samuil comes for me. He takes it away. He slaps me, and he brings me with the rest, because in the papers I signed was my oath to God that I would come here, to America.

"On the plane, I pray. I pray for death, so that I will be with my Alisa. But that is no good. She is a blessed angel in heaven.

When I die, I will burn in hell. But I pray anyway. I think maybe Alisa can hear me."

He paused again, shoulders hunched. Then he straightened and turned to look me straight in the face.

"It is when we have come here. I am finish the cleaning at the motel, and I go to the ocean. I think about drowning, but I don't know how. I close my eyes and I pray to my Alisa.

"It is then that he comes to me, this other blessed angel, and he says...he says that I may be redeemed in him. If I open my soul to him, and help him recover his love, who was unjustly torn from his arms—if I will do this, he will bless me, and when I die, I will rise to heaven, and be with my Alisa."

I took a careful breath.

"Have you seen him, this angel?"

"Yes. He is very beautiful, and his wings are steel rainbows."

As fair a description of my Varothi as anyone could wish.

"But," Vassily said, shaking his head sadly, "if you wish to speak with him, you are too late. He has left me, and I think now that I will never be blessed."

CHAPTER THIRTY-THREE

Mr. Ignat' was inside the operator's area, greasing the dragon's front axle. I ducked under the fence and joined him.

"Good morning," I said.

He glanced at me over his shoulder with a smile that faded a little as he turned completely around to face me.

"Have you been having adventures, Pirate Kate?"

"You could say. I absorbed a bunch of stray *jikinap* that somebody had carelessly left in a configuration that could have damaged the Gate. It made me sick, so I gave it back." I tipped my head, seeing the flames dancing in the centers of his eyes. I didn't want to ask the next question, but I figured it was better to know.

"Is something wrong?"

"Wrong?" Mr. Ignat's brows pulled together, and he turned back to finish his greasing.

"I wouldn't say *wrong*. You may find that you know some things that you never learned, if you take my meaning."

"Because the . . . other Ozali knows it?" I asked, feeling a little queasy.

"That's right," he said. "When powers mingle, information is shared."

I thought back to those moments when Mr. Ignat' and I had faced each other across a cement table in Fountain Circle, and he had insisted that I take his hands. Of course, Mr. Ignat's power hadn't tried to kill me, because Mr. Ignat' loved me. And I hadn't gotten the sense that we had *mingled*, so much as gotten the true measure of each other.

This business of having mingled *jikinap* with the Varothi was... unnerving, and slightly nauseating, but not, I told myself firmly, *threatening*. Even less so, if Vassily was telling the truth—and he was, according to the land—and the Varothi had left the building.

Right, then, I thought. *On to the reason for the visit.*

"There's a citizen of Kashnerot hiding at The Last Mango," I said, as Mr. Ignat' returned to the axle. "She was brought here against her will, and she'd really like to go home now. Her clan amulet is being used to anchor her. She's tried calling it, but it won't—or can't—come to her."

"Is there a reason why she cannot physically recover it?" Mr. Ignat' asked. "Power is *a* tool; not the *only* tool."

"Actually, yes; there is a reason. She's at The Mango because the man who's holding her prisoner beat her up pretty bad. She ran away or he threw her out—I'm not sure which. In either case, it's probably not wildly safe for her to go back to his house in search of jewelry."

Mr. Ignat' finished the axle, and snapped the lid onto the grease can.

"I was wondering," I continued, when the can was sealed and he still hadn't said anything, "if you might be willing to help her get a fix on her amulet; and either call it, or walk me through the process."

He held up a finger—*wait*, that was—and carried the can and rag into the shed. He came out, and closed the door.

"I believe that you want Arbalyr for this," he said when he was back with me.

"If he's willing to help, I'm more than willing to have him," I said.

"Well, let us see."

Mr. Ignat' closed his eyes.

Two blasts echoed over the whole of Fun Country, announcing that the park was open.

Mr. Ignat' opened his eyes.

"I've put the question," he said. "You should have an answer quickly."

He ducked under the safety fence and mounted the stairs to the operator's station.

I walked out from under the shade cast by the boarding platform's roof, into the sunshine. Right now, it was pleasantly warm. Later, when the sun was at zenith, the tired asphalt that was Fun Country's common ground would act as a reflector, baking happy thrill-seekers from below while the sun burned them from above.

The good news was that there would be thrill-seekers aplenty, according to what the land showed me about the crowd entering the park. I might have a hard time navigating Baxter Avenue against the river of bodies.

A shadow flashed, momentarily turning the gray asphalt interstellar black. I glanced up, and spied a largish black bird spiraling lazily above me.

Apparently, Arbalyr had decided to take the job.

"Thank you," I called to Mr. Ignat'.

He looked over his shoulder and up, then gave me a smile and a nod before turning back to his controls.

I'd ducked out of the park via the service alley, and jogged down Grand Avenue, across the least-crowded edge of Fountain Circle, and into the midway.

At first, it didn't seem as if the crowds were as strong here, then I turned the corner into the little half-street where The Mango was situated—and I hit gridlock.

The land growled.

I blinked, sent a query, and turned my head, my eyes drawn to a young man in new jeans and a plain T-shirt, who seemed to be...watching, but not like he was happy with what he saw.

I tried to inch forward, and bumped into the side of a shirtless teen boy.

"Cool it," he said, automatically.

"Sorry," I said. "What's the holdup?"

"Couple guys up ahead not letting anybody past. Says there's a repair being made, and it'll just take a couple minutes."

That...wasn't how Fun Country did business. Any repairs that had to be made were done in the dead of night, not when paying customers were roaming the grounds. Unless one of the juicers had gone on the fritz, and Peggy had to call in a repair-man. But...

The land growled again—and I suddenly saw The Mango, admirably isolated, fruit littering the asphalt, along with the mangled remains of the cheery red hanging baskets, and a smashed rectangle of plastic, that might've once been a cell phone.

There was the sound of things being broken; I thought I heard someone laugh.

The land, though, was focused on the unequal struggle between a beefy guy in T-shirt, jeans, gimme hat, and businesslike boots—and a small, roundish woman with pink hair. He had her by the arms, and she was fighting as best she could. With the land's ears, I could hear her yelling, but it wasn't getting through the noise of the crowd. She kicked, hard, but she was off-balance, and missed his balls. He was going to have a helluva bruise, though—and he wasn't happy about it.

"Fat *bitch!*" he snarled. He shook her so that her head snapped, and spun her, one arm up behind her back. She gasped—*and I had to get over there!*

I pushed, trying to run—air whooshed in my ears; the crowd and the alley smeared into a rainbow of colors; I momentarily lost track of my body—and recovered it abruptly as I slammed to my knees by the edge of the fence, directly behind the guy who was holding Peggy.

Gasping, I grabbed a handful of *jikinap* and spun a shield—an invisibility spell, you would say—and laboriously climbed to my feet. After a moment, I created a net of *jikinap* and stretched it from one side of the alley to the other. That would keep helpful folks out, and mischievous folks in.

At least for a little while.

"She too much for ya, Sam?"

Another guy in the same jeans-tee-boots ensemble stalked toward them; he looked right at me over Sam's shoulder—but the spell held firm.

"Here, I'll help." He swung a casual arm, and backhanded Peggy across the face.

"Quiet, bitch."

"Stop it!" Ulme rushed out of The Mango, and ran toward the three of them. "I will not allow you to hurt Peggy!"

The nameless guy turned.

"How you gonna stop us? The same way you stopped the Coasties from picking up Julie's crew? Stupid cow." He stepped forward into his swing, but Ulme ducked, and the blow went past her.

"Keep a lid on it!" snapped the third member of the crew, a wiry woman in what seemed to be the crew's uniform. She had a beer bottle in one hand, and a lighter in the other.

"We're here to deliver a message, that's all. If you mess around in Joe Nemeier's business, you get messed up. You followin' this, fat girl?"

There wasn't an answer. The boy who'd backhanded Peggy grabbed her by the hair, and yanked. Peggy cried out.

"She's talking to you, cow."

"Leave it," the woman said. "She's listenin'. So, Ulme." She smiled. "Think you can run away and hide with your friends? You do that, then Joe sends us, we hurt your friends, then we take you back to Joe. What Joe does to you . . ." She shrugged, her smile widening.

"But before we take you home to be spanked, we need to finish cleaning up here."

She flicked the lighter, and lit the beer bottle's wick. Then she threw it over Ulme's head . . .

. . . into the The Mango.

Glass shattered, and flames roared, licking hungrily up the wooden frame.

Peggy screamed.

From the side of my eye, I saw a stocky figure moving up behind Sam, the guy holding Peggy. Felsic put long hands on Sam's shoulders, and he seemed to lose focus . . . to sag, as if his bones weren't quite as strong as they had been, just a moment ago. He let go of Peggy, and turned to face Felsic.

I darted forward, low and quick, caught Peggy and pulled her back with me behind the invisibility spell. Once we were out of sight, I made a request of the land, and was pleased to see the asphalt soften immediately under the boots of the boy who had hit Peggy, then firm up again, locking his heels to the ground.

Nobody seemed to have seen me, or Felsic, or noticed that Peggy was gone. The second guy was watching the fire hungrily, not even aware that he was bound.

"Oh, and?" The woman reached into her pocket and pulled out a chain, a glittering disk at the end. "I hear you can't go home unless you have this—is that right?"

"Yes!" Ulme cried.

The woman smiled.

"So you want it bad, then." She gathered disk and chain slowly into her hand, then jerked her arm back and threw the bauble into the heart of the fire.

"Go fish."

With no hesitation whatsoever, Ulme turned and leapt over the counter, vanishing into the leaping flames.

"No!" Peggy screamed.

I threw my arms around her, pushing her face into my shoulder, so she wouldn't have to see.

"She'll be fine; she'll be fine," I whispered, watching the flames—the whole booth was engaged, now. "She'll be fine."

"*Fine!*" Peggy struggled and I let her turn, keeping a hand on her shoulder, in case she decided to run.

I'm pretty sure I was the only one who saw the black-winged shadow swoop into the engulfing flames. Everyone else was staring at Ulme, as she stepped casually out of the wall of fire, if anything, more beautiful than ever, and not even marked with soot. Both hands were up and behind her neck, as if she was fastening a chain.

"What the *hell!*" snapped Joe's female enforcer, moving forward.

The asphalt rippled before her; she staggered, snatching at the air for balance, catching it—and losing it.

She hit her head hard when she went down, but the land told me she was still alive. I pulled a thin strong string of *jikinap* out of my supply, and trussed her up, nice and tight.

The guy with his boot heels stuck in the asphalt tried to run. That was comical. He got trussed up in turn.

That left Sam, who was standing quiet and scarcely seeming to breathe under Felsic's hands.

"Let him go, Felsic," I said, walking over. "We've got a limited time to clean up before the cops get here."

"He hurt Peggy," Felsic said calmly. "He will not survive that."

"Not your call," I snapped.

Felsic looked at me . . . and smiled, showing teeth.

"Felsic!" Peggy snapped, voice strong despite her bruises. "If you hurt him, we're through."

The truth jolted through me like electricity. The woman was *serious.*

Felsic thought so, too. One long look at her bruised face, and Felsic thrust Sam at me. He staggered; I administered the magical equivalent of a cosh to the head and wrapped him up, too.

Then I turned to Ulme, who had been standing politely out of the way.

"The fire's out," Peggy said suddenly. "Who put the fire out?"

"A firebird came, and drank it," Ulme said helpfully.

"That's right," I said briskly. "Now, Ulme, I'm sorry to rush you, but we've got a very tight window of opportunity here. We need to get you on the way home before the cops arrive and everything gets *a lot* more comp—"

I felt something stir along my magical nerves, and turned toward the charred remains of the juice stand.

As if my words had created it, a window was forming in the smoky air. A window that was getting more solid the longer I looked at it. I went forward to meet it. Out of the corner of my eye, I saw Felsic step to Peggy's side and put an arm around her waist, preventing her from following me.

I pulled a defensive spell to my fingertips, and held my breath.

The window... opened.

A slightly pudgy man, a shock of Crayola-red hair standing straight up on his round head, peered out. I eased another step forward, and he looked at me.

He blinked, mildly. I felt *jikinap* flutter over me, and withdraw.

"I beg your pardon, Ozali," he said. "I felt the presence of one of my clan, distinctly here. Have you perhaps—"

"Great Flame, Great Flame!" Ulme practically threw herself to her knees before the window. "Here I am! Please, *oh please* take me home!"

The Great Flame extended a hand and placed it on her head.

"Ulme, child, we've been so worried! Why didn't you call before?"

Ulme shook her head, obviously speechless, and raised both hands to grip his wrist.

I cleared my throat.

"She was brought here by a criminal, who separated her from her amulet. That has just been returned to her. It was to be my next act, sir, to send her back to you. If you would take her now—and treat her gently. Her time here has not been easy."

"I see, I see," the Great Flame murmured. "But she found a champion, and..." He gazed myopically into the dissipating smoke, "and a friend. That is well done. I thank you for your care, Ozali...Kate Archer, and Peggy...Marr. Our clan is in your debt."

"If I may suggest speed, sir..." I said delicately, and the Great Flame smiled.

"Else the soot will be much more difficult to clean from the fingers, eh? Of course. Come, Ulme. Your mother has been distraught..."

Flames erupted from the window. Peggy squeaked. The flames died.

Ulme, the window, and the Great Flame—were gone.

I heard the sound of wing against air above me, and flexed my knees to take the shock when Arbalyr landed on my shoulder.

"Well done," I said, and raised a hand to stroke his chest feathers before I turned to look at Felsic and Peggy.

"One more thing," I said, and stepped forward. "Let's take care of you, Jersey; you look a sight."

She gave me a rumpled grin and held out her hand. I took it between both of mine, asked for, and received, the land's benediction.

"All right," I said then, stepping back, and releasing the crowd-control divider I'd stretched across the alley. "Let's let 'em in."

CHAPTER THIRTY-FOUR

Low Tide 4:41 P.M. EDT

Joe's three kiddies were handcuffed and hauled off by Archers Beach policemen and -women. It may have interested no one but myself that cops and prisoners were accompanied off the property by a pair of summer people in brand-new shorts who didn't look like they were having any fun.

Nothing was said about what might have befallen the couple guys who had been blocking the street earlier. I figured if nobody else wanted to talk about them, then I didn't, either.

That made it fairly easy to give statements that were for the most part truthful. Unless you're a stickler who counts sins of omission.

In any case, mention of Ulme was omitted; certainly any mention of windows opening in the smoke. Our three gentle visitors were by testimony reduced to petty thugs out for random mischief. They'd torn down the baskets and smashed the fruits, and when Peggy got her cell phone out to call for help—they'd snatched it out of her hand and stamped it beneath their boots.

The cops gathered up the poor smashed remains as evidence.

I, so the story went, had arrived while play time was in session, and had managed to subdue the attackers by dint of not being too squeamish about smacking heads against hard objects.

The cop folded up his book, and said he'd be in touch to have us sign statements, and neither Peggy nor I was to leave town. He didn't mention Felsic; hadn't questioned Felsic; hadn't apparently *seen* Felsic, though Felsic had been standing right next to Peggy when the cops arrived on the scene. I made a note to talk to Felsic about that.

The fire department, the fire inspector, and the remediation specialist were still doing their various things when the cop left us. I pulled Peggy aside and asked her how she was holding up.

She sighed, and ran her fingers through her pink hair.

"I've got soot on my face, I bet."

"It was a hell of a party. You wouldn't be doing justice to its memory if you didn't have soot on your face."

She snorted.

"Yeah, well. I'm going to have to call Arbitrary and Cruel; and somewhere I'm going to have to come up with a new cell. Dammit; I *liked* that phone."

"Well, here's what," I said. "It looks like The Mango's closed for the rest of the day. Why don't you come with me? I'll introduce you to Gregor; we'll see if he has any prepaid phones. Then I'll buy you lunch at Bob's."

She looked at me doubtfully; I could see the to-do list getting longer as she stood there.

"C'mon, Jersey, you don't want to call the bosses on an empty stomach."

She sighed and gave me a reluctant grin.

"There's that. Do you know anybody in town who can look the booth over and give me an estimate on—"

"I'll take care of that," Felsic interrupted, putting a hand on Peggy's shoulder. "Let Kate take care of you; call Management; have a bath. Should I come past, tonight?"

"Yes," Peggy said with a smile.

"I will, then," Felsic said, smiling, too, before stepping back. "Go on, then, the pair of you. The midway'll come to no harm."

"That sounds like marching orders to me," I said, tucking my arm through Peggy's. "C'mon; I don't know about you, but I'm starving."

Gregor had a prepaid candy bar with 60 starter minutes preloaded hanging on a card behind the counter. When he heard what happened to Peggy's phone, he threw in an extra 120-minute card for free, and pointed at the door.

"I'll get it activated and bring it over to Bob's. You girls need to sit down and relax. Big and tough, right? Picking on somebody their own size, sure! Lucky it wasn't worse, that's all." He peered at Peggy. "I hope this ain't put you off us, deah."

Peggy smiled and patted his hand.

"No, I met Kate first, so I knew this was a good town."

"Well, there." Gregor looked pleased, then pointed at the door again, making shooing motions with the hand that held the minute card.

"Go on! Go sit down 'fore you fall down!"

So it was that we were sitting in a booth in Bob's nearly deserted main room, ice tea to hand, and lunch on the way.

Peggy was looking wilted and pale, no shame to her. I sipped my ice tea—unlike his coffee, Bob's ice tea is pretty darn good—and put the glass on the table.

"So," I said, by way of keeping her awake. "I didn't know you and Felsic were an item."

She stirred and reached for her glass. "That makes us even, right? I didn't know you were the Great and Powerful Wizard of Oz."

I grinned. "That warning about not looking behind the curtain..."

"Too late for that," Peggy interrupted. "I'm dating Felsic. I saw a woman throw herself into a living fire, and walk out of it like I walk out of the shower. I'm right here behind the curtain with the rest of you."

"Then you know there's nobody here who's all-powerful."

"Neither was Oz."

She took a long drag on her straw, and sighed, deep and heartfelt.

"Here you are, ladies." Bob put a bacon, lettuce, tomato and cheese sandwich in front of me, a cheeseburger in front of Peggy, and a plate of fries bigger than my head between us.

"Look okay?" he asked, standing back, and watching us sharply.

"Looks *won*derful," Peggy told him. "I really am hungry."

Bob grinned. "I'll leave you to it, then. Holler if you need anything; I'm just in the back."

He bustled off, pushing through the kitchen door with energy.

"Is Ulme going to be okay?" Peggy asked, applying a liberal coating of ketchup to her burger.

"I think so. Her Great Flame didn't look to me like a man who'll be fooled twice. Whatever Joe did to snatch Ulme in the first place isn't going to work again. Us, though..."

I paused. Peggy was tired, maybe even a teensy little bit shocky.

I'd drawn on the land's energy, but I could own to being tired, too. Not really the time to be introducing more stress into either of our lives.

"What about us?"

I picked up half of my sandwich and gave her a straight look.

"Well, I'm thinking of Joe as I know him. He's not going to be pleased with us, and he's not a man who's shy about letting his feelings be known."

I took a bite, feeling lettuce crunch.

"What're the chances Kyle will get him?"

Chewing, I blinked. "Kyle?"

"Ulme said Kyle was hunting Joe, remember?"

"So she did." I thought about that, reaching for a french fry. "Well, fuck."

"What?"

"If Kyle's hunting Joe, then he's MDEA—"

Peggy blinked.

"Maine Drug Enforcement Agency," I expanded. "Which means he's not likely to be making me a carousel animal, like he said he would."

"You think a cop's gonna rip you off?"

"Let's just say that I'm alive to the possibility."

She nodded and turned her full attention to her burger. I did the same to my BLT. At some point, Bob came by and refilled our glasses; the fact that I didn't notice him was kind of a testament to how tired I was. Peggy must be out on her feet.

The street door opened, bell jangling.

"Good. You're still here!" Gregor called, coming quickly to our table.

"Taking our time," Peggy said.

"That's what you need." Gregor put the phone down at the edge of her plate. "I just loaded in that extra one-twenty while I was at it. Sorry it took so long; had me on hold forever. But you're all set now."

"Thank you," Peggy said, giving him a smile that was just a little ragged at the edges. "I really appreciate your help."

"No problem at all. You need anything else like this, you come see me." He gave me a nod. "Kate."

"Thanks, Gregor," I said, dredging up a smile of my own. "You've been a big help."

He colored a little, nodded.

"You two have a good rest of the day, now. See you."

I looked at Peggy. She had picked up her new cell and was frowning at it.

"God, that's an ugly thing."

"Tomorrow, you can call your cell company, explain what happened to your phone, and talk them into replacing it for free. That'll be fun, won't it?"

She brightened considerably.

"You know, it will."

"So, if you're taking suggestions—home, a shower, and then a call to Management?"

"Sounds like it might be the bet," she said. "Then beer. What about you?"

"Shower and nap, I think. Got a date tonight."

"You need to look your best, then! How do we settle?"

"Bob!" I called. "How much do we owe you?"

"On the house!" His voice came from the kitchen.

"Bob—"

"Can't hear you, Kate! Wicked noisy back here."

I rolled my eyes. Peggy got up, cell phone in hand, and jerked her head toward the door.

"C'mon, we'll gang up on him later."

"Deal."

We walked up Dube Street. I saw Peggy to her door, and safely inside, then started up the steps to the porch.

My cell phone gave tongue. I sighed and fished it out of my pocket.

"Katie," my mother said urgently. "I need you here—now. There are intruders in the Wood." There was a small pause before she added.

"They aren't dead. Yet."

It isn't far from the midway to Heath Hill. It's a lot farther when lives are hanging in the balance. Running down Grand, I asked the land to show me what was going on in the Wood.

That got me a head full of shadows, and looming, tentacled horrors. I thrust my will forward and into the land, demanding that the trees attend to the land's Guardian.

That . . . wasn't too bright.

They paid attention, all right. I was hit with a spike of enmity so strong that my link to the land evaporated in a blast of static. The land howled—defiance, not panic—and we were united again, sharing a very lively fear for the intruders' lives.

The Wood...I had never felt the Wood's *anger* before. To me, it had always been a measured, peaceful place—and it hit me that I wasn't going to be in time; the trees were too angry; people were in mortal peril, and I couldn't run fast enough. I needed to be there. Needed to be there *now*.

And once again, in response to my urgency, it came, that whooshing blur, and the sense of not quite being—and then I was being again, all right. I was on my knees well within the boundary of the Wood, a vine-wrapped man under my right hand.

The air inside the Wood was cold—I mean to say, bone-chilling cold. There came a faint, soft growl inside my ears, which I ignored as I took a breath, and said, as calmly as I could manage. "It's Kate."

There was a pause, stretching out. I used the time to look about me. We were in a clearing so small it could be argued that it was only a clearing at all because the thickness of the surface roots made it impossible for anything else to take root here. Those that had were hulking brutes of trees, their leaves as sharp as knives, and their branches like the twisted fingers of murderers.

The man under my hand was trussed up handily. His ankles and wrists were bound in the vines of fox grape and honeysuckle, twigs and dirt were tangled in his light brown curls, and there was what appeared to be a stringy, flexible rootling around his throat.

His eyes were closed, he was breathing, and I knew him.

I let go the breath I had been holding, and looked around me, aware that I hadn't had any kind of acknowledgment to my announcement. A gleam drew my eye, and I saw my mother crouched behind a small shrub directly across from me; Arbalyr the firebird perched in a branch above. She shook her head when she saw that I'd seen her.

I looked away, keeping my hand on Kyle's shoulder, and said, more loudly, "It's Kate."

A breeze tickled the inside of my ears, but that was all. Right. Time to pull rank.

"I am the Guardian of this Land, and in the absence of the

Lady, I am empowered to arbitrate with the Wood. I know this man, and I vouch for him. I do not believe that he came into the Wood with intent to despoil or destroy. If you have evidence that refutes this, I will see it now."

Nothing. Out of the corner of my eye, I saw my mother shift, her eyes narrowing.

He should not have come here, the Wood informed me, coldly.

"He should not have come here," I agreed. "Plainly, he was in error. Did he offer the Wood harm?"

The others *wished to harm us. He followed them.*

"Maybe he wished to forestall them," I said, and rose to my feet. "I will see these others. Preserve this man until I have learned what I might."

Silence.

"Well?" I asked, irritably. "I don't have all day, you know."

A path opened before me, and I followed it, not far, as such things are measured in the Wood.

Two people—a man and a woman—were bound hand and foot, and very deeply unconscious on stony ground littered with twigs and pine cones. Not your most comfortable sleeping situation. I knelt down so I could get a good look at their faces.

The man was a stranger, but I recognized the woman.

She'd tried to kill me a few weeks back, and it was only luck and the land that she'd murdered my favorite commuter mug, instead. It really is an aid to memory, almost getting shot.

"There was a disturbance at the house," my mother said from beside me. "A lot of cars and police cars, and—these two were out back, and when they understood what was happening—that the house was being raided, they ran down the hill and into the Wood.

"The other one—he did come after them, but I think he meant to arrest them, Katie."

"I think so, too," I said. I sat back on my heels and rubbed my forehead. "This," I told my mother, "is turning into a very interesting day. Remind me to tell you about it."

"All right," she said. "What are you going to do?"

That was a good question, but really, there was only one thing *to* do.

"I'm going to wake up Kyle," I said.

❋ ❋ ❋

"This man," I told the trees, as I knelt again beside Kyle, "came into the Wood on purpose to protect it. I propose to awaken him, and have him take the two despoilers away."

They are ours, the Wood said, and there was enough menace in the voice of the trees that I shivered.

"Times have changed. If you kill them, men will notice you. The Lady has lately avoided notice, hasn't she?"

Silence, then an answer, very nearly petulant.

She has.

"Then, in the Lady's absence, that's how we'll play it."

I put my hand on Kyle's shoulder.

"Please unbind him."

For a count of three, nothing happened; then the vines unwound from his legs and arms, and the rootling withdrew from about his throat. I heard a rustle and glanced to my right, watching my mother place a gimme hat, a handgun and a bottle of Poland Spring water on the ground by Kyle's shoulder, before she once again withdrew to the shrubbery.

I considered the handgun without favor, then I reached to the land and nudged Kyle awake.

"Hey!" he said, sounding faintly surprised.

He opened his eyes, and met mine, blinking like he'd looked into a lamp that was too bright.

"Good morning," I said cheerily. "How're you feeling?"

"Lousy," he said, keeping his eyes on mine. "And also like I might be losing my mind."

"Lucky I happened by," I said, nodding to his right. "There's a bottle of water there for you, if you're thirsty."

"Thanks."

He sat up cautiously, turned his head, and looked at the things Nessa had put there on the grass for a longish time before he sighed, put out his hand—and took up the bottle of cold spring water.

"I guess my question is *how* you happened by," he said, after he'd cracked the seal and taken a swig.

"Truthfully? Got a phone call that there was a trespasser in the woods. This land here belongs to my family."

Kyle looked at me, holding the bottle a little away from his mouth.

"*The trees tried to strangle me!*" he said, like he'd rather be saying almost anything else.

I nodded, as matter-of-fact as I knew how.

"They're old trees, set in their ways, and they don't like strangers." I shrugged. "You really shouldn't've come in." I glanced significantly at the gun, that he'd left out in plain sight on the ground.

"MDEA?" I asked.

He shook his head. "FBI."

I sighed, making it as theatrical as possible.

"I guess this means I'm not getting my horse."

"What?" He blinked, and for a second it looked like he had no idea what I was talking about, and then the penny dropped. "Oh, hey, no! You'll get the horse—Mike's working on it now."

"Mike?" I suddenly had a bad feeling. "The guy in Glen Echo? You didn't ship that wood to Maryland, did you?"

He shook his head.

"No; he's here at the shop. We brought him up once I had the in with you. Since we didn't know how long this would take to crack, or exactly what your relationship with Nemeier's operations was, we figured we'd best produce the horse." He pressed his lips together, but his eyes said he knew he'd let the cat out of the bag.

"You thought *I* was working for or with Joe Nemeier?" I demanded. "Do I look like a smuggler to you?"

"Does *he* look like a smuggler?" he countered, jerking his head toward the top of the hill. He had another swig of water. "And there were questions enough about you—including where the hell *did* that horse go, and what was in it?

"But you're not a smuggler, are you?" he continued. "You're— what? A sorceress? A—an *earth spirit*?"

I was impressed; the boy could think outside of the box. 'Course, being entwined and throttled by the Wood might broaden anybody's outlook.

"I'm what's called the Guardian; job's been in the family for generations. Now, I don't want to be rude, but I also don't want to try the trees' patience much further. The kiddies you chased in here are alive, but if we don't move them soon, they won't be. What I propose is that we drag them outta here, before you call for backup. Okay?"

He took a breath, nodded, and reached for his hat.

"Okay."

❋   ❋   ❋

"Did you get Joe Nemeier?" I asked, as we stretched our prisoners out on the grass at the edge of the Wood. "In the raid."

"Far's I know," Kyle said, flipping open his phone.

"Good. And before you make that call, I'm leaving, and you never saw me, right?"

He looked at me, face resigned.

"My boss is a real down-to-earth kind of guy. He doesn't handle...unusual situations well, and the team tries not to upset him."

"Then he's going to love how you're not going to tell him about Ulme, who was a victim, and who's gone home now."

"To the world next door," Kyle muttered. "You bet I'm telling him *that*."

"Go up to St. Margaret's any Sunday morning, and they'll tell you a story that sounds remarkably similar," I said.

He gave me a sour look. Clearly, he wasn't in the mood for philosophy.

"All right, then! I'll just leave you to your work," I said, and left him at the edge of the wood, cell phone in hand.

CHAPTER THIRTY-FIVE

Sunset 9:02 P.M. EDT

"I'll call that a busy day followin' a frantic yesterday."

Borgan had been waiting when I got home, one hip resting on the porch rail as he gazed out to sea.

"Oh," I said. "Damn!"

He turned his head and looked down at me, eyes glinting.

"You forget our date?"

"No and yes," I told him, coming up the stairs slowly.

Borgan had dressed for a *nice* date: salt-white shirt embroidered with seashells in glistening silver thread; black jeans; boots. The nacre stud was in his ear, and I caught the gleam of a silver bracelet under the edge of one cuff.

He was so beautiful that my chest hurt, just looking at him. He raised an eyebrow.

"You want to reschedule?"

"No!"

Halfway up the stairs, I stopped, looking into his face. I didn't want to reschedule; I was sick and tired of people, but I *wasn't* sick and tired of Borgan. I wanted him with me. I wanted...

I swallowed, hard.

"How 'bout a change of plans?" I asked.

311

"To what?"

"You go to Lisa's and buy us a pizza; get a bottle of wine—no, get two bottles!—from Ahz. While you're hunting and gathering, I'll take a shower, and order my thoughts so I can present the most entertaining version of how I didn't forget our date, but managed to be totally unprepared to find you standing here."

Borgan considered it, head to one side, then nodded.

"I can work with that. Only two bottles of wine?"

"Use your judgment," I told him, earnestly.

He grinned, and I could move again. I gained the porch and stood aside to let him pass me.

Except, he paused at my side, and ran his fingers lightly down the side of my face. I shivered, and turned my head to kiss his knuckles. He caught his breath; his other hand rose toward my cheek . . .

And fell away.

"Pizza," he said, his voice husky, "and as many bottles of wine as Ahzie will sell me. I'll be back, Kate."

"I'll be here," I promised, and watched him jog down the stairs and walk briskly toward Grand Avenue. Nice jeans.

"*Shower*, Kate," I told myself sternly, and turned to open the door.

It was something of a shock, a little over an hour later, to come downstairs, dressed for my date in the maroon shirt I'd bought for the pre-Season opener, and my best pair of jeans, to find him in the kitchen, the pizza in the center of the table, and a bottle of wine breathing next to it. Plates were set, with wineglasses, and napkins. Borgan was rummaging in the silverware drawer, his back to me.

For a moment, I thought I'd forgotten to lock the door.

Then I remembered that I'd given him leave to enter, and truly said that he was welcome in my home.

That gave me another pleasurable shiver, and I wanted to walk up behind him and put my arms around his waist and rub my cheek against his back. I didn't do it, though, and a second later he'd turned 'round, and smiled.

"Hope you're hungry," he said. "That's Lisa's extra large with everything, right there."

Now, all that was left of the pizza were a couple of sad crusts; and the second bottle of wine had been opened. My story had been told, and I was out of words.

Borgan considered the toes of his boots.

"I can see you'd be tired, after all that," he said, looking up with a wry smile. "Best I help you clear up," he added and stood up to do just that.

I stood, too, stacking the dishes in the sink to wash tomorrow while he folded the pizza box until it was small enough to fit in the trash can.

"Well, then," he said, looking around as if he didn't know what to do next. "I'd better be taking myself off. Let you get some rest."

The last thing I wanted, I realized, was *rest*. And I certainly didn't want him to go.

I wanted Borgan's hands on me; I wanted him to kiss me, hard; I wanted him . . .

If you want to go faster, woman—go faster!

"There's something I didn't tell you," I said, moving closer to him.

He tipped his head.

"What was that?"

"I'd been talking with Peggy about relationships. Turns out she's bad at them, too."

Borgan was watching me closely. He made no objection when I put my hands on his chest.

"Still, you know, advice is free. Hers was that if I wanted us to get past kissing and cuddling, I was going to have to move things along. Because—this is her theory, now—you're too nice a guy to rush me."

"There's something wrong with my kissing?" Borgan inquired.

"As far as I know—which, mind you, isn't very—there isn't a damn' thing wrong with your kissing."

The corner of his mouth twitched.

"This is your notion of moving things along, is it?"

"I am," I told him seriously, while I tentatively worked at his top shirt button, "a novice." The button came open and I moved on doggedly to the next one. "I do admit that this seems a little slower than I'd anticipated. Maybe I should just take my shirt off?" I looked up at him. "Or would that be forward?"

He laughed, and lifted me in his arms. I wrapped my legs around his waist, and laughed down at him.

"Now, I've got you where I want you," I told him, and put a hand on either side of his face. His skin was warm, and ridiculously

soft. I stroked my thumbs up his cheekbones, feeling his breathing speed up as he looked into my eyes.

I bent closer, holding him between my hands, and kissed him,
hard and deep.

We broke to breathe and I kissed him again, or he kissed me.
No . . . we kissed each other. One or both of us moaned, and I
wanted him, I *ached* with wanting him.

He carried me to the sofa, and lay me down, guidebooks and
maps sliding off and scattering across the floor.

"Half a minute," he murmured, and withdrew, leaving me
bereft—and then breathless as he finished unbuttoning his shirt,
and dropped it to the floor.

Some bad seed in the very back of my brain tried to suggest
that I should be terrified now, but I wasn't listening. I ran my
hands over his chest, and laughed, my voice sounding breathless in
my own ears. He nuzzled my neck, sliding his hands beneath me
and under my shirt, his fingers molding my back and shoulders.

I stroked his back, hard, and he raised his head to look down
into my face.

"You're sure about this?" he murmured.

"Yes," I said, with the full force of the land behind the word.
His eyes widened; his fingers tightened, and I kissed him again.

CHAPTER THIRTY-SIX

Sunday, June 25
Low Tide 5:29 A.M.
Sunrise 5:01 A.M. EDT

Something woke me, cleanly and completely.

I was curled on my side, back comfortably pressed into a broad, warm chest, and I smiled even while I strained my ears for an echo, or a repeat, of an unusual sound.

All I heard was the faraway whisper of the surf striking the sand, and, much closer, Borgan breathing deep and even in sleep.

The sound of the waves was too much a part of the usual to wake me, though I'd've been awake in a shot, if it had someway stopped. I didn't think Borgan's breathing had woken me, though if I thought about it, the fact that I was sleeping with somebody might begin to unsettle me.

I decided not to think about it.

Instead, I opened my eyes and looked at the clock on the bedside table. Two-two-two read the illuminated red digits. Something moved in the darkness beyond the clock—but it was only the curtains, blowing in the breeze from the open window.

And then I felt it.

A vibration, deep inside my chest cavity, as if someone had plucked a single string of my heart.

Or as if someone had unraveled one of my workings.

"Fuck!" I sat straight up, my blood suddenly cold.

Borgan muttered sleepily, then sat up as I threw the covers back and jumped out of bed.

"Kate?"

"The carousel," I said rapidly, grabbing a pair of jeans from the chair and skinning into them. "I forgot to ward it tonight. And somebody—"

The plucked string vibrated *hard*. I staggered, caught my balance, and yanked open the closet door, finding a sweatshirt by feel and yanking it over my head.

"Somebody's releasing the prisoners," I gasped, as another string was plucked, and another still.

Borgan already had his jeans on.

"I'm with you," he said.

"I've *got* to get down there!" I snapped, terror feeding urgency.

And, as I'd done twice before in the last day, I...shifted.

This time there was no blurring, no sense of dislocation at all. It was as if I had pushed open a door and stepped from my bedroom into the carousel enclosure.

The air burned with magic; the carousel was spinning in the eye of a maelstrom of power; the animals writhing as if they were alive. I saw the moose shake his antlers; the coon cat raised one paw as if it were about to smack a mouse.

Vassily came into view, crackling with power; his feet braced against the decking, his arms flung wide. His hair, the hood, his clothes stood away from his body, as if he were underwater.

It was a stupid thing to do with so much power in play, and yet, I had to see what he was doing; if he had begun the opening sequence...

Even in Side-Sight it was hard to understand what he was doing. I spent precious seconds looking for a coherent spell before I realized that the plan depended on brute force, and a dizzying expenditure of *jikinap*.

Mr. Ignat' would be *very* disapproving.

Brute force had, however, been effective. The enchanted sleep was shredded; the prisoners were awake...

The last prisoner who had left the carousel had done so by transforming the wooden body she'd been bound to. Vassily had broken the binding spells, too, and the prisoners were emerging from their prisons.

I saw a thick, glowing braid of complex powers writhe out of the wolf's wide jaws. Possibly that was a viable shape in whichever of the Six Worlds the emerging being called home, but in the Changing Land, it wouldn't last five minutes.

I ran forward, the binding spell already formed and ready. With so much magic in play, I was going to have to get close, to be sure that the spell wasn't deflected—or absorbed—before it struck its intended target.

I gathered myself to jump to the deck, and yelled as a steam locomotive hit me in the side, sending me head over heels on the cement floor.

"Jailer! I will kill you!"

Twisting to my feet, I ducked a blast of unformed *jikinap*, its edges burning bright. The woman who had thrown it was naked, and I could feel the power burning in her blood, even in the chaos around us. One of Ulme's countrywomen, I thought, and then I was too busy parrying her attacks to think much more.

I threw the binding spell at her, that being what I had in hand. It clung to her and she screamed, throwing herself to the floor.

Good enough.

I jumped onto the decking, an offensive spell on the tips of my fingers. The wolf, the woman of Kashnerot, even the angry storm of power—those things were distractions. I needed to get to Vassily.

And prevent him from opening the Gate.

I rounded the wheel's curve and there he was, floating a few inches above the decking now, power rippling and flowing, infusing him until I doubted he would survive it, poor mortal thing that he was.

Two more running steps—I wanted to be close, to be sure of a strike, rather than just dispelling my working into the general confusion.

Vassily turned, lazily, and flicked his fingers. Power blossomed, raising my hair and crackling along every magical nerve I had, and I threw my offensive spell even as I realized that it was all smoke and mirrors—a diversion.

And a blast of raw, burning power struck me in the back.

I dropped and rolled, felt another blast go over me; snapped the second offensive spell to the fore, came up on my elbows, and released it point-blank into the woman's chest.

She screamed; it seemed to my magic-saturated eyes that she simply...unraveled, and collapsed bonelessly to the decking.

I came to my feet, heard a roar, and was knocked backward, off the decking and onto the floor. Rolling, I called for my third, and last gun, got my feet under me—

And smelled the rich smell of the ocean, heard a sound like wave striking iron, and, in a moment, a hand under my elbow, easing me to my feet.

"Borgan." I almost fell against his chest.

"You could've waited for me," he said mildly.

"I didn't know it was going to happen again. I wish to hell I knew what it was and how to get a grip on it. I *will be* talking with Mr. Ignat'."

It struck me that it was 'way too calm and quiet, and I glanced over my shoulder. Chaos was still ongoing, but there seemed to be a wall between it and us.

"Raised some peaceful waters," Borgan said. "Won't last long in this. What's the plan?"

"Stop the boy who's trying to open the Gate. Rebind the prisoners. Mop up. Get drunk."

He nodded. "Let's do it, then."

The heat, confusion, and noise returned.

The noise—the godawful racket that meant the Gate was open.

I ran, Borgan at my side, but it was too late; the Gate *was* open, and two rainbow-winged beings stood in a pall of shadow that washed out over the deer, the otter, and giraffe, coating them and the decking, and the spare, crumpled figure in a gray hoodie, his lips parted, and a line of blood running from his nose.

The winged beings embraced; I felt the shock of their passion in my gut, and for a moment I was truly frozen. Arms and wings about each other, the Varothi turned, and I shook myself free of paralysis, looked into and through the Gate's energies, to the particular piece of mosaic that I had to remove in order to close it. I extended my will—

And lost my concentration, as Borgan grabbed me around the waist and swung me against him.

"Let them go!" he snapped. "They don't belong here, and they never did."

"But—" I began, and then I stopped, because it was true; they *didn't* belong here. They were dangerous to this land, and all that lived on and in it.

The land of which I was Guardian.

And so we stood there, Borgan and I, and watched the Varothi walk into the shadow. A damp and cooling breeze sprang up, smelling of leaves and grass. The burning air cooled, and *jikinap* flowed through the Gate in the Varothis' wake.

Somewhere, a hound belled. The shadow lightened, relinquishing Vassily and the poor, dumb animals.

Silently, the Gate closed.

Borgan let me go. The air still stank of *jikinap*, but the chaotic energy was gone. It felt…peaceful inside the carousel's storm gates.

Peaceful and very quiet.

I left Borgan's side, mounted the decking, and knelt next to Vassily. Despite the thin line of blood, he looked peaceful, too. My eyes filled with tears, and I wondered if the Ozali of Varoth had made good on his promise.

I put my hand against his cheek—and almost fell backward.

Alive! the land shouted, barking in equal parts joy and relief.

"Alive," I said, my voice shaking.

"Good. Best let him sleep until we get the rest of it cleaned up," Borgan said, which was only common sense.

But it turned out that there wasn't much cleanup.

I could see the carousel's decking through the misty body of the woman from Kashnerot, a mist that faded into nothing as we watched. I felt a thrill of guilt, and heard my grandfather's arms master in memory, "A warrior kills what he intends to kill."

"The boy I hit's gone, too," Borgan said from the floor. "So that's two accounted for."

"Three, counting the Varothi," I corrected, and walked around the decking until I came to the wolf.

It was, as I had suspected, empty. The goat, the knight's charger, the unicorn, and the hippocampus were likewise empty. Of all the animals on the carousel, the only one touched by magic was the fiberglass rooster.

"They're all gone. We killed two; the Varothi's lover escaped. I wonder where the other two are?"

"Prolly got themselves out of here as fast as they could sing the words," Borgan said. "No reason to stay in the Changing Land, is there?"

"I wonder if they'd know where to go, without their memories," I said. "Unless the Varothi managed to give them back."

"Can't really take a man's memories," Borgan commented. "Not to say *take them*. For one thing, where would you put 'em? If it was me doin' it, I'd just build a nice wall inside my man's head and put his memories right behind it."

"So, once the Varothi started breaking the place up, the prisoners would have gotten access to who they were again? That would explain the Kashnerot woman wanting to kill me for being her jailer."

He nodded.

"Excuse me just a sec," I said, and closed my eyes to query the land.

"If they're here," I said eventually to Borgan, "they're hidden good."

"Who's hidden good, Katie?" asked Mr. Ignat', stepping through the hole in the storm wall. "And who came through the Gate?"

I sighed.

"We'll all go down to my place for coffee and I'll tell you all about it," I said. "First, let me tend to Vassily."

I sat cross-legged on the decking next to him, and asked the land to nudge him awake.

His eyes opened, brown and dazzling. He extended a hand, and gripped my arm where it rested across my knees. He smiled at me; a smile of benediction and blessing. A smile you might expect to see, if you were blessed beyond the normal ken—on the lips of an angel from heaven.

"Kate Archer," he said, his voice trembling with what I thought was awe. "I have been redeemed."

CHAPTER THIRTY-SEVEN

High Tide 11:49 A.M. EDT

"So, let me see if I have this right," I said, handing Mr. Ignat' a coffee mug.

Mr. Ignat' alone had taken me up on the offer of coffee and conversation at my place, Borgan excusing himself by reason of having to fish. He'd given me a thorough kiss before we parted, though, just as if my grandfather hadn't been standing right there, beaming at us benevolently.

"Come by *Gray Lady* after work, if you like it, Kate," he said, and left us at the water's edge.

"All right, Katie, dear," Mr. Ignat' said, as I settled on the sofa next to him. "If it will make you more comfortable to review, please do, though the concept is quite simple. I did tell you that power carries information."

"You did," I agreed, peaceably. After all, it wasn't his fault that I hadn't thought through the ramifications.

"So, having shared *jikinap*, and by extension information, the Varothi just stripped what he needed right out of my code—the structure of the binding spells, how to open the Gate safely— *everything* he needed. Then he returned through his link with Vassily, and set his nefarious plan in motion."

"It really was," Mr. Ignat' murmured, sipping coffee, "quite elegant."

"You weren't there for the carnage part," I said, and sighed. "I feel like such a pushover."

"I think, when you've had a chance to examine the information you obtained from the exchange of *jikinap*, that you were up against someone who has quite a bit of training and control. He seems a splendid tactician. To manage all that, with minimal loss of life—of course, he knew he wouldn't be able to harm you, Katie, since your powers were entwined, but—"

"Wait." I held up a hand. "Wait."

Mr. Ignat' raised his eyebrows and sipped more coffee.

"When I have a chance to examine his information," I repeated slowly. "How do I do that, exactly?"

"That's a very good question. All you need to do is open yourself to your power, as you open yourself to the land. You already have the Varothi's information; you only need to bring it into consciousness."

Or, I thought, *I have the file; all I have to do is open it.*

I leaned forward and put my mug on the coffee table.

"Will you watch for me?" I asked.

He smiled gently. "Of course, Katie."

I closed my eyes, and asked the land to be very, very quiet. Then I centered myself, and tried to clear my mind.

Nothing happened.

I considered the possibility that the Varothi had found a way to withhold his information, to lock the file, in essence, in order to protect Jaron, if for no other reason—and only see how well I had protected Jaron! Taken by my enemies, and locked away, his life reduced to a single function—leash. *My* leash, by which my master would ensure that I come to heel...

Mr. Ignat' had made a second pot of coffee. When I opened my eyes, he was at the counter, sawing bagels in half. Sun was flooding through the French doors.

"Hello, Katie. Breakfast?"

"Thank you," I said. "Breakfast would be good."

I stood, carefully, and stretched, then I walked out onto the summer porch and stared over the dunes, to the sea.

Pretty day, I thought, *going to be a hot one, too.*

I felt a slight disturbance in the air, and knew that Mr. Ignat' had joined me.

"The Varothi imprisoned in the carousel—Jaron—was set up," I said. "He was taken and imprisoned to ensure his lover's cooperation with a certain political faction. My Varothi..." I smiled slightly. "*My* Varothi is Prince Aesgyr. He's old and he's sneaky, and I no longer feel like a doofus before him. He'd give *you* a run for your money."

"If I were so foolish as to put myself in his way," Mr. Ignat' murmured.

I laughed. "In other news, the wild gate was his; he used it to enter the Changing Land. He'd originally thought to use it as his escape route, too, but then I went and closed it. And he hadn't anticipated the problems connected with figuring out which prisoner was who. Also..."

I sighed.

"Also, they—Aesgyr and Jaron—they didn't go back to Varoth." I turned to look at Mr. Ignat'. He met my eyes with a smile.

"They went to Daknowyth. Aesgyr intends to place Jaron under the protection of the Opal of Dawn."

"A *splendid* tactician," Mr. Ignat' said, with clear approval.

"*If* he can keep the jailbreak quiet," I said. "He's only good for so long as the guys holding his leash believe that Jaron's still fastened to the other end."

"Ah."

"I'd been wondering," I said, "if I should call the Wise. All of their prisoners gone; they're not going to like that. When they get around to noticing. But now I'm thinking that the Wise aren't wholly above little things like politics and extortion."

"It might be so; they're wise, not infallible."

I nodded, looking out over the water. There were a couple of kayaks out, just beyond the breaker line, paddling upcoast, toward Surfside.

"Not infallible," I said, nodding. "And it's really none of my business what they do in their spare time. When it becomes my business is when they use the land of which I'm Guardian—and the business that's been in our family for years—to do their dirty work. We didn't ask to be the jailers for the Six Worlds. And I reject the proposition that we have to sully our honor and endanger our people on the whim of the Wise."

There was a small silence. The guys in the kayaks were making good time; at this rate, assuming they were following the coast, they'd be in Cape Elizabeth in time for a late lunch.

"Will you be calling the Wise, then, Katie, and giving them your decision?" Mr. Ignat' sounded only politely interested.

I turned my head and smiled at him.

"No. And I won't be telling them that the prisoners are gone, either." *And I won't spoil Aesgyr's surprise*, I added silently. He'd trusted me with his secret; he'd trusted me, so I gathered from his information, to be a woman of honor.

Well. At least I was a woman who knew how to keep her mouth shut.

"The Wise," I told Mr. Ignat' out loud, "can go fish."

Mr. Ignat' laughed, and wrapped me in a downright exuberant hug.

"Excellent!" he said. "Oh, *excellent*, Pirate Kate!"